Praise for the novels of

Elizabeth Lowell

"This author delivers
pure, undiluted excitement."
Jayne Ann Krentz

"Romantic suspense is her true forte."
Minneapolis Star-Tribune

"Lowell manages to balance
the right amount of intrigue [and] romance . . .
[Her] characters come alive."
Columbia State

"Romance and suspense . . .
[with] likable characters blessed with Lowell's
knack for witty and enjoyable dialogue."
Grand Forks Herald

"Spellbinding . . .
intrigue, passion, and danger."
Florida Times-Union

"Lowell's keen ear for dialogue and intuitive
characterizations consistently set her
a cut above most writers in this genre."
Charlotte News & Observer

By Elizabeth Lowell

THE SECRET SISTER • DEATH IS FOREVER
THE COLOR OF DEATH • DIE IN PLAIN SIGHT
RUNNING SCARED • MOVING TARGET
MIDNIGHT IN RUBY BAYOU • PEARL COVE
JADE ISLAND • AMBER BEACH

WINTER FIRE • AUTUMN LOVER
ENCHANTED • FORBIDDEN • UNTAMED
ONLY LOVE • ONLY YOU
ONLY MINE • ONLY HIS

EDEN BURNING • THIS TIME LOVE
BEAUTIFUL DREAMER • REMEMBER SUMMER
DESERT RAIN • WHERE THE HEART IS
TO THE ENDS OF THE EARTH • LOVER IN THE ROUGH
A WOMAN WITHOUT LIES • FORGET ME NOT

And in Hardcover

ALWAYS TIME TO DIE

ELIZABETH
LOWELL

THE SECRET SISTER

(Originally published as *The Secret Sisters*)

AVON BOOKS
An Imprint of HarperCollinsPublishers

This book was originally published, with the author writing under the name Ann Maxwell, as *The Secret Sisters* by HarperCollins in May 1993 and reissued in May 1999.

AVON BOOKS
An Imprint of HarperCollins*Publishers*
10 East 53rd Street
New York, New York 10022-5299

Copyright © 1993, 2005 by Two of a Kind, Inc.
ISBN-13: 978-0-06-051110-4
ISBN-10: 0-06-051110-9
www.avonbooks.com

First Avon Books paperback printing: November 2005
First HarperCollins special printing: May 1999
First HarperCollins paperback printing: May 1993

Avon Trademark Reg. U.S. Pat. Off. and in Other Countries, Marca Registrada, Hecho en U.S.A.
HarperCollins® is a registered trademark of HarperCollins Publishers Inc.

Printed in the U.S.A.

10 9 8 7 6 5 4 3 2 1

Chapter 1

Manhattan
Friday morning

Call Jo-Jo.
   Urgent.
   Christy McKenna looked at the date on the message call slip. Three days old. Just one of the many notes that had built up during her two-week vacation. But reading this note made her stomach feel as though the bottom of the world had just fallen out.
   She hadn't heard from her younger sister in twelve years. It had been bad news then.
   It would be bad news now.
   Christy felt the old familiar mixture of love and guilt and unease wash through her. Jo-Jo couldn't help that she'd been born with the kind of beauty that literally made people stop and stare. It wasn't Jo-Jo's fault that most people tripped over themselves in their rush to please her. Against an everyday setting, the kind of beauty she had was stunning.
   As a result, Jo-Jo thought the universe revolved around her perfect body.

You like people because of certain things, Christy reminded herself wryly. *You love them despite certain things. Like a beauty that's equaled only by her selfishness.*

For better or for worse, Christy loved her dazzling younger sister. She always had. Twelve years couldn't change that. Nothing could.

But Christy really wished she could like her sister.

As she flipped through more telephone messages the cool breath of the past chilled her spine. After twelve years of silence, Jo-Jo had called five times in two weeks.

What's gone wrong in my baby sister's life that a smile and an extra swing of her fabulous hips can't fix?

Nothing answered Christy's silent question but the equally silent slips of paper clenched in her hand. She had a gut-deep certainty that something was very wrong.

Something Jo-Jo would expect Christy to fix.

"Shit," she muttered.

Nobody responded to the unhappy word. She was alone in her office with the door closed because she didn't want to be interrupted while she did triage on the work that had been piled on her desk while she was gone.

"Why me, Jo-Jo?"

That was easy enough to answer. There wasn't anyone else left of their "family" but the two of them.

"What makes you think I'll drop everything and come running?"

Silence.

Twelve years of it.

Christy had never entirely forgiven Jo-Jo for taking whatever caught her eye on her way through life—Christy's clothes, shoes, boyfriends, girlfriends.

Grandmother McKenna's gold nugget necklace.

Of all that Jo-Jo had taken, only the necklace still rankled.

It was the only piece of the past that Christy wanted. Jo-Jo had known it.

That was why she took it.

"So what?" Christy said impatiently to the messages. "Gramma is dead. I'm in New York. Jo-Jo is wherever Jo-Jo wants to be. I'm doing what I love. Right?"

Silence.

Silence and years and guilt for not being able to make it all turn out right.

Frowning, Christy looked around her office. The shelves were still crammed with books on art, fashion, philosophy, and human adornment, from Stone Age body painting to Tiffany's most astonishing diamond necklaces. The lone window still needed washing and still had a view of another Manhattan high-rise an arm's length away. The nameplate on the door still said CHRISTA MCKENNA, CONTRIBUTING EDITOR.

Nothing had changed.

Yet she had an uneasy feeling that everything had changed. Maybe it was as simple as wanting a few more weeks of vacation. Maybe it was as complex as the restlessness that had overtaken her in the months since her thirty-second birthday.

Maybe it was the past, wounded, bleeding, never healed.

Call Jo-Jo.

The past, and the hope that this time would be different. This time the old wounds would be healed because Jo-Jo was finally old enough to understand that other people hurt, other people cried, other people bled. Not just Jo-Jo. Everyone.

Even her older sister.

Christy reached across her desk for the newest *Horizon* magazine and flipped to Peter Hutton's standing six-page ad package. The layout had been shot on the deck of a yacht off Martha's Vineyard and featured Hutton's signature model, an internationally famous beauty known to the world by only one name: Jo.

Leggy, blond, innocent and wicked in the same instant, Jo-Jo wore a pastel silk pullover sweater and white silk slacks. The sea wind swept her straight hair to one side, letting her look up from under dense eyelashes at the world. She had wide green eyes. Cat eyes. Waiting for the next stupid mouse to move.

Christy stared at the ad, looking for some reason, some hint that would tell her why Jo-Jo was calling after all these years. Nothing came but the sheer physical presence of an internationally successful model.

Jo-Jo wasn't a swizzle stick kind of clothes rack. Her waist was as narrow as a girl's, but she had a woman's hips and high, full breasts. The weave of the silk sweater was so loose and the yarn so fine that her nipples stood out clearly. The silk of the slacks was equally thin, almost sheer. A brunette would have had to shave up to her navel to get away with the pants. On Jo-Jo, the clingy material was an "accidental" striptease frozen just before the moment of total nakedness.

Pure Hutton. Pure Jo-Jo. Seemingly casual, sexually challenging, and manipulative as hell.

Hutton's vision of fashion skated dangerously close to being coarse, yet somehow always managed to avoid the label. Jo-Jo's sheer beauty had a lot to do with it.

"What's the matter?" Christy asked the ad. "Did Hutton finally discover you aren't his alone? Is he going to throw you out on your fantastic ass?"

Urgent.

Christy shivered and set aside the magazine. She could no more ignore her sister's needs now than she had been able to long ago, far away, in another part of the country.

Get it over with. Call and find out what's wrong. Because you know something is.

The call-back number had an area code of 305. Christy pulled out a phone book and flipped to the map in the front.

Colorado.

For a moment she was too surprised to do more than stare. Jo-Jo hated the West even more than Christy. At least Jo-Jo had felt that way years ago, when she used her body as a one-way ticket out of the shit-kicking boondocks.

With clipped motions, Christy punched the number into the keypad. Somewhere in Colorado a phone rang. It was answered abruptly, with a single word.

"Yes."

But the clear, sexy alto was all the identification Christy needed. She could send her own ID along the line, too. She knew of no other person on earth who called Jody McKenna Jo-Jo.

"Hi, Jo-Jo. What's wrong?"

There was a starkly drawn breath followed by silence.

"Hold, please." Jo-Jo's voice was neutral, the tone of someone talking to a phone solicitor.

Christy waited, puzzled and irritated. And guilty.

Where Jo-Jo was concerned, nothing much had changed. Christy still felt that the breach between them should have been fixed by her. She was the one who understood human nature. She should have been able to teach Jo-Jo more. Maybe Jo-Jo was right. Maybe Christy was too jealous to do anything but undermine her younger sister.

Through the phone came the sound of a chair being pushed back, a door closing, and Jo-Jo returning. When she spoke again, her voice was animated, teasing, faintly taunting. It was the old Jo-Jo to the last full stop.

"Hi, Christmas. Bet my call rocked you back on your prim little ass."

Christmas.

Red hair and green eyes. It had been a long time since anyone had called Christy that.

It had been a lifetime.

"You shocked me," Christy agreed. "You were the one who told me never to bother you again. You were the one who never answered my letters. Now you're calling me. So what's wrong?"

"I read your stuff all the time," Jo-Jo said, ignoring the question. "Must be nice to be admired for your mind."

The uneasiness in Christy doubled. "What's wrong, Jo-Jo?"

"What do you mean?"

"You need something from me or you wouldn't have called."

Jo-Jo's laugh was like her voice, smoky, sexy, subtly mocking. There was a pause followed by the quick intake of breath as she lit up a cigarette. She exhaled softly.

"Christmas?"

Jo-Jo sounded wistful, and something more.

Something that made cold fingernails march down Christy's spine.

She leaned back in her chair, trying to relax, trying to tell herself that she hadn't heard a plea in Jo-Jo's husky voice. She hadn't heard loneliness. She certainly hadn't heard stark fear.

But she had.

"I turned thirty this year," Jo-Jo said.

"Consider the alternative. Besides, most people don't have the consolation of your success at thirty."

"I've only had one success."

Huskiness had given way to bitterness.

"You only need one success if you're Peter Hutton's signature model," Christy said.

There was the quick sound of Jo-Jo taking a drag on a cigarette. The exhalation that followed was like a sigh.

"So tell me," Jo-Jo said. "You're the international style maven. What do you think of the new layout?"

The subtle current of defiance in Jo-Jo's question told Christy that her sister already knew. As a child, Jo-Jo's sporadic efforts to win her older sister's approval had torn out Christy's heart. Time had filled the hole with guilt.

"Jo-Jo," Christy said gently, "if we have different tastes or see the world differently, it doesn't matter. That's what growing up is all about."

"Is it? You were the only person who could hurt me. You still are."

Christy suspected she was being manipulated, yet she was touched. Her throat ached around tears that had waited years to be shed.

"What about Gramma?" Christy asked. "Didn't you care about her approval?"

"You were always her pet."

"You were everyone else's."

"I wanted to be hers."

The sound of Jo-Jo drawing in smoke and exhaling and drawing in more smoke came over the line, defining rather than filling the silence.

"You know why I left home, don't you?" Jo-Jo asked after a moment.

"To hurt Gramma."

"I wanted you to be free to go off to a fancy eastern school and be a big success," Jo-Jo said, "so I split."

Christy winced. She thought she'd outgrown feeling guilty over taking the East Coast scholarship, her personal ticket out of the rural hell of Wyoming. But she hadn't outgrown guilt.

And she'd never gone back. Not once.

"I was really proud of you winning that scholarship," Jo-Jo

said with a subtle hint of mockery balanced by an odd sincerity. "And what you're doing now, too. You're really tough, you know?"

"I have to be. People wouldn't pay attention to a pansy writer."

Jo-Jo laughed. The huskiness of her voice was edged with malice and cigarette smoke.

"Peter swears you're the best in the business, even if you've cut him to ribbons a couple of times. Was that because of me?"

The incoming-call light blinked on Christy's phone, distracting her.

"Was what?" she asked.

"Would you like Peter's designs better if I wasn't his model?"

"No." The intercom buzzed, summoning Christy. She ignored it. "Hutton doesn't care what I think. He doesn't need me. He's a household name on five continents. So are you."

"I'd rather be twenty-one again."

"Time only runs one way, darlin'," Christy said with a faint High Plains drawl in her voice. "Where are you?"

"A place called Xanadu."

"Where and what is Xanadu?"

"It's a nifty ranch in southwest Colorado. Peter bought it last year."

"We must have a bad connection," Christy said. "I thought I heard you say 'ranch' and 'nifty' in the same breath."

"The West has changed. People are much more aware of the primal forces of the land than they were when we were growing up."

Christy grimaced while the intercom buzzed. Her sister's words had the cadence of a publicity release, something memorized and then repeated often enough to remove the natural rhythms.

"You'll see when you get here," Jo-Jo said.

The intercom stopped buzzing.

"What are you talking about?" Christy asked.

"You're coming to Xanadu."

"What?"

"Hasn't your boss told you?" Jo-Jo asked. "I figured it was all set up by now. That's why I tried to get hold of you before you left."

"I left, but not for Colorado. I've spent the last two weeks on vacation."

The intercom buzzed again. Christy wondered if it was her boss, trying to tell her what Jo-Jo already had.

"When you come," Jo-Jo said in a rush, "you might hear some things about me that aren't true."

Christy became very still. Her instincts told her that Jo-Jo was finally getting down to the reason she'd opened up the lines of communication after twelve years.

"I've made some enemies," Jo-Jo said. "Men. You know. . . ."

"No, I don't. Men are crazy for you."

"Yeah, well, that can be a problem. Some don't like it when you say no or yes. Some get really pissed. Like Cain."

"Who?"

"Aaron Cain. So stay away from Cain when you come here. Do you hear me? He hates me now. He's not safe."

"You're not making any sense. What's wrong?"

This time there was no question in Christy's voice. It was a flat demand, big sister to little.

"I'll give you Gramma's necklace if you get here in three days," Jo-Jo said. "I need you."

The line went dead.

Christy stared uneasily at the phone, wondering how much of what Jo-Jo had said was truth and how much was lies. As a teenager, Jo-Jo had had a taste for psychodrama and a malicious flair for involving others in her adrenaline head trips.

Yet the undercurrent of fear in her sister's voice had seemed very real.

It couldn't have been, Christy thought. *I must be wrong. It's been twelve years. I don't know her anymore.*

Then she shook her head and stopped trying to lie to herself. She'd held Jo-Jo through too many long hours while nightmares shook the beautiful golden-haired child. Christy knew what her sister sounded like when she was afraid.

And Jo-Jo was afraid now.

Chapter 2

The intercom buzzer shrilled, dragging Christy back into the world of *Horizon* magazine. She punched in the button and spoke automatically.

"McKenna here."

"About time," said Amy, the editorial secretary. "Myra is on me every three seconds. She wants you in her office."

"Now?" Christy asked. "Technically, I'm still on vacation."

"You should have left word where you'd be while you were gone."

"The point of a vacation is to take time off."

"Tell it to Myra."

Christy hung up and gathered herself for the showdown to come.

Myra was no friend. She represented a certain stratum of Manhattan—smooth, polished as a marble sphere, and just as warm.

The fundamental differences between Christy and Myra were reflected in everything from their politics to their clothes. Myra followed trends. Christy analyzed them. Myra wouldn't wear anything that hadn't been approved by the very fashion world *Horizon* covered. Christy had long since realized that what models wore wasn't necessarily what looked good on her.

The intercom buzzed again, a harsh reminder that Myra was waiting.

With a silent curse at office politics, Christy headed for the managing editor's suite. She hesitated outside Myra's door, then opened it and stuck her head in.

"You called?" Christy asked.

Startled, Myra looked up from the stack of color prints on her desk. She scowled and snatched a pair of tortoise-shell glasses from her nose, as if annoyed at being caught using them.

"I didn't hear your knock," Myra said.

"Sorry. I gave it up after Howard threatened to fire me on grounds of formality."

Myra smiled rather grimly as she straightened her pastel jacket over her dainty print skirt. Both were Peter Hutton designs. She lifted her manicured hand to the single strand of pearls she wore, letting the silence build while she counted the beads of her WASP rosary. While her fingers moved slowly, she eyed Christy's clothes—no-name jeans, cotton shirt, and a faded black blazer.

"Were you out on the pistol range playing Annie Oakley again?" Myra asked coolly.

"We can't all be brave and wealthy enough to choke muggers with a rope of pearls."

"Unless other arrangements have been made in advance," Myra said coldly, "staff is expected to be in the office by nine, and *dressed for business*."

Silently Christy prayed for Howard's rapid recovery. "Of course," she said aloud. "I was counting this as a vacation day. I still have more than a month coming to me."

Myra's smile was as cool and perfect as her pearls. "Would you shut the door and sit down, dear?"

Christy shut the door, sat down, and waited, knowing she wouldn't like what was coming next.

"Howard died yesterday," Myra said.

Pain twisted through Christy, surprising her with its intensity. Three times in the past twenty months, Howard Kessler had been hospitalized with complications from AIDS. Each time he'd recovered and returned to work, thinner and more frail, yet with renewed wit and sharpened sensibility. As a result, the staff had believed that Howard would beat the odds and survive until a cure was found.

Christy tried to speak, but knew her voice would break. She closed her eyes for a few seconds, fighting for self-control.

"Tomorrow," Myra said, "I will be named editor in chief."

"Congratulations," Christy managed.

Myra looked at her for a long moment, then nodded. "Thank you. Although we've had our, ah, differences in the past, I'm certain things will run smoothly in the future."

Christy nodded and said nothing. She was still caught in the painful moment of discovering the depth of her feelings for Howard. She'd been very different from him, but they had been bound together by a shared fascination with the ways human beings use clothing, jewelry, and objets d'art to express their own unique and individual selves.

"We will be doing things a bit differently now," Myra said. "I'm rethinking your piece on diamonds. I feel it was a bit too gushy when it came to the *nouveau* . . ."

She paused, looking for the right French word.

It didn't come.

Christy didn't offer to fill up the silence.

"Your provincial prejudice against tradition and continental sophistication was just too obvious," Myra said finally.

Christy felt her temper gnawing through her self-control. First Myra quietly gloated over Howard's death, then she attacked a piece of writing that Howard had regarded as one of Christy's best.

"The article was designed to showcase some of the exciting new Pacific Rim jewelry designers," Christy said evenly. "Was I too kind to the new kids, or was I too hard on some of the high-priced hacks who advertise with us?"

"Are you suggesting that an advertiser could pressure me?"

"They wouldn't have to. As Howard so often pointed out in staff meetings, you have a gift for celebrating the costly mundane."

Myra's narrow mouth flattened into a line of distaste. "Your unnecessarily hostile piece on the makers, buyers, and sellers of important jewelry will go on the hook for the time being. I have something much more meaningful for you to work on."

Deliberately she straightened and folded her small hands on the desk, waiting for a reaction.

Christy did her best not to show what she felt. Most of the anger she felt was at herself. She'd been naïve at best and stupid at worst. She'd assumed that good work and an enviable reputation for intelligence, integrity, and taste would assure her editorial freedom.

She'd been wrong. Her decade of hard work at *Horizon* was as fragile as a giant shimmering soap bubble.

And Myra Best was sitting with a needle ready in her hand.

"Sounds irresistible," Christy said neutrally. "What is it?"

"*Horizon* has become too unpredictable, too undisciplined, too tangential," Myra said quickly. "Our readers aren't interested in bizarre little trends and no-name Japanese designers who might or might not be in business tomorrow."

She looked at Christy.

Christy looked back at her.

"We must pay closer attention to the best-known people in

fashion and design," Myra said. "Those are the names the public recognizes, because they are the names on the labels the public buys."

"And those are the labels that advertise most heavily in our pages. Friends helping friends," Christy said, remembering Jo-Jo's blunt summary of how business was done.

"Advertiser influence has nothing to do with it! If you even hint at such a thing again inside or outside this office, you will be fired. And then you will never work again in fashion in this city."

Christy didn't doubt it. Myra had connections that went back farther than the *Mayflower.* Christy had nothing but intelligence, a flair for style, and the discipline to make it all work.

"Do we understand each other?" Myra asked.

"Completely."

There was a tight silence. Then Myra nodded slightly and went back to her carefully prepared presentation, the one she'd given to every staff member who mattered to the magazine's future.

"*Horizon* is one of the great fashion magazines of the world. Naturally the greatest designers advertise in our pages. Inevitably those same designers will create new styles that will take the international fashion community by storm. Peter Hutton is a case in point."

Myra paused and looked narrowly at Christy. "You don't approve."

"I haven't seen his new designs. How can I approve or disapprove?"

Spots of color appeared on Myra's pale cheeks. "My dear, why don't you put that shrewd little Irish brain to work on pulling with me instead of against me?"

"Scots," Christy said evenly.

"What?"

"I have a shrewd little Scots brain."

"Irrelevant," Myra said, waving her hand. "My entire point is that *Horizon* must move in a new direction, and I am telling you what that direction will be."

Christy braced herself.

"We will record megatrends, not obscure Japanese or South American metalworkers," Myra said. "We will show-case the design studios and designers whose work is sold in every world capital and whose fashions are worn on the most exclusive streets in Paris, New York, London, Rome, and even—God forbid—Los Angeles and Tokyo."

Christy had told herself she wouldn't argue, but she couldn't let that one by. "Peter Hutton isn't the first name most people would have chosen for a piece on the best of international design. He's hardly at the top of his game anymore."

"Don't be ridiculous."

"Sales are down in his own stores, retail chains are reluctant to feature his lines, and there have been rumors that—"

"Nonsense," Myra cut in. "This industry is always full of groundless rumors. Peter Hutton is the most recognized name in contemporary American fashion. You see his logo everywhere."

"Yes. Everywhere."

Myra frowned delicately, not liking the reminder that a designer couldn't be exclusive and at the same time be sold in shopping malls across America.

"Peter is on the verge of announcing an exciting, entirely new line," Myra said firmly.

Christy waited.

"I've previewed some of the materials and motifs," Myra said. "I'm convinced this will be his biggest success yet. It will also be a *Horizon* exclusive."

As Christy listened, she felt her whole life slipping out of control. Myra had already decided what *Horizon*'s position on Hutton's new collection would be. She was expecting praise for a designer whose work had become increasingly marginal, humdrum, and predictable.

"I know you'll do a wonderful job of capturing the spirit of Peter's bold new venture and delivering its excitement to our readers," Myra concluded.

Her smile dared Christy to object.

Christy wanted to, but the memory of Jo-Jo's plea was too fresh.

Jo-Jo, what have you gotten me into? Christy asked in silent bitterness. *I should tell this smug-faced piece of Brie to lie down in traffic on Fifth Avenue.*

But she couldn't. All she could do was pray that she found a new job before Myra ruined her old reputation.

Maybe Peter Hutton has rediscovered his original vision.

Maybe pigs sing.

"That's an interesting idea," Christy said aloud.

It was her all-purpose response to certain types of modern art and music.

Myra smiled with real relief. "Thank you for signing on with the new program. Your reputation within the avant fashion elite will be a boon to *Horizon*."

"And Hutton?"

Myra frowned. "Amy has your plane reservations on her desk."

"Isn't Hutton showing in Manhattan?"

"No, no. His preview showing will be in the same place where his vision first came. A place called Xanadu. Rather like the Native Americans and their vision quests."

"Did the Indians smoke opium?" Christy asked.

"What?"

"Coleridge did."

Myra gave Christy a blank look and returned to her own agenda. "I expect you to generate copy and coordinate with photographers for a package that will be due here in Manhattan in thirteen—no, twelve and a half days."

"That's not much time to research a story of this magnitude."

"You'll find a research file with your tickets. If you read quickly, you should be fully briefed by the time your plane leaves tomorrow. If not, there's always the plane trip itself. Coach class is so boring." She smiled brightly. "Do keep in touch, darling. It's so annoying to track you down like some kind of international rock star. Now, if you'll excuse me, I have so much to do. Howard let everything slide, poor dear."

Myra picked up a stack of glossy color photos and began sorting through them.

Christy left the office without a word.

As soon as she closed the door behind her, Christy stood and tried to control the shaking of her hands. After several slow, deep breaths, she headed for her office, mentally revising her résumé and drawing up a list of job prospects.

The list was frighteningly short. Jobs like hers were made by an editor/mentor. She didn't have one anymore. It would take time to find a new one. If she could. People with Howard's rapier mind and unerring taste were rare.

But she couldn't worry about that now. First on her worry list was Jo-Jo and Xanadu.

And the fear in her sister's voice.

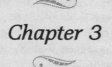

Chapter 3

La Guardia Airport
Friday night

Christy waited in the airport with her bag at her feet. Every few seconds she glanced at her watch and looked in the window of her cell phone. Not that Nick would call her. To him the cell phone was sacred for business. The rest of life could be reached over landlines.

"Come on, Nick," she muttered. "If you aren't through customs real soon, we'll barely have time to say hello before I have to run for my own plane."

It wouldn't be the first time. Nick Warren was an international investment banker whose one real passion was making deals. He'd spent the past three weeks in London, negotiating yet another addition to his bank account.

A glance at her watch told Christy that she had eleven minutes before she had to run. The window of opportunity between Nick's arrival and her departure was closing. There wouldn't be time to say hello, much less to talk about something as personal as a secret sister.

The first-class passengers filed slowly in from customs,

then past the secure area to the terminal where Christy waited. Nick was the third person off the plane. Normally a stylish man, at the moment he resembled a street person. His pima cotton shirt was rumpled from neck to tail. His trouser legs looked like broken accordions.

He smiled wearily at her. "You look as tired as I feel, Christa. Don't tell me you were awake all night too?"

She forced herself to smile. Nick's greeting was so like him, civilized and dispassionate, disdaining the use of her nickname no matter how many times she told him that she preferred being called Christy.

She gave him a quick, light kiss. He brushed a kiss over her forehead in return.

"Hi," she said. "Other than that, how was your trip?"

"Worth every bit of your temper when I missed your vacation," he said with satisfaction.

Her smile slipped, but she didn't say anything about Nick's broken promise to spend a couple quiet weeks with her. She'd hoped the time would lead to the next step in their relationship.

And it had. It just hadn't been in the direction she'd thought.

"I heard about Howard in London," Nick said. "I'm sorry."

"Myra isn't. She's the boss now."

"Too bad. This isn't a good time to be looking for another job. Everyone is cutting back and playing safe."

"I've noticed. Come on, I'll walk you as far as the security checkpoint."

For the first time Nick saw the carry-on bag at Christy's feet.

"Going somewhere?" he asked.

"New assignment. Colorado. Rush job."

He frowned. "But I haven't seen you for *weeks*."

Christy bit back what she wanted to say, which was that he

was the one who hadn't kept the promise, not her. She glanced at her watch.

"In thirty—no, now it's twenty-nine minutes," she said, "I'm off to preview Peter Hutton's new line. With any luck I'll be back in three days."

"More likely three weeks," Nick said irritably.

She shrugged. "Whatever it takes. Just like your job."

"Oh, well, it's only temporary," he said, smiling.

"What?"

"Your job. We both know it will be a race to see whether you quit before Myra fires you."

Christy wanted to argue but didn't bother. He was right. She picked up her bag and headed for the main security checkpoint.

"Don't worry," he said, catching up. "I've got a better job offer for you. Have you given any thought to what we talked about last month?"

She glanced sideways at him and tried to head off the inevitable.

"Home, hearth, and heathens?" she asked lightly.

He looked pained. "I'm serious, Christa."

"If I'm not on that plane, Myra will fire me. That's as serious as it gets."

"No." There was a hard edge to his voice. "I've been doing a lot of thinking."

"Too bad we couldn't have done it together."

"That was business," he retorted.

"So is this."

Christy shut up and kept walking, hoping to avoid the discussion. But that was the thing about inevitability. It couldn't be avoided.

"I have no wife, no children, no real home," he said. "In a week I'll be forty. That's serious, Christa. The rest of it is crap."

"Then why did you fly off to London after promising me—"

"I told you," he interrupted impatiently. "It was business. The deal couldn't wait."

"But I could?"

"Bloody hell, are we going around this track again? I make a hundred times as much as you. Quit and we'll spend a lot more time together."

"You're right. This is the wrong time and the wrong place. Let's not go around this track right now."

"I can support you. Hell, I can support twelve like you out of petty cash."

"Well, hurry along, darlin'. You've got a week to find twelve like me to support. But if they're really like me, they'll support themselves."

He made an impatient gesture. "You're so damned touchy about your work. It's just a job. I'm offering you a life!"

Christy stopped at the end of the security line.

Nick pulled her stiff body closer and kissed her forehead. "I'm tired and jet-lagged and I want a home to go home to. Make me a home, Christa."

Guilt snaked through her. She liked Nick, had even thought she might love him, but she no longer believed they had a future together. It wasn't simply the broken promise or his eighty-hour weeks and long absences overseas. It was something more. Something fundamental that no amount of talking would overcome.

He just wasn't . . . passionate.

The realization startled her. Nick's cool, unruffled style had been much of his attraction for her. But the weeks alone on Fire Island had given her a lot of time to think.

Nick was the wrong man for her.

She was the wrong woman for him.

The security line moved forward quickly. Soon she'd have

to leave him behind. She faced him, frustrated that there was never time to do anything properly with Nick.

Even break up.

"I can't pass up this assignment," she said. "It involves my sister."

"I didn't know you had one." His expression was one of mild surprise and total lack of interest.

"I haven't seen her in twelve years."

"So what's the rush? A few weeks more won't matter."

"Apparently she's on a tight schedule."

"Another career girl?"

"She's Peter Hutton's signature model."

Nick's jaw literally dropped. "Jo? *The* Jo?"

"Yes."

"Incredible! Fantastic! I can't wait to meet her."

Christy looked at him coolly. "Jo-Jo and I haven't spoken in twelve years."

Nick stared at Christy, but she knew he wasn't really seeing her. He was comparing her to Jo-Jo.

Suddenly Christy's temper flared. The speculation and comparisons in his eyes were why she never mentioned her relationship to the screamingly sexy model in the Peter Hutton ads.

"She takes after our mother," Christy said flatly. "I favor the McKenna side of the family."

"Your mother must have been gorgeous."

"She was. Like Jo-Jo. And like Jo-Jo, she was a user."

"Jo could use me anytime." He grinned.

Christy looked at the briskly moving line.

"What did you do to make Jo angry?" he asked.

What makes you assume it was my fault? Because I'm not outrageously beautiful like she is? But all Christy said aloud was, "I got a scholarship. When Jo-Jo found out I wasn't going to stay in Wyoming, she seduced her boyfriend's father, got pregnant, and talked him into running off with her. On the way out of town, she stole Gramma's gold necklace. The scandal broke my grandmother's health. She died of a stroke."

"Was the necklace valuable?"

Christy grimaced. Trust Nick to be curious about the money rather than the emotions. "At most, the necklace was worth a few hundred dollars."

"So how did Jo end up in the big time?"

"I don't know. She refused to talk to me and never answered my letters. All I found out is that she had an abortion, traded up in men, and was a cover model before she was twenty-one."

"No surprise there. A face and a body like hers come along once in a century. Did you call her while you were on vacation?"

"No. She called me."

"Why?"

"Good question. I don't have an answer. Good-bye, Nick."

She showed her ID and e-ticket to a guard, leaving Nick standing on the other side of the security line.

She didn't look back.

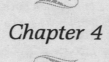

Chapter 4

Colorado
Saturday morning

Christy sat on the edge of her hotel bed and waited while the desk clerk checked for messages.

"Christy McKenna?" the hotel clerk muttered.

"That's me. Room 308."

"No messages. Sorry."

"Thank you," Christy said automatically, hanging up the phone.

She checked her cell phone. Nothing new. Nothing old, either. In Remington, her cell service went without warning from barely usable to complete silence. She might as well carry around a paperweight.

With an impatient motion she tossed the cell phone on the bed. It landed next to the laptop computer that she hadn't found an Internet connection for yet. If she wanted one, she had to go to the local coffee shop and wait in line behind the pencil-neck townies, who then would read everything on her screen as fast as she did. Just one more of the joys of rustic life.

The only good news was that it was driving Myra nuts not to be able to micromanage her reporter.

The bad news was that Jo-Jo was nowhere to be seen.

Well, I made it here in less than three days, but there's no gold necklace waiting for me. Not even a "Hi, Christmas, got you again, huh?"

Irritated at losing the old game, Christy checked her watch.

Too much time.

She wasn't due at Hutton's private prepress showing for several hours. Plenty of time to bathe. Plenty of time to change. Plenty of time to wonder why she was such a sucker for Jo-Jo's games.

At that instant Christy knew that she wasn't going to wait around the phone like the carrot-topped teenager she'd once been, praying for a date.

I'm too old for this.

She grabbed her faded black blazer and clattered down the hotel stairs. When she strode out onto the sidewalk, the sun poured hot and clean through the cloudless sky.

Leaving her rental car in the hotel lot, she headed on foot for the art gallery she'd seen advertised in the guest literature stacked by the phone in her room. She wondered if the gallery would be as pleasant a surprise as the hotel had been. She'd been expecting linoleum floors, knotty pine furniture, and wallpaper covered with fake western brands. What she got was elegant pseudo-Victorian decor.

Halfway to the gallery, Christy realized that Remington itself was rather like an old frame home that was being made over one room at a time into an upscale bed and breakfast. Some of the storefronts were expensively refurbished, with beveled or stained-glass insets in the doors and hand-carved wooden trim freshly painted. And some of the stores hadn't been painted for longer than Christy had been alive.

Remington was a work in progress.

The gallery wasn't far away because the town didn't cover much ground. There was only one stoplight and one paved road. The side streets were dusty, but the items in the Main Street shops were both expensive and surprisingly cosmopolitan.

Christy stopped in front of a boutique whose windows offered French lingerie, Italian sunglasses, Ecuadoran weaving, and modern Navajo jewelry. The cultural mixture was subtly electrifying, a reminder of how small the world had become.

She began to have real hope that Hutton's line would be good after all. The most exciting styles had always come from cultural collisions, cultural tensions, cultural fusions.

Without realizing it, she took a slow breath and put her Manhattan worries and do-it-yesterday pressures on a back burner in her mind. What she was looking at now was real, vital, and new. More relaxed, she glanced around the town with renewed interest, measuring both the old and the new. Glittering arty boutiques and a True Value hardware store down on a side street.

It was the hardware store that brought back long-buried memories of her childhood. There was a woman who moved with the unmistakable sore-footed walk of a tired waitress. Three schoolgirls shrieked and giggled because they were still young enough to believe they wouldn't end up like their mothers. Two working cowboys wore faded jeans, down-at-the-heel boots, and an arrogant tilt to their hats. There was a slight stiffness to their gait and a complete disregard for streetlights and any traffic that had wheels instead of hooves.

There also were tourists—flatlanders, outsiders who were dressed more like California or New York than Colorado. There were some young men who wore the western look without much success. Their clothes were new and their bodies hadn't been broken by bad horses, worse weather, and rotgut whiskey.

Christy watched the drugstore cowboys with a disdain she didn't bother to hide. Imitation might be a high compliment, but it was a sad excuse for individual style.

The vehicles parked diagonally along the street were a mixture of visitors from the outer world and Christy's memories of the insular West. A few exotics such as BMWs, Range Rovers, and Japanese baby pickups were sprinkled among the inevitable full-sized American pickup trucks with gun racks—and often guns—hung across the back window. The local vehicles were dirty and carried the dents and scars of ranch use. The exotics had out-of-state license plates and the sheen of good wax beneath recent road dust.

In front of the Two-Tier West Gallery was a vehicle that didn't quite fit in either the exotic or the local category. Intrigued as always by anything different, Christy studied it.

It was a one-ton truck and it was American, but there were four doors instead of two. The truck bed was enclosed, giving it the appearance of an oversized, muscular station wagon with cargo doors instead of a tailgate. SUBURBAN was written in chrome letters on the black body.

Oversized tires and high-lift suspension hinted at off-road use. Dings, dents, and parallel horizontal scratches along the body confirmed it. Everything was caked with dirt except the front windshield and side mirrors. They were spotless. The paint beneath the dirt had the gloss of good care. The license plate was local.

Now, there's someone who doesn't fit in either tier of the West, old or upscale.

After a second glance, Christy went to see what the gallery had to offer. The Two-Tier West had genteel alarm wires around its plate-glass windows and a generic cardboard placard announcing that the gallery was open. A bell pealed sweetly at the top of the door when Christy pulled it open.

Two people were inside. One was an Indian woman with the broad, serene features and solid build of an R. C. Gorman model. She dressed the part with a floor-length dark green velveteen skirt and a heavy maroon satin blouse. Her smile lit up the white-walled gallery space like a floodlight.

The second person was standing at the counter. He definitely wasn't a drugstore cowboy, but he didn't quite look like a ranch hand. He wore a heavy, closely cut beard and a slate-gray Stetson with a low crown, medium brim, and the look of hard, sweaty use. There weren't any pheasant feathers, conchos, or other decorations on the hatband.

The hat was right for a local cowboy, but the beard wasn't. The shirt was just right, blue chambray with steel snaps instead of buttons, and faded from long use. A gallery case hid his feet, so Christy couldn't tell whether he was wearing cowboy boots or something more comfortable.

If the man smiled in return at the Indian clerk, it didn't show in his profile. Hawk-featured with hooded eyes, he looked proud and rather grim. He was somewhere in his thirties, dark-haired, tall, and long-boned. There was both strength and stillness in him.

"Can I help you?" the woman called to Christy.

"Just browsing," Christy said automatically.

"If you need me, my name is Veronica."

"Thanks."

Veronica turned back to the man who didn't fit. He was carrying a cardboard carton, which he set carefully on the counter.

Christy sensed the restrained excitement in the Indian woman and wondered whether the man or the carton was the source. Curious, she drifted closer to the two while she cata-

logued the contents of the gallery with eyes that had seen the
best and the worst of many cultures and styles.

". . . long time," Veronica said.

The man's reply was a low rumble of sound that could
have meant anything.

Christy strained to overhear.

"Danner said you weren't coming back ever."

"Danner is a horse's ass."

The man's voice was baritone, clear and faintly drawling.
Either a native or someone with a good ear who had picked
up local accents.

Pretending to study a nearby necklace, Christy watched as
he handed Veronica an envelope. Without another word he
turned and went out the front door. He moved with the easy
gait of an athlete or a hiker rather than a cowboy more used to
horses than walking. And he was wearing scuffed hiking
boots, not cowboy boots.

She watched the man the whole way, conscious of staring
but not able to look away. She'd seen more handsome men—
Nick, for instance—but she'd never seen a man who ap-
pealed to her senses more.

But she was damned if she could figure out why.

He went straight to the black Suburban parked out front.

Figures, Christy thought, oddly pleased. *The man who
doesn't fit owns the truck that doesn't fit.*

She turned back to the gallery's offerings. A decent contemporary painting on the wall behind the counter caught her
eye. The painting was a stylized neon-blue cowboy against a
glaring crimson and black backdrop that could have been
Times Square or the Las Vegas Strip. The cowboy radiated a
masculine intensity and lean power that was much older and
more enduring than the twentieth-century techniques of the
artist.

Stepping back, she studied the painting, drawn by it in a way she couldn't name.

The front bell rang again, announcing the man's return. He was carrying another carton. He set it down on the counter across from Veronica and went to work on the fastenings. When he pulled something out of the carton, Veronica set aside the papers she had been reading and gave a low whistle.

"Did you take photographs in situ?" Veronica asked.

"What do you think?"

Veronica laughed. "I think you have a batch of them."

For a moment there was quiet while they admired the bowl cupped in the man's long fingers.

Christy watched from the corner of her eyes, intrigued both by the obvious excitement of the gallery owner and the way the man was holding the bowl. She'd never seen a man touch anything so carefully, like it was a butterfly or a woman's breast rather than pottery.

"Have you shown it to anyone else?" Veronica asked.

"For sale? No. I had Mike over from Mesa Verde to look at it, though."

"What did he say?" she asked.

"That he wished he'd found it."

The front door opened with another cheerful peal and closed with a bang.

A big, hard-shouldered man in white shirt and light straw stockman's hat strode in. He wore a tooled gun belt with a white-handled revolver in the holster. Silver gleamed in his hair, and a five-pointed silver star glinted on his pearl-buttoned shirt. He was perhaps fifty and physically fit in the manner of a man accustomed to hunting game and riding rough trails on horseback.

Christy had seen smaller bulls.

"Afternoon, Sheriff Danner," Veronica said. "What can I do for you?"

"You can stop buying pots from that Moki-poaching, high-grading son of a bitch."

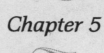

Chapter 5

Christy was close enough to overhear Veronica's unhappy hiss. "Shit."

Danner wasn't.

Nor could the sheriff see the change that went over the man who held the pot. In the space of a breath, he went from relaxation to predatory alertness.

Instinctively Christy stepped back.

The man returned the pot to its carton with great gentleness. Yet when he turned to face the sheriff, there was nothing gentle about his expression or his stance. His eyes were wolf's eyes, pale amber, unemotional, unflinching, revealing nothing.

"Danner," the man said.

"I want to see papers on those pots," the sheriff said curtly.

"I'm sure you do."

Silence grew until Danner realized that nothing more was going to be said unless he said it.

"Get them."

The man didn't move.

Veronica did. She scooped up the papers she had been reading and handed them across the counter to Danner.

"All in order," she said. "Landowner's notarized signature, in situ photos, USGS map coordinates, the works."

The sheriff scanned the papers quickly. Too quickly. Christy suspected that Danner either didn't know what he was looking at or didn't care.

The way Danner threw the papers back on the counter said he didn't give a damn.

"All in order, right?" Veronica said with forced lightness.

"This time," the sheriff said coldly.

"Every time," she said, "and you know it as well as I do. Everything in my gallery is aboveboard and top quality."

Danner didn't answer. He'd already dismissed Veronica. He was focused on the younger man, who was watching him with cool disdain.

"You disappoint me, boy," Danner said.

The man's smile said he knew he wasn't anybody's boy.

"Because I'm still alive?" the man drawled.

"Because you don't have enough sense to stay out of places you aren't wanted."

"Last time I checked, it was a free country."

"Seems to me," Danner said, "a kid who had a bullet in his lung a few months back would have better sense than to try the high country again."

Christy flinched at the sheriff's casual words.

A bullet in his lung.

She stared at the younger man. For the first time she saw that his clothes were a bit loose, as if he'd lost weight recently. Brackets of pain or anger cut into either side of his mouth so deeply that even the thick, closely trimmed beard couldn't conceal them.

"Don't worry about me," the man said. "I'm a survivor."

The sheriff wasn't impressed. "What do you want here?"

"Same thing I always did. To be left alone like every other law-abiding citizen."

"You better move on, boy. I'm going to ride you like a green pony."

"Why?"

Danner seemed surprised by the cool question. "We don't take to murderers around here."

"Then why aren't you looking for the man who tried to murder me?"

The sheriff straightened up fully and dropped his hands to his sides. His right palm brushed against his holster.

Christy wondered why he needed to reassure himself about the gun. The sheriff was at least eighty pounds heavier than the other man.

"I've only been in office a few months," the sheriff said. "That's hardly enough time to draw up a list of your enemies, much less talk to them. Anyway, it was just someone after spring venison, and you know it."

The younger man's teeth showed in a quick, cold smile. "I don't know anything of the sort. As for your busy schedule, you might have more time for investigations if you spent less time playing security guard out at Xanadu."

"Look here, you—"

"But I can see how Hutton's campaign contributions—"

"—son of a bitch! You have no—"

"—might be more important than solving a shooting."

"—right to question me!" Danner finished angrily.

"Ten thousand dollars is a lot of money in a county like this."

"What's that supposed to mean?" Danner demanded.

"You tell me, *Sheriff*. You're the one cashing Hutton's checks."

"And not Larry Moore, is that it? You're pissed off that your buddy didn't get elected sheriff."

"Larry couldn't be bought."

Danner turned his head a little and squinted, like a man

who didn't think he'd heard correctly. He hooked his thumb into the gun belt just ahead of the holster. His palm curled back over the hammer of the gun.

The other man faced the sheriff and hooked his right thumb into his own belt, a clear and conscious mimicking.

Christy blinked. She couldn't believe the unarmed, recently injured man was facing the threat of a gun so calmly. The closest thing he had to a weapon was his sterling belt buckle. As weapons went, it wasn't much—a palm-sized silver oval mounted with a circle of fine turquoise.

"I wasn't bought," Danner said. "I got *elected* to keep bad actors like you from getting in the way of good citizens."

"I did my time," the man said flatly. "I don't owe you anything. I don't owe the state of Colorado anything. The only person I owe is the son of a bitch who shot me and left me to die. I always pay my debts. Ask anyone."

"You better watch that mouth, boy. Might make a man nervous enough to cause another hunting accident."

The man with the beard became very still.

Instinctively the sheriff started to back up, then stopped himself. His hand closed over his gun.

Christy's breath clogged her throat. *This can't be happening. This is an art gallery in the twenty-first century, not some saloon in the Wild West.*

"Are you trying to tell me something, Danner?" asked the man.

"I'm only telling you the same thing your doctor told you. Remington isn't a healthy place for a lung-shot ex-con. Everyone would be better off, including you, if you'd just drift."

The man's laugh was even harder than his smile. "Every western town needs an outlaw to keep the tourists happy. Looks like I've just been elected."

He turned his back on the sheriff and spoke to Veronica. "I'll be by tomorrow to talk about these pots."

Christy watched the man walk out of the gallery and get in the Suburban.

The sheriff swore under his breath and left without a word.

When the bell over the door shivered into silence, Christy forced herself to draw a deep breath.

"A decade doesn't seem to have changed the average western male very much," she said.

Veronica gave a hoot of laughter. "Yeah, that's one hell of a man, isn't it? Six-foot-two of trouble on the hoof."

"He looked taller than that. Must have been the gun."

"Gun? Oh, you mean Danner. Yeah, he's six-four. But I was talking about Cain."

"Cain?" Christy asked faintly.

"Aaron Cain."

She shook her head, feeling disoriented. The man with the dark beard was the man Jo-Jo had warned her against.

"If I was a betting woman—and I am—I'd back Cain in a brawl against anyone."

Christy hardly heard. She stared out the window at the man her sister had warned her against.

"What's a Moki poacher?" she asked finally.

"A thief."

"Is that why he was shot? Was he stealing something?"

"Cain? He's no Moki poacher, no matter what the university types say."

Christy looked as bewildered as she felt.

Veronica smiled and began carrying one of the cartons Cain had left into a back room, talking all the while.

"People around here take their Anasazi sites seriously," she said. "If you have a degree from a fancy school and dig up pots, you're an archaeologist. If you don't have a degree, you're a grave robber, even if you're well educated, careful to record what you do, and have a landowner's permission to dig."

Veronica vanished into a back room but kept talking.

"But if you dig on public lands, you're a pothunter and a Moki poacher."

"And a son of a bitch?" Christy offered dryly.

Veronica's laughter rang again.

"Well, Danner and Cain never had much good to say for each other," Veronica admitted, grabbing the second carton. "Danner liked giving orders even before he was elected sheriff."

"Cain doesn't look like he takes orders worth a damn."

"Not that boy. Then there was their little disagreement over Hutton's model, that fancy blonde."

Christy was glad Veronica couldn't see her reaction. By the time the gallery owner came back out, Christy had her expression under control.

"The one they call Jo?" she asked carefully.

"That's the one."

Veronica disappeared into the back room again.

"What happened?" Christy asked.

"Danner wanted her. He didn't get her. But I saw Cain and the blonde over in Montrose one night, working the honky-tonk trapline."

Jo-Jo and Cain? Christy shook her head.

"She was all over him like a rash," Veronica said. "It was the only time I saw them together, but . . ."

Veronica's voice faded as she vanished into the back again, leaving Christy to wonder if Cain had been the man able to teach Jo-Jo that there were some things beauty couldn't buy. And that's why Jo-Jo hated him.

The thought went through Christy like a shock wave, unsettling everything in its wake.

Maybe that's why Jo-Jo called and offered the gold necklace. Maybe she's finally grown up and wants to mend her fences.

Maybe Aaron Cain was a miracle of reality in Jo-Jo's relentlessly self-centered life.

Christy almost smiled. Cain didn't look like a walking miracle, but stranger things had happened between men and women.

Something very like hope bloomed in Christy.

Maybe he touched the Jo-Jo I always believed was there, deep beneath the selfishness, a woman who could be reached with enough patience, enough understanding, enough love.

Maybe Jo-Jo is finally able to love and laugh and share.

Maybe she's able to feel pain that isn't hers.

A sister in more than blood.

That was the ultimate lure, the irresistible one, the shining promise of a childhood healed.

Suddenly Christy couldn't wait to see Jo-Jo.

This time. This time it will be different.

Chapter 6

Colorado
Later Saturday morning

Empty cattle vans rocketed past Christy, heading for the high country to bring cattle back down to the valleys for the winter. The slipstream of the big trucks made her little rental car shake.

"One more thing that hasn't changed," Christy said under her breath. "Big trucks and narrow roads. Welcome back."

And her damned cell phone still couldn't find anything to talk to.

On either side of the two-lane highway, small dirt tracks led off between barbed-wire fences to ranch houses that were more than a hundred years old. Even in the bright warmth of the sun, there was a feel of winter's depths in the run-down brick and turn-of-the-century frame houses.

Christy knew how houses smelled, how they felt, how they creaked when the wind blew in the middle of the night and tree branches scratched against the glass. She knew what it was like to be a teenager staring through tears at a cheap dresser mirror and asking herself why God had given her a brain instead of a face and body that brought men to heel like hound dogs with long tongues hanging out.

Part of Christy had never stopped wondering. She'd just given up on ever finding an answer.

She put away the often bitter, sometimes sweet childhood memories and concentrated on the narrow road and the wide land. The last weeks of September lay serene in the long meadows and lofty divides of the Rockies. On the hard shoulders of the mountains, the highest aspen groves had already turned a pure, burning gold. Above timberline the wild peaks varied from dark red to steel gray and black. The sky was a blue so vivid it blazed even through sunglasses.

Remington County had the same compelling, muscular grace as the landscape of her childhood. She was drawn to the land even though it revived unhappy childhood memories. A stubborn, unchanging part of her still loved being surrounded by the grandeur of untamed mountains rising against a wild blue sky.

She turned off the road onto a narrow paved lane that led to Xanadu. Ahead, a lush stand of spruce grew right up to the road. A new snake-back fence zigzagged alongside the pavement on both sides. The fence was picturesque, but it also carried a message.

Keep out.

The message was reinforced by a guard in a self-consciously rustic shack at the edge of a spruce grove.

When Christy stopped in front of the shack, she realized that the folksy appearance was barely skin deep. Underneath the shack's cedar shingles there was a gleaming steel security center with high-tech connections to the rest of the world. Whether for vanity or necessity, Peter Hutton had built an efficient, expensive, armed barrier between Xanadu and the rest of the world.

The guard stepped out of the shack. He wore blue jeans

whose crisp look came from being ironed, and probably starched as well. His white western shirt was equally crisp and definitely starched.

She suspected it was the same for his underwear.

"What can I do for you, ma'am?" the guard said.

No question in his voice. He was polite, but just barely. His tone and his body language said that his job wasn't to help. He was wearing a pistol and a five-pointed star like Sheriff Danner's. The nameplate beneath it said SANDERS.

Christy wondered if the people of Remington County cared that their tax money was being spent to guard a fashion designer's privacy.

"I'm Christy McKenna from *Horizon* magazine in New York."

Sanders pointed back the way she'd just come.

"All reporters are supposed to check in at the press center in the hotel in town," he said. "The media party isn't until tomorrow night."

She took off her dark glasses and looked at him with eyes that were more gray than green. When she spoke, her voice was every bit as cool as his.

"I'm not here for the press party. I'm here at Mr. Hutton's personal invitation."

The guard looked skeptical, checked a clipboard, and shook his head. "McKenna?"

"Yes."

"I've got a list of special guests, ma'am. Your name isn't on it."

Christy smiled without warmth. "Check with your supervisor."

Sanders reached for a phone just inside the door of the shack, punched in a number, and waited.

She waited too, wondering why such aggressive security was necessary in Remington County. The West of her childhood was one of unlocked doors and unchained gates.

The deputy's voice came heavily through the silence. "This is the front gate. I've got a Miss McKenna here from some New York magazine, says she's supposed to see the Man."

Christy couldn't hear the reply. She didn't have to. She saw its effect immediately.

The deputy shot a fast, rather disbelieving glance at Christy. "Yeah," he said to the phone. "Okay."

He listened some more.

"Yes. Yes, sir. Right away."

Sanders hung up, stuck his head out of the shack, and whistled shrilly through his teeth. "Yo! Hammond! Front and center!"

A younger deputy trotted into the sunlight.

"Sorry about that, Miss McKenna," Sanders said to her. "Nobody ever tells us anything down here. You're to go right on up."

"Thank you."

"Deputy Hammond will show you the way. If you have any luggage, Hammond will take care of it. Mr. Hutton has one of the guest suites ready for you."

Not only security, but gofer too. Interesting. "That won't be necessary. I have a room in town."

"But Mr. Hutton—"

"Thank you for your help," Christy said over the deputy's objections. "Mr. Hutton knows—or should know—that I'm a reporter, not his personal guest."

"Uh, yeah. Sure. Whatever."

Shaking his head, Sanders leaned back into the guard shack.

Deputy Hammond slid into the front seat beside Christy. He looked fresh out of high school. He wore a badge and carried a pistol like a real deputy, but didn't have anything close to command presence. He glanced sideways at her quickly, almost shyly.

The heavy wooden gate slid open.

"Drive right on through the gate, ma'am," Hammond said in a soft voice.

For the first half mile, spruce trees and snake-back fences lined the road. The brighter green of pastures gleamed through gaps in the trees. Very beautiful, but . . .

Something was wrong.

She frowned, trying to figure out what it was.

The road climbed up a long grade to the top of a sandstone mesa that was studded with dwarf cedar and juniper.

"I don't get an armed escort very often," Christy said finally. "Is the West really that wild?"

Hammond touched the gun on his hip self-consciously and shook his head. "No, ma'am. Mr. Hutton just likes to treat his really special guests well," the young deputy said as they crested the mesa.

"So I'm a really special guest?"

"Yes, ma'am."

"Do you have many?"

"I don't know. I'm new to the deputy trade."

New but trained well enough to keep his mouth shut around reporters, Christy noticed. She gave up talking and concentrated on the scenery, letting impressions sink into her. The afternoon air was like polished crystal. She rolled the window down and inhaled old familiar scents, meadow grass and pine, sunlight and clean, silky air.

After two miles the hardtop gave way to a broad, graveled ranch road that had been graded recently. The road crossed the mesa, dropped into a narrow meadow, and wound upward into scattered tall pine trees.

The shadow of a hawk riding the wind caught her eye. She watched the bird's graceful, predatory ease and wished she could ride the winds of change half as well. The fan of the hawk's tail was a startling russet, the color of fire burning just beyond reach.

"What a gorgeous color," Christy said.

The deputy glanced at her, then at her hair.

"You and that bird related?" he asked with a wide grin.

At first she didn't understand. When she did, she laughed, totally unaware of the change smiling made in her looks.

Hammond wasn't. His eyes narrowed with sudden male calculations that were much older than his smooth face.

The road brought them to the far edge of the mesa. Reflexively Christy braked to a stop and stared at the beauty that was Xanadu.

The valley lay between two red-gold sandstone mesas. A mile wide and three miles long, Xanadu was mostly meadow and pasture. The grass was a green so deep and rich it could only be described as emerald. Graceful cottonwood and willow lined the watercourses that snaked down from the mesas.

At the head of the valley, on the steep slopes that led up to the San Juan Wall, stands of aspen blazed bright yellow against the cobalt sky and stark white afternoon clouds.

Like the land itself, the ranch house had uneven levels and surprising angles, a redwood and glass mansion with soaring windows that faced the wall of mountains on one side and the western sky on another. The huge house sat on a knoll at one edge of the valley, like a god overseeing the earth below. On the flats, a huge barn with outbuildings and corrals spread out in the balanced asymmetry of boulders in a Japanese garden. Like gems in a well-designed setting, the buildings blended rather than clashed with the uncluttered landscape.

"Gorgeous," Christy said simply. "How far does the ranch go?"

"Way up into the mountains and clear across both mesas.

Boundaries are kind of hard to pin down when you're talking about this much land. Darn shame it's all going to waste."

Puzzled, she looked at the deputy.

"Not one head of working stock," Hammond said.

Abruptly she understood why Xanadu's beautiful meadows and pastures had seemed wrong to her.

"The only cows on this place are the ones they'll be barbecuing for tonight and tomorrow," he said. "Some of the best pastureland in the state too. Put a lot of ranch hands out of work when this turned into a playground."

She suspected the young deputy was one of them. "An idle ranch for the idle rich?" she asked.

Hammond shrugged and let the empty land speak for itself.

"What happened to the stock?" she asked.

"Sold. I guess Mr. Hutton didn't like cow flop on his pretty grass. Or maybe he was afraid they'd wander onto his target range and stop a few bullets."

The deputy's contempt was strong enough to override his training about loose talk and reporters. He was drawing Hutton's wages, but he was still pissed off by the changes a wealthy outsider had brought to a hardworking western town.

Christy wasn't surprised by the young deputy's attitude. You couldn't dump a mega-millionaire outsider like Hutton on a community like Remington without ending up with envy, resentment, and a half-shamed, general stampede by the locals to suck up any crumbs falling from the rich man's table.

In Manhattan, Peter Hutton was just one among many ultra-rich people.

In Remington, he was the cash cow for an entire county.

Chapter 7

As she released the brakes, Christy wondered if that was part of Remington's allure for Hutton. He was a man of amazing vanity.

Silently they drove through the city man's dream of a well-designed West.

The meadow with its landing strip and apron for small planes spoke eloquently of quick, expensive transit across the wide-open spaces.

A shooting range lay on the opposite side of the meadow, well away from the landing strip. The bold targets were set at distances that suggested both pistol and rifle.

"Six-guns at twenty paces?" Christy suggested ironically.

Hammond almost smiled. "Hutton's not bad with a pistol for a city sli—uh, man. One or two of his boys are pretty good with a rifle too."

"Especially for city slickers?" she asked innocently.

The deputy looked uncomfortable. "Uh, yeah."

"Relax. I grew up in Wyoming, hours from anything I'd call a city now."

"Yeah?"

"Yeah."

"It sure don't show," Hammond said.

"Thanks. I think."

He laughed.

She pointed to an area in front of the barn where a dozen carpenters were hammering like they were being paid by the nail. "What's going on over there?"

"They're building a dance floor out of rough lumber. The barbecue pits are over there. Going to be a big party tomorrow night."

Off to one side another work crew was sweating over a fire that was slowly turning a side of beef into a feast for the smaller private party tonight. Four damp mounds of earth marked the locations of fire pits big enough to contain whole pigs.

"Looks like quite a shindig," Christy said dryly.

As the outbuildings fell away on either side, the road passed through an elegant wrought-iron arch and wound up the hill to the big house. As soon as Christy parked and opened the car door, a silver-haired man dressed like a drugstore cowboy came out to meet her. The white boots, dark pegged pants, and pearl-button white shirt were as expensive as they were amusing.

"Ms. McKenna, I'm Ted Autry, Peter's administrative vice president," he said.

Before Autry could help Christy, she was out of the car. She gave him a professional smile and a handshake to match.

"You're just in time for a glass of wine," he said. "Peter's giving a few friends an unscheduled look at the Sisters Collection."

"The Sisters?" Christy asked rather sharply.

"Sorry, I forgot. You haven't been briefed about the background of the collection. Myra Best wanted you to see the designs cold."

"Here I am." She smiled. "As cold as they come."

Autry was a good vice president. He caught the edge in her voice and tried to smooth things over.

"The designs are drawn from a stunning archaeological find Peter made right here on Xanadu." His smile invited Christy to share the excitement.

She resisted.

"He actually discovered an old Anasazi site," Autry said. "It was dedicated to two sisters. Princesses."

"Royal sisters?" Christy's voice invited Autry to keep talking.

He resisted.

"I'll let Peter have the fun of filling in the details," Autry said. "He loves to tell the story."

She didn't doubt it.

Autry escorted her across a manicured lawn, onto a smooth redwood deck, and into a huge room that took up one entire end of the ranch house. The cathedral ceiling rose almost three stories above the floor, giving a sense of vast space within a sacred enclosure.

Two of the three exterior walls were entirely of glass. The third wall was an extraordinary mosaic of hand-crafted wood. Suggesting an altar, a freestanding stone fireplace in the center of the room soared to the full height of the ceiling. There was a panoramic mountain view from deck to roof. Mellow afternoon light filled the room, making everything glow with a special beauty. The wood floor had a warm reddish cast and a superb grain. Glass display cases were scattered cleverly about. Western art and artifacts lay within the glass, waiting to be admired.

Christy spotted a Remington bronze. Genuine, no doubt. Hutton's ego wouldn't settle for less. A dozen paintings with western themes and/or artists hung on the walls. They in-

cluded a Catlin, a Bierstadt, and a Moran. There was a small
O'Keeffe, some very good watercolors, and a Charlie Rus-
sell with the trademark vivid colors.

Now she understood the guards and guns. Hutton's spec-
tacular secular church had several million dollars in art grac-
ing its various altars.

Gradually she focused on the people in the room. They
had gathered around a huge glass case in the most prominent
display area. She recognized several of the other guests immediately: Tim Carroll, a dark-haired Hollywood actor who
made $10 million a picture; Shannon Prell, his girlfriend,
whose ditzy-blonde roles made her the highest-priced actress
in the trade; Frank Rohrlick, a New York author with a string
of blood-drenched bestsellers to his credit.

Christy didn't recognize the rest of the guests by name,
only by type. Everyone had the air of well-dressed confi-
dence that she associated with the wealthy at play. Hutton's
trophy guests were a cross section of the Beautiful People,
the jet set, the top tier of the two-tier West that had grown
when nobody east of the Rocky Mountains was looking.

Autry put a finger to his lips, smiled, and gestured for
Christy to join the others.

No one looked up from the display case when she walked
across the room.

". . . so all the evidence suggests that the two women were
members of an aristocracy. They had magnificent jewelry.
Lots of it. Several kilos of turquoise and six thousand pieces
of jet."

Everyone murmured appreciatively.

Hutton kept talking. "The body of the tortoise is solid
argillite a kind not found anywhere but the Queen Charlotte Islands of British Columbia. The mother-of-pearl inlay
is from California abalone shell. My archaeologists tell me
there should be another tortoise somewhere in the dig, be-

cause the sisters were probably priestesses. I can't tell you how wildly impatient I am to find that other tortoise."

He straightened up from his position over the case. Tall, spare, curly-haired, he had the sculpted features of a male model, the lazy smile of a sybarite, and the supple voice of the Broadway actor he'd wanted to be until he realized how much more money there was in dressing rich women than in entertaining them.

"What you're seeing is mother-of-pearl," he said. "Abalone shell, to be precise. The nearest abalone beds are in Malibu, California."

More awed sounds rose from the people as they leaned closer, trying to see better.

"In other words," Hutton said, "this tortoise proves that the people of the Chaco empire were powerful enough to reach out a thousand miles for materials and for the artistic vision to create a piece of grave goods that is every bit as elegantly stylized as anything from an Egyptian tomb."

He paused and smiled his trademark smile. The women who were watching smiled back.

Christy didn't. She just wondered if Jo-Jo enjoyed looking at her sexual opposite in Peter Hutton, or if the competition made her uneasy.

"That's why I'm so enthusiastic about this find," he said. "Not only is it an inspiration for me artistically, it's also a real breakthrough in our understanding of ancient Mesoamerican cultures. Until this find, the Anasazi were dismissed as backwater clods. Now people will be forced to admit that one thousand years ago an important imperial culture existed from the New Mexican desert to the Colorado Plateau."

Hutton glanced around, measuring the enthusiasm of his audience. When he saw Christy, his expression changed.

"Excuse me for a moment," he said to the people gathered around the case.

He crossed the huge room toward her with the odd, flowing grace of a runway model. While his chiseled Grecian beauty wasn't to Christy's taste, it was compelling in the way that all good art is compelling.

Jo-Jo had the same effect on the senses. People stared because they couldn't believe such physical perfection existed anywhere short of heaven or a movie screen.

"Christa? We've almost met so many times, and now I find out you're Jo's sister. I'm still in shock."

Hutton took both Christy's hands and held them with every evidence of pleasure.

"Hello, Mr. Hutton."

"Never. For you I'm Peter, and you're Christa for me." He smiled, a curve of the lips that was just for her.

For the first time in her life, Christy was grateful that she'd spent a childhood in Jo-Jo's glittering orbit. Otherwise Hutton's sheer physical beauty might have left her speechless and scrambling for balance.

But she smiled because it was impossible to be the focus of Hutton's smile and not return it.

"Mr. Hutton—"

"Peter," he interrupted firmly.

"Peter." She shook her head slightly. "You're everything people said you were."

"Oh, I hope not." He winked, sharing a secret with her. "People say some pretty awful things and forget to say the nice ones."

"That's the first thing a reporter learns."

Hutton leaned down and said in a low voice, "For instance, Jo never mentioned that you were a beauty in your own right."

"Jo-Jo is beautiful. I'm well turned out."

He laughed. Then he looked Christy over from the crown of her head to her feet.

"I beg to differ with you, darling," he said. "And I'm the acknowledged world expert on female beauty."

With a confident pressure of his hand over hers, Hutton drew Christy toward the case.

"I was just giving some friends a preview of the treasure of Xanadu," he said. "You can't imagine the magic of these pieces."

As he approached the people grouped around the case, they looked up expectantly at him.

Christy didn't blame them. There was a vividness to Hutton that colored everything within reach.

"Mind your nasty tongues, children. The press has arrived," he said.

Christy watched the predictable result with a mixture of resignation and amusement.

"Such shocked looks," Hutton said. "Relax, Tim, she's not going to mug you for some sleazy tabloid."

The movie star grimaced. The rest of the group laughed.

"Christa McKenna is class all the way. She's the guru—or is it guress?—of taste and style in the U.S. If you don't believe me, ask *Horizon* magazine."

A wave of interest went through the people as they looked at her.

"Shannon," Hutton said, "you're blocking the case. I, personally, don't mind, but I'm sure Christa would rather look at the artifacts than your heart-shaped ass."

Laughing, the actress stepped to the side.

Christy saw instantly why the guests were so fascinated by the display. Every piece in the case was marvelously preserved and presented. None showed the rude execution that she associated with Anasazi works.

The turquoise fetishes and strings of jet beads were tiny and immaculately polished. The pottery's painted designs were both irregular and artistically inevitable. The baskets had breathtaking elegance and intricacy. The arrowheads and the stone and bone implements were superb in their execution and timeless in their balance and purpose.

Most compelling of all, some of the artifacts transcended the limitations of form and function to become art.

"What do you think?" Hutton asked, watching Christy with shielded intensity.

"Elegant, elemental, and extraordinary," she said.

His smile was genuine, relieved, and triumphant. "And you haven't even seen the best!"

He set a simple rosewood display box lined with soft green velvet on top of the case and gestured to her. When she hesitated, he pushed the box closer.

"Look," he said in a hushed voice.

A tortoise effigy rested on the velvet. The pendant was as big as a man's palm. The creature's shell was made of highly polished black argillite. The potent head and neck were mother-of-pearl inlay, as were the legs. The collar at the base of the neck was turquoise inlay. The eyes were polished turquoise spheres.

Beyond the age of the object, beyond its superb craftsmanship, beyond its rarity, there was an aura about the tortoise that fairly sang of longevity and reverence, wisdom and fertility.

It was a god effigy from a sophisticated culture.

"Isn't he marvelous?" Hutton said.

"Yes," Christy said simply.

"I believe he's the highest expression of Anasazi art ever to be found." Hutton's voice was rough with excitement. "For my money, this is one of the highest expressions of ancient art of *any* culture."

She let out a breath she hadn't been aware of holding. "This came from Xanadu?"

"Yes." His voice softened. "Everything in this case came out of a sandstone cave we found last year."

She bent closer, inspecting the icon intently. A tiny piece of abalone inlay was missing from one foot. Somehow the loss reassured her, made the piece more genuine, more human.

Imperfect, and therefore real.

"Go ahead," Hutton said, picking up the tortoise with heart-stopping casualness. "Touch it. Hold it."

Reverently Christy took the object in her hand and touched the polished shell with her fingertips. The surface was smooth, cool, almost seamless. The inlays were so carefully made that she had to concentrate to feel where stone ended and mother-of-pearl began.

"My archaeological consultants tell me that the cave was a tomb for two royal sisters," Hutton said.

"When I studied the Anasazi in college," Christy said, "we were told they were simple farmers."

"Textbooks are being rewritten as we stand here. Hundreds of Anasazi sites are being uncovered every year, all across the Colorado Plateau and the Southwest."

She glanced up at the excitement in Hutton's voice. Then she went still, caught by the beauty of his eyes, as deep and vivid as the mountain sky.

"The latest thinking is that the Anasazi were an imperial people," Hutton explained. "Their capital was in Chaco Canyon, New Mexico. They maintained a system of roads that reached all the way into Colorado."

But even his excitement and mesmerizing male beauty couldn't keep Christy's attention from the icon for long. Both timeless and atavistic, the tortoise enthralled her.

"Our archaeologists believe Xanadu's cave is the northernmost reach of the Chaco empire," Hutton said. "Not far from where we're standing lies the edge of one of the greatest ancient empires in the world."

"Why, it's like finding King Tut's tomb right here in Colorado!" Shannon Prell said.

"Anyone have the movie rights?" Tim asked idly. "I could make a hell of a film out of it."

Hutton smiled, but he didn't look away from Christy. Gently she placed the ancient tortoise back in its modern rosewood box.

"It must have been thrilling to discover this," she said, looking at the object. "I can't wait to see the cave."

Hutton's disappointment was immediate and intense. "I'm sorry. It's not safe."

"It can't be more dangerous than midnight in Manhattan."

"It's so bad they're not digging, they're stabilizing walls."

She looked away from the tortoise. "Sounds serious."

"It is. Besides," he added sheepishly, "the archaeologists would have my balls if I went back in there. They're still screaming about the stuff I already took out. But I couldn't leave *everything* there. What if the rest of the ceiling came down and buried the tortoise forever?"

"May I assume the tortoise is what inspired your new fashion collection?"

"Naughty, naughty," Hutton said, shaking his finger slowly at Christy. "You can't be a reporter until tomorrow tonight. Tonight is just for a few of my friends."

"No problem. I really came to see Jo-Jo." Christy looked around at the glittering crowd. "I'm surprised she isn't here."

He gave Christy a puzzled look. "I haven't seen her since yesterday, when she flew off to New York to meet you."

Chapter 8

"**D**amn!"

Another dead end.

Christy slammed the phone into its cradle and leaned back against the headboard of her hotel bed. Her shoulders were stiff and her neck muscles were in knots from seventy minutes on the telephone. She'd checked every message center, every link, every point where she and Jo-Jo might have missed connections.

Nothing.

No messages at the *Horizon* office.

Nick, groggy and grouchy from being awakened, said no one had called her since she left.

Jo-Jo's modeling agency hadn't heard a word, and her favorite Manhattan hotels had not seen her. Same for Hutton's headquarters in New York.

Christy's mouth was a flat line of frustration and . . . fear. With clipped politeness she battled the hotel switchboard long enough to reach the private number Hutton had given her. It was answered immediately.

"Autry speaking. May I help you?"

"This is Christa McKenna. Is Mr. Hutton available for a moment? It's rather urgent."

"For you Peter is available anytime, anywhere. But he's up to his ass in party alligators, so don't keep him too long, okay?"

"Sure. Thanks."

"Hang on."

A few moments later Hutton answered the phone, sounding harried. "What's up?"

"I can't find Jo-Jo."

"Did you try the Beverly Hills Hotel?"

"They haven't seen her for a month."

"How about— Wait a minute."

Hutton's voice faded as though he was holding the receiver aside while he fixed a petty crisis involving vegetarian guests who might be offended by barbecued meat.

"Did you try her agency?" he asked finally.

"She hasn't checked in for a week."

"Even with her personal agent?"

"Yes."

"Then maybe . . ."

Hutton's voice faded again into a muttered dialogue with Autry.

"Sorry," Hutton said into the phone a minute later. "It's a little crazy here."

"Aren't you worried about Jo-Jo?"

There was silence, then laughter. "That's a joke, right?"

"No."

"Babe, Jo is thirty years old. We are, as they say, an item, but not of the till-death-do-us-part variety. She comes and goes as she pleases. So do I."

"Without telling you?"

"If she wants me to know where she is, she'll be the first to tell me. Until then, I might as well whistle for the wind. It will come to heel sooner than Jo will."

The flat certainty in Hutton's voice told Christy that he'd tangled with Jo-Jo on that subject.

And lost.

"Isn't she modeling tonight?" Christy asked.

"The regular runway girls can fill in for the private showing."

"What about the press showing tomorrow night?"

"If—wait, Autry, I'd better talk to him myself—Christa, I've got to run. You're coming tonight, aren't you?"

"I don't know. Either way, I'll be at the formal press showing."

Her last words were spoken into a dead line.

She hung up, stared at the phone for a few minutes, and felt tension knotting her nerve endings. Some things never changed. Jo-Jo was still manipulating the people around her with sulks and disappearing acts.

Come out, come out, wherever you are.

But Jo-Jo wouldn't. Not until she was good and ready.

Christy jumped to her feet and began pacing. She wished she had a big swimming pool within reach. Twenty laps would have gone a long way toward working the tension out. She measured the length of her room three times, but only felt more confined for it. Like a wolf in a cage.

She needed to be outside.

A barbecue at Xanadu was better than waiting around her hotel room for a call that likely wouldn't come.

I don't play your games anymore, Jo-Jo. When are you going to outgrow them?

Christy showered and dressed in black silk slacks, a loose black silk pullover, and a pair of low black shoes that were dressy enough for a barbecue and comfortable enough for a hike. There was a lot of Xanadu to pace around in.

When she finished tying off her French braid, she checked her appearance in the mirror. With a grimace, she turned away from her reflection. Basic black went everywhere, but it required at least one piece of jewelry. She'd brought this outfit expecting to showcase Gramma's necklace against the black silk.

But the necklace was still beyond Christy's reach, and she hadn't brought anything else suitable.

So what? I'm not the one on display.

She yanked on an unstructured black linen jacket and went to the hotel lobby. She thought about driving herself to the ranch and decided it wasn't worth the hassle at the gate. She'd ride the shuttle with the rest of the hotel guests—the B-list folks who hadn't been invited to stay the night at Xanadu.

Outside, the evening air was cool. A full moon was just sliding up over the San Juan Wall, pouring silver light over the land. A gleaming white van wheeled up to the entrance of the hotel. A driver in a cowboy hat leaned out.

"Xanadu?" the driver asked.

Three couples who had been waiting climbed into the rear seats of the van, leaving Christy to take the front seat next to the driver. She didn't feel like being chatty, so she simply turned her head and looked out the side window.

Even without joining the conversation, she learned a great deal about her fellow guests before they reached the top of the rocky mesa. The most vocal of the group was a wealthy Seattle brain surgeon and his wife who collected Anasazi artifacts. They were traveling with a primitive-art gallery owner from Houston and his wife.

Conversation swirled around the van, the boasting and shouldering of full-time, wealthy collectors.

"At the Tucson show, he paid twenty-nine thousand for a pot I wouldn't have pissed in."

"That's nothing. Herman was bidding on a basket that went to fifty-three."

"Did he get it?"

"Shit, yes. He always gets what he wants."

Christy looked out at the moon-silvered land and tried to imagine what it would have been like to live and die within the same handful of square miles, having known nothing but the sun, the sky, and the land itself. The idea seemed a melancholy counterpoint to the avaricious conversation behind her.

". . . grave goods from Springerville. Only these were special."

"Turquoise?"

"I should hope to shout. Buckets of it."

"So?"

"So it was wrapped around seven skeletons like a winding sheet."

A soft whistle came out of the silence. "Were they complete?"

"Except for a few toe bones, and those will probably turn up. Even had some hair."

"Male or female?"

"Female."

"Why wasn't I called? I've got a standing order for female bones. Nobody pays more than I do."

"These aren't for sale."

"Everything is for sale. Look at the McElmo grayware that came on the market last month. We both know where we saw that last."

"Yeah, and we know where it is now. Damn Japanese are driving prices over the moon."

"The Germans are worse. They'll buy anything Anasazi, even a piece-of-shit potsherd I wouldn't step on. In fact—"

"Shelby, can you talk about something besides dead Indians and greedy foreigners for just two minutes?"

There was laughter at the woman's long-suffering complaint. The conversation shifted locale but not subject matter, from Colorado to a private showing in Sedona—pots, fetishes, and the skull of a baby inlaid with turquoise.

Christy watched the moonlight on the top of the mesa, grateful she had never been possessed by the urge to collect. The only object she'd ever really wanted was Gramma's necklace.

I'll get it and to hell with Jo-Jo's games. That necklace is mine.

The conversation shifted to real estate prices in Telluride, Aspen, Santa Fe, and Taos.

She began to get the feeling that the West was being overrun by looters of all kinds—those who sacked archaeological sites for artifacts and those who sacked old ranches for condominium sites. Like that young cowboy-turned-deputy. He'd been crowded off the land when a fashion designer's millions had changed the way his part of the West was run.

Shutting out the voices, Christy watched the land flow by in dreamlike shades of black and silver. If the light was just right, her window became a bottomless mirror reflecting her and the country in strange unity. She stopped thinking and let herself be mesmerized by light and dark flowing through her and the land.

When the shuttle arrived at Xanadu, some thirty couples were already dancing on the rough-lumber floor she'd seen being built earlier that day. Another hundred people— fashion groupies, Hutton executives, and art collectors—had gathered around tables laden with food, wine, and beer.

In what had once been a pasture and now was a carefully groomed meadow, hired pilots had tied down small planes near a moon-bright runway. Other planes circled in the high, clear air, waiting for their turn in the landing pattern.

A Range Rover waited off to the side, ready to whisk newcomers a whole one thousand feet away to the party.

Peter Hutton appeared for a moment, framed in the doorway of the barn, talking to someone who was out of sight inside.

When Christy reached the big, gambrel-roofed building, she saw that it had been turned into a makeshift dressing room. In a quiet frenzy, seamstresses and dressers made last-minute adjustments for a dozen models.

Jo-Jo wasn't one of them.

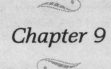

Chapter 9

Lighting technicians went over the script with the narrator, who was a New York stage actor brought in for a one-night gig. He was the kind of beautiful celebrity that Jo-Jo loved drawing into her orbit.

But Jo-Jo wasn't here.

Christy caught glimpses of flowing fabric with lightning-stroke designs that reminded her of the Anasazi pots in Hutton's house. She saw several pieces of jewelry in the turtle's turquoise, black, and mother-of-pearl motif. There was a breathtaking gown in white silk with a glittering black design that was like a curving variation of a child's stick figure. The design had extraordinary energy.

When Hutton spotted Christy he walked toward her, flashing his trademark smile. "Glad you decided to come tonight. You class up the place."

"Thanks," she said politely.

"I'd like to show you around, but—"

"No problem," she cut in. "Just one quick question."

Hutton raised his pale, arching brows. "Sure, babe."

"Do you know a man named Aaron Cain?"

Hutton's eyes narrowed. "That bastard. What about him? Last I heard he was in a hospital in Grand Junction."

"He's in Remington now."

For a moment Hutton looked as primitive as a stone club. Then he shrugged casually. "Doesn't matter. He won't be around long."

"Would he know where Jo-Jo is?"

"Jo did lots of slumming around Remington and Montrose. I doubt if she kept in touch afterward."

Someone yelled Hutton's name.

"Sorry, babe." He brushed a fast kiss across Christy's cheek. "Catch you after the show."

Within seconds he'd disappeared into the whirl of fabric and female flesh that would miraculously become a fashion show.

The smell of food drifting from the barbecue pits reminded Christy that it was well past dinner hour, Manhattan time. She hadn't eaten much on the plane or during the drive to Remington. She hadn't eaten at all since she'd arrived. She'd been too busy, too angry, or both.

But now the cool night air and the fragrance of the barbecue teased her appetite. She walked over to the buffet tables groaning beneath platters heaped with three kinds of meat. Pans of chili, bowls of salads, and plates of vegetables filled in the spaces between mounds of fresh bread and tortillas. Beer chilled in a tub, side by side with white wine for the city types and Dom Pérignon for those foolish enough to think champagne really did go with everything.

Christy ate barbecued pork tenderloin, a square of tender buttered cornbread, and a casserole of red-and-white Anasazi beans with chilies and molasses. She washed it down with a pale Colorado ale. She half expected the combination of Xanadu's seven-thousand-foot altitude, jet lag, and alcohol to knock her on her butt. Instead, the food gave her new energy.

And the tastes and scent of the barbecue, the textures of the western night itself, brought memories. She pushed them away as she'd done for so many years.

Restless, edgy, not knowing what to do about it, she set aside her plate and glass. She strolled around the edge of the crowd, looking for the flash of Jo-Jo's blond hair, listening for the husky laughter that made everyone who heard it feel part of a delicious conspiracy.

When the band took a break, the workmen descended, carrying a runway into position for the fashion show. The separate knots of people slowly began to converge on the stage, anticipating a preview of the fashion event of the year.

Without warning all the anger and disappointed hope exploded in Christy. She was damned if she'd wait around like ugly wallpaper for Jo-Jo to make her entrance.

Jamming her hands in her pockets, Christy strode away from the strings of lights and groups of laughing people. A hundred feet from the perimeter of the barns, she was alone. She let out a long breath of relief. She wasn't up to the demands of her professional role as a *Horizon* reporter or her social role as the dirt-plain sister of the heavenly Jo-Jo.

Once, just once, Christy wanted to rock her sister back on her perfectly shaped butt.

The thought was tantalizing.

Jo-Jo knows what the necklace means to me. That's why she dangled it in front of me when she thought I might not come.

All Christy had to do was sneak into the house, take what was hers anyway, and then enjoy the look on Jo-Jo's face when she finally swept in—and saw Gramma's necklace around her sister's throat.

A quarter mile away the beautiful glass and wood house

gleamed like a beacon on the knoll. A road wound up to the front door.

Christy didn't follow the road because she wasn't sure whether Hutton's security troops would be on duty. What she wanted to do was too personal to explain to some stranger. She'd just have to play Hide and Seek with all the ex-cowboys wearing badges.

Sparse brush and grass covered the knoll. She stumbled a few times until her eyes adjusted to the darkness. The altitude and the beer she'd had made her a bit light-headed. Moonlight added to the sense of unreality.

By the time she reached the edge of the lawn that wrapped around the house, she was breathing rapidly. Dew sparkled on the grass, drenching her shoes. Lights burned inside the house, but she didn't see anyone moving around. At the far end, away from the display room and its walls of glass, there was a kitchen big enough to service a restaurant. Pans hung from hooks on the wall.

As Christy walked closer to the house, she saw that the kitchen was empty. All the caterers were busy out at the barn. Feeling slightly foolish and very determined, she looked around to make sure she was alone before she went up to the open kitchen window and listened. Somewhere inside a radio was playing country music. No one was singing along with Merle Haggard. No one was making any noise at all.

The kitchen door was locked.

She circled around behind the house, trying several more doors. She was about to give up when she found one open. Walking softly, she entered and closed the door quietly behind her. Then she looked around, trying to orient herself.

Her heart beat frantically.

She hadn't felt this foolish and little-girl frightened since Jo-Jo had talked her into hiding spiders in the teacher's desk.

*And guess who paid for that bit of mischief? It sure wasn't
the beautiful little angel.*

After two attempts Christy found the corridor leading off
in the direction of the house's residential wing. The dew-wet
soles of her shoes squeaked on the tile floor. To her
adrenaline-heightened senses, the tiny sounds were as loud
as clashing cymbals.

The corridor opened into the huge room where Xanadu's
treasures were on display. Flames danced cheerfully in a fireplace big enough to roast an ox.

The room was empty.

Christy retraced her steps and found another hallway. This
one led to what she hoped was Hutton's quarters. She walked
down the hall very quietly, not sure if Jo-Jo and Hutton
shared a bedroom as well as a bed.

The hall was lined with paintings. Each canvas had its own
light. She glanced at the art as she went through the hall. One
of the paintings stopped her cold.

The painting was a surrealistic drawing of a sunset storm
sweeping across the red-rock mesa country. Inside the dark
crimson storm cell lurked faces of ghouls whose eyes and
cruel smiles were human skulls. The squall itself was a vicious demon raking the land with talons of lightning.

Wherever the talons touched, wounds appeared.

Within the wounds were headless skeletons. Their gleaming ivory arms were extended upward, fingers clawing toward the missing skulls that would be forever beyond their
reach.

Technically, the painting was expert. The artist had a keen
appreciation of force and energy, light and shadow, color and
shading. That was part of the picture's horrifying impact.
The rest came from the enjoyment of pain that radiated from
the demon's cruel smile.

With a shiver, Christy turned away, feeling chilled to the center of her own bones. She could no more have lived with that demon-ridden painting than she could have used a corpse as a coffee table. She hurried away from the ghastly art.

An open door farther down the hall led to what was clearly a guest bedroom. The decor of the room was as expensive and impersonal as a suite in a five-star hotel. The room was so clean and orderly it felt like it had never been used.

A second door opening off the hallway was locked. At the end of the hall she tried a third door, found it open, and let herself into a large master suite. Expensive men's clothing hung in the walk-in closet.

Hutton's quarters.

An odd, half-familiar scent tickled Christy's memories. She breathed in deeply, trying to place it.

Baby powder?

Not very likely. She inhaled again.

Baby powder.

Even with the smell of a nursery in the air, there was a decidedly masculine feel to the bedroom. The decor was lean and sinewy, dramatic, red and black with silver accents.

Another intense work by the artist who put ghouls in his rain clouds hung over the bed. The gleaming silver-white of skeletons and lightning from the hallway painting appeared as accents in small sculptures around the room.

It was like walking into hell.

How could anyone sleep here?

Off to one side of the room she saw another door. It led to the adjoining room. This door wasn't locked.

The next room was another bedroom. A life-sized nude photo of Jo-Jo dominated the wall of this room. The color combination of creamy skin, pink lips and nipples, golden hair, and emerald eyes echoed in the off-white walls, the pink-and-gold fabric of the canopy bed, and the emerald accents supplied by carved crystal perfume bottles placed in artful disarray across the white-and-gilt dresser.

The effect of the room was rather like Jo-Jo herself—creamy, sensual, with gemlike flashes of temper.

Gotcha, sister mine.

Chapter 10

Christy started to close the door behind her, but thought better of it. There might be an automatic locking system. Very carefully she left a finger's width of space between the edge of the door and the frame.

Then she took a deep breath and looked around quickly, reviewing Hutton's house in her mind. The French doors off of Hutton's room opened onto the cantilevered deck that overlooked the grounds. There weren't any doors like that in Jo-Jo's room. Even better, the curtains had been drawn against the night.

She wouldn't be spotted by anyone wandering around outside.

Feeling both elated and foolish, she headed for the white lacquered jewelry box on top of the dresser. It didn't take long to go through. Jo-Jo had always known instinctively that her aura of primal sexuality was undermined rather than enhanced by flashy accessories.

Gramma's necklace wasn't there.

"Liar," Christy whispered. "You hocked it after all."

But she wouldn't give up until she was certain. She had

come this far and she was damned if she'd tuck tail and run until she'd searched all the usual places.

And a few of the unusual ones while she was at it.

It wouldn't be the first time Christy had searched her sister's room for forbidden fruit of one kind or another. But, with luck, it would be the last.

The ornate, vaguely Louis XIV dresser held enough sexy lingerie to stock Frederick's of Hollywood. Christy ran her hands underneath the drawers, checking what had once been Jo-Jo's favorite hiding place for small things. All Christy found was that the dresser undoubtedly was expensive, but it hadn't been finished worth a damn. The wood was rough enough to leave splinters.

She made a quick run through the bedside tables, the bed, and between the mattress and springs before she turned toward the double doors that shielded the walk-in closet. A huge, knobby, old-fashioned brass key rested in a scrolled brass keyhole. A single turn opened the lock.

Inside, the closet was filled with the sharp aroma of cedar. The faintly astringent odor was pleasing after the room full of cream and gilt, perfume and lingerie, lorded over by Jo-Jo's naked perfection.

After a bit of fumbling, Christy located a light switch. *Lordy, lordy, as Gramma would have said.*

Unbelievable.

Jo-Jo had always loved clothes. Finally she'd been able to indulge that passion. Rank after rank of costumes hung on padded hangers—sports outfits, cocktail dresses, winter sweaters, slacks, skirts, and some swirls of fabric whose name Christy couldn't guess.

Shoes, boots, sandals, and slippers of every color stood in rainbow array in an alcove made just for the purpose. A full set of Hartmann luggage was stacked at the back. The soft leather cases were scuffed, which meant that Jo-Jo would be shopping soon. She'd never understood that even the most beautifully made tool was supposed to be used.

The order in the closet told Christy that a maid had straightened it. No matter how great her passion for clothes, Jo-Jo had no patience for picking up after herself. That chore had been left for Gramma or Christy to do.

She dismissed the clothes and went to the built-in chest. The top three drawers held socks of all colors and fabrics. She patted the carefully matched pairs. Nothing was hidden inside or beneath. She ran her hand beneath the drawers. Nothing.

The fourth drawer was full of starched and ironed Hutton dress shirts, man-styled but in the soft colors Jo-Jo preferred. Nothing concealed underneath the shirts.

No necklace.

The fifth drawer held jeans, ironed, no starch. Nothing between the folds. Nothing on the bottom of the drawer.

Nothing.

Damn it! Did you really sell that necklace just to get back at me for something I never did?

Christy's flying fingers almost missed the key taped beneath the sixth drawer. She hesitated, caught between disappointment that it wasn't the necklace and triumph at finding anything at all. If Jo-Jo had taken the trouble to hide the key, it was important.

Maybe she'd trade it for the necklace.

Gently Christy eased the drawer free of its tracks, turned it upside down, and peeled off the tape. The key had the blank anonymity of a public washroom. Plain steel, not a curlicue or flourish of gilt anywhere.

Hardly Jo-Jo's style.

The key showed signs of long casual use, as though it had passed through many hands. Clearly it didn't fit a lock in any of Jo-Jo's fantasy bedroom furniture.

Frowning, Christy replaced the drawer, wondering where the lock that fit the key might be. She moved closer to the closet light and held the key up. The metal was so worn she couldn't make out the words that had been stamped in it. No matter how hard she stared, a vague ". . . SP . . ." and a faint ". . . ot Dupl . . ." was all she could read.

Then she heard the sound of someone walking down the tiled corridor from the main part of the house. Without stopping to think, she flipped off the light switch and held her breath like a child sneaking through a graveyard on a dare.

The sounds came closer, then stopped.

She guessed that whoever had made them was still in the corridor. Maybe it was just a bored guard walking a beat that included the display cases and the ghoulish but undoubtedly first-rate paintings on the walls.

Breathing very softly, she listened with every bit of her concentration.

She didn't hear anything.

Cautiously she opened the closet door and tiptoed across the bedroom to the hall door. Putting her ear against it, she held her breath. All she heard was the blood roaring in her ears. It didn't make her feel better.

Necklace or no necklace, it was time to get out of Jo-Jo's fantasy.

Christy shoved the key into the pocket of her black slacks and headed for the hall door straight from Jo-Jo's room. She didn't want to face the demons in Hutton's bedroom again. As she reached for the doorknob, she noticed the rheostat on the wall. When she twisted it cautiously, the light in the room dimmed. She twisted a bit more and then even more until the room slowly slid into darkness. With great care she turned the door handle, praying it wouldn't squeak.

It didn't.

Letting out her breath in a soundless rush, she eased the door open just enough to peek into the hall.

The man was huge.

He stood with his back to her, a darkness that seemed to fill the hallway from floor to ceiling and wall to wall. His face was hidden by the straight brim of a big Stetson.

Frozen by shock, she watched the man kneel in front of the locked door that lay between the display room and the entrance to Hutton's bedroom. When he moved his hand, small pieces of metal glinted and rang softly.

She'd never seen a set of lock picks, but she was certain she was seeing them now.

The man was working on the locked door, but he wasn't having a lot of success. A metallic snap, a muttered curse. Metal gleamed and clicked as he tried a new probe.

Somewhere in the house a door closed and boots rang like shots on a tile floor. The steps were confident, open, loud, and headed from kitchen to display room.

The huge burglar straightened, listened, and glanced down the hall in Christy's direction, a man looking for a fast, silent exit.

The confident footsteps came closer, then muffled when they went from tile to one of the Navajo rugs scattered around the display room's floor. The sound of the steps became clear again, then faded.

Obviously one of Hutton's guards was making a circuit of the display room. It took no particular brains to figure out that the hallway paintings would be next on his rounds.

The burglar sure thought so. He stood swiftly and stared toward the display room.

The instant the man's attention shifted, Christy eased Jo-Jo's bedroom door shut. Heart pounding, she headed for Hutton's bedroom. The escape route through the French doors onto the deck was her only hope of avoiding a discovery that would be embarrassing—and, with the burglar around, dangerous.

She was reaching for the knob of the connecting door when she heard one of the French doors open and shut. Someone else had just entered Hutton's bedroom. The burglar's escape route was cut off.

So was hers.

She spun around and felt her way through darkness back to Jo-Jo's closet. When she opened the door, her hand brushed against the oversized antique key in the lock. She pulled out the heavy brass key and shut the door quietly behind her. Working in the dark, she tried to insert the key quietly into the back side of the lock.

Her hand was shaking too hard.

By steadying one hand with the other, she managed to fit the key into the thumb-sized opening. As she turned the key, she prayed that the lock was as old-fashioned as the key itself.

It was. The key turned and the mechanism clicked. Anyone who tried the door from the outside would find it locked.

The key slipped out of her shaking fingers and fell to the carpet. She stood in the dark and shivered with the adrenaline racing through her body. Her heart was beating so fast and hard she was afraid it could be heard all the way to the barn.

The hall door into Jo-Jo's room opened and closed, followed by the sounds of someone blundering around in the dark. The burglar, no doubt. A guard would have turned on a light.

She held her breath and desperately wanted to be invisible.

Chapter 11

"Jack, where the hell are you?" a guard yelled.

"Hutton's bedroom. Anything in the hall?"

"I thought I saw someone go into Jo's room."

"Check it out."

A light switched on. A shaft of brightness poured through the closet's empty keyhole, piercing the darkness with light.

Shouts and curses exploded.

By the time Christy dropped to one knee and peered through the keyhole, the brief struggle was over. Two of Hutton's security guards faced the big burglar. One of the guards was Deputy Hammond, who had ridden with her from the gate. The other guard was older and had his gun out. Both guards wore the bright silver stars of Remington County deputies.

"Turn around, you son of a bitch," the older deputy said. "Hands on the wall right now. Do it!"

The guard underlined his orders with a wave of his chrome-plated revolver.

The prisoner shrugged, then turned and faced the wall.

"Frisk him, Jack."

Hammond stepped forward and patted the burglar down, careful not to get in his partner's way.

When the prisoner looked over his shoulder at the deputies, Christy saw that the man was Native American, darkly handsome. A scar ran from beneath his eye to the point of his chin. The cut had gone deep. The right side of his face didn't move when he spoke or smiled.

"Hey, Jack, I'm just looking for a head," the burglar said to Hammond.

"Bullshit, Johnny," Hammond said. "You know where the heads are."

"Check it out, man," Johnny said.

"Crap," Hammond said in disgust. "Hutton would never invite a no-account Moki poacher like you to his party. What are you doing up here?"

"Aw, c'mon, I was just—"

The big Indian started to turn away from the wall as he spoke, but Hammond stepped in close and delivered a quick, hard kidney punch.

"Don't move," the deputy snarled.

"Aw, Jack, you know I'm not going to jump you."

"Face the wall," the senior deputy ordered with a wave of his gun. "What were you after?"

The Indian glanced over his shoulder, then spat in the direction of the two guards.

The senior deputy stepped forward and slammed his pistol across the right side of Johnny's face. Blood sprang from a new cut close to the scar on his face, but his expression didn't change. It was like the blow had never happened.

Johnny spat blood carelessly. "Do that again and I'm gonna get pissed off."

"Cuff him," the senior deputy ordered.

He rested the muzzle of his pistol against Johnny's neck

while Hammond fished a pair of handcuffs out of his hip pocket. The deputy's motions were awkward. He was more used to putting pigging strings on calves than handcuffs on prisoners, but he got the job done. He snapped one cuff on Johnny's right wrist and dragged it down into the small of his back.

"Gimme the other hand," Hammond said.

When Johnny moved too slowly, the senior deputy rammed the muzzle of his gun into the Indian's throat.

"Do it!"

Unwillingly, Johnny dropped his left hand and let it be cuffed. Hammond closed the metal bracelet in place.

"Tighter," said the senior deputy.

Hammond squeezed hard until the cuffs bit into flesh. When he was certain Johnny was helpless, Hammond drew his fist back and delivered another kidney punch.

"That's for that bar over in Montrose," Hammond said, "when you busted Shorty's skull."

This time Johnny groaned softly and went to his knees. "I'll get you for that, you—"

Johnny's words were cut off by a gun barrel raking across his mouth.

"What are you doing here?" the senior deputy demanded.

Johnny's response was a mumbled curse that could have been English or some older language.

Another raking pistol blow stopped the words.

"What are you doing here?" the senior deputy asked again.

Silence.

The senior looked at Hammond, who shrugged.

"I know this ol' boy," Hammond said. "You can hammer on him till your arm's sore and he won't say nothing he don't want to say."

"Autry isn't going to like this."

Hammond shrugged again.

The senior guard pulled a small portable two-way radio from his belt and spoke softly into it.

The Indian spat blood. "Yeah, call Autry. Tell him I want to talk to him."

The senior deputy ignored Johnny.

The Indian grinned, exposing bad teeth outlined in his own blood. "You better get Hutton up here, too."

"Mr. Hutton doesn't want to talk to your kind."

"Tell him it's about Kokopelli's sisters." Johnny spat again. "That'll bring him on the jump."

The two deputies exchanged puzzled glances.

"Kokopelli," Johnny growled. "Tell him."

The guards stepped back a few feet and conferred in whispers for a moment. The senior deputy shrugged, then looked at Johnny and frowned. Hammond went over and jerked the big Indian to his feet.

"Walk or git dragged," Hammond said.

"I'll walk. But you gotta get Autry."

"Yeah. Sure," the senior deputy said. "Just as soon as we cool you off."

The two men shoved Johnny ahead of them in the direction of the hall.

Christy drew a deep breath and swallowed hard, fighting the beer and barbecue sauce that were trying to crawl back up her throat. She'd seen bar brawls in her Wyoming childhood, but she'd never seen a bound man deliberately beaten. Even knowing that Johnny was a burglar didn't make it less sickening.

When she couldn't hear any more sounds from outside, she groped around on the closet floor until she found the big brass key. It took her three tries to unlock the door, and three more tries before the door locked again behind her.

The blood the big Indian had spat lay bright and red on the carpet.

Her stomach clenched and threatened to rebel all over again. She swallowed. It was past time to leave the horror show behind.

Letting out her breath, she made a wide circuit around the blood, crept to the hall door, and listened. Somewhere at the other end of the house, a heavy door closed. One of the guards came back into the hall from the kitchen. The men's voices carried clearly in the silent house.

"He ain't gonna die in that meat locker, is he?" Hammond asked.

"Not real quick. It's only about forty degrees. But when we drag him out in half an hour, he sure won't be running his mouth at us anymore."

The deputies came down the hall from the kitchen as far as the entrance to the display room.

Christy shrank back from the door. If she went out that way, she would be spotted and recognized instantly.

"Look here," the senior deputy said.

"Where?"

"There. See? He must of had someone with him."

"What?" Hammond asked.

"Jesus, Jack, get some glasses. See those shoe prints on the tile? They're way too small to be ours, much less Johnny's."

"Oh, Christ. They're still damp. We'd better go through the place again."

"Yeah. And this time we'd better do it right, or Autry will kick our asses right out of Colorado."

The closet wouldn't be good enough this time. Christy had to get out of the house, and she had to do it *now*.

She ran for the door that connected Jo-Jo's room with Hutton's. The door was still ajar. She leaped through, raced

across the bedroom, and headed for the French doors. The
door latch wouldn't work.

Come on, come on, open!

She wrenched and twisted the lock until it finally opened.
The doors seemed way too heavy to her frantic, fumbling
hands. Suddenly cool, clean air rushed over her.

She was free.

She sprinted across the big deck. There was an eight-foot
drop down to the bushes. She hesitated, heard a man's voice
from Hutton's bedroom, scrambled over the railing, and
hung by her hands for a moment. Before she could change
her mind, she let go and fell into the shrubbery below.

The ground had just been worked by the gardeners. It was
soft and loose, cushioning her fall. She scrambled to her
feet, tripped over a sprinkler head, fell, and tumbled into the
decorative shrubs. The low branches of an evergreen raked
over her.

She didn't fight the prickly embrace. She just curled
tightly beneath the branches, terrified that she'd hear the
guards yelling after her—or worse, shooting at her. She
prayed that the black of her clothes would blend completely
into the moon shadow of the thick shrubbery. But she didn't
look up or try to see anything happening on the deck. She
knew how an animal's eyes gleamed when caught by a
flashlight.

Breath held, heart pounding, she heard a guard walk to the
edge of the deck and stop.

"See anything, Jack?" the other guard called from the
bedroom.

"Thought I did."

"Check out the front. I'll take the side."

Hammond cursed but did as his boss said.

Barely daring to breathe, Christy waited while steps overhead faded away into the house. She gathered her courage, pushed herself to her feet, and fled down the back side of the knoll, racing for the best safety she could find.

Off to the right, a graceful stand of spruce marked the bottom of the slope. Straight ahead, across the meadow, runway lights flared and graceful, leggy women glided like colored shadows through the night.

Once Christy got to the barn, she could blend into the crowd. No one would know she had ever been inside the house. But the meadow between her and the party was drenched in moonlight.

If she went that way, the guards couldn't miss her.

She sprinted for the trees off to the right. As their shadows closed around her, she caught a flicker of movement from the corner of her eye. With a hoarse sound she flung herself aside.

Too late.

A hard hand clamped across her mouth, stifling her scream. A long arm went around her shoulders and jerked back, pinning her, dragging her farther back into the trees.

Silently, desperately, she twisted and clawed against a strength much greater than her own. Suddenly her feet were kicked out from under her. She went face first onto the cold ground.

The man followed her down, pinning her until she no longer struggled. She would have screamed then, but she didn't have the breath or the strength to get away from the hand clamped over her mouth.

She went slack, hoping to make him believe that she'd given up.

The world spun dizzily as the man flipped her over with frightening ease, like she was made of shadows rather than solid flesh. He turned her head toward the moonlight. His smile was a bleak flash of white against a face hidden by darkness.

"Jackpot," he said softly.

Christy recognized the voice and stiffened.

Aaron Cain.

Chapter 12

"**S**ettle down, Red," Cain said in a low voice. "I'm not going to hurt you. Do you hear me?"

Christy heard.

But she didn't believe him.

"I'm going to lift my hand," he said calmly. "Before you scream, think about it. You listening?"

Slowly she nodded.

His white smile gleamed briefly. "Good. You keep on thinking and listening and you'll be all right. Hutton's guards are local boys—cowboys and hunters and miners. You run fast for a city girl, but they'll track you down real quick."

Cain's matter-of-fact tone cut through her fear. So did the fact that he wasn't hurting her. He was just holding her hard enough to make sure she didn't run or scream, giving away her position.

And his.

Hesitantly she nodded.

"I'm not going to hurt you," he said again. "I'm going to help you get out of here. Is that what you want? To get out of here?"

She nodded again.

After a long moment, the hand covering her mouth lifted slightly. She drew in quick, aching breaths, her body jerking against his while she pumped air into lungs starved by effort and fear.

He looked down into her eyes and saw that she was frightened but not panicked. Watching him. Wary of him. She wasn't screaming, but she was a long way from trusting him. He rolled aside and waited to see if she would try to get away.

The sudden freedom was as dizzying to Christy as being captured had been. After the heat and weight of Cain's body restraining her, the night felt cold and limitless.

"Ready?" he asked softly.

"Why are you helping me?" she whispered.

White teeth flashed.

This time she was calm enough to understand that his smile was cold rather than comforting.

"Good question, Red. When I have an answer, you'll be the second to know. Got your breath back yet?"

"I'm working on it."

"Don't take too long. The word has gone out."

She followed his glance. On the hillside leading to the house, four flashlight beams swept the grass. Other flashlights flickered on the flats as more guards abandoned the dance floor and headed toward the house.

Sooner or later, someone was bound to notice the trail she'd left across the recently watered lawn.

"I'm ready," she said quickly.

Cain didn't waste any time talking. He came to his feet, pulling her with him.

His casual strength irritated Christy, reminding her all over again how much of a disadvantage she was at when stacked against the average male, much less one with Aaron Cain's height and lean power. When he took her arm to lead her through the night, she pulled back.

Or tried to.

His hand tightened, chaining her as efficiently as the deputy's steel manacles had chained Johnny.

"Easy," Cain murmured. "I know the way. You don't."

"I can walk without—"

"Quiet." Though soft, there was no doubting the command in his voice.

She wanted to yell at him, but it was the wrong time and place to tell him how she could get along just fine without him. Silently she let him draw her through the trees to a narrow game trail.

"Follow me," he said in a voice that carried no farther than her. "Try not to make any noise."

He was like the night. Quiet. He blended into the darkness with no more fuss than a wolf. He moved like a wolf too. Tireless, relentless, following a trail she couldn't see.

She followed as quietly as she could, not complaining even though the pace was just short of a run. It irritated her that she wasn't nearly as quiet as Cain, but what really made her mad was that she was rapidly running out of breath.

She'd have to double her time at the gym.

Cain didn't stop until he came to a small dry ravine cutting through the trees. The sides of the ravine were four feet high and nearly vertical. He slid halfway down the bank until he found solid footing. Then he reached back up, caught her beneath her arms, and lifted her down.

She barely bit back a startled cry. She wasn't used to being lifted. Her fingers clenched around his shoulders. When she felt dry sand under her feet, she stumbled, still off balance.

He steadied her, then released her slowly.

Her heart jerked. She was certain she'd felt his palms brush the sides of her breasts as he let go.

But nothing in his manner suggested that he'd noticed the intimacy, or cared about it if he had. He was already walking off through the lighter shade of darkness that was the bed of the ravine. His low voice floated back in the darkness.

"Move, Red. Or do you want me to carry you?"

With a muffled word, she followed. She felt breathless, off balance, thoroughly irritated with herself, with him, and with the night itself.

Moonlight turned the sand into a pale, rumpled highway. When the dry watercourse deepened and widened, Cain waited until Christy came alongside.

"No noise, now," he said in a voice that barely carried to her ears.

She nodded. Together they walked carefully, quietly, following the gently winding ravine.

Men's voices came from somewhere off to the right.

She froze even as her heart raced. When Cain's hand closed around her arm and pulled her toward deeper shadows, she didn't fight him.

Flashlight beams flickered through the woods, but no cry of discovery followed. So far no one had found Christy's trail across the grass.

Standing in the chill clarity of the night, she was aware once more of the thin air at seven thousand feet. That, more than fear or exercise, was making her breathless.

Cain tugged at her hand, urging her forward once more. His long legs covered the ground at a speed that made her work. She concentrated on controlling her breathing so she could keep up. After five minutes, he finally slowed.

She noticed that his breathing was easy yet quick. She wondered if the altitude was getting to him. Then she remembered that he'd been shot not very long ago. He might move like a wolf, and she had no doubt that he could run or walk her into the ground, but he wasn't a machine. He had to breathe too.

The thought comforted her. She let out a long breath.

He turned and looked at her in silent question. She smiled

in equally silent reassurance. He squeezed her hand and turned back to the trail again.

She wondered where it led.

Safety would be good.

Then she smiled at her wistful thought. Cain might be helping her right now, but anywhere he went had to be a long way from safe. He just wasn't a safe sort of man.

After a few more minutes, a second dry wash came in from the left. Cain pulled Christy into the shadow of a clump of willows. Then he pulled her right up against his body. Before she could protest, he was speaking against her ear. His mouth was so close she could feel the warmth of his breath.

"Quiet," he breathed.

She wanted to ask why. She didn't. Even if he answered— not likely—this wasn't a good time for questions.

Motionless, silent, she stood close to him in the black and silver darkness, feeling the heat of his body on one side and the cold of the night on the other. She heard nothing but the soft sound of breathing, her own and his. The sense of isolation and intimacy was both disturbing and strangely exhilarating.

She'd never been so completely alone with a man, any man, much less a stranger.

"All right," he murmured.

He tugged on her hand and started walking again. Within fifty steps they turned a bend in the ravine. A low, open Jeep loomed out of the darkness. The vehicle all but filled the narrow watercourse.

"Yours?" she whispered.

"Your fellow burglar's."

"What?"

"That's his Jeep."

"He's not *my* burglar," she said.

"Quiet."

"But—"

"Later," he interrupted ruthlessly.

He circled the Jeep and kept walking quickly, pulling her along in his wake. A quarter mile farther down the dry wash, the black bulk of his truck loomed beside a clump of willows that looked silver in the moonlight.

Cain led Christy to the passenger side, unlocked the door, and opened it. No interior lights came on. She was still absorbing that—and the fact that it was a big step up into the truck—when his hands closed around her waist. Before she could say a word, he tossed her up into the passenger seat.

The door closed quickly and very quietly behind her.

He circled around and got into the driver's seat. The truck's engine fired instantly. Smoothly he eased into gear and started forward.

"Aren't you forgetting something?" she asked.

"What?"

"Headlights."

His smile gleamed coldly. "No, I'm not forgetting them."

Cain drove expertly despite the darkness and the obstacles in the streambed. The truck made twice the pace a fast-walking man could have managed.

Christy knew she was staring at him, or at least at his black profile against the lighter side window, but she couldn't help it. His long, lean hands held the wheel with a casual skill that fascinated her. She'd forgotten how much harder driving was in a riverbed as opposed to a highway. There weren't a lot of dry riverbeds to drive in Manhattan.

I've been away too long.

Or maybe not long enough. It was just this kind of lean, confident, take-charge-or-else man that had made New York look good.

Chapter 13

Cain drove several miles in the bed of the creek before he came to a dirt road that led down through cuts in the bank. He turned onto the road and shifted out of four-wheel drive. Little more than a dirt track, the road was almost as rough as the creek bed had been. Ruts led up a steep hill and then across a flat red-rock mesa. After more than a mile, the road dropped down through a slot into another canyon.

"Time for headlights?" Christy asked.

"No."

"Why?"

Silence.

A deer leaped out of the scrub right in front of the truck. Cain hit the brakes hard.

There wasn't any red flash from the brake lights. Like the interior lights, the taillights had been put out of commission. The big truck was nearly invisible as it moved over the backcountry.

And this "Moki-poaching son of a bitch" accuses me of being a burglar? she thought sardonically.

Finally he snapped on the headlights and picked up speed.

The black truck rattled and banged over the rough surface of the dirt.

"Home free?" she suggested.

"We're getting there."

"How did you and Johnny get separated?" she asked. "Or were you the lookout?"

"What?"

"Oh, come on. I don't think that ravine is one of the usual parking spots for Peter's guests."

Cain grunted.

"You weren't in the house with Johnny," she said, "but you were watching the house. You called him a burglar, so you knew he was inside with a handful of lock picks. It stands to reason you were the lookout."

"Got it all figured out, haven't you?"

"I'm working on it."

"Do you spend a lot of time with burglars and ex-cons?" he asked.

The question was so calm that it took a moment for her to understand. "Excuse me?"

"You don't seem worried about being off alone in the ass end of nowhere in the middle of the night with a man who you think is a burglar and you know is an ex-con."

That answered the question of whether Cain had noticed Christy eavesdropping in the Two-Tier West.

He had.

"So," he said, "either you're used to crooks or you're the kind of woman who just can't wait to get in a murderer's jeans and see if he's different from the other men you've screwed."

Her breath came in sharply. His voice was calm, but so bitter she felt like she'd been slapped.

"Stop the truck," she said flatly. "Now."

He ignored her.

She reached for the door handle.

He flipped the master lock switch.

"Let me out!" She tried to keep the fear out of her voice, but didn't quite make it. Not surprising.

She was frightened.

"Settle down," Cain said. "The truck is going too fast for a dramatic exit. You'll break your silly neck. Waste of effort. I'm not going to hurt you."

His tone was tired and disgusted, though whether it was with himself or with her was up for grabs.

"Go to hell," she said distinctly.

"Been there."

She didn't doubt him. It didn't make her feel better.

"What do you want from me?" she asked finally.

"I saved your ass. Don't you think you owe me something?"

"Forget it. I'm not going to crawl into bed with you just—"

"I want answers, not sex," he cut in coldly. "Jesus, why do women think that all a man wants is to get laid by any woman who'll spread her legs?"

"Because it's true."

"Not always."

"Bullshit."

Surprisingly, he laughed. "Come down off the adrenaline jag, honey. You're safe with me."

"How stupid do I look?" she retorted.

"If I was thinking about raping you, I'd done it back when I had you laid out beneath me on the ground. You felt real good that way, especially when you breathed hard."

The matter-of-fact words literally took away her breath. She started laughing, only to stop abruptly when she heard echoes of hysteria in her own voice.

"You're not used to this, are you?" he asked after a time.

"To what? Being kidnapped? No, I'm not."

"The adrenaline. You're not used to it. You don't know that

it makes you irritable as hell after the first rush. Then, a while later, it lets go of you and you feel like you've been run over by a truck."

She let out an explosive breath. "I'm not at that point yet."

"You'll get there."

The moonlit night turned cold, as the big truck descended from the last mesa into a broad canyon. The shape of the land seemed familiar to Christy. After a few minutes she realized that they were approaching Remington from a different direction. The lights of the little town danced in the far distance like a band of fireflies.

Cain drove toward the lights for a few miles. Then without warning he turned off and headed up a graded gravel road. Ahead the spruce forest fanned down from the dark peaks like a ragged slice of midnight. Soon the truck was in the forest, growling happily and taking the road like a smooth black beast.

When Christy was certain her voice wouldn't show fear, she asked, "Why aren't you taking me back to the hotel?"

"That's the first place Hutton's county mounties will look for you."

"County mounties—oh. The deputies. I don't think they saw me."

"How sure are you?"

She thought about it. There was no guarantee Hammond hadn't caught a glimpse of her as she went across the balcony. And if he had, he'd know who she was.

Red hair could be a real pain in the ass.

"Not that sure," she admitted. "Where are we going?"

"My place. No one will look for you there. Tomorrow I'll ask around. If it's safe, I'll take you back to the hotel."

"Won't the deputies be suspicious if I'm seen with you tomorrow morning when you drop me off?"

Teeth flashed in the darkness of Cain's beard. "They'll assume the obvious."

"Love at first sight?" she said ironically.

"Something like that, Red."

"I'll take your word for it. I've never been there, done that."

And she sure didn't plan on starting now.

For a time she just sat and tried to understand how much her world had been rearranged by her sister.

Again.

But thinking was impossible. She was caught between the night and Cain's reflection in the window. With each breath she took she felt adrenaline retreating from her blood, stranding her in a kind of numbing fatigue.

Five minutes later he turned off the main road onto a side road that led up into a stand of tall, elegant spruce. The headlights glinted on glass windows and picked out the shape of a small cabin with a pitched metal roof. A wood corral stood in front of a small hip-roofed barn.

"How about Johnny?" Cain asked as he turned off the engine. "Will you take my word for him too?"

"What do you mean?"

Without answering, Cain got out, walked around to her door, and opened it. He stood in the doorway, keeping her in the truck.

"I wasn't Johnny's lookout," Cain said. "I don't even know what he was after inside the house—assuming he was after anything."

"He was."

"How long have you known Johnny?"

"Know him? I never even saw him until tonight."

"Then how did you know it was Johnny up in the house?" Cain asked reasonably.

Christy tightened, remembering the instant she'd first spotted the big Indian crouched over a door.

"Bigger than Sheriff Danner," she said rapidly, "no movement in the right side of his face, handsome despite that, a handful of metal rods that had to be lock picks."

"That's Johnny." Then Cain asked casually. "Since you'd never met him, how did you know his name?"

"One of the guards called him Johnny."

Cain whistled through his teeth. "Guards, huh? Did they grab him?"

"Yes."

Something in her tone made Cain look at her, really look at her. In the moonlight, his eyes had a feral gleam.

"What happened?" he asked.

"My turn," she said tightly.

"What?"

"If you weren't with Johnny," she said, "why were you following him?"

"To see where he was going," Cain said dryly.

"Whose side are you on?"

"My own. What happened when the county mounties found Johnny?"

"Why do you care?"

"Because I think he's the back-shooting son of a bitch who tried to murder me four months ago."

Chapter 14

Christy opened her mouth but nothing came out. She tried again with the same result.

Cain's hands slid underneath her arms.

"The first step is a big one," he said. "Ready?"

"No. I just discovered how Alice felt on her way down the rabbit hole."

This time his smile was genuine, and warm. "It's not that long a step, honey. Hang on."

He lifted, swung, and lowered. The ground came up beneath her feet, but her knees gave way. She hung on to his forearms, bracing herself.

Despite the coolness of the night, his shirtsleeves were rolled back to his elbows. The flesh beneath her palms was warm, hard, and roughened by hair. He smelled like wood smoke and evergreens.

She was so close to him that she could see the pulse beating in his throat.

He was alert but calm.

She was neither.

Running water laughed somewhere nearby. A light breeze teased the trees. Branches brushed over glass; sounds that took her straight back to her childhood and a pain she still couldn't heal.

Exhaustion washed over her in a soundless black wave, pulling her down, drowning her. Distantly she realized that she was holding on to Cain like salvation and at the same time trying to push him away.

"Red? You okay?"

"Sorry," she said faintly. "I think I was just run over by that truck you mentioned."

An instant later the world tilted and then righted itself again. She looked up into his face in disbelief as he started forward, carrying her like a child.

"I can walk," she said.

"I can do it better. You're shaking."

"I'm not."

He smiled. "Okay, what do you call it?"

"Um. Okay. I'm cold, that's all. But you're not. How did you get used to adrenaline?"

"Jail."

"What?"

"For killing a man, just like Danner said."

"My God."

"Too tired to panic?" he asked coolly. "Good. Hang on while I open the cabin door."

Numbly she waited while he opened the door and maneuvered through. Inside, he set her down but didn't let go.

"I'm not going to faint," she said irritably.

"Yeah? Your skin is white."

"I'm a redhead. And I'm a lot tougher than I look."

He smiled slightly. "What's your name, tough lady?"

"McKenna. Christy McKenna."

"Aaron Cain," he said.

"I know."

"The gallery," he agreed.

Holding on to her with one hand, he reached over with the other to a wall switch. Light flared, revealing a large open living space that looked like a combination of museum and workshop.

The first thing she saw was a worktable littered with pottery and sherds. A large pot with geometric designs rested, half repaired, on a potter's wheel in the center of the table. Several dozen sherds of the same color and design lay next to the wheel, waiting like pieces of a jigsaw puzzle to be put into place.

At the other end of the worktable, a mud-crusted pottery bowl the size of a large frying pan waited patiently to be cleaned. The bowl was intact except for a crescent-shaped chip missing from the rim on one side. There was an intricate, sophisticated design of black diamonds and chevrons just beneath the layer of red clay.

She didn't doubt that the pattern had been hidden for centuries.

"You have that Alice-down-the-hole look again," Cain said.

"If you offer me a cup of tea, I'll hit you."

"Brandy?"

"Please."

She spoke without looking away from the artifacts that were stacked in every part of the room. Pots and bowls and mugs, some black on gray, some red on white, and some a clean white with brown or black designs. All of them were ancient. Most had a timeless beauty.

Many were clearly art.

Lured by a culture and an artistic style that were both new and intensely pleasing to her, she went from room to room in the cabin. Excitement energized her, making her forget how exhausted she'd been just a few minutes ago.

The cabin was much bigger than it had looked from the outside. It was jammed with art and artifacts of all sorts. In addition to the marvelous Anasazi pottery, there were examples of contemporary Native American art side by side with antiques that had once belonged to white settlers and frontiersmen. She saw stone axes, hand-forged steel trade tomahawks, and a powerful wooden bow where eagle feathers dangled in a silent statement of the former owner's rank.

A cast-iron Dutch oven that had been blackened by the fires of a hundred years stood on a shelf next to a lustrous old grandfather clock. Nearby was a cherrywood fiddle so old the varnish had begun to crack. The varnish had already cracked on several of the paintings on the wall. The paintings were landscapes of the West as it hadn't been for more than two centuries.

Throughout the rooms, like crystalline punctuation marks, there were mineral specimens whose like Christy had not seen short of the Smithsonian Museum of Natural History. Spikes of quartz older than the oldest civilization on earth flashed and glittered from every corner. Some of the crystal spikes were smoky. Some were opaque. Many were as clear as spring water. All were museum quality.

She stopped in front of a bookcase that was crowned by a golden sunburst shooting through the heart of a cluster of crystals that were so clear they were nearly invisible.

Beneath the incredible specimen, the old wood gleamed with a once-living grain. The glass doors of the bookcase reflected back Christy's image and Cain's. He was standing in the doorway with a brandy snifter in his hand, watching her.

"Is it—" she began.

"Yes," he said before she could ask. "The sunburst is pure gold."

She started to turn around, but the books themselves

caught her eye. From their good condition she'd assumed they were modern.

Suddenly she wasn't sure.

She lifted the glass shelf and selected a volume whose title was as familiar as her childhood. The book had been required reading in the Wyoming school system. The volume in Cain's bookcase was much older than her school text had been. Gently she opened the book. The title page said it all. She was holding a first edition of *Banditti of the Plains,* published privately in Wyoming in 1893.

"It's an account of the Johnson County war," he said, coming up behind her. "The cattlemen lost the war but they tried to limit the damage by buying up every available copy of the book."

She nodded absently, enthralled to be holding a piece of history.

"Michael Cimino tried to turn it into a modern epic," Cain added. "The result was *Heaven's Gate.*"

"Almost as big a fiasco as the original," she said dryly.

"Real people died in the Johnson County war. Only reputations died in Hollywood."

Something in his voice reminded her that he knew very well how men died. Carefully she closed the old book and eased it back into place behind the safety of glass.

"If that book is what it says it is—a first edition—it must be worth a great deal," she said, changing the subject.

"It is."

Christy thought back to the avid collectors she'd met on the ride to Xanadu a few hours earlier. A few hours and a lifetime ago.

"Are you a collector?" she asked.

His smile wasn't warm. "Do I look like a rich man?"

"Your clothes don't. Clothes can be changed. What can't

be changed is the eye that selected all these things." She gestured around the cabin. "You have an extraordinary eye. Are you a dealer?"

"Only when I can't afford to hang on to something any longer, or when I find something better."

Silently she wondered if he selected women on the same principle—keep them until something better came along. If he did, he was definitely Jo-Jo's hidden lover. When it came to physical perfection, Jo-Jo was museum quality.

"Well-made things last longer than any of the people who own them," Cain said. "A good cooking pot, clay or cast iron, is like the land that way. It connects you with something that endures a hell of a lot more years than one human life."

She nodded, surprised by his matter-of-fact acceptance of mortality, his own included. "Most people don't like to think about that."

"Most people don't like to think, period." He nudged her fingers with the snifter he was holding. "Drink this while I start a fire."

She took the fragile crystal glass and lifted it to her mouth. As she breathed in, tasting it, she made a surprised sound.

"Armagnac," she murmured.

"What did you expect, wood alcohol with a twist of chewing tobacco for flavor?"

She ducked her head, hoping that he couldn't see the flush on her cheeks. In truth, she hadn't been expecting much in the way of finesse from a Moki poacher's liquor cabinet.

"Sit down." He gestured to the furniture behind him. "I'll have the fire going in a minute."

She looked at the sofa. It was small, almost a love seat. If two tried to sit on it at once, they would feel every breath the other took. She'd been forced to be that close to him more than once tonight. The thought of any more intimacy unnerved her.

She passed up the couch and sat in the big easy chair near the fireplace. As soon as she settled into its depths, she realized that it must be Cain's favorite chair. It smelled faintly of him, evergreen and wood smoke, soap, and the elusive, indefinable scent that was the man himself.

I wonder if he scents me this clearly?

Her pulse jumped. She wasn't used to thinking about men and women in such primitive terms—scent, strength, danger, death, life itself.

Rather grimly she took a drink of the Armagnac. The clean, complex, heady liquid spread through her like sunrise.

"You didn't get this at the state liquor store in Remington," she said.

"No," he agreed.

"As a matter of fact, I think they were pouring it at Hutton's party tonight."

He looked over his shoulder at her through narrowed eyes. "Yes. And yes, this probably came from Hutton's private stock."

"Are you friends with him?"

"No." Cain turned back to tend the fire.

"Then it's the fabulous Jo who is your—ah, *friend*," Christy said.

"With Hutton's slut for a friend, a man wouldn't need any enemies."

The casual contempt in Cain's voice shocked Christy.

"Sounds like a man scorned to me," she said.

"Not as scorned as she was."

"What does that mean?"

"What do you care, Red?"

"I'm a reporter," she said quickly. "I ask all kinds of questions."

"A reporter. Jesus."

"You make it sound worse than being a burglar."

"Honey, I'd rather have a burglar any day. At least you know up front what their game is."

Chapter 15

Christy watched as Cain stood and went to a liquor cabinet that had been an icebox in the previous century. He pulled out a bottle shaped like a banjo and poured two fingers of Armagnac into a second snifter. Then he leaned against the fireplace and cradled the snifter against his palm, putting the stem between his long, surprisingly elegant third and fourth fingers. He held the snifter unself-consciously, the way a man would if he was alone and knew that Armagnac needed human warmth to be fully released.

And he watched her with eyes the same golden color as the fire he had just kindled in the hearth. But unlike the flames, his eyes were cool, a wolf's eyes studying something new, trying to decide whether it was dangerous, edible, or simply meaningless to a solitary predator's life.

"Is that what you were doing in Hutton's house tonight?" he asked finally. "Research?"

"After a fashion." She smiled slightly.

"What does that mean?"

"Just a pun. I write for *Horizon* magazine."

He waited.

"That's a magazine about international style," she explained.

"I've seen it."

"Oh." She started to take another sip.

"So you're doing another one of those fawning Hutton pieces," Cain said.

"I don't fawn in print or in person. I dissect style in the same way a critic dissects art."

Cain saluted her ironically with his snifter.

"So," he said after a moment, "you're doing another one of those pieces that tell women why they should buy Hutton's crap even though it looks like dried flower arrangements from the five-and-dime."

She nearly choked on the potent liquor she was swallowing. Gasping, laughing, coughing, she wiped her eyes. When she could see again, he was still watching her.

This time there was a smile in his eyes.

"I'm no fan of floral arrangement fashions, dried or otherwise," she said huskily. "I leave that to Myra."

"Who's she? Another model?"

"My boss. Until she fires me."

"Is that likely?"

Christy shrugged. As she did, she realized that Cain had diverted her questions about him and turned them into questions about her. It was a neat trick, an interrogator's or reporter's trick, one that few people could play successfully on her.

"Is that what you were doing tonight?" he asked. "Stealing a look ahead of the competition?"

"You'd probably like Hutton's new designs," she said, not quite answering the question. "Anasazi motifs all the way."

Cain bent over the snifter, swirled the liquid gently, and inhaled the aromatic fumes of the brandy. After a moment he tilted the crystal and let a bit of the tawny liquor slide down his throat.

"Anasazi?" he asked casually. "Are you sure?"

"Yes."

"How do you know?"

"The usual way." She sipped. "I saw the designs."

"When? In the house?"

"In the barn."

"Let me get this straight," he said. "You're here to cover Hutton's latest fashion twitch, but when the show began down by the barn you weren't there."

"I missed the formal show, but I saw some of the fabrics earlier. Grays, black, whites. Unusual geometries in the designs. Like that bowl on the worktable."

"Late Pueblo," he said.

But his eyes said he knew she was changing the subject.

"Very striking," she said. "There was an odd, curving stick figure too. Many of the designs revolved around it."

"Kokopelli."

The barely leashed intensity in Cain's voice and glance told her that there was more to the matter than a simple design. Then she remembered Johnny using the word "Kokopelli" to summon Autry. And Peter Hutton.

Apparently Kokopelli was some kind of code word.

She wondered if Jo-Jo knew it too.

Quickly Christy ran through the few facts she had. Johnny had used that word. Cain thought Johnny had shot him. Hutton was connected to Johnny. And to Jo-Jo.

Is that why Jo-Jo is afraid of Cain? Is he why she's hiding?

"What does Kokopelli mean?" Christy asked.

"He's the Anasazi Pan. A hunchbacked, oversexed flute player."

"A fertility symbol?"

Cain smiled slightly. "More like a symbol of unleashed sexuality."

"An odd choice for women's clothing designs."

"Not with Jo doing the modeling. Hutton knows what he's selling, and he knows just how to sell it."

The shades of scorn and something worse in Cain's voice made Christy feel cold in spite of the brandy and the cheerful hearth fire. Yet she wasn't afraid of him. Not really, not in any personal way.

Wary, yes.

Watchful, yes.

Off balance, certainly.

But she was positive at some primitive level that he wouldn't hurt her physically. He wasn't the kind of man who took pleasure in giving pain.

Yet he'd killed someone.

And someone might have tried to kill him.

Suddenly she realized that the silence had gone on too long. Cain was watching her with amber eyes that saw much too clearly. She started talking about the first thing that came to her mind that didn't have to do with death, near death, and Jo-Jo.

"Fabric isn't as rigid as clay," Christy said, "yet Hutton's designs work very well. They're mysterious, enigmatic, and primitive, while being sophisticated in the timeless way that balanced asymmetry often is."

Cain didn't say a word.

"After all the pastels and cloying designs he's been flogging these past few seasons," she said, "it's refreshing."

"You don't like Peter Hutton, do you?"

She was dismayed by Cain's insight. Usually people couldn't read her that well. Or maybe it was just that she usually hid her reactions better.

"It's my job to write about Hutton's fashions," she said, "not to like or dislike him."

"Have you met him face to face?"

"Of course. Why?"

Cain's smile was thin and cold. "Most women come into heat when they get that close."

"I'm not most women."

"No, you aren't. You're the woman I caught running flat out down the hill while Hutton's guards beat the underbrush."

She took a sip, stalling. Real soon she'd have to stop fencing with Cain and tell him the truth or tell him to go to hell. Of the two, she'd rather tell the truth. She was more used to it. And she couldn't fight the growing certainty that she could trust Cain—up to a point.

That point was Jo-Jo.

The heady fumes bathing Christy's face were almost as intoxicating as the liquor itself. She took another sip and then another. The tawny Armagnac burst softly inside her, sending shock waves of warmth through her chilled flesh.

Distantly she realized that the top of her head had come off, drifting, floating, flying. . . .

Uh-oh. Altitude, alcohol, and an adrenaline jag are a bad mix.

Deliberately she set aside the snifter, but it was too late. The gleaming crystal was empty.

He leaned over, took the snifter, and poured another two fingers in.

"No, thanks," she said quickly. "I've had enough."

"'In wine is truth,' which means I don't think you've had nearly enough yet."

She gave him a wary glance. "I've had as much as I'm going to right now."

"So give me as much truth as I'm going to get from you right now."

She blinked, then smiled slowly. Not all the truth and no outright lies. The reporter's way.

"I was looking for Jo," Christy said.

"Why?"

"Some people in New York told me she and Hutton weren't as close as they had been," Christy said, choosing her half-truths carefully. "I thought she might be able to give me some—um, new insights into Hutton's character."

"Why were you looking for her in the house?"

"She wasn't in the barn with the rest of the models. Where else would she be?"

He didn't answer.

"Some people hinted that she had a new lover," Christy offered.

Cain drank. Whatever he was thinking didn't show on his face.

"Do you know who it is?" she asked.

"Half the state of Colorado."

"Are you speaking from personal experience?"

"With Jo-Jo?" he asked sardonically. "No way. She doesn't have a personal bone in her body."

Jo-Jo.

Shock cut through the Armagnac's glow, shaking Christy. She was the only person who'd ever called Jo by that childhood name, which meant that no matter how much Cain might scorn Jo-Jo now, he'd once been close to her, so close that he knew about her childhood. If he knew about that, he could well know about the older sister who'd given Jo-Jo her nickname.

My God, what have I gotten myself into?

Chapter 16

Without thinking, Christy reached for the snifter again. She took a reckless sip, swallowed, and blinked away the tears drawn by the powerful liquor.

"Jo-Jo?" Christy cleared her throat. "Is that what people call her?"

"It's what she called herself," Cain said.

"Really? Any special reason?"

"Jo-Jo didn't need reasons. She thought just being sexy was a good enough excuse for everything she did."

"Did she tell you anything else about herself?"

"Why would she?" He breathed in the aroma of fine brandy. "Like I said, nothing personal. She just wanted to see if screwing a murderer would feel any different."

Christy shuddered, relieved and horrified at the same time. "You hate her."

It was an accusation, not a question.

He sipped, swallowed, and lowered the snifter, revealing the grim lines of his face. "Okay, Red. You didn't find the divine Jo-Jo in the house. What *did* you find that scared you?"

"I saw—" Her voice broke as she remembered. "The guards. They beat Johnny."

The memory of the blows with pistol and fists, and the blood and the pain, made her feel cold all over again. She closed her eyes and took another swallow of the fiery liquor.

"They beat Johnny in front of you?" Cain asked skeptically.

"They didn't know I was there."

"Where were you hiding?"

"Jo's closet."

"Why were they beating him?"

"He tried to break into a room down the hall," she said. "He spent several minutes working on the lock. Then he heard a guard and ran into Jo's bedroom to hide. I heard him coming and hid first."

"Must have been a hell of a lock."

"Why?" she asked.

"Johnny went to postgraduate burglary school—three years in jail." As always, the mention of jail made Cain's expression even more bleak. "What did the guards want from Johnny?"

"They wanted to know what he was after."

"What was it?"

"I don't know," she said. "He didn't tell them."

"So they beat him."

"Yes." She sipped more brandy. Too much, but she couldn't stop herself. The remembered taste of fear was too strong in her mouth. "I think they were afraid of him. Physically."

"Smart men. Johnny's a famous brawler. He can take a lot of hammering. He can give even more."

"Tonight, he was taking it." Christy swallowed. "They hit him in the face with a pistol."

"Doesn't sound like Hammond."

"It was the other one. He liked hitting Johnny. I could see it. He . . ."

She took a quick drink, covering the taste of fear and nausea in her mouth.

"Then what?" Cain asked, but his voice was more sympathetic than his words.

"Johnny got scared. He wanted to talk with one of Hutton's aides."

"Anyone in particular?"

"Mr. Autry."

"Bringing Autry in would be like throwing a drowning man an anchor."

"He seemed pleasant enough when I met him," she said, "despite his drugstore cowboy clothes."

"Autry is a retired FBI agent."

"I can see how a man in your position wouldn't think much of him."

" 'A man in your position,' " Cain quoted coolly. "As in ex-con?"

She took refuge in another sip of brandy.

When she looked up again, he was watching the fire. She'd never seen such raw intensity in any man as she saw in him right now. Automatically she lifted the brandy to her lips, trying to drive away the persistent chill that had begun with Jo-Jo's call and had done nothing but get worse the closer she got to her sister.

"Red?"

She looked up.

"Why were you really up in Hutton's house?"

While Christy tried to figure out what to say, he watched her with a curious expression on his face. It was like they were on a first date and he was trying to decide whether or not to kiss her good night. But his eyes were measuring rather than playful. He knew she'd been lying to him. What he didn't know was why.

She closed her eyes.

Big mistake. Alcohol, altitude, and the aftermath of an

adrenaline jag made her sway. Chills chased over her. She was cold. Shivering cold. Bone-deep cold.

Instinctively she wrapped her arms around her body and held on, trying to hold in her own body heat.

"Are you going to faint on me after all?" he asked.

"No," she said, her voice ragged. "I've never fainted. Ever."

She struggled to her feet and stood with her back to his, swaying slightly.

Before she could take another breath, his hands were beneath her elbows, steadying her. He was close, almost as close as he'd been when he grabbed her in the stand of trees. She remembered the strength of his grip then. It was just as strong now.

And just as careful of her softer flesh.

"What kind of trouble are you in, honey?" he asked gently.

"I'm cold. That's all."

And she was. All the way to the marrow of her bones.

Cold.

Cain's fingers tightened for an instant before he let out a long breath and accepted that she wasn't going to trust him tonight. Maybe not ever.

"All right," he said. "We'll play it your way for a while. Sure as hell my way isn't getting us anywhere."

"What does that mean?"

"It means if you're cold, I've got just the thing for you. Can you walk or do you want me to—"

"I can walk," she cut in quickly.

"Damn. And here I was looking forward to carrying you."

His lazy, teasing tone startled her. She gave him a swift look over her shoulder. His smile was as warm as the firelight reflected in his eyes.

"Don't look so worried," he said, amused. "I may be an ex-con and a Moki-poaching son of a bitch, but I'm a gentleman where good women are concerned."

She smiled uncertainly. "You forgot the bit about high-grading."

Cain laughed and shook his head at the same time. "You'd sass Satan himself, wouldn't you?"

Her smile widened.

"What is a high grader, anyway?" she asked.

"Someone who skims the best of a mine's ore and leaves the rest for the legal owners."

"Oh. The mineral specimens?" Christy looked at the golden sunburst radiating up through natural crystal spires.

"Yeah. They're legal, by the way. I have a permit to hunt specimens in a lot of the old mines around here."

"And the Moki poaching?" she asked neutrally.

"I have permits for that, too. Digs on private land are perfectly legal. Ask Hutton."

"Why would he know?"

"My best stuff came from the old Donovan ranch before Hutton bought it, fenced it off, and started digging himself."

She remembered the fantastic artifacts she'd seen that afternoon. The "stuff" must indeed have been good. She didn't blame Hutton for wanting to keep it to himself.

When Cain led her out into the night, the cold air bit right through her silk blouse and jacket.

"This is going to warm me up?" she said.

"Trust me, Red. On this, at least."

She looked up into the darkness but could see only the dense black silhouette of a tall man. The width of his shoulders blocked out part of the starry sky. His eyes were hidden. So was his expression.

But the hand beneath her arm was patient, not demanding.

He was waiting for her decision. She could go back into the house and the certainty of a fire in the hearth, or she could trust Cain and follow him into the cold night.

"All right," she said simply.

Chapter 17

Christy sensed rather than heard the long breath Cain let out. His fingers curled caressingly around her arm for a moment, then relaxed.

"The moonlight should be bright enough," he said, "but if you want a flashlight, I'll get one."

She looked out at the silvery light flooding the mountainside, making the world both beautiful and unreal. Far above timberline, patches of white snow glistened like quicksilver against the darker peaks. Nearby, black groves of spruce whispered and sighed beneath the breeze.

"No flashlight." Then she added in a tone of surprise, "I've missed the night."

"Too many city lights?"

"Yes."

Where the path entered a spruce grove, there was a sudden rustling in the underbrush.

"Are you afraid of dogs?" he asked quickly.

"No."

An instant later she wondered if she'd spoken too soon. The animal that appeared in the moonlit path wasn't a tail-wagging puppy-friendly critter. Big-boned, long-legged, rangy, the dog looked more like a wolf than man's best friend.

"Hey, Moki," Cain said as the dog trotted forward. "I hope you caught dinner, because I didn't bring any for you."

A long bushy tail waved in response to Cain's casual ruffling of the animal's ears, but it was Christy who was the center of the dog's attention.

"He won't bother you unless you ask," Cain said. "Maybe not even then. He's been on his own since I got shot."

"You left him to fend for himself?"

"Better hungry and half wild than locked in a pen," Cain said flatly. "Moki wouldn't have lasted more than a month at the end of a chain."

His voice said more than his words. The time he'd spent in jail had given him a hatred of being penned, locked up, chained.

She shivered, but it was from the thought of being in a cage, not from the cold.

In the moonlight, Moki looked lean and predatory. Yet there was something endearing about the set of his ears. She dropped to one knee and held out her hand.

"Hi, Moki," she said softly. "I don't blame you for being wary of strangers, but you're okay with me. I won't hurt you or tie you up. I'd even feed you if I had anything worth eating."

Drawn by her low, calm voice, the dog came to her like a black ghost, sniffed her hand, and then nudged her palm with his nose in a frank invitation to be petted.

She laughed lightly and gave the dog his due.

"You sweet old fraud," she said. "You're not a big bad wolf after all, are you?"

Moki grinned, showing double rows of gleaming teeth.

She laughed again, not at all afraid. Talking quietly to him, she scratched his ears and down his muscular chest, enjoying the warmth and the sensation of lean, sinewy health the dog radiated. It had been years since she'd touched anything but city dogs with fine pedigrees and the kinds of neuroses that come from living in tiny apartments and walking on cement.

"Come on, Red," Cain said after a time. "Moki will soak up that kind of loving until you go numb from the cold."

"He's warm."

"So am I. Want to scratch my ears?"

She laughed and stood again. When she started forward into the brush, Moki fell in along her left side. Bracketed by lean male animals, she felt both amused and safe from whatever the darkness might offer.

From the path ahead came the sound of running water. As they approached, spruce trees gave way to a clearing where a small stream murmured and dreamed in shades of silver through the night. Water tumbled down the rock face of a little ledge, crossed the clearing, and disappeared again in the trees.

Cain guided her toward a small rock pool off to one side of the stream. At first the little pool seemed a part of the stream itself. Then she realized it was separate, although it was connected to the creek by a rock-lined channel that had been made by man rather than nature.

The pool was twenty feet across and so clear it looked like a condensation of moonlight. Wisps of steam rose gracefully from the surface.

"A hot spring?" Christy asked, hardly able to believe her luck.

"This country is volcanic. There are lots of hot springs around."

He dropped to one knee, tested the water, and made a pleased sound. "I used to dream about this pool while I was in the hospital. Couldn't wait to soak out the aches. Better than any painkiller out of a bottle."

He went to the head of the pool and added rocks to the gate

across the channel from the stream. No more water flowed into the pool. The surface of the hot spring became very still, with only lazy swirls at the center to mark the slow upwelling of water from far below.

"The stream is meltwater," he said. "Starts with snowfields at twelve thousand feet. Doesn't warm up much on the way down here, but we'll be grateful for that once the pool starts heating up."

He stood and undid his shirt in a ripple of steel snaps popping open. He was too far away for Christy to see anything more than the vague gleam of moonlight on naked skin.

There was a lot of it.

"Cain—"

"If you're too shy to strip, use this as a bathing suit," he said, tossing his shirt to her.

She caught it automatically. The cloth was warm with his body heat. A shiver of sensation went through her that had nothing to do with the cold air.

"What about you?" she asked.

"I'm about as shy around you as Moki is."

"He has a fur coat."

"So do I." White teeth flashed in a grin that vanished when Cain turned his back to her. "I'll wait to finish undressing until you're in the pool. Don't dawdle. It's damn cold with that wind off the snowfield."

Remembering his earlier words, she looked at the gently steaming water and then at him: *I'm a gentleman where good women are concerned.*

"Cain?"

He made a rumbling, questioning sound.

She hesitated. "Am I a good woman as far as you're concerned?"

"Yeah."

"Just like that? No qualifications, no questions about my past?"

"Just like that."

She took a deep breath. "Okay. I'll holler when I'm in the pool."

"Watch your step. It gets deep real fast. I built in some high-backed wooden benches underwater along the left side."

She undressed quickly, shivering when the air bit into her unprotected flesh. She paused over her bra and panties, then stripped them off too. Two wisps of black lace were more of a tease than a nod to modesty.

Shivering in the breeze, she put on his shirt. The cuffs came over her fingertips and the tails dragged well below her knees. When she reached for the last snap, she discovered she'd fastened them crookedly in her haste to get into the warm pool.

"Tough," she muttered.

She hurried to the pool and stepped in. It wasn't rough, as she'd expected. Cain had covered a lot of the bottom with smooth river pebbles, all rounded and gentle on bare feet. The water was hot, but after the first shock it felt delicious rather than painful.

The benches he'd warned her about were angular black shadows just beneath the silver surface of the water. The seats were set at different depths in the pool, where the rock shelved steeply down. She settled cautiously onto the closest bench. The water rose to her collarbones and stopped.

His shirt billowed and floated around her like a tent. The sensation of liquid warmth against her naked skin made her feel weightless and free.

"Ahhhhhh," she groaned. "God, that feels good."

"Are you hollering, Red?"

"I'm whimpering with pleasure."

"I'd rather hear you holler so I can come in out of the cold."

"Holler holler holler!"

His laughter rang in the night. "Keep your shirt on. I'm coming."

"It's your shirt, remember? But I'm keeping it on just the same."

Still smiling, he sat down on a rock and started to unlace his boots. She watched him in the moonlight as he pulled off his shoes and socks with quick, efficient motions. The play of silver light and dense shadow on his shoulders both revealed and then concealed his lean power.

Like Moki, Cain was furry. Unlike Moki, the hair was concentrated on Cain's chest before narrowing into a pencil width and vanishing below the waistband of his jeans. He stood and undid his jeans with the same casual efficiency he'd unlaced his hiking boots.

As he started to peel off his pants, she realized she was staring.

He knew it too.

Chapter 18

If taking off his clothes in front of a strange woman bothered Cain, it didn't show. Jeans and underwear together slid down his body far enough that the pencil line of fur flared suddenly into a wedge.

Hastily Christy looked somewhere else.

Anywhere else.

"You worked as a male stripper, did you?" she muttered.

"Several weeks in a hospital. Close enough."

The distinct sound of metal buttons hitting stone came as he dumped his jeans on top of a boulder.

"Catheters and bedpans and hundreds of sponge baths given by lots of different nurses," he said. "After a while, modesty is just a word."

She studied the patterns of the current right under her nose. Random splashing sounds told her that he was wading into the pool. Then came a soft groan of pleasure and a swirling displacement of water as he slid onto the other end of the bench, an arm's length from her.

"Okay, Red. It's safe to look now. I've got my back to you."

The laughter in his voice irritated her. "I'm not a prude," she said under her breath.

He heard. "Who said you were?"

"You did."

"Not me. It's damned refreshing to find a female who can still blush."

"You've been chasing the wrong kind of women."

"More like vice versa. Ever since Hutton showed up, his high-priced whores have been going through the local men like grass through a goose. Especially Jo-Jo. She loves flat-backing with cowboys, Indians, and dangerous western trash like me. *Fighting* men."

The contempt in his voice was enough to chill the pool. Christy turned toward him, but the protest on her lips died when she saw the ragged, barely healed scar that gleamed between his spine and his shoulder blade.

Cain eased down onto the next bench below and the scar vanished beneath the blackly gleaming water.

"Oh, God," he said in a low voice.

"What's wrong?"

"Nothing," he said through clenched teeth. "That just feels better than it should."

"What are you, some kind of closet Puritan? It feels as good as it feels."

"God help me, a philosopher as well as a reporter."

With that, he slid all the way under the water and stayed there for what seemed like a long time. When he surfaced and drew a deep breath, he sounded like a great sleek dolphin rising from a midnight sea.

He stretched, arching his back as if trying to make supple the muscles that had been ripped by a bullet and were still healing.

"You shouldn't have been carrying me," Christy said unhappily.

He turned toward her.

"You weigh a lot less than the iron I pumped to rebuild my right side," he said. "You're a lot more fun, too."

The lazy, teasing note was back in his voice. The white flash of his smile and the dense, water-slicked black of his beard were dangerously attractive to her. And the clear, still waters of the hot spring didn't hide nearly enough of him.

The moon was like a searchlight.

She closed her eyes and concentrated on the delicious heat of the pool rather than on a more dangerous kind of heat.

"Chicken," he said.

"Cluck cluck."

He laughed, took a breath, and slid beneath the healing water again.

She sensed that he was more pleased than irritated by her retreat.

"Cain?" she asked when he surfaced again.

He made a rumbling sound that said he was listening.

"Sheriff Danner said you weren't supposed to come back up to the mountains. Is that true?"

Cain took so long to answer that she thought he was going to ignore the question. She knew she should let it go, and she knew she wasn't going to. She needed to know more about Cain with an intensity that went beyond her customary curiosity as a reporter.

"Cain?"

"Whoever shot me was used to killing mule deer," he said after a time.

"What does that mean?"

"He used a soft-nosed slug. I lost some of my right lung. It collapsed."

She made a low sound and wished she hadn't asked.

"The pulmonary specialist said I'd run the risk of collapsing the lung again for a while," he added. "He said I'd do better down on the flats for a year or two."

"Then why did you come back?"

"I wanted to look around before the snows came."

"But—"

"I haven't had any problems so far," he said, talking over her objection.

"You were breathing hard when we were running down the creek bed."

"So were you."

"I haven't been at this altitude since I left home," she said.

"A western girl, huh?" he asked, changing the subject.

"Why do you say that?"

"Land doesn't come this high back East."

She hesitated, then shrugged. "Yes, I was raised in High Plains country."

"Wyoming?"

"Yes."

"Not a city miss after all," he said.

The satisfaction in his voice irritated her.

"I was born in Wyoming," she said. "I *chose* Manhattan. I'm city all the way."

"Bull."

"Crap."

He laughed quietly. "Boyfriend waiting for you?" he asked after a moment.

She made a sound that could have been taken for agreement.

"A city man?" Cain persisted.

"Very much so. An investment banker. Manhattan, London, Tokyo, Cali, Los Angeles, Bonn."

"Sounds like he spends more time in jets than with you."

"And vice versa."

"A modern relationship," Cain summarized.

"I suppose." She yawned deeply, unraveled by the heat of the pool.

He went underwater again. When he surfaced, the two of them sat quietly, letting the pool draw out the last of the adrenaline jag.

Knots of tension Christy hadn't even been aware of loosened. The hot spring was as comfortable as any European spa she'd ever visited. The only thing lacking was the chlorine stink of water that had to be chemically treated to be safe.

She half closed her eyes and lay against the back of the bench, listening to the quiet night sounds and the liquid murmurings of the stream. Above her night flexed in an ebony arch that glittered with a million, million stars. Nearby the wind combed gently through the evergreens, making a long whispering sound, as if trees and stream were trading secrets.

With a deep sigh, she arched her back and spread her arms, letting them float just beneath the surface. She was as close to perfectly comfortable as she could remember being. Ever. Jo-Jo and Peter Hutton and all the rest of her worries seemed a million miles away.

And Cain was very close.

It should have worried Christy, but it didn't. She was too wonderfully unstrung to worry about Cain right now. Like Moki, his ferocity was more apparent than real.

At least when it came to people.

Cain had a very fierce love of the artifacts that filled his house. His words about *Banditti of the Plains* had been casual, but not his eyes. They'd held a combination of leashed excitement and unleashed hunger that reminded her of nothing so much as Howard Kessler, the man who had taught her about the tangled relationships between human emotion and human style.

Cain and Howard both understood that there was a connection between an artifact and the human being who once had made it. The connection was elemental, compelling, and intangible.

It was the human connection that mattered, not the price the artifact commanded in the marketplace.

It's simple, Christa. Artifacts are reservoirs of human memory and emotion. Next to that, what is dollar value but something to amuse people who have no imagination? People who have money and no imagination follow fashion. People who have imagination and no money fashion styles.

As Howard's words echoed in her mind, she smiled. Cain and Howard had more in common than anyone would have suspected from just looking at the men.

For one thing, both had been immune to Jo-Jo.

At least, Cain said he was.

Far above the hot spring, a jet tunneled with a faint roar through the night sky. Christy thought of Nick, a man who flew so frequently his body never knew when it was at home.

Nick was a modern man, a man who never showed anger or passion or pain, a man who lived much of his life forty thousand feet above the rest of the world. No scars, no fears, nothing but the numbers on a balance sheet at the end of the month.

And now, floating in the vast western landscape of her childhood, she finally understand what she'd known and never admitted.

Nick's the wrong man for me.

I'm the wrong woman for him.

Nothing personal. Just a case of mistaken identity. And the certainty that there was no going back.

I should feel sad.

What she felt was relief.

Her thoughts drifted, wrapped in heat and the glitter of diamond stars. Slowly all thought drained away, leaving her utterly relaxed.

"Unwinding?" Cain asked in a lazy, rumbling voice.

"Unwound." She yawned. "My brain is guacamole dip."

There was silence, another yawn.

"What were you really doing in Hutton's house?" Cain asked.

The words were so casual that it took a few moments for her to understand. When she did, she felt like she'd been manipulated in a particularly unpleasant way.

"So that's what the kid-glove treatment was all about," she said coldly. "You were just softening me up for another round of questioning."

"Red—"

"My name is Christy," she cut in, "and why do you care what I was doing?"

"Because I think you know something about a connection between Hutton, the Secret Sisters, Johnny Ten Hats, and the slut who set me up to die."

"What?"

"You heard me."

"Jo?"

"The one and only."

"No. Never. She couldn't." Christy's voice was flat, certain. She didn't believe that Jo-Jo had any part in Cain's shooting. Jo-Jo was self-centered and spoiled and wild, but that didn't make her a murderer.

"Yeah?" Cain looked at her intently. "So, how well do you know the great Jo?"

Christy looked at the naked, powerful, and very intelligent predator who had neatly outmaneuvered her and was now watching her. The cold fires in his eyes were burning again. His bleak intensity poured over her like midnight.

"Sheriff Danner thinks the shooting was an accident," she said.

"Sheriff Danner is full of crap."

"What about the rest of the town? What do they think?"

"They think someone was after a little spring venison," Cain said, "and I got in the way."

"But you don't believe that. You think Jo had something to do with it."

"Yeah."

"Why? What reason would she have? It's ridiculous."

Cain looked at Christy for a long time before he said, "That's one of the things I wanted to ask Johnny."

"Johnny? What does he have to do with any of it?"

"I told you. I think he was the trigger man."

"Why?" Christy asked starkly.

"That was the other thing I was going to ask Johnny, just as soon as I got my hands on him."

"If you really believe Jo was part of it, why not ask her?"

"That lying bitch? I wouldn't piss on her if she was on fire. She knows it too. She's made herself real scarce since I've been back."

Christy opened her mouth, then closed it. There wasn't anything she could say to the man who hated her sister so savagely. A chill that no hot spring could banish sank into Christy's soul.

No wonder Jo-Jo is afraid of Cain.

And no wonder she's hiding somewhere. He blames her for a hunting accident that wasn't really anyone's fault.

Cain was wrong about Jo-Jo, but there was no point in telling him that. What Christy had to do was convince him he was wrong. The quickest way to do that would be to tell him the truth.

Except for Jo-Jo being her sister. If she told Cain that, he wouldn't listen to anything else she had to say.

So what? Why should I care?

The answer made Christy flinch. She had to find Jo-Jo, and to do that she had to stay in Remington. But if Deputy Hammond had recognized her jumping over the balcony, staying here could be a problem. She'd need someone on her side. Someone who knew the territory. Someone who wouldn't cringe at a little casual pistol whipping.

Someone like Cain.

God, what a mess. Thanks, Jo-Jo. Thanks all to hell.

But all Christy said aloud was, "Kokopelli."

"What?"

"He's more than one of Hutton's design motifs."

Cain waited.

She took a deep breath. "Johnny told the guards he wanted to talk to Autry about Kokopelli's sisters."

Cain sat so silently that she wondered if he'd stopped breathing. Then he let out a sound that was both a laugh and a soft curse.

"Son of a bitch," he said. "I was right."

"About what?"

He didn't answer.

"About what?" she demanded.

He simply laughed again.

Everything that had happened in the last twenty-four hours boiled up in Christy. As though standing outside herself, she watched as she did something rare. She lost her temper.

She wanted to hit him but knew it wouldn't do anything except hurt her fists.

Hell.

She surged to her feet and splashed out of the pool, not caring that she might as well be naked for all the cover the clinging shirt gave her.

"You son of a bitch," she said, clipping each word.

"What the—"

She kept talking. "What we have here is the usual old-fashioned western relationship. The dumb little woman gives and the smart big man takes."

"What are—"

"Thanks for the lesson," she continued savagely. "I'd forgotten that western bastards like you are the biggest reason western women like me can't wait to go *east*."

Chapter 19

Christy awakened slowly, trying to piece together her reality. It was early. Something had split the gray light of dawn into four squares. A dormer window. She was in a sleeping loft.

It was cloudy outside.

Something on the bed beside her moved. She felt the pressure of another body along her leg, and the warmth of something resting on her hip.

It felt like the weight of a man's hand.

"You worthless son of a bitch. Enjoy it, because it will never happen again." Despite the words, Cain's voice was soft and amused.

The pressure along Christy's leg and hip shifted as Moki raised his head and glanced toward the bedroom doorway. His tail beat once on top of the down cover, then again.

"Red, you awake yet?" Cain asked, flipping on the light.

He was standing in the doorway with a bundle of cloth under one arm and a cup of coffee in his right hand.

"Go to hell," she said.

"Still mad that I wouldn't take you back down the mountain last night?"

She gave him a look that would have frozen the hot spring.

"Whew," he said. "How about a truce?"

"How about jumping off a cliff?"

"I'd rather have a cup of coffee. What about you?"

She looked at the steam gently rising from the mug in his hand. The heady aroma told her the coffee was made the way Gramma had always done it—strong, thick, boiled. It would clear the cobwebs out of her brain and put the sun right up in the sky.

She tried to think of a way to get the coffee and still ignore Cain. She couldn't.

A look at his gleaming eyes told her that he knew it.

"Coffee," she said in a clipped voice.

"You're welcome."

"Sorry, am I down on my etiquette? Are kidnappers expecting to be thanked these days?"

"Bullshit," he said without heat. "I haven't done one damn thing except refuse to drive down a mountain road after drinking brandy and soaking my brains out in a hot spring."

"Does that mean I dare to hope for my freedom this morning?"

"You can hope for whatever you want. Maybe you'd like me to call Danner and tell him you're coming in to talk about Johnny Ten Hats, Hutton's house, and Kokopelli?"

Her stomach clenched. "You wouldn't."

His eyes narrowed. "Don't bet anything important on it, Red. Someone tried to kill me. I'm going to find out why."

She closed her eyes.

"Mexican standoff," he said. "You won't tell me why you were sneaking around in Hutton's house. I won't take you back to the hotel until you do."

Her eyes flew open.

He watched her, waiting.

"What's for breakfast?" she asked through her teeth.

"Oatmeal. Wear these. The slick city stuff you had on last night got shredded up pretty bad when you went over the railing."

He tossed the bundle under his arm to her. It unraveled into a pair of white denim jeans, a blue-and-white windbreaker, a fuzzy white silk pullover sweater, and a man-styled shirt in pale blue.

Jo-Jo's clothes.

"Where did you get these?" Christy demanded.

His black eyebrows rose at the tone of her voice.

"Jo-Jo came prospecting here a while back," he said ironically. "She left in such a hurry she forgot to pack."

With a hand that trembled slightly, Christy reached for the clothing. Though sturdier than the silk she'd slept in, the jeans and blouse were still lightweight.

Spring weight.

"Don't worry," Cain said sardonically. "I had them disinfected."

She let out a long breath. Jo-Jo hadn't left the clothes in his cabin lately. She wouldn't have been caught dead in spring fashions after May first.

"They won't fit," Christy said.

"Honey, from what I saw last night, they'll fit just fine."

She turned toward him so quickly that her hair fanned out like wind-driven fire. "What?"

"When you stalked out of the pool, my shirt fit you like black paint. Anyone ever tell you that you have nice legs? And a really *fine* ass."

Her mouth dropped. "I don't believe this."

"Yeah, it set me back too. Spent a long time thinking about it before I got to sleep. You sure you're a good woman?"

"You're just doing this to—to—to keep me off balance!"

His smile flashed against his black beard. "Works both ways, honey. If I hadn't been sitting down, seeing you that way last night would have brought me to my knees. Breakfast in five minutes. Don't be late, or I'll feed yours to that no-good dog who slept where I wanted to last night."

Cain left, taking the cup of coffee with him.

Three minutes later she walked into the kitchen. To her amazement, he'd been right about the fit of the clothes. She'd left the waistband unbuttoned to make room for breakfast, and the pant legs were nearly two inches short, but the rest fit as though made for her.

She'd put Jo-Jo's key in her left pocket. Now she wondered if the pants were tight enough to show the outline.

"Shoes and socks by the chair," he said without turning away from a bubbling pot on the stove. "See if they fit. It's rough country where we're going."

"Where is that?"

"To see if we can track down Kokopelli and his 'sisters.' "

She looked at the Gore-Tex walking boots and the white socks. She knew they would fit. She and Jo-Jo had shared shoes since the eighth grade. Or, rather, Jo-Jo had regularly raided her older sister's closet.

"Are prisoners allowed telephone calls?" Christy asked as she put the shoes on.

"Not if they keep harping about being prisoners when they know damn well they could leave anytime."

Her teeth clicked together. "May I use your phone?" she asked carefully.

"Sure."

"Is it a land line?"

"Nothing else works out here."

No shit.

She strode to the phone on the kitchen counter and called the hotel, wishing the place had voice mail so she wouldn't have to parade her business past the hotel desk. She suspected that the locals liked it that way. Nothing else interesting was going on in the town.

"This is Christa McKenna in room eight. Any messages for me?"

"You have one from Mr. Hutton."

"Read it, please."

" 'Sorry I didn't have more time with you. What did you think of the show, or were you too busy looking around Xanadu to watch?' Signed, Peter."

Her heart paused, then beat more quickly. It could be a veiled hint that Hammond had recognized her. Or it could be a polite way of letting her off the hook if she didn't want to talk about her response to Hutton's designs.

"Any other messages?" she asked.

"Yes."

"Read them all, please."

" 'Staff librarian says no more material on Hutton or Xanadu. Call me when you've seen the designs.' It's signed Myra. There's one more. No signature."

"Read that one too," Christy said impatiently.

" 'Thinking about you. Are you thinking about me?' "

Damn it, Jo-Jo, you know I am.

"That's it?" Christy asked.

"Yes."

"Nothing else? No one asking about me?"

"No, ma'am. But the day is young."

The clerk's dry reminder that it was barely dawn made her flush. She had no doubt that the locals were being kept fully up to date on the immoral comings and goings of Hutton's guests.

"Thank you," she said stiffly, and hung up. "If Sheriff Danner is after me, he's keeping it quiet."

"Cops usually do," Cain said.

"I'll bow to your superior knowledge of law and disorder."

"You do that, Red, and we'll both be better off."

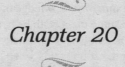

Chapter 20

The silence lasted until Cain pulled the steaming pot off the stove and dished oatmeal into two soup bowls.

"No fried steak, fried eggs, fried potatoes, flapjacks, and toast?" Christy asked. "What's the West coming to?"

"At altitude, you need your blood for carrying oxygen, not for digesting a bellyful of grease. Later, you'll thank me for it."

"Hold your breath."

"I'll pass, thanks."

He put a cup of coffee in front of her and sat down opposite her. They ate in a silence that slowly became companionable.

It was hard to be angry with a man who was eating mush across a small table from you.

She ate almost as much as he did before she remembered the top button of the jeans. After he finished his second bowl, he stood and began clearing the table with the easy motions of someone doing a familiar task.

"You cooked, I'll clean up," she said, falling into the child-hood pattern of dividing chores.

He raised his eyebrows but said only, "I'll get a few things and warm up the truck."

"How long will we be gone?"

"However long it takes. All day, likely."

She started to object that she had to wait around in case Jo-Jo tried to get in touch. Then she thought of the taunting message—*Are you thinking of me?*—and decided to let her beautiful sister stew for a change.

The kitchen took only a few minutes to straighten up. Christy was drying the soup bowls when she heard the truck rumble to life. A minute later she was outside, feeling her spirits lift just because of the clean air and shining sky.

The morning was chilly and calm. The air carried a quiet promise of winter coming soon. The sweater, blouse, and windbreaker she wore just barely kept the cold at bay. Her breath hung like smoke in the still air. She wanted to laugh for no reason she could figure out.

Moki trotted past her to the idling truck. Its white exhaust plume was like a long exhalation from a great beast. The dog sat on his haunches beside the rear cargo doors. His rakish ears were held at an expectant angle.

"Okay, boy," Cain said.

Moki leaped through the open cargo doors like a deer clearing a garden fence.

"Warm enough?" Cain asked, looking at Christy, frankly approving the fit of her jeans.

"So far."

"Let me know if that changes. There's an extra wool shirt in the back you can use as a coat." He smiled. "If it's too big, we'll just wet it down and let it shrink to fit."

"Is that before or after I turn you into toad droppings?"

"Glad to see you've got your sass back." Grinning, he dropped a full leather knapsack near the dog and closed the door.

From the corner of her eyes, she watched Cain. He was wearing a lightweight down vest and a long-sleeved wool shirt over his jeans and work boots. He'd traded his Stetson for a black knit watch cap. As he climbed into the front seat, he offered a similar cap to her.

"It'll be windy in places up on the mesa," he said. "If you keep your head warm—"

"—the rest of you will stay warm," she finished for him. "Followed by, 'It's easier to stay warm than to get warm.' "

"Your mama didn't raise any dumb ones."

"My mama didn't raise any, period, dumb or smart. But thanks for the cap. Cold ears were the curse of my childhood."

He headed the truck back in the direction they'd come the night before. Color was just coming on in the east, behind the San Juan Wall. In the west stars were dissolving into a sky that was more deep indigo than true black. There weren't many other vehicles on the road.

Cain tuned the radio to the local Remington station. The six A.M. local newscast was of the neighborhood bulletin board variety. Cattle prices, road repairs, bar brawls, and snow level in the passes.

"No bodies discovered in the ditch beside the road," Cain said after listening for a while. "No strange disappearances reported. No prowler caught in Hutton's house. No prowler *not* caught in Hutton's house."

She looked sideways at him. "Meaning?"

"Either Johnny talked his way out of trouble or they haven't found the body yet."

"But then, the day is young," she said dryly, remembering the desk clerk.

The weather forecast was more serious than the local news. Brisk northern winds and the expectation of snow flurries at higher elevations. Cain shut off the radio when feed prices, hog futures, and the price of light sweet crude became the focus.

"How high are we going?" she asked.

"What we're looking for has never been found above eighty-one hundred feet."

"Just what are we looking for?"

"I'm not sure. A ruined house and a grave, most likely."

"Lovely. You're a real ray of sunshine this morning."

"Beats being toad droppings."

Christy smiled in spite of herself.

Wind outside buffeted the heavy truck. A chill passed through the steel doors into the interior. She pulled the windbreaker more firmly around her. When a cold nose nudged her ear, she jumped.

"It's just Moki poaching a little affection," Cain said.

Turning, she saw what he meant. The dog had leaped out of the cargo area and onto the back seat. As she watched, he braced his hind feet on the cushion and his front feet on the console between the people in the front seat. She reached for the dog's shaggy neck and worked her fingers into his thick fur, enjoying his sheer animal warmth.

"What's a Moki?" she asked a few minutes later.

"It's what the local people called the Anasazi long before eastern professors arrived and started digging."

A dirt road came into the highway. She turned and looked at it as they sped by. "Isn't that the road we were on last night?"

"Good guess."

"What makes you so sure I'm guessing?"

"Most city folks can't find their way around any ground that isn't named, numbered, and nailed down by concrete."

Five miles farther south, he turned off the main road onto a dirt track that headed across the scrub flats toward a white sandstone mesa.

"Do you know where we are now?" he asked.

"We must be close to the south edge of Hutton's ranch."

"Dead on. You haven't been in the city long enough to lose your sense of direction and distance."

"I had a detailed research package on Xanadu."

"Good. From here on out, you can tell me if I'm on Hutton's land. That way we won't trespass any more than we already have."

"I thought he'd fenced all of it."

"He tried," Cain said. "But along the back side, where the plateau unravels into a thousand nameless little canyons and gullies, Hutton sort of ran out of steam."

"How did the rancher who owned it before Hutton—"

"Donovan."

"—keep his cattle from wandering?"

"The locals let God and the red-rock cliffs take care of most of the fencing. The rest got sorted out at roundup."

Christy frowned. It had been a long time since she'd been anywhere that wasn't laid out in a grid and measured down to the last inch.

"What about GPS?" she asked.

"Same as cell phones. Doesn't work down in a lot of the little canyons and creases. Great for the flats, though."

"My cell phone isn't."

"Yeah, well, we noncity types don't have that much to say to each other."

She rolled her eyes. Then she looked out at the vast, uneven, unfenced country. She didn't have to be western-raised to know how easy it would be to get lost in broken country.

"Do you at least have a U.S. Geological Survey map?" she asked.

"Hip pocket. Want to get it?"

She gave him a sideways glance.

He grinned. "Maybe when you know me better. Right now we're about half a mile south of the technical boundary of Xanadu."

"Who owns the land on either side of the road?"

"We do."

"Yeah, right."

"The Bureau of Land Management just administers it for us," he said. "Nice of them, huh?"

She laughed.

"Tell me when you figure we've crossed back onto Hutton's land," Cain said.

"Okay."

He smiled slightly, knowing what was ahead. In the next mile, the gravel road deteriorated to a dirt road and then to a set of tracks that meandered across a heavily grazed meadow and started up a short chute canyon.

He slowed and reached over to pull the transfer case lever down into four-wheel drive. "You do know how to drive, don't you?" he asked. "Just in case something happens to me out here."

Like a deer hunter out for other game.

"I drove a tractor years before I got my first period," she said.

"Yeah?"

"It's one of the few things about the West that I miss."

His smile gleamed against his beard. "Having a period?"

She snickered. "Driving. But you can have the tractors. What I miss is this kind of driving."

"Four-wheel freedom."

"Exactly."

"It's something big-city folks just don't understand," he said. "Same way I'll never understand how millions of people a day can march down piss-stained stairs into the underworld and commit their lives to a bunch of coked-out Puerto Rican subway jockeys."

"Let's hear it for the all-white West," she said sardonically.

"My mother's mother was born in Chihuahua. My father's

mother was Sioux. Two of my great-grandparents were Scots. The rest were garden-variety third-generation American mongrels."

She looked curiously at him. "Quite a mix."

"Common as dust out West. My only quarrel is with the choices people make, not their bloodlines. Cities give me a rash."

There was a finality in his tone that struck her.

"Was it a city where you . . . ?" She hesitated, not sure quite how to ask. "Is that where you got in trouble?"

His smile reminded her of Moki's toothy grin, more than a bit savage.

"Yeah, a city was where I killed a man. Boy, actually."

"Why did you kill him?"

"What makes you think it wasn't just for the hell of it?"

"Because you aren't a just-for-the-hell-of-it kind of man," she said impatiently.

"Thanks. I think." He flexed his hands on the wheel and let out a harsh breath. "I was a boy too. Rob was twenty. I was eighteen. It was a rowdy beer bar in Oakland."

She waited, holding her breath without realizing it.

"We were both students," Cain said evenly. "The judge called it 'mutual combat.' "

"Then why did you go to jail?"

"Under California law, mutual combat is good for a manslaughter conviction."

Christy tried to think of a tactful way to ask her next question. There wasn't one. "How long were you in jail?"

"Two years, two months, and six and a half days."

She looked at Cain and tried to imagine him locked up. He was so fiercely independent. "It must have been hell."

"The second half of my sentence was spent in a forestry camp called Susanville, up near the Oregon border."

"At least . . ." She winced and didn't say any more.

"I wasn't caged the whole time?" Cain finished bitterly. "Yeah, semi-freedom is better than none. But anything less than real freedom isn't worth the name."

The little canyon narrowed to a slot, then suddenly widened out again into a mile-long valley. On both sides white and rust-colored sandstone cliffs rose more than five hundred feet high.

She was amazed at how quickly and unexpectedly the land could change, and at how many nooks and crannies time and weather had carved in the edges of the mesas. The land was like the man next to her, full of surprises, rough yet compelling, alive its own way and on its own terms.

"Well, Red? Are we on Hutton's ranch yet?"

She thought back over the twists and turns in the road and shook her head. "Without a compass and a map, I wouldn't even guess."

"Even with a compass, it's impossible to be certain. God didn't get around to painting geodesic survey lines here."

"That's why you like it."

"It's a place where a man can be as free as he wants to be," he agreed.

Her hand touched his arm and she pointed to the left. "Look," she said in a hushed voice.

A herd of eight dark, shaggy elk broke and scattered across the valley, startled by the truck's sudden appearance. The leader was a big bull with a rack of horns that spread like a wall trophy waiting to be claimed. He stood his ground on a little rise and bellowed a challenge.

"He won't feel so confident in a month," Cain said.

"Why?"

"Hunting season opens."

"Ah, yes. Blood sports. Welcome to the Wild West."

"You think the beef you ate at Hutton's party volunteered for the job?"

She sighed. "No. And yes, I loved each politically and medically incorrect bite."

He laughed. "Supermarkets and plastic wrap insulates you from reality."

"Some of it. On the other hand, I don't think you'd be able to walk past a psychotic or simply alcoholic human being in Manhattan with anything like the callousness I've had to learn."

"Is living in the city worth it?"

"It's better than what I came from."

"I didn't know farm life was so bad," he said.

"You were never a poor girl who was smart instead of pretty," she said in a clipped voice. "You were never raised in a rural hell where men looked you over like a pony they might want to ride or a heifer they might want to breed. Nothing personal. Just another farm animal."

"Pretty girls always—"

"I wasn't pretty," Christy said flatly. "My sister got all the looks in the family. I got the brains."

The certainty in her voice amazed Cain. He looked at her and saw she wasn't fishing for compliments. She believed every word she'd said.

Amazing.

"Your sister must be drop-dead beautiful," he said after a moment.

"She is. What about you? Sisters? Brothers? Parents?"

"Yes. Parents in San Francisco. One sister in London, married to a diplomat. Another in Seattle running a coffee shop. A brother in Boston. Lawyer. I see them all when I make my rare-book rounds."

"Your . . . When do you do that?"

"Winter. Too cold to do much else then. What about your sister?"

"What about her?"

The complex emotions in Christy's voice made Cain glance sideways at her.

"Not close, huh?" he said sympathetically.

"Not the way you mean. But in other ways . . ." She hesitated.

He waited.

"Our parents died when I was eight," Christy said. "Not that I noticed. Dad was in and out of jail so often I barely knew him."

"So that's why you didn't run the other direction at the thought of an ex-con."

She shrugged. "Jail was a fact of life. Dad was a drinker. Mother drank right along with him. They had a high old time, right up until they drove into a train at eighty miles an hour."

"They missed a hell of a daughter."

Startled, she turned and looked into Cain's amber eyes.

"Who raised you?" he asked.

"Gramma. Mother's mother. She died the year I left home."

"What about your sister?"

"She takes after Mother. Wild. But—" Christy stopped abruptly. She could barely explain it to herself, much less to Cain.

"But?" he asked in a soft voice.

"She's all I have left," Christy said with barely leashed emotion, wanting him to understand. "In a whole world of strangers, she's the only one alive who shares the first half of my life, of my memories, of myself. There are times I want to strangle her, a lot more times I want to scream at her to grow up, but I love her anyway. I just don't always like her a whole lot."

He smiled crookedly. "Sounds like me and my brother. Don't get along most of the time, but when it counts, we'll back each other right to the wall, no questions asked."

"Yes," she said. "And each time, you hope this time it will work."

She didn't notice his look or the intensity of her own voice. She was caught up in a dream that was as old as her childhood and as deep as her need to love and be loved in return.

Right to the wall.

"This time," she said fiercely, "this time it will be different."

Chapter 21

"How much do you know about the Anasazi?" Cain asked without looking away from the road.

Christy blinked and realized it was the second time he'd asked the question. She took a deep breath and let the past go for the moment. And wished she could get rid of the past forever. Or some of it.

Most of it.

"I know the Anasazi are called Moki by the locals," she said.

He smiled slightly.

"And Peter gave me the spiel yesterday afternoon," she said. "All about the new theories of the Anasazi empire in the San Juan Basin."

"What Hutton knows about the Anasazi empire could be put into a one-paragraph press release."

"So says the Moki poacher."

"This Moki poacher has a Ph.D. in archaeology."

She stared at him.

"Like I said, there's not much to do around here in the winter," he added dryly.

"Should I call you doctor?"

"I won't answer. I studied because I wanted to know, not because I wanted the world to know I knew."

Tilting her head, she studied him the way she would a design of unknown origin and fascinating complexity.

"You're looking at me the way Moki looks at a rabbit," he said after a minute.

"Cultural synthesis."

"You do and you clean it up."

Smiling, she shook her head. "Too late. You've already given the game away. You're not a tongue-tied cowboy. You're not a stump-dumb bar brawler. You're quite civilized under all the—"

"Don't count on it," he interrupted roughly. "A fancy degree doesn't make silk out of pigskin."

"No, but it makes some really intriguing patterns on even the toughest hide," she shot back. "The most elegant and powerful designs often come from cultural synthesis."

He steered the truck around a hole in the road. "The story of humanity. Thesis, antithesis, synthesis. Repeat as necessary."

"You studied some philosophy along with pots and bones."

"Like I said. Winters are long."

"What did you specialize in for your doctorate?" she asked.

"Guess."

She smiled. "So, Professor, according to your studies, what did the Anasazi do to amuse themselves during the long winters?"

"Beyond the obvious?" he asked, grinning. "I've found small polished pieces of bone that could have been markers in various games."

"But no sign of written language?"

He shook his head. "They almost certainly had a fine and

complex oral tradition. The Pueblo Indians still do. Much of it is secret, though."

"Medicine men?"

"Medicine women."

From the corner of his eyes he saw the *gotcha* expression on Christy's face.

"Matriarchy," she said with satisfaction. "Those Mokis were no fools."

"I don't know about matriarchy. I suspect it was more a matter of women being given half of the cosmos to look after and men taking care of the other half."

"Good God. A nonabsolutist approach to the universe. What makes you think the Anasazi were that unusual?"

"The Pueblo tribes today have a system rather like that. Each sex has vital work to do in ensuring the continuation of the clan and the universe."

"Yin and yang," she said softly. "The most subtle, elegant, and powerful symbol yet devised by human beings. Of course, because the Chinese created it, the women got the short end of the symbol."

Cain laughed outright. "Only in the written description. The symbol itself is neutral. Male in the heart of all that is most female. Female in the heart of all that is most male."

She gave him another surprised look.

"The Anasazi were sophisticated," he said. "Their empire spread all over the San Juan Basin, everywhere you can see from here."

Christy stared out over the rugged land, trying to imagine an empire spreading away on all sides. Wherever she looked, mountain peaks either distant or close rose like elegant stone crowns.

"What you're looking at is a geologic feature called the Colorado Plateau," he said. "It's a maze of piñon and cedar, big sage, and creeks lined by willow and alder, mesas, mountains, aspen, and a sky as big as God."

Without hesitating, he steered around a boulder just slightly smaller than the truck.

"The Anasazi lived all over the Colorado Plateau?" she asked.

"Yes, but it was along the southern and western edges they built cliff houses into the bones of the land itself, in places where the plateau eroded down to the desert in a series of mesas separated by finger canyons and joined by the endless sky."

She looked at the rugged land, as beautiful as it was empty. "It's hard to believe there was ever an empire in the San Juan Basin."

"Maybe not an empire in the way you mean," he said. "Armies and cities and a single powerful emperor. I don't think things worked that way. There was power, but it wasn't just one person's."

She turned from the land to the man who was more interesting the longer she was with him. That alone was enough to surprise her. Most people she met became less intriguing as they became more familiar.

"I think we're talking about informal domination," Cain said, "an integrated system of communities with its religious and social center in Chaco Canyon."

"Where's that?"

"Over in northwestern New Mexico. We're at the far northern reach of the Anasazi empire or sphere of direct influence or whatever right now."

Christy frowned, vaguely remembering something she'd read years before. "I thought Mesa Verde was the northern edge of the Anasazi range."

"The academics used to think so too. The locals knew

better. You can't walk out here without kicking up some sherds."

He slowed the truck, letting it creep over a patch of deeply rutted road.

"Then how did we miss the signs of the Anasazi for so long?" she asked.

"You don't find what you're not looking for."

"Okay. Why are we looking now?"

"A few years back, Uncle Sam decided that a place couldn't be flooded, filled in, paved over, or even plowed if there were signs that the area might have archaeological interest."

"So?"

"So every time someone wants to put in a road to a distant site to wildcat for oil, or the Army Corps of Engineers pursues its mandate to dam up everything bigger than a stream of piss, potsherds and walls are found."

"You're joking."

He shook his head without looking away from the bad road. "There are thousands of sites in the San Juan Basin. Hundreds of thousands, more likely. Hell, there were more people living in some parts of the basin seven hundred years ago than there are today."

"Good-bye dams and oil drilling."

He gave her a sidelong glance. "You really think so?"

She grimaced. "No. How do they get around the rules?"

"They use other rules. The construction crews call in archaeologists to go over the site and see if there's anything really unique that has to be saved."

The tires thumped and Moki's claws scrabbled for purchase as the truck "walked" over another rough patch of road. Christy braced the big dog, much to Cain's amusement.

"If the site looks special," he said, still smiling, "the archaeologists work like hell to save what they can before the bulldozers arrive or the dam is finished and the site is flooded."

"Does that happen often?"

"So often there's a name for it. Salvage archaeology."

"Sounds grim."

"It's better than no archaeology at all," he said. "There are probably five hundred professionals digging and exploring in the San Juan Basin right now, and the more work that's done, the more sites they find to explore. The situation sort of defines an embarrassment of riches."

The truck settled onto a less rugged course. He didn't accelerate. He knew the road would just get worse. Much worse.

"How rich?" she asked.

"Most of the Colorado Plateau could quite easily fit the definition of an archaeological site, which wouldn't leave room for the people who live here now."

"I find that hard to believe."

"Why? They've discovered a network of roads that reaches all the way over into Utah and up into this part of Colorado," Cain said.

"Roads? Real roads like the Roman roads in Britain?"

"As real as it gets. Thirty feet wide and straight as a ruler, come hell or high mountains. When the terrain got too steep for roads, they cut stairs."

"Must have been the male half of the Anasazi power structure that built the roads," she said. "Women are smart enough to go around an obstacle."

Cain's smile showed white against his short black beard.

She knew she watched for that smile more than she should. The contrast of light and dark, laughter and bleakness fascinated her.

"The Anasazi built those roads long before the Spaniards

came," he said. "There were no wheels or four-footed beasts of burden to worry about on the stairs."

"So what did they use?"

"Slave labor is the most logical possibility," he said, "though a lot of the university folks would as soon lynch you as discuss it. They prefer to think white men invented slavery, war, disease, sin, and everything else bad."

Christy tried not to laugh, but gave in. "I hope you got your degrees by correspondence course."

Laughing quietly, he shook his head. "Reality has a way of sneaking past ivory towers. The Anasazi weren't simple, noble savages or New Age collectivists. Despite their lack of written language and metallurgy, they developed a unique, sophisticated civilization. Astronomers have even found evidence that Chaco Canyon could have been laid out as a giant solar and lunar observatory."

"Like Stonehenge?" she asked, startled.

"Same principle, different means. Same need."

"Religion?"

"Survival. When your growing season is measured in weeks rather than months, planting at the best time is a matter of life and death."

Christy listened, watching the man rather than the land. The excitement buried in his voice reminded her of herself on the trail of a new style, one that transcended simple fashion and became something very close to art. Half closing her eyes, she settled more deeply in the seat, enjoying the intensity of Cain's deep voice as he talked about something he obviously loved.

"Lots of new information is turning up every day," he said. "So much that the universities can't keep a lock on it. Hell, they can hardly keep a handle on it. Even we *Moki poachers*—that would be the folks who don't work on university digs"— he explained sardonically, "have been invited to attend some of the university conferences and talk about what we've found. But we have to translate it into professor-ese and document it their way. No oral traditions for university types."

"If they tolerate you, they must be desperate for your information," she said blandly.

He gave a crack of laughter. "That they are. We've found trade goods in Anasazi sites that could only have come from thousands of miles away."

"Argillite and abalone shells from the Pacific."

Cain looked at her in approval. "And copper bells and parrot feathers from the interior of Mexico. Trade routes almost two thousand miles long."

"Quite an empire. What happened? Where did it all go?"

"No one knows."

Christy blinked. "Why not?"

"No written language. All we know is that the empire began to collapse in the twelfth century, just about the time the Chaco community was reaching its zenith." He slowed the truck to a crawl. "That's where the Sisters come in. And this is where we leave the road."

"What road?" she said. "I don't see any."

"In a few minutes, you'll remember this little track with great fondness."

"Yeah. Right."

"Trust me on this one, Red." He stopped and shifted the truck into low range.

Then he turned right and headed up a sandstone slope.

"Cain!"

He grinned. "Weren't you the one singing hymns to four-wheel freedom?"

"But—"

"Hang on, honey. It looks a lot worse than it is."

The slope was broken and weathered, a long rough ramp

onto the top of another mesa. He let the Suburban set its own speed. The truck rocked from side to side unpredictably—unpredictably because the angle of the ramp was so steep that the hood hid everything but the sky.

She held on to the door with one hand and Moki's ruff with the other, bracing both of them until the truck gained the top of the mesa.

"Moki's going to wonder what he ever did without you," Cain said.

There was another faint track out through the scrub forest of piñon and cedar. Though rough, the way was better than the sandstone chute had been.

"Those are the Sisters up ahead," he said.

Her head whipped around. "What?"

"The Sisters. At least that's what some people call them."

He pointed to two rock spires that rose a hundred feet above the mesa. Like massive stacks jutting up from a piñon sea, the Sisters were the remnants of a long-vanished, much larger rock formation.

"Is that where we're going?" she asked.

"Yeah."

"How far away are they?"

"Several miles."

The columns stood together and had generally similar shapes, but they were distinctly different colors. The smaller was a reddish sandstone that rose in slender elegance above the land. The other was nearly white toward the top, the color of the mesa's cap rock.

"The Sisters are hard to see from the flats, even when it isn't cloudy like today," Cain said. "From most angles, only the white one shows. But once we get over to them, you can see damn near to Arizona and New Mexico."

The intensity of his eyes as he watched the Sisters was almost tangible. He was like a wolf sighting prey.

"Why are the Sisters so important to you?" Christy asked.

"I have a theory about the Anasazi, why they settled in some of the unlikely places they did. If my theory is right, there will be Anasazi sites clear up here, close to the mountains."

"And you want to be the first to find them."

He glanced at her. "You have a problem with that?"

"I'm old-fashioned," she said after a moment. "I think archaeological sites should be explored by professionals rather than stripped by even the most highly educated pothunter."

"I'd agree with you, if it was that simple."

She raised auburn eyebrows but said nothing.

"There are thousands and thousands of sites that the academic archaeologists won't get to for decades, if then," he said evenly. "Some of those sites are on public lands. A lot are on private ground, farms and rangeland."

"Still—"

"What's the local bean farmer supposed to do when he plows his most productive fields in spring and turns up artifacts?"

"Call in the university," she said.

"Then what? He could wait a long time before the professionals show up to do their research, particularly since neither the state nor the federal government has the funds to properly explore and document the sites that are *already* known, much less new ones."

She began to understand what he'd meant about the sites being an embarrassment of riches. She might have lived in the city since she was nineteen, but she hadn't forgotten the intractable rhythms of the seasons. Kicking up potsherds in a field and doing the right thing by calling in the authorities could bankrupt a small farmer.

"Planting time doesn't wait," she said, sighing.

"Modern farmers and ancient Anasazi have that in common. Short growing season. If the farmer knows his discovery means taking that field out of production for years, he'll keep his mouth shut, plow the whole damn thing under, and plant beans so he can support his family."

"So in come the salvage archaeologists."

"Yeah. Not a perfect solution, but not as bad as plowing everything under. We get to look at something new and the farmer gets on with the job of making a living on marginal cropland."

Christy thought about the designs Peter Hutton had borrowed from the finds on his own land. Despite the protests of his hired archaeologists, he'd simply gone in and taken what he wanted when it had been found, and to hell with the rest of the process.

Not a perfect solution either.

Yet having seen the extraordinary turtle, she doubted that she would have gambled on leaving it behind in its academically proper place, and perhaps losing it to storms or falling stones or true pothunters, the kind who grabbed and ran.

"Life is incurably messy," she said.

"That's why the road to hell is paved with good intentions."

He braked the truck at the edge of a five-foot-deep channel in the rocky top of the mesa. "End of the line for wheels. We go on foot from here."

The two massive pinnacles Cain called the Sisters were still more than a mile away from the truck, but they were close enough to reveal that the red sandstone column was straight-sided and clean. The white spire, though taller and thicker at the top, was shot through with cracks and miniature fault lines. Sections of pale rock had fallen away in several places, leaving the column with an appearance of being humpbacked, twisted, oddly misshapen.

Christy didn't see a trail anywhere.

Chapter 22

When Christy opened the door, Moki leaped across her seat to freedom. The dog dashed off a dozen yards, sniffed around beneath a spreading cedar tree, left his mark, and came trotting back.

She stood next to the truck. She still didn't see anything like a trail. There was a wildness in the wind blowing through the stunted junipers and piñon pines. Overhead, the gray clouds seethed and parted. A shaft of golden light flowed across the red pinnacle but soon vanished as the clouds flowed together again.

"You picked a fine morning for a hike," she said as Cain joined her.

"Talk to your friend Hutton. We could have driven a lot closer than this if he wasn't so damned touchy about trespassing. We're close to the edge of his deeded land now. Then it becomes federal land. Of course, he leases that and treats it like he owns it, but so does every other western rancher."

With that, Cain scrambled down the near side of the runoff channel that had halted the truck. A few moments later he climbed up the other side and headed off through the broken country.

Moki jumped down onto a rock, leaped across the channel with muscular, four-footed grace, and trotted after his master. Cain disappeared behind a screen of head-high brush without so much as a backward look to see how she was handling the rough land.

"That will teach me to call him a pothunter," Christy muttered.

Nothing answered but the wind.

She scrambled through the channel with less grace than Moki, but she got the job done. A gust of chill wind combed through her hair as she climbed up the far side. She zipped the windbreaker, pulled the watch cap over her head, and trotted to catch up with Cain.

He strode along easily, his vest unzipped and his hat back on his head. Against the gray clouds, his eyes gleamed like citrine. For all the ease of his stride, there was an intense wariness in him that made her nervous.

"Is something wrong?" she asked.

He shot her a surprised look. "Not yet."

"Are you expecting something to go wrong?"

"No, but I wasn't expecting anything the last time I was here either."

"When was that?"

"The day I got shot."

She felt a chill that had nothing to do with the wind. She waited, but he didn't say anything else.

"Did you get shot right here?" she asked.

"No. Closer to the base of the Sisters."

"What were you doing?"

"Walking along through a stand of piñon pines, just like we are right now."

"And someone just shot you? No warning?"

He nodded.

"Why?" she asked.

"If you believe Danner, somebody thought I was a deer."

She looked at Cain. There was nothing the color of deer hide anywhere on him.

"I suppose it's possible," she said slowly. "God knows a lot of range cattle buy it every hunting season."

"This wasn't hunting season."

"Were you out Moki poaching?"

"Red, Moki poaching may be a joke to you, but it's a felony," he said in a flat voice. "An ex-con would find himself in jail real quick if he picked up so much as a stinking potsherd without the landowner's signed, notarized permission."

Her eyes widened. "I'm sorry."

A flashing sideways look was his only answer. Then he said something under his breath, yanked off his watch cap, and raked his long fingers through his hair.

"I'm a bit touchy on that score," he said. "I don't have permission to dig here. Hutton won't let anyone on his land, and the Bureau of Land Management won't let anyone dig, period."

"Then why are we here?"

"You can hike on BLM land. That's what we're doing. Hiking. If you pick up so much as a rock chip, I'll make you put it back."

"Why are we hiking here, if it's such a problem?"

"Because here is where I'll find evidence to support my theory about the extent of the Anasazi empire."

"Like what?"

"Ruins, grinding holes, potsherds, anything," he said.

"Why here?"

"Jesus, you're a regular fountain of questions."

"I'm a—"

"Reporter," he said, interrupting. "Yeah. I've noticed."

They walked quickly for a few minutes.

In silence.

"Well?" she said.

"Well, what?"

"Why do you think the Anasazi will be here when nobody else thinks so?"

"I'll give you a copy of my dissertation," he said in a clipped voice.

She sighed and tried another tack.

"Is it likely you were shot by some jealous rival archaeologist, either professional or amateur?" she asked.

He laughed.

"Well," she retorted, "it makes as much sense as someone thinking you were a deer."

"Most archaeologists are good at hunting pots and lousy at moving targets."

"So?"

"Whoever shot me was good enough to bring me down at three hundred yards."

Christy's hand wrapped around Cain's arm, stopping him.

"How do you know he was that far away?" she asked.

"I felt the bullet hit me and throw me back. I was on the ground, trying to figure out what had happened, when I heard the report."

A small sound escaped her lips. Without realizing it, her hand moved slowly, almost caressingly, on his arm.

"I'd estimate the time between the shock and the sound at not quite two seconds," he said evenly. "That means a range of three hundred yards. It also means that whoever shot me had a telescopic sight."

Cain started walking.

Christy stared, then hurried to catch up and walk beside him, thinking hard. She snatched a twig off a cedar tree as she walked past it. The scent of the flat green needles was rich and astringent, like Jo-Jo's closet. With a shudder of memory, Christy threw away the twig.

"Can you see much detail through a telescopic sight at three hundred yards?" she asked.

"You sure as shit can see the difference between a deer and a man, especially when the man is standing out in the open."

"Can you see enough to identify someone?"

Cain didn't say anything.

She waited.

"Maybe," he said finally, "but only if you knew him on sight already."

"Do you hear what you're saying?" she asked in an unhappy voice.

"Yeah. Whoever shot me knew exactly who I was. Not an accident, Red. Murder, plain and simple."

Chapter 23

Christy stopped and stared at Cain as the reality of what had happened broke over her. Until now she really hadn't believed the shooting had been a deliberate act. She'd assumed that he was simply making an accident more understandable, more meaningful, by saying that the shot had been deliberate rather than a random bit of rotten luck.

But it hadn't been random and it hadn't been luck.

Murder, plain and simple.

Even now, she had a hard time accepting it. No one murdered without a motive, yet Cain didn't know of one, and if anyone should know, it was the man who'd nearly died.

No motive.

No reason.

And no doubt that the shooting had occurred. Cain had the scar to prove it.

I've been in the city too long, she thought bleakly. *I find it easier to accept random violence than the idea of premeditated murder.*

"Hello-o-o," Cain said, waving his hand in front of her face.

She gave him a startled look.

"You keep staring at me as though I've just grown a set of antlers," he said, smiling.

"It's not every day a man calmly tells me that somebody tried to kill him."

"It's hardly the first time I've said it."

"But it's the first time I've—"

"Believed it?" he finished.

She nodded.

He turned away.

"Damn it, Cain," she said fiercely, "how would you feel if a stranger walked up to you with a story that someone was trying to kill him but everyone else thought it was just an accident?"

After a moment of hesitation, he ran a big hand through his hair, yanked the watch cap back into place, and looked over his shoulder at Christy.

"Come on," he said. "We've got some rough country to cover before those clouds decide if they're going to get together and rain."

Moki came dashing in from some piñons with a predatory gleam in his eyes and his long pink tongue hanging out. There was no doubt the dog loved the wild land and the even wilder wind. He nudged Cain's hand and danced over to Christy, vibrating with life.

"What does he want?" she asked.

"Not much. Just a little company when he's lonely or has something to share."

Before she could answer, he walked off with long, lithe strides. Moki yapped excitedly and took off running again.

Christy shut her mouth and followed.

The sun was warm in protected places. Everywhere else the wind stripped heat from land and flesh alike. Yet she found herself enjoying the clean chill of the air and the slow-motion boiling of the clouds high overhead. The mountains that rose behind the mesa were already on fire with aspens turned gold by the frost. Deer and elk at the higher elevations would begin to gather and drift toward the valleys, following summer as it retreated down the mountain slopes.

Vast change. Vast sameness.

She thought she'd left all that behind, the untamed land, the exhilarating freedom, the wind from a distance that was just as wild. Yet it had always been there, always waiting for her just a handful of hours from Manhattan.

And it always would be here.

Once that would have dismayed her. Now it comforted her in a way she didn't understand, just as she didn't understand the depth of her attraction to Aaron Cain.

But like the land, the attraction was real.

When they approached a thick stand of piñon, Moki caught a hot scent and bounded into the thick of the trees. The grove exploded with noise and flashes of dark blue as birds flew up in all directions. The birds were bigger than robins and four times as loud. The blue of their feathers had a shiny, misty sheen, like the bloom on a plum.

Smiling, Cain and Christy watched the birds' wild flight, enjoying the bright blue specks of life racing before the wind. The birds jeered and called back and forth while they reformed into a new flock. A few hundred feet away, they settled into another stand of piñons and attacked the ripe cones, stuffing the bounty of rich, oily seeds down their throats.

"Piñon jays," Cain said.

He bent over and picked up a deep blue feather that one of the birds had dropped. The feather seemed much darker now than any of the birds had been. Absently he held the feather next to Christy's red hair. His eyes said the contrasting colors pleased him.

Then, as though realizing what he'd done, he opened his fingers and let the wind take the gleaming feather.

"Free and glad of it," he said. "But they've got a lot of work to do before winter, if they expect to survive. Out here, there's no such thing as a free lunch."

Calling Moki away from the jays, Cain resumed his swift pace. Christy's eyes followed the brief, erratic flight of the single feather. She went to the shrub that had captured the feather, plucked it free, and tucked the fragment of blue into her pocket. Then she hurried to catch up.

As they approached the Sisters, they could hear the faint whistle of air currents playing around the twisted form of the white spire. The sounds were eerie, ghostly, flutelike in their purity. They belonged to a world and a time when spirits had walked with mankind in uneasy unity.

Moki reappeared and walked beside Christy. Cain's pace slowed as his eyes scanned the landscape, seeking something only he knew.

"What are you looking for?" she asked finally.

"Anything that's out of place."

"Such as?"

"If I knew, I would have found it by now."

She looked at the Sisters and the raw, rocky land. Fallen slabs of red and white sandstone lay in heaps at the base of the two spires, but the disorder looked quite natural. It was the result of eons of wind and water erosion. The rest of the mesa top was windswept and almost clean, like a well-kept floor.

The more she looked, the more she absorbed the rhythms of the land. For all its appearance of permanence to human eyes, the sandstone mesa was only temporary. Wind and weather and time ruled here, dissolving rock grain by grain and creating red sand that blew away on the wind.

The same forces worked on life. In the sheltered spots, the cedars and piñons were straight and healthy. In open spots where the wind blew freely, the trees were knotted and hunched, like old men with bodies twisted by time.

Cain walked to a small rock cornice that was a hundred yards from the base of the white spire. He checked an angle over his shoulder, then scrambled up.

Silently Christy watched as he inspected the rock.

"This is where the killer shot from," he said after a few minutes.

"How do you know?"

"It's where I'd shoot from if I expected to kill a man exploring around the Sisters."

He quartered the stone ledge until he finally settled on a spot that was sheltered behind two waist-high boulders. He hunkered down behind the rocks and went through the motions of a sharpshooter looking for a place to rest a rifle barrel in the notch between the boulders.

When he found the best position, he raised an imaginary rifle and mimicked the actions of firing, working the bolt and reloading. His eyes traced the arc a spent cartridge case would make when it was ejected. He scrambled over to that spot and dropped out of sight, searching for something behind the boulders.

Alone with the wind, Christy waited for Cain to reappear. It took some time, but he finally emerged from the shadowed spot in the rock and jumped down. His smile was grim and triumphant.

"Three-oh-eight, just like I thought," he said.

He held out a dark metal cylinder the size of a pencil stub and dropped it into her palm.

"It's spent brass," he said. "A shell casing."

"I know. I'm from Wyoming, remember? I've seen a lot of old brass. But that was worn and dull from years out in the rain and snow. This casing is bright. It could have been dropped yesterday."

"Makes you feel good to know the sheriff has done such a thorough job of investigating my shooting," Cain said.

"How could he miss this?"

"Easy. He never looked."

Cain took the casing from her and dropped it into his shirt pocket.

"Shouldn't you wrap it up in cloth or something?" she asked. "Can't someone use it as evidence, even if the sheriff doesn't know his butt from a warm rock?"

Cain's smile flashed, then faded. "Half the deer hunters in southwestern Colorado shoot that caliber Winchester. Unless I can come up with a weapon—and a motive—it would be like hunting red sand on the Colorado Plateau."

"But somebody tried to kill you!"

"You sound like you believe me now."

"I do."

"There was more than one 'somebody,'" he said.

"How can you be so sure?"

"I was there, Red. Remember?"

"At three hundred yards," she said in a rush, "without binoculars, lying on your back and wondering what hit you—how could you be so sure it was deliberate, much less that Jo was involved?"

For a moment, he was too surprised by her intensity to respond.

"You said you weren't ever lovers," Christy continued fiercely, driven by fear and something more, emotions she couldn't name and didn't want to examine. "What motive would she have for wanting you dead?"

His eyes narrowed. "You sound like you changed your mind about believing me."

"I believe someone tried to kill you. I have a hard time believing any man would turn down a woman like Jo."

"She had a hard time believing it too. But I wasn't nineteen anymore."

"What does that have to do with it?"

"A smart man needs only one Jo-Jo in a lifetime," Cain said. "I had mine when I was nineteen." The look in his eyes was a warning not to ask any more questions.

Christy ignored it. "You're not making sense."

"How about trusting me?"

"How about trusting *me*?"

For the space of several breaths, the only sound was the spectral fluting of the wind around the Sisters.

"Jo-Jo came on to me just like she did to every other man between the age of eighteen and eighty," Cain said in a clipped voice. "When I didn't send back the right signals, she got curious. We talked."

Christy waited, breath held.

"Down underneath that beauty, she was a strange, scared kid," he said. "But you had to dig damned hard to get under the varnish."

"What was she afraid of?"

"Growing old. Getting ugly. Living. Dying." He shrugged. "You name it. If she couldn't control it with sex, it terrified her."

Christy's ragged sigh was covered by the eerie notes of the wind.

"From time to time she would show up at the cabin," he said. "She wanted a place to sleep because Hutton was mad at her. At least, that's what she said."

"You didn't believe her?"

"I don't think she knew the difference between truth and lies. Whatever worked was fine with her."

"So you think she came up there because she just couldn't wait to trip you and beat you to the floor?" Christy asked acidly.

His mouth curved in a smile that was as thin as a new moon. "Jo-Jo would have put out for me if I'd asked. But that wasn't what she was after."

"Was she really afraid of Hutton?"

Again, Cain shrugged. "What interested her was my Anasazi stuff."

"Jo?" Christy said, startled.

"Yeah, it surprised me too. But she was really excited about it, kept asking me questions."

"So you let her stay."

He nodded curtly.

Christy remembered what Cain had said earlier about what Moki wanted from people. *Not much. Just a little company when he's lonely or has something to share.*

Cain had wanted to share his love of the Anasazi culture.

Jo-Jo had been willing to listen.

"Then," he said, "I came back from a trip last winter and found Jo-Jo shacked up in my cabin with Hutton's hotshot jet jockey. I threw both of them out so hard they bounced."

Christy winced.

"Later I discovered some of my Anasazi bowls were missing," he said.

"And you think Jo took them?"

He nodded.

"Why would the world's best-paid model need to steal Anasazi artifacts?" she asked reasonably.

"Jo-Jo's like that. She sees something she wants and she takes it."

Christy thought about Gramma's necklace. Jo-Jo had taken it, but not for the usual reasons. The money value of the nuggets didn't matter to her. It was the loss to Christy that mattered.

Simple vengeance against someone Jo-Jo couldn't control. Someone like Cain.

"Were the artifacts especially valuable?" Christy asked, her voice raw.

"Just to me. They were key pieces of evidence supporting

my theory of Anasazi settlement patterns. My paper had been accepted, but suddenly the best evidence was gone. If I cared about academic recognition . . ."

"It could have ruined you," Christy finished.

"It sure didn't help. Even with all the in situ photographs, I had a hell of a time getting the dissertation published."

"So that's why you hate Jo."

"No."

"Then why?"

"Leave it alone, Red."

"I can't," she said starkly.

For a long moment, he watched her out of bleak eyes.

"Jo-Jo liked having men fight over her," he said in a flat tone. "After I threw her out, I ran across her in a bar in Montrose. She had Johnny Ten Hats panting after her, but it wasn't enough. She did everything but a hand job to get me interested. Then she tried to get me to fight Johnny over her."

Christy stood so still she ached with tension. Like attempted murder, she didn't want to believe it. But she did. "What happened?"

"Johnny was willing. Hell, he'd go to war over a bent penny. But I wasn't nineteen anymore. I wasn't going to fight over a lying piece of ass again. I walked away."

A chill went over Christy. "Again? The fight in California? It was over a woman?"

He didn't answer.

He didn't have to. She saw the old rage and pain in the instant before he narrowed his eyes, shutting her out.

"I understand now why you hate Jo," Christy said after a moment. "But . . ."

The look on Cain's face was closed and cold. She took a deep breath and chose her words carefully.

"But just because Jo tried to get you to fight Johnny,"

Christy said in a low voice, "is that any reason to think she tried to kill you?"

"Look around."

She started to object, then did as he asked. She didn't see anything that she hadn't seen before.

"You see any way a man could follow me here and then scramble up into that niche without my spotting him?" Cain asked.

She looked around again, carefully, before she turned back to him and shook her head slowly.

"A few days after I walked out on Johnny in that bar, Jo-Jo called me," Cain said.

An odd stillness settled over Christy. She wanted to tell him to stop talking, to stop telling her more than she wanted to know about the beautiful little angel who had grown up into something ugly. But she didn't ask him to stop. Stopping wouldn't change the truth.

Jo-Jo, what happened? Were you always like this and I just couldn't see it?

"She apologized for taking the bowl that had a drawing of the Sisters with Kokopelli and his flute," Cain said. "To make up for it, she told me she'd found a little ruin up here on the Sisters mesa."

"No."

He didn't hear Christy's low, ragged voice. He was caught in his own moment of agony when he'd nearly died trying to breathe icy air through a bullet hole in his chest.

"She said she wanted to explore the ruin but didn't have—"

"No," Christy whispered again.

"—time, so she thought she'd pass it on to me as a way of telling me how sorry she was."

"There must be a mistake."

"Yeah. It was made by the man who didn't quite murder me."

"Jo is selfish and sometimes cruel, but I can't believe she'd set up a man for murder. *I just can't.*"

Christy's words stopped when she realized that Cain was watching her with predatory intensity.

"You sound like you know her real well," he said.

"Yes." She heard her own words and added quickly, "I have the same file on her that I have on Hutton."

Black eyebrows lifted.

"Besides," she said. "It's . . . hard . . . to believe that beauty isn't more than skin deep. I can't believe that Jo . . ."

There wasn't any comfort in Cain's smile. "Yeah, I had a hard time myself. But I learned the truth of that old cliché at nineteen. Pretty is as pretty does."

Christy opened her mouth to say, *But she's my sister!* Then she closed her mouth and looked away.

"As far as I'm concerned," he said, "women like Jo-Jo are literally as ugly as sin. Any more questions?"

"No," she said in a low voice.

"Good. Now let's see if we can find that ruin."

"You don't think she lied about that too?"

"She might have, but this doesn't lie."

Cain held out his hand. On his palm was a potsherd crossed with black lines.

"Where did you find it?" she asked.

"Over there," he said, gesturing with his hand.

"Today?"

"No. Just before I was shot."

Chapter 24

"**Y**ou take that side," Cain said, pointing to the column of red rock rising up to the sky.

Without a word, Christy turned toward it. She wanted to talk about Jo-Jo some more, to protest more, to do something that would take the ice and nausea from her stomach.

But there was nothing to do except pull up her socks and help the man her sister had tried to murder.

"Look for pictographs or petroglyphs," he said.

"Oh, sure," she said. "I never remember which is which."

"Pictographs are painted on. Petroglyphs are hammered in."

"Got it."

She circled out from him, following the irregular base of the red spire. She didn't see drawings of any kind on the blocks of rubble or on the face of the pinnacle itself.

"Anything?" she asked when she met him on the other side.

"No. Let's try the white Sister next."

Christy circled one way and he went the other while the wind fluted its eerie music all around. When they met in back, neither had found anything.

"I was afraid of that," he said. "Too exposed."

"What is?"

"The Sisters. The wind has sandblasted them. Any drawings the Anasazi left are long since worn away."

She studied the outlines of the two stones, Sisters that had spent unimaginable eons standing next to each other. She wondered if they understood each other any better for all the time together.

She doubted it.

"What did they look like a thousand years ago?" she asked.

"About the same as now. A thousand years isn't a long time for rock."

"The drawing in the bowl."

"Yes?"

"How was it oriented?"

Cain glanced at Christy thoughtfully. Abruptly he nodded. "Good idea, Red."

With that he turned and began walking so fast that she had to trot to keep up.

"Where are we going?" she asked.

"To look at things from another angle."

She made a frustrated noise. Smiling slightly, he touched her cheek. The caress was gentle and so swift it was over before she had time to react.

"The Anasazis' closest surviving relatives are the Pueblos over in eastern New Mexico," he said as though nothing had happened. "Their shamans have one job—to keep track of the place the sun rises each morning."

He scrambled up a low rock ledge onto another flat stone platform. The mesa top had many of them, frozen waves of sandstone. The tops of the low stone waves had been worn off by time and wind into random broad steps that came from nowhere and led nowhere.

"Here," he said, holding out his hand. "It's steeper than it looks."

No sooner had she reached for him than his hand closed around her wrist. He pulled her up onto the new level with an easy strength that went against the idea he'd ever been shot, wounded, bleeding on stone.

But she knew he had. She'd seen the scar. She'd seen the pain in his face when he stretched a certain way.

"The most important day on the solar calendar is the solstice," Cain said.

She followed his intent glance. He was examining the stone wall in front of him as though he expected to find a treasure map.

"What are you looking for?" she asked.

"Any indication that this was a place of power and importance for the Anasazi. If it was, it would have to do with solar events."

"Then we're out of luck. The sun is hiding."

His smile flashed briefly. "It will burn through before noon."

She glanced up and saw that he was right. As the sun climbed, it slowly ate the clouds. Even behind the misty cover, the sun was an incandescent circle far too bright to look at.

Slowly Cain walked until he could see the sun disk bracketed by the Sisters. He circled to his left, walked a dozen paces, then stopped and stared back toward the Sisters. The red spire now blocked the sun. He adjusted his position a few feet, then gestured with his hand toward the gap between the rock needles.

"The sun would rise on the morning of the solstice right there," he said, gesturing toward the eastern sky. "The first light would be visible back there somewhere."

"How do you know?"

"I'm a shaman," he said dryly. "Come on."

Together, they headed across the windswept mesa toward a spot a quarter mile away. Behind them the wind swirled around the sandstone needles, wailing like a lost child.

When they came to another of the broad stone steps, he levered himself up and offered her his hand again. Moki danced around on the lower level and finally leaped up and scrambled over the rim. He stood between them, facing the wind and waving his plumed tail proudly.

Cain put his hands on Christy's shoulders and turned her until she faced the Sisters.

"On the summer solstice," he said, "from here the sun would rise directly between the two spires. This side of the mesa top would have been a very special place for the Anasazi. There has to be a kiva around here somewhere."

She was keenly aware of the weight and warmth of his hands on her shoulders. It felt good.

"What's a kiva?" she asked, her voice almost husky.

"The navel of the world."

She looked over her shoulder at him. He was so close that she could sense the warmth of his breath on her cheek. He smiled at her.

"A kiva," he said, "is also a circular room dug into the earth and roofed over with cedar beams and plaster."

"Into the earth? Why? In this country wouldn't it be easier to build above the ground?"

"Probably. But the Anasazi believed that all the clans originally emerged from the underworld on their great journey toward the sky. Going to and from the kiva mimics that journey. Some say that it also mimics the womb, and birth."

She frowned. "So a kiva is a kind of church?"

"A church. A social club. A clan headquarters. A symbol of secrecy. The kiva could have been all those things."

"Or none of them?"

A smile flashed through Cain's short black beard.

"Or none of them," he agreed. "All we know for sure is that the kiva was very important to the Anasazi. They went to a lot of trouble to build kivas next to their apartment buildings. The Pueblo people do the same today."

Releasing Christy, he turned and examined the mesa behind them, looking for any sign that once, long ago, people had built here, lived here, died here.

Nothing showed but the rough mesa top itself, marked with dark evergreen and red rock, swept by the restless wind. The abrupt, rocky platform where they stood was close to the edge of the mesa. Nearby, a deep slit canyon cut through the sandstone. Beyond the slit, the land fell away into the distance, leaving a sheer stone precipice behind.

"How are you on heights?" he asked.

"I live on the forty-third floor."

"How are you when there aren't any elevators to take you up and down?"

"I'll manage."

"Good. Come on."

He leaped down from the small stone platform. When she started to follow, he lifted her down as he'd done once before, when they had been fleeing from Hutton's guards. And again, she was sharply aware of Cain's palms gliding lightly over the sides of her breasts.

She saw an answering flare of awareness in his eyes before he released her and turned away.

Moki barked eagerly from atop the rock platform.

"You got up there yourself," he told the dog. "You can get down the same way."

Moki barked again, circled the little platform, then dashed to one edge and jumped. He touched a small outcropping of rock on the way down. The rock gave way suddenly, dumping the dog to the ground. He scrambled up, shook off the surprise like rain, and raced off over the mesa once more.

"Is this something useful?" she asked.

Cain turned in time to see her pick a white fragment from the fresh fall of dirt that had come loose when Moki had kicked the rock out of its resting place in a crevice.

"What is it?" he asked.

"Something that doesn't fit," she said.

When he held out his hand, she dropped the fragment into it. He brushed a thick layer of red silt from the surface and smiled. There was a pattern of black crosshatched over white.

"A potsherd!" Excitement rippled in her voice and gleamed in her eyes.

"Your first?" he asked, trying not to smile.

She nodded so quickly that locks of red hair slipped free of their moorings beneath her watch cap.

"How did it get there?" she asked. "I don't see any ruins around."

"Some Anasazi probably did what we did—climbed up there for a look around. He might have broken his canteen or a seed pot he was carrying. He walked on, and the pieces stayed behind."

She looked back at the windswept little platform with wonder in her eyes.

"It's quite a feeling, isn't it?" he asked softly. "Sharing just for a moment the life of someone who died centuries before you were born."

"Yes," she said, and the word was close to a sigh.

"Too bad we didn't find this over on Billy Moore's land," Cain said, handing the sherd back to her. "He wouldn't mind if you kept it."

"But the owner of this land would?"

"Yeah. You keep that and you've committed a felony. The feds will harass your ass into an early grave."

She looked around the mesa. "This is all federal land?"

He nodded.

"Where's Xanadu?" she asked.

"It starts somewhere over by the edge of the mesa."

"Where?"

"You'd have to be a surveyor to know for sure. Hutton's ranch is a hodgepodge of leased grazing land and deeded land."

"But he doesn't run cattle."

"He'd rather pay the grazing fees and keep other folks' cattle out," Cain said. "Come on. Let's find the rest of the pot."

She looked at the damp reddish earth where the stone had fallen away. There was some more dirt in the crease, but not enough to hide a pot. With a sigh, she put the sherd back in its place.

"We won't find the rest of the pot here," she said.

"The first rule of potsherds is that they go downhill."

He crossed the strip of wind-smoothed sandstone that separated the low stone platform from the edge of the mesa. A nose of rock extended out into the canyon. The wind was stronger at the edge but felt less chilly. The ground below the lip of the canyon still held summer's warmth.

When Christy walked out and stood next to Cain, she gasped in surprise.

The canyon floor was a long, long way down.

Below her feet, the black backs of ravens gleamed as the birds floated on the wind, calling sharply to one another. She was swept by a feeling of being weightless, of soaring and falling in the same instant.

Without realizing it, she took a step closer to the edge.

Chapter 25

Cain's hand shot out and gripped Christy's arm, but he didn't pull her back. Instead, he moved to stand just behind her, letting her enjoy the view. If the dropoff made her dizzy, he'd make sure she didn't fall.

"Heady feeling, isn't it?" he said.

His voice was calm and low, very close to her.

"It's incredible," she said.

"The Anasazi loved the mesa tops too," he said after a moment. "They must have been sorry to leave. There's no place in the world like this."

The soft morning air rushed up from the canyon below like a great, fragrant sigh.

Slowly Christy's perceptions adjusted to the vast distances revealed by the shearing away of the land. What looked like small shrubs at the base of the sandstone wall were really full-sized trees. A narrow path was really a dirt road. The featureless canyon bottom was really rugged and tumbled, filled with boulders the size of Cain's cabin.

Small side canyons occurred wherever runoff channels had carved through the rock. Like everything else in nature, the edge of the mesa was asymmetrical and unexpected, a work in progress designed not by graph paper and blueprints but by wind and time and storms.

The small nose of rock they were standing on was little more than an irregularity on the edge of a vast, ragged shawl of stone whose fringe was cliffs, and the spaces between the fringe were deep canyons filled with sun and silence.

"That's a big place to find something as small as a pot," she said finally.

"We're not going way down there. I'll look just underneath the rim."

Gently she eased forward and craned her neck, trying to see straight down. "Looks like more of the same to me."

"If there are rooms or storage cysts or anything like that, they'll be tucked just under the overhang of the rim, away from the weather."

She turned and searched Cain's face for signs that he was teasing her. What she saw was the intensity he showed when he was in pursuit of something he loved.

"Are you telling me that the Anasazi chipped out places to live on the face of this cliff?" she asked.

"No. Nature took care of the chipping out. The Anasazi just filled it back in with buildings."

"I don't understand."

"Imagine two slabs of stone," he said, holding one hand over the other parallel to the ground.

She nodded.

"The top slab depends on the bottom to hold it up," he said. "If the bottom slab is softer than the top, it wears away more quickly and an alcove or shallow cave is created."

As he spoke, he bent the fingers of his lower hand, making them shorter.

"The roof is solid stone," he said, moving his top hand. "The second layer holds the alcove. All the other layers underneath are still solid."

"Home sites by Mother Nature," she said. "Nifty."

"Yeah, until the weight of the ceiling overhang becomes too great and it falls."

"Does that happen often?"

"In a human lifetime? No. Over the span of a thousand years? Often enough, I suppose."

She shuddered. "Not a happy thought."

"Life's a gamble, honey. The only guarantee is that nobody gets out alive."

"Wow, does that ever make me feel better. What will those buildings look like if we find them?"

"Lines of rubble, most likely, but oddly shaped rubble, like someone piled flagstones around and then gave up and walked away before finishing the patio."

Cain saw the disappointment on her face. Smiling, he tugged lightly at a flyaway lock of red hair.

"That's good news, not bad," he said. "If there were well-preserved ruins up here, somebody would have spotted and mapped them already—right after they looted them down to bedrock and masonry walls."

Slowly, he let the lock of red hair slip free of his fingers. When he had only the memory of silk on his skin, he turned back to face the mesa edge. Nothing moved but wind and ravens.

"It's too close to noon for the shadows to be any help," he said. "So search just beneath the rim of the canyon, where pale rock meets rock the color of your hair."

Christy took in a long breath and forced herself to turn away from the man who became more compelling to her each time she looked at him. It took her a moment to focus on the land rather than on the memory of the gentle tug of his fingers sliding over her hair.

"Look for debris slopes that show gray or black areas," he said. "The Anasazi burned wood and threw their ash and garbage over the front porch into the canyon below."

"A long, thin layer of black?" she asked.

He followed her glance. "That's a seam of coal. Anasazi middens—garbage heaps—occur in patches rather than in long lines." Suddenly he leaned forward. *"Like that."*

She followed the line of his finger. Two hundred feet away, and a dizzying drop below the rim, there was a dark stain in the debris slope that fringed a small alcove.

"See it?" he asked.

"Yes. There's another one to the left."

"About a hundred feet, yes. See that dark green weed?"

"The stuff all over that second little slope?" she asked, wondering what he was so excited about.

"Yeah. That's Moki weed."

"Why do they call it that? Did the Anasazi eat it?"

"No," he said. "It only grows in Moki middens."

"Then there are ruins there?"

"Near there. Somewhere. There must be. The Anasazi didn't take a long walk to dump garbage."

Frowning, he studied the canyon walls for a time. Nothing more caught his eye. He shrugged off the small backpack he wore, pulled out a pair of binoculars, and studied the wall above the streak of green Moki weed.

"If there are any ruins, they're damned well hidden," he muttered. "Must have eroded away to nothing at all."

Silently he continued studying the walls.

"What are you looking for now?" she asked.

"A way down."

"That? It's a cliff!"

"You sure?" he asked dryly.

Uneasily she waited while he finished studying the rock

face. When he was done, he handed the binoculars and back-pack to her.

"There's a network of ledges and creases that go down to the midden from the top of the mesa," he said. "Stay here while I check it out."

"But can't I—"

"No way," he interrupted flatly. "You're staying."

The mutinous look on her face made him sigh.

"It's going to be a bastard of a climb," he said. "I'm not sure I can do it myself."

"I wasn't shot last spring. Let me at least try."

"No. You don't recognize the limits of your own strength."

"And you do?" she asked sarcastically.

"Yes."

She glared at him. He simply shook his head.

"Look," he said finally, "if you go, I'll have to watch you like a mother hen because you won't ask for help even if you need it. The trail is too rough for that kind of game. We both could get hurt."

She closed her eyes and thought fast. She couldn't push him into doing something he clearly believed would be un-safe for him. Nor could she demand that he let her get herself out of any trouble she got into. He would help her out, even if it meant risking his own neck. That was just the kind of old-fashioned man he was.

"Damn," she muttered, accepting defeat.

"Sorry."

"If I get bored, I suppose I can throw rocks."

"Don't get bored, honey."

With that, he bent over, kissed her hard and fast, and walked off. Before she caught her breath, he vanished over the rim.

Cautiously she went to the edge of the mesa and watched him pick his way along the small ledge he had found. It led to a tongue of steep rock-studded dirt where scrubby cedar and stubborn piñon had taken root. He moved over the rough, uncertain ground with surprising speed, completely at home.

"What are you," she said under her breath, "part mountain goat?"

Then she stopped breathing when he dropped from a rock platform onto the first dark patch, the one where no weeds grew. Immediately he began to slide downhill toward another, much longer drop.

"Cain!"

Even as she screamed his name, he caught his balance, threw himself to the side, and found solid ground.

With fingers that trembled, she picked up his binoculars. The slippery slope leaped into focus. It was spread out in front of a small overhang, but the alcove sheltered beneath the rim was empty. She watched while he searched for building blocks or potsherds, remnants of walls, any sign that man had once lived there.

"Anything?" Christy called when she couldn't stand the suspense any longer.

"Not yet," he yelled back.

He went farther into the alcove. The angle of the rock hid him from her. He emerged a few minutes later.

"This dark patch isn't a midden," he called to her. "There's a spring at the back and a crack leading up to the mesa top. Runoff water has washed the alcove clean."

Disappointed, she watched while he scrambled around an outcrop of sandstone and into the next alcove. When he was out of sight, she hurried overland to the rim just above him, hoping to see more from there.

All she saw was air, distant ravens, and fully grown trees that looked the size of thumbtacks.

"Lord," she said, stepping backward quickly. "That first step is forever."

She found a spot to sit down at the base of an elegantly twisted cedar. From time to time she could hear Cain moving below the rim, even though she couldn't see him.

Moki appeared from nowhere, panting with pleasure from a recent run. He flopped down on the slick rock beside her.

She looked south across the ragged country. The lid of clouds was scored and thinned by the great burning torch of the sun. As she watched, mountains condensed in the distance. A network of incandescent blue appeared across the sky. Golden heat spilled through the gaps in the clouds.

With a sigh of pleasure, she opened her jacket, leaned back against the wind-smoothed tree, and enjoyed the feel of the sun on her face. Cloud shadows dappled the red sandstone, making the mesa country ripple like a great animal breathing, alive.

Eyes half closed, she let the kaleidoscope of cloud and landscape play across her awareness, sinking past her rational self to the most primitive levels of her mind. Slowly the world of second hands and concrete sidewalks slid away, freeing the underlying, elemental rhythms of sun and earth, wind and time.

A shadow eclipsed part of the design. At first she thought it was just another passing cloud. When it lingered, she sat up and looked around.

The sun had gone behind the white sandstone Sister. The spire was throwing a long, wide shadow that wouldn't lift for some time.

"And I was just getting comfortable," she said.

She stood up and looked for a new spot in the sun. Moki scrambled to his feet and waited expectantly while she surveyed the mesa top.

A dozen yards to the left, a slice of white-hot sunlight lay across the sandstone like a giant knife. It took her a moment to realize that the bright blade came from a shaft of sunlight passing between the two Sisters. The white slide of light was no more than ten feet wide.

It pointed directly across the mesa to the rim above Cain.

The effect was striking. Eerie. It reminded her of what Cain had said about the sun being important to the Anasazi.

"What would the Anasazi have made of a slice of sunlight like this?" she asked Moki. "Would they have worshipped or feared or celebrated it? Sure as sunlight they couldn't ignore it."

The dog panted happily.

She walked into the blade of light. With Moki at her heels, she followed the shimmering path to the very edge of the mesa. A vague pattern appeared at her feet. The hair on the back of her neck rose as the pattern condensed into an ancient drawing.

On the rim of the canyon, a hunchbacked flute player called to the ravens far below.

Chapter 26

Christy didn't remember calling to Cain, but she must have because he scrambled up over the rim and ran to her, afraid that she was hurt.

"I'm fine," she said. "It's right over there. Hurry, the sun is moving so fast."

"The rock sure isn't," he said, breathing hard.

Yet he didn't object when she took his hand and all but dragged him to the lip of the mesa thirty feet away.

The sun had indeed moved. Now it highlighted the petroglyph.

"Son of a bitch," he said reverently.

He sat on his heels next to the drawing, running his fingertips very light over the rough surface of the rock. Kokopelli's figure was faint, eroded, and unmistakable. The universal Pan, bursting with sexuality and life.

The point of the dagger of sunlight burned only on his magical flute.

Cain looked up at Christy. His eyes, like the flute, burned with light and life.

"You're good luck for me," he said.

"What's luck got to do with it?"

"Everything." He glanced back toward the two Sisters, then checked his watch. "Noon. Or close enough."

"So?"

"Do you know what day this is?"

She thought for a moment. "September twenty-first?"

He nodded.

"So?" she asked.

"It's the autumnal equinox, the day of balance when the sun is directly over the equator. Day and night are of equal length."

Cain's voice was like his eyes, full of life, a vitality that tugged at her as surely as the wind and wild land.

"See?" He pointed. "The narrowest part of the shaft of sunlight is touching Kokopelli's flute at noon on the equinox—give or take a minute or so. Nothing stays precisely the same over time."

"The Anasazi knew that the light would touch the flute at the equinox?"

"If you had a growing season that was just barely long enough to produce corn or beans, what would you give to know that the days were lengthening or shortening?"

"A tenth of my crop," she said dryly.

He smiled. "The standard religious tithe. I suspect the price of Anasazi peace of mind was a lot steeper."

Again he ran his fingertips just above the figure of Kokopelli. The combination of strength and delicacy in his touch reminded Christy of how he'd held the Anasazi bowl when she first saw him in the Two-Tier West. Now she saw what she'd missed before, his love and respect for the artifacts chance brought his way. He was far more complex than she'd thought at first.

In terms of second hands and concrete blocks—rational terms—it had been only yesterday that she'd met Cain.

In terms of sun and land, wind and time—elemental terms—it had been a lifetime.

"Honey?" he asked.

Her breath caught at how natural the endearment seemed.

"What?" she whispered.

"Did you touch this at all?"

"No. As soon as I saw it, I must have started hollering for you. I don't remember. I just knew it was something I had to show you."

A smile gleamed momentarily against his beard. Then his mouth settled into a hard line as he looked from the sandstone dust on his fingertips to Kokopelli.

"What's wrong? Isn't it real?" she asked. "Did some cowboy make it or—"

"It's real," he cut in. "So real someone tried to erase it. If this hadn't been in full blazing sunlight, you'd probably never have seen it."

"Why would someone vandalize a piece of ancient art? Sheer meanness and stupidity?"

"Maybe. And maybe it wasn't Kokopelli someone tried to destroy. Maybe they were trying to hide something else."

Slowly he looked around, searching for anything else that might have been overlooked.

Moki's sudden, aggressive barking made both of them turn toward the sound. It came from below the rim.

"Did he fall over?" Christy asked, alarmed.

"Doubt it."

But Cain followed her to look over the rim into the canyon below.

Moki stood on a rounded boulder eighty feet below, wagging his tail like a battle flag and looking up at them expectantly. When they didn't move, he barked again, impatient to get going.

"Is he all right?" she asked.

"He wouldn't be wagging his tail and dancing around if he'd fallen there. There must be another way down."

"Was Kokopelli pointing the way?"

"Could be. Maybe that's why someone tried to blot the old boy out."

Cain quartered the rimrock until he came to a small cleft in the rounded sandstone. "This is as good as it gets."

He eased into the cleft.

"Cain?" she asked hopefully, wanting to follow him.

"Let me check it out first."

She watched anxiously when he disappeared into the cleft. A curse and the sound of pebbles rolling floated back up to her. Just when she'd decided she'd be left behind again, he reappeared.

"It's a hell of a lot better than it looks at first," he said. "Still want to play mountain goat?"

She grinned.

"Hand me the backpack, then," he said, grinning back.

He put on the backpack and held out his hand once more. She took it—and started sliding toward him. Fast.

"Yikes!"

"I've got you," he said.

He caught her, held her until she found her feet, then released her with a slow smile that said he'd liked feeling her body against his.

"I could get to enjoy hiking rough country with you," he said. "Watch your footing, now. It's not what you expect it to be."

"Neither are you."

He gave a crack of laughter, touched her cheek, and turned away to lead her farther beneath the mesa's eroding rim.

The cleft became a gap between two massive chunks of sandstone stacked on each other like a giant's toy blocks. The gap quickly became a tunnel that was hidden from above and lit only by sunlight from either end. Despite Cain's warning about the uneven footing, Christy stumbled more than once.

"Hell," she muttered.

"Yeah, these stairs are hard for people used to modern steps."

"Stairs?" she asked blankly. "Where?"

"Under your feet. Look at the surface of the stone. See those pockmarks?"

She squinted into the gloom. "Yes. Barely."

"Those were left by a hammer stone wielded by some poor son of a bitch who was told to chip steps out of solid rock."

"Ouch. Glad it wasn't me."

She walked slowly, amazed at the work that had gone into making a steep watercourse into a path. As she settled into the rhythm of slope and stairs, she found herself stumbling less.

"Heads up," he warned.

The ceiling of the tunnel was dropping. He was bent over already. Soon she was crouching right along with him.

"If this keeps up we'll be on all fours," she said.

"Starting real soon."

Twenty feet ahead, the burning blue of the sky and Moki's excited barking promised an end to the tunnel. Cain and Christy had to crawl on all fours for the last ten feet. His shoulders were too wide to fit the exit. He had to twist and slide through sideways, pulling the backpack behind.

"Very neat," he said, grunting as he forced himself past the narrow opening. "A ten-year-old with a sharp stick could hold off an army."

"When I went to school, I was told the Anasazi were peace-loving subsistence farmers."

"Your professors were left over from the hippie-dippy sixties," he said, amused. "Nobody builds and lives on the face of a cliff because they like losing toddlers and old folks over the edge."

"You make cliff dwelling sound irresistible."

His hand came back through the opening. "Grab hold. Tight."

When she did, he pulled her out of the tunnel and into the sunlight. The first thing she noticed was that there was nothing in front of her but air.

Lots of it.

"Steady," he said as he shrugged into the backpack again. "There's not much room on this ledge."

She made an odd sound.

"You okay?" he asked.

"Give me a second to get used to the idea of walking on air."

"Stone, actually."

"Says you. Looks like air to me."

Breath came out of her in a long sigh. When she looked up, he was watching her closely.

"I'm okay," she said. "Really." She took another deep breath. "And I take your point about living on cliff faces. You'd need a really good reason to do it. Sheer survival comes to mind. Nothing else would be good enough."

Moki came bouncing across the rock face like a rubber ball, urging them on. The dog had the advantage of four sure feet and he was headed straight for Christy.

Cain's hand moved in a short, sharp motion. Moki stopped so fast he skidded. Another brief motion of Cain's hand and the dog stood as though nailed to stone.

"Impressive," she said.

"He would have made a fine hunting dog."

"You don't like to hunt?"

"Ex-cons can't own firearms."

His voice was matter-of-fact rather than bitter. He was absorbed in studying the rock.

"More steps," he said. "Follow me and do what I do. Exactly. Like a child's game, only damned serious. Understand?"

"Yes."

His eyes pinned her for a moment. Then he smiled. "I'd kiss you again, but it has a bad effect on my sense of balance."

"It doesn't do much for mine either."

Something flared in his eyes. Then he turned and started walking.

She followed him across the rock on steps so faint and weathered she wasn't even sure they were there at all. It was faith in him that drew her, not any evidence of her own senses. She put her feet where his had been.

Exactly.

Slowly they made their way for fifty feet along the face of the cliff. From the corner of her eye, she gradually became aware that their path was leading them out and away from the talus slope and over a steeply slanting section of mesa wall whose front had broken away and fallen to the canyon bottom far below.

"Am I the only one who doesn't see anything below us but air?" she asked uneasily.

"Don't look at the air. Look at the rock. Especially here."

He stopped and pointed to a place where the steps came at a different interval than they had before.

"Stop and switch feet here," he said. "Most people lead with their right foot on a stairway. Lead with your left from here on or you'll find yourself down on the canyon floor."

A single look at his face told her that he was quite serious.

"Left foot, huh?" she said. "Okay. Left foot it is. But why? Did they measure the steps wrong or something?"

"It's an old trick, like a long step thrown in with a bunch of short ones. Causes no end of grief to outsiders who don't know the key."

"Peace-loving, huh?" she asked.

"You bet. Gentle, fruit-eating apes, every last one of them."

She snickered. "I'd love to have seen you in academia."

He smiled lazily. "It was fun."

She watched and changed leads at the spot he indicated. Walking that way was awkward at first but she quickly caught the new rhythm. They made their way across the rock face for another fifty feet before he stopped.

"No wonder nobody ever found anything up here," he said softly. "Look at the size of that flake."

"Flake?"

He gestured.

She realized that the "flake" he was talking about was a sandstone slab as big as a basketball floor and nearly as thick as Cain was tall.

"That," she said, "is one big flake."

From a short distance away, the sandstone slab appeared to have broken neatly off the canyon rim and slid thirty or forty feet down the face of the mesa. In geologic time, the event was recent. The edges of the sandstone slab looked newer, brighter, less weathered than the rest of the mesa face.

"Look at the steps," he said in a hushed voice.

The faint path of worn steps led directly up to the edge of the fallen slab and vanished.

"End of the line?" she asked, disappointed.

"Maybe. Maybe not. Look up there."

Five or six feet above the path, there was a little hollow, almost like the sandstone slab had fallen over the front of a small alcove, concealing it. The hollow was in full shade.

Christy stared and then stared again, feeling excitement sweep through her.

"Is it . . . ?" she asked breathlessly.

"Yes."

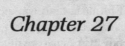

Chapter 27

Without looking away from the flake, Cain held his hand out. When Christy took it he squeezed hard.

And then he laughed.

Suddenly she was laughing too. She forgot her uneasiness at being perched on the exposed rock face. There was no need for fear. She knew what it was to fly like a raven above an ancient, timeless land.

Ahead of them the corner of a man-made wall loomed from the shadows.

"Look at the thickness of those vigas," he said.

"I would, if I knew what they were."

"The cedar roof supports."

Moki emerged from the shadows at the edge of the fallen slab. His whole body vibrated with eagerness for them to join him, but he didn't race forward or bark. He was on his best hunting behavior now, watching his master's hands for instructions.

The order was to stay put.

Christy nearly laughed at the dog's visible disappointment. "Poor baby."

"I don't want him to go through a kiva roof or trash a pot while chasing rats," Cain said.

"Rats?"

"Not the New York kind. The Moki kind. Pack rats. They move into ruins and fill up the storage cysts and lath walls with nests."

"Rats are rats. I hope Moki's part terrier."

"Moki is part everything."

When they reached the tumble of rocks where Moki waited, Cain stopped Christy with a hand hard around her wrist.

"No farther," he said. "Ruins can be dangerous. The walls are usually unstable. So are kiva roofs. And the alcove stone itself . . ."

Warily he measured the massive sandstone flake that had fallen within historic times, shutting off the alcove except for a narrow window or doorway at each end. The sandstone slab looked like it was teetering on the edge of falling again. When it did, it would take a lot of the rim with it.

Just a matter of time.

"I don't like the looks of that flake," he said.

"Are you going in anyway?"

"Yes."

"Then so am I."

He turned to argue with her and saw she wasn't having any. "Okay, honey. But be real careful where you put your feet."

He started up the rubble pile to the entrance of the alcove. The sandstone debris seemed to be stable, as if it had been wedged together during the fall.

Halfway up the ramp, a fist-sized chunk of stone came tumbling out of the pile. The rock hit the ledge at Christy's feet and bounced down the steeply sloping stone face until it disappeared soundlessly over the edge.

Cain looked at her.

"Whither thou goest and all that," she said through her teeth.

"What happened to the woman who said cluck cluck?"

"She discovered her wings and flew away."

Smiling, shaking his head, he stepped onto the little sill of rock that ran across the alcove window. After a moment, he motioned for her to follow.

A faint breeze stirred within the shadow-filled alcove. When she reached the sill, she saw another wedge of sunlight on the far side.

"Let your eyes adjust," he said. "When you can see into the shadows, let me know."

As her eyes slowly adjusted to the gloom, she saw what lay behind the huge sandstone curtain.

"My God," she breathed.

"Amen."

The alcove held a well-preserved cliff dwelling, intact except for a fallen wall across the front of the structure. The corner of wall and roof they'd seen from below was part of a block of rooms that stretched for almost a hundred feet across the alcove. There were from two to four stories in the building, depending on the slope of the alcove roof.

"Is this as good as I think it is?" she asked softly.

"It's better, honey. It's like a time capsule. I don't know of another ruin in the Southwest that's been protected like this."

"How old are the buildings?"

"I can't say for sure, but the doorway style looks a lot like Mesa Verde. Mid–twelfth century. About the height of the Chaco empire. And about the time things started coming apart."

Cain took another look around. His left hand moved slightly. Moki bounded past them and into the ruins.

"Change your mind about letting him in?" she asked.

"Yeah. He's better at sensing bad footing than we are, and better able to get himself out of trouble if something gives way."

"Is that likely?"

"Hell, yes. In ruins this size, some of the floors will be lucky to support themselves. And no, you're not going with me if I go exploring."

One look at his set expression convinced her to wait now and argue if and when he went exploring.

Moki appeared atop one of the rooms close to their window, tail wagging and coated with what looked like twigs. The breeze from the interior of the alcove suddenly smelled rank.

"Yuck," she said.

"Moki found a pack rat's nest."

"Wonderful," she said without enthusiasm.

He smiled. "I hope you don't mind getting dusty and dirty. These ruins haven't been cleaned for nearly a thousand years."

He eased down onto a low wall that once had run along the lip of the alcove. The masonry was thick and strong.

"The kid-catcher is still solid," he said.

"Kid-catcher? Oh, the low wall. Is that what it's called?"

"That's what I call it." He looked around. "This must have been one of the first rooms built."

"How can you tell?"

"It's full of rubbish now. The Anasazi often filled in old rooms and built new ones. Sometimes they buried the dead in the rooms. Sometimes they threw them in the midden with the rest of the garbage."

She frowned. "A status thing?"

"Some say yes. More say no."

"What do you say?"

"No one that I know of has ever found grave goods with human bones in a midden. Grave goods have been found in room or crevice burials."

"Status."

"Looks that way to me, but I'm just a Moki-poaching son of a bitch."

Christy winced.

He went a little farther along the wall, testing his footing and the stability of the ruin every bit of the way. When nothing gave, he returned.

"If I tell you to stay here?" he said.

"I will, for a while."

"How long?"

"Until you turn your back."

His eyes narrowed. "About what I figured."

"I'm your good luck charm, remember? You don't want to leave me behind."

Unwillingly he smiled. "Okay, my redheaded rabbit's foot. Move softly, like a ghost. I don't trust that sandstone flake. I swear I felt it shiver when I leaned on it."

She looked at the heavy slab, swallowed hard, and nodded.

Cain walked back along the wall, his shoulder only inches from the tons of rock he'd felt shiver at a touch.

Christy followed carefully, steadying herself with one hand on the massive slab of rock. It felt cool and steady enough, but she wouldn't have trusted it no matter what Cain had said.

"This looks like an apartment building," she said.

"Close enough."

The second room they came to was empty except for a huge mound of sticks and debris. The musty smell was thicker here, almost overwhelming.

"Thousands of generations of pack rats have lived there, adding their little bit to the pile," he said. "Reminds me of New York. Except it smells better."

"New York does?"

"Not in summer. It stinks."

"You sound like you spend time there," she said.

"Only when I can't help it."

She rolled her eyes. "That's so western."

He smiled. "Now you're talking."

The floor of the third room was flat and relatively clean. He ducked in through the low doorway and let his eyes adjust to the near darkness inside. She followed and stood close beside him.

Gradually they made out the details of the room's construction. The walls had been plastered with red mud. In places the mud had fallen away, revealing a lattice of sticks beneath the plaster.

"Willow," he said in response to her unspoken question.

"Look," she said. "The pattern."

Her hand traced a ragged ellipse of tiny white stones that had been set into an unusually thick layer of mortar.

"This didn't add to the wall's strength," she said. "It was done purely to please the eye."

"Like the paint."

Startled, she looked up. The upper part of the room had once been painted in designs that reminded her of the pottery she'd seen.

"Look closely at the plaster," he said. "See the handprints?"

She eased closer to examine the wall. He was right. There were many clear handprints in the plaster surface. Lightly she laid her hand over one of them.

The hand that had built the room was smaller than her own, with short, blunt fingers, but her own palm fit easily in the cool depression that had been made almost a thousand years ago. She ran her other hand gently over the rest of the wall, trying to absorb through sheer touch what the life of those other people had been like.

"So much time," she whispered. "So human."

He laid his own hand over hers, measuring the difference in their sizes. The act was curiously intimate.

"Yes," he said simply. "So human."

Delicate currents of warmth shivered through her. She was caught between the cool plaster surface of the past and the living warmth of the present.

"And nobody's touched this place for a thousand years," she whispered.

He was on the point of agreeing when something caught his eyes. "Well, *shit*."

He lifted his hand, bent over, and snatched up something from the floor. He held his fingers in the vague light coming in through the doorway so she could see too.

"Oh, no," she said.

"Oh, yes."

He was holding the burned butt of a very modern, machine-rolled cigarette. He held it to his nose and grimaced. "No more than six months or a year old." He turned the butt over and read the small print on it. "Dunhill."

"Dunhill? Do you know him?"

"Not him. It. Dunhill is a brand of cigarette."

She looked blank.

"The Remington Super-Valu doesn't stock them," Cain said. "Westerners like their cigarettes plain and simple. It takes a self-consciously exotic type to smoke Dunhills."

A chill replaced the warmth Christy had felt only a moment ago. Memories came, a beautiful blond fourteen-year-old who'd seen a cigarette ad in a fashion magazine and driven the local boys crazy until one of them somehow found a way to get her a pack.

"Do you—" She cleared her throat. "Do you know anyone who smokes Dunhills?"

"Guess."

"Jo," Christy whispered.

It wasn't a question, but he answered anyway. "Yeah, the cowboys' walking, talking wet dream."

With a hissed word, he flicked the butt into a corner and wiped his fingers on his jeans. "Well, let's see how badly her boyfriend trashed the place."

"Hutton?"

"Doubt it. Last I saw Jo-Jo, she was flat-backing with the Indians, not the drugstore cowboys."

Christy wanted to protest his contempt, but didn't. The more she learned what her sister had become, the less she liked it. *Wonder what I'll find out next.*

Then she shivered as though a dead finger had touched her nape.

Chapter 28

Cain ducked back underneath the lintel and into the alcove. Moving quickly, no longer worried about accidentally damaging something, he strode along the low wall at the front of the room block. He stopped at each doorway to stare into the dark recesses.

Only once did he step into the darkness. When he came out a moment later, there were potsherds in his hand.

"They cherry-picked the entire site," he said harshly. " guess they didn't think this was worth taking out."

The sherds joined perfectly, becoming the painted bowl of a ladle. Even with the handle missing, it was a handsome piece.

He tipped his palm and let the pieces slide to the floor. She started to object, but when she saw him wipe his palms on his jeans as though he'd touched something unclean, she bit back her words. He had a bone-deep contempt for Jo-Jo and all she stood for. Everything she touched.

Looking at the wreckage of beauty, so did Christy. A child's selfishness was one thing. This was adult.

This was criminal.

Jo-Jo, why?

But the cry was only in Christy's mind, echo of a past when anything had been possible, even an unselfish Jo-Jo.

I never really knew her.

Now I never want to.

And that hurts me more than it does her. Nothing has changed. Except one thing. I'm through letting her hurt me.

It's finished.

With tears burning the back of her eyes, Christy watched Cain climb up a short, irregular stairway of rubble to the second story of the building. The rooms were even smaller there. Some of the walls were smoke-blackened. Every space was bare. Except for a broken clay mug and a few rough, tiny corncobs preserved perfectly in the dry air, the rooms had been looted to their floors.

Operating from instinct and experience gained in the exploration of a hundred ruins, he picked his way to a block of rooms that formed a right angle to the line of the original building. He stood there, staring down at the remnants of a small plaza in the crook of the L-shaped structure.

She paced him on the ground level. As she stepped over a low wall onto the floor of the plaza, there was a low, hollow groan, as though she had stepped on a ghost. She jumped back, more in surprise than fear.

"Stay put," he said quickly. "There's probably a kiva under that debris. Don't trust the roof to hold your weight."

She skirted the little plaza, peering into gloomy corners. When a metallic glint caught her eye, she eased a little closer.

If he hadn't already told her about Anasazi underworld myths, she might not have recognized the square black hole in the plaza floor as an entrance. A few inches of aluminum ladder stuck up out of the hole.

"There's a ladder here," she said.

"Wait where you are."

Using one of the thick vigas, he swung down off the roof

of the room and walked toward her, skirting the level area that was a kiva roof of uncertain strength.

Moki looked out from one of the upper windows of the building block. He was thoroughly filthy and quite pleased with himself. Resting his chin on the windowsill, he watched his master below.

Cain poked around in a pile of rubble until he found a piece of cedar bark. From the pocket of his shirt, he pulled a pack of survival matches and lit one. The bark flared quickly into flame, casting an eerie, flickering light on the walls of the alcove.

Leaning down into the hole with the makeshift torch, he looked around the kiva. "Cleaned out."

His voice was like the line of his mouth. Flat. Hard.

She ducked underneath his arm and looked into her first kiva. The wavering light showed a dusty, circular chamber beneath a low, roughly plastered ceiling that was supported by four straight log pillars. Niches had been carved into the curving walls of the kiva.

"They look like stations of the cross," she said.

"You've got it. You're looking at an Anasazi church whose icons have been looted for sale to the unbelievers."

The bark torch guttered. Its fading light caught something shiny on the kiva floor.

"Hold this," he said.

He handed the nub of bark to her, showed her where he wanted it to be held, and dropped quickly down the ladder. A moment later he struck another match, touched it to the wick of a kerosene lantern, and lowered the glass chimney in place.

Christy dropped the makeshift torch just as her fingers became uncomfortably hot. The fire winked out before the bark reached the kiva floor.

"Come on down," he said. "See what real Moki poaching looks like."

Silently she climbed down the ladder into a room that seemed to vibrate with his cold rage. It didn't take her long to understand why he was furious.

The poachers had attacked the floor of the kiva with pick-axes and shovels. They'd hacked at one of the log pillars for no reason Christy could see. Pale potsherds mixed with dirt and twentieth-century plastic trash.

Kneeling, Cain scooped up a double handful of the sherds and examined them.

"This pot could be salvaged," he said. "They just junked anything that wasn't whole."

Angrily he put the sherds back when he'd found them. As he straightened, he saw a hint of pattern. He froze, utterly intent on the low, curving sill that went around the whole kiva. Parts of the sill had been cut away. The segment that remained was painted with an unusual design featuring Kokopelli in many incarnations.

"I've never seen anything like that," he said in a low voice.

"What?"

"The painted sill. Once it must have gone all the way around the room."

"Is that unusual?"

"The sill? No. But to have the painting preserved . . . it's a miracle. And those bastards hacked it up like firewood and hauled it out of here."

She knelt where some of the rubble showed painted surfaces. Carefully she fitted several together. As she did, a distinctive black-on-white pattern formed, a flowing abstraction that was a pure distillation of style. Unique, vivid, the design was a painted message sent from one millennium to the next.

Ancient, yet oddly familiar.

After a few moments Christy figured out why. "Oh, my God," she said, horrified. "This looks just like one of the motifs Hutton is using in his new collection."

"You going to write about that in your magazine, Red?" Cain asked bitterly. "You going to tell all the fashionable folks how Hutton raped a priceless Anasazi site to come up with the inspiration for some city threads?"

She winced at his tone but didn't throw it back in his face. There was no defense for what had been done to this ancient place.

He snatched the lantern and held it head high, inspecting the shambles of the past with naked yearning on his face.

"God, but I wish I could have seen what it was like," he said in a low, intense voice. "There may not be another kiva this good in the whole world. And now it's . . ."

She closed her eyes, not wanting to see his pain.

"Gone," he said. "Just *gone*. All the king's horses and all the king's men couldn't put this mess back together again."

He kicked at a pile of rubble. A piece of thin rough rope sprang free of the dirt. The rope was attached to a small mat of fibers.

"This was a shoe," he said. "A sandal made of yucca fiber. Not as rare as cloth or turkey feathers, but a miracle of preservation against the odds just the same."

His fists clenched. He drew in a quick, ripping breath.

"And they threw it away like it was trash," he said savagely. "God knows what kind of stuff they kept. A king's ransom. Feast for a hundred scholars. And for what? For a few thousand dollars to keep a lying slut happy. Christ. If Johnny wasn't so stupid I'd feel sorry for him."

"Johnny Ten Hats?"

"Yeah. He's the cigar-store idiot who was banging Jo-Jo

when I was shot. Of course, that was six months ago. She's probably had a hundred like him since then."

Contempt resonated in the space within the kiva. Cain was like a priest enraged at the desecration of a church. Christy tried to find words that might ease his anger, but there weren't any. Something irreplaceable had been lost for no better reason than greed. In the face of that barbaric act, anger was not only justified, it was necessary.

Silently she went from niche to niche in the kiva, hoping to find some hint of the artifacts that once had been the focus of Anasazi religious tradition. In the fifth niche, she found a small fragment of smooth black stone. It had been worked into a bead, perhaps part of a necklace. No one would ever know, now. Whatever the bead belonged to was gone. All that remained was the polished bead itself, overlooked in the destructive rush to wealth.

She held the rounded stone between her fingers. It had a smooth, cool, soapy feel.

"Is there any way of salvaging the site?" she asked quietly.

"No. They might as well have gone through here with a backhoe."

"They might have overlooked something."

He made a curt gesture. "Sure, some of the pots might be put together again. More might be discovered. But the potential for knowledge is gone."

She looked around at the combination of plastic garbage and ancient debris and hated to her soul that Jo-Jo had had a part in the rape of a sacred place.

"Can't something be salvaged?" she asked finally.

"The layers are trashed. Fireplace ash from the early years is mixed in with the later ashes. There's no way anybody could even get a decent date out of the hearth. It's a total write-off. Null. Zero."

Silently he lifted the lamp and looked around the interior again, hoping to find something the looters had overlooked. There was nothing but blackness receding before the lamp, then flowing back to claim the kiva as the light moved on.

The lantern light cast eerie shadows in the dark niches and irregularities of the curving kiva walls. Shapes glided and vanished, only to reappear as though squeezed out of the stone itself.

Christy's skin prickled with a primal sense of *other*. There were spirits here. Some were benign. Some were as vicious as the ones she'd seen in the paintings in Peter Hutton's hallway.

"All those niches," Cain said grimly. "I haven't seen that many outside of Pueblo Bonito."

"Where is that?"

"Chaco Canyon."

For a few more breaths he studied the kiva in silence. Then he made an inarticulate sound of pain or rage.

"No ruins have been found this far north," he said. "From the size of this kiva, this was an important place to the Anasazi. A vital place. And now we'll never know why. *Goddamn all pothunters.*"

He lowered the lantern with a speed that made light and shadows mix dizzyingly. "I've seen about as much as I can take."

Lantern in one hand, he climbed back to the plaza. Christy followed without a word. There wasn't anything she wanted to say. The lantern gave new illumination into the destruction of the little village that had been hidden behind the sandstone slab. Protected, but not well enough.

He walked from room to room. Everywhere he looked there were telltale pits where pots or other artifacts had been dug out and carted off with no thought to their intrinsic worth. Only money counted in the world of the Moki poacher.

In a corner close to the sill where he and Christy had entered, there was a partially collapsed wall. At first glance it looked like it was a keystone holding the rest of the block of rooms in place.

"If you have to come in here," he said softly, "don't kick anything. Don't even sneeze. This place is waiting for an excuse to fall."

He eased closer to see if the area was as dangerous as it looked. His breath came in with a harsh sound. Along the back wall of the alcove, there was a framework of modern timbers. Not enough for the job. Not nearly enough.

"No closer," he said flatly.

"Why?"

"Some fool used toothpicks to hold up the mesa rim."

He turned up the wick of the lantern until it smoked. Then he made his way carefully over a fallen rubble pile to the far wall of the alcove.

She didn't follow. She'd seen the frail patchwork and had to remind herself to breathe.

It can't be as dangerous as it looks.

But it was.

Chapter 29

By the wavering light of the lantern, Cain examined the "support" with a delicate care that said more than any words could about the danger. Christy watched, breathing shallowly, rolling the black bead with her fingertips. She took an odd comfort from its ancient, smooth surface.

A cold nose pressed against her wrist, startling her. Moki had given up on pack rats for now. Ignoring the grit and bits of straw clinging to the dog, she took her hands out of her pockets and thrust her fingers deep into Moki's fur. She wondered what was the proper prayer for holding up the sky. And then she wondered if the people who built the kiva knew the words.

Thinking about that kept the cold sweat from gliding down her spine.

After a few minutes, the dog pulled away and went to lie down on a slab of cool sandstone. In the gloom, Moki was invisible except for the occasional flash of his eyes as they caught the lantern light.

Cain trimmed the lantern wick and walked back to Christy.

"Well?" she asked through gritted teeth.

"There's a chunk of sandstone about fifteen feet square that looks like it's suspended in midair. There's a crack behind it big enough to crawl into."

A primitive claustrophobia swept over her. She shoved her hands back in her pockets. This time her fingertips touched the metal of Jo-Jo's key as well as ancient stone.

Hello, enigma, Christy thought with a humor that wasn't far from stark fear. *Meet the mystery bead. May all your secrets be little and safe.*

But she doubted it.

"What about the shoring?" she asked. "Will it hold?"

"Whoever was here before us had some mining experience. He jerry-rigged some braces to stabilize the stone."

Breath held, she waited.

Cain didn't say anything more.

"For me," she said tightly, "ignorance is no particular bliss."

"The flake of stone must weigh twenty tons. You don't handle that kind of weight with four-by-four timbers."

She let out a long breath. "Finish it."

He threw her a surprised look.

"If the flake was all you were worried about," she said, "you'd have dragged me to the lip of the alcove before you said a word."

He smiled. "You know me pretty well, honey."

"Well enough to know you're not telling me all you know." Her hands clenched in her pockets. The bead was smooth. The edges of the key cut into flesh.

She wasn't telling him all she knew either.

"The flake is supporting a second slab," he said finally. "The crack separating it from the cliff looks like it goes all the way to daylight. The gap is so big the Anasazi built storage cysts in it."

He ran his hands through his hair, displacing the watch cap. Absently he stuffed it into his hip pocket.

"The whole ceiling of the alcove is ready to drop away," he said bluntly. "The second slab is bigger than the one that closed the alcove. When it goes, they'll hear it all the way to Denver."

Automatically she looked at the ceiling of the alcove, where the rock spread above them like the canopy of a dome tent. The sandstone was darkened with the soot of thousands of fires and dampened by seepage from millions of winter melts and summer storms.

"It looks so . . . solid," she said.

"It was, once. But there are always cracks. Water gets in. It dissolves the glue holding sand grains together. In winter the water freezes, forcing the crack deeper into the stone. When the crack is big enough, gravity wins."

Silently she tried to imagine the subtle forces at work, water that froze and expanded in winter, prying stone apart. Then the time of melting came and water became a gentle acid dissolving away stone.

Drop by drop, season by season, stress by stress.

Then one day, one hour, one instant, and the massive flake broke away. When the last crushing echo faded and the fine dust settled, a new balance was achieved.

Then the whole cycle was repeated. Drop by drop, season by season, stress by stress.

"Are you saying we should get out?" she asked, her voice not quite steady.

"I'm saying I'd hate to be in here in a thunderstorm. One good roll of thunder could trigger one hell of a crash."

"That bad, huh?"

"It's a matter of luck. The ceiling has held this long. It should hold a while longer. Then again, why shouldn't it fall? No reason I can see."

Christy shuddered.

"If you want to wait outside the alcove," he said, "do it. I sure don't blame you."

"What about you?"

"I saw something along the edge of the building block. I want to take a closer look at it before I get out of here."

He picked up the lantern again and headed toward the massive slab of sandstone that had fallen sometime after the Anasazis had nearly filled the alcove with their cliff house.

After a moment's hesitation, she followed him. Moki watched but showed no desire to follow.

"What are we looking for this time?" she asked.

"I think there's another kiva over near the other window at this edge of the alcove. It looks like the ceiling caved in when that slab fell. Somebody spent a lot of time digging at one side."

The second kiva was situated well beyond the block of rooms. Lantern light showed a tangle of splintered cedar-log roof timbers. The ceiling was completely collapsed. The upright pillars that had once supported the roof were broken in half. Dirt and chunks of stone nearly filled the sunken room.

A mound of loose dirt had been piled beside a small tunnel at one edge of the kiva. The tunnel dropped down beneath the collapsed dome, then widened out into a small chamber the size of a telephone booth.

Together they knelt at the mouth of the tunnel and peered into the chamber.

"It's a pile of jackstraws," he said, surveying the tangle of broken timbers and tumbled rock. "Whoever did the digging must have had cast-iron balls."

"What were they after?"

Careful not to brush against the sides, he crept a few feet into the tunnel, just far enough to shine the lantern into the darkest corners of the chamber.

"It looks like a cyst of some sort. They got down below the floor level of the kiva, almost like they were—"

Abruptly he reached into the chamber and scratched in the dirt.

At first Christy thought he'd unearthed another potsherd, but when he handed the fragment back to her, she knew instantly it wasn't pottery. Something about its shape made her uneasy. Or perhaps it was the texture.

When he backed out of the opening, she handed the fragment to him as though it was burning her fingers.

"Here. Take it," she said.

"You don't like it?"

"No."

He brought the lantern to bear on the fragment and grunted. "Just as I thought. Bone."

"Human?"

"The head of a femur."

She swallowed hard. "Do you run into bones often?"

He shook his head. Then he put the scrap of bone aside and scratched through the loose dirt.

"What are you looking for?" she asked.

"The rest of the skeleton. This is the biggest Anasazi grave I've ever seen."

He scooped out several handfuls of soil and set it aside. Then he scratched some more. Nothing came to light. Gently, carefully, he kept going until the hole widened enough to trigger a miniature cave-in along the back edge.

A flicker of color caught Christy's eye. She snatched up the lantern and held it closer. "Look!"

"I see it."

Very carefully he leaned into the chamber, stretched, and gently retrieved a flat green pebble that was smaller than a postage stamp.

"My God," he said softly. "Turquoise. Some pothunter really struck it rich in this grave."

The size and shape reminded her of Hutton's extraordinary inlaid tortoise. "If that wasn't turquoise, I'd swear it came from Hutton's collection."

"What do you mean?"

"He has an abalone, turquoise, and argillite tortoise that came from somewhere on his ranch," she said. "But the turquoise inlay was intact."

Cain's narrowed eyes gleamed in the lantern light as he looked from the turquoise fragment in his hand to her.

"Then why does this remind you of his artifact?" Cain asked.

"The shape and size is the same as the inlay on the tortoise's head. An odd kind of partly curved polygon."

Thoughtfully he turned the piece of turquoise over in his hand. The shape of the piece was indeed odd. Despite his previous orders to her about not picking up so much as a pebble, he put the turquoise into his pocket. Screw regulations. He'd risk jail again before he left the ancient turquoise to be crushed during the next thunderstorm, or the one after that.

"Can you describe the tortoise?" he asked.

"My business is describing things. Four legs retracted so that only the clawed feet were visible. Tail barely a nub. Extremities of abalone inlay. Head and neck not retracted, frankly phallic in shape. Eyes made of two tiny turquoise spheres. Turquoise collar. Argillite shell."

"Any more?"

She frowned. "As big as my palm, two-dimensional rather than sculptural, sophisticated rather than crude, curvilinear more than angular, meant to be viewed from one side only, like a pendant. The workmanship was very fine. And there was something . . ."

Her voice faded.

"What?" he asked.

"It was more than the sum of its parts," she said simply. "Whoever created it was an artist. The tortoise was invested with a sense of wisdom and longevity and fertility that was breathtaking."

He let out a long sigh. "I'd like to see that. It sounds like a fetish from a very wealthy, very powerful clan."

"That's pretty good guessing, for a white man."

The gravelly voice came from the darkness behind them.

Cain spun and held the lantern above his head, sending a wash of light into the shadows.

Johnny Ten Hats stepped into the light. In one big hand was a shotgun with a sawed-off stock and barrel. His finger was over the trigger.

The barrel was pointing right at them.

Chapter 30

"Hello, Johnny," Cain said. He gave a low, curt whistle. "Somebody worked you over pretty good."

"Don't come any closer," Johnny snarled.

"I'm not moving," Cain said easily. "How's it going?"

Christy stared, unable to believe how casual he was. He flicked a sideways glance at her.

The look in his eyes made her cold.

When Johnny turned and glanced quickly over his shoulder, Cain made a brief motion with his hand, as though warning her not to move.

"Somebody on your trail?" Cain asked.

"Back away from that hole," Johnny said. "Put the lantern down on that rock and keep your hands where I can see them."

Carefully Cain set the lantern down and moved away from it. He watched the big man with cold, predatory intent, waiting for an opening.

"Not that I need to worry much about you," Johnny said with faint contempt. "You won't fight me. You proved that before you were shot."

She stared, unable to believe that Johnny didn't see the

battle-readiness in Cain. It fairly shouted to her, scraping her nerves until she felt like she was bleeding under her skin.

"Some things just aren't worth fighting about," Cain said. "A professional piece of ass is one of them."

"Shut up." Johnny lifted the shotgun to chest height and pointed it at Cain's head.

Fear froze Christy. The bore of the shotgun looked as big as a railroad tunnel and as black as death itself.

Cain simply watched, expressionless. Johnny was staring at Christy. Not good. Cain moved to one side slowly, trying to draw attention back to himself.

"Hold still!" Johnny said roughly.

"Take it easy, man. You on speed or something?" Cain asked.

The Indian shook his head, in denial or in response to some private pain. "I gave that shit up."

"Good thing," Cain said easily. "Makes you paranoid."

Johnny blinked and wiped sweat and blood off his forehead with the back of his left hand. The muzzle of the shotgun in his right hand didn't waver.

"You the one that looted this place?" Cain asked.

Johnny grunted.

"You sell it all for dope?" Cain asked.

The big man glared blackly.

"Yeah, well," Cain said, shrugging, "I warned you how much Hutton's whore would cost."

Johnny's response was a stifled sound that might have been a laugh. He took a ragged step closer, trying to intimidate Cain by pure bulk.

When Johnny moved, the side of his face that was toward Christy came out of shadow. She made an involuntary sound. He looked like a dead man walking. His face was bruised and covered with crusted blood from several cuts. Other cuts were still bleeding. He held his left hand stiffly, as if it was injured.

"You don't look real good," Cain said.

"I look better than you will if you don't shut up and stand still." Johnny gestured curtly with the shotgun.

Cain showed his empty hands. "I'm not dumb enough to go bare-handed against a shotgun."

"Hell, you won't go bare-handed against nothin'."

"Coming from you, that's funny."

"What's that mean?"

"How does it feel to shoot someone in the back?" Cain asked. "Did it make you forget what a fool you are for paying for a piece of ass every cowboy in Remington County had for free?"

Johnny took a step, stumbled, and caught himself on a waist-high chunk of sandstone. He sagged against it like an old man sinking into a rocking chair. Then he grinned in the lantern light, revealing a mouth full of broken teeth.

"So you think it was me," Johnny said. He laughed thickly, then spat off to the side, blood and saliva darkly mixed.

Cain waited, measuring his chances.

Christy bit back a scream. Johnny was too far away, the shotgun too dangerous. Cain would be killed before he took one step.

Then she noticed it was Johnny that Cain watched, not the gun. His actions told her that the man was the more dangerous weapon.

"How much did you take out of here, Johnny?" Cain's voice was matter-of-fact, a man making casual conversation with an acquaintance.

But his eyes weren't casual. He watched Johnny with reptilian intensity.

"Who says I took anything out of this place?" Johnny asked.

Cain laughed softly. The sound was like a rasp on stone. "This ruin was a cultural gold mine. Now it's trash. That's your style. You destroy a whole site for a few good pots. I know you, Johnny. I've seen your sign all over the San Juan Basin."

Johnny wiped the back of his hand across the corner of his mouth. His hand came away dark with blood and dirt. "You got any water?"

"In my backpack."

"Where is it?" Johnny said, glancing around.

Cain eased forward in the instant before the Indian looked back at him.

"I'm wearing it," Cain said. "I'll just take it off and—"

"No! Don't move. I don't trust you," he said in a rising tone. "I don't trust no one no more!"

"Easy, Johnny," Cain said. "You're fine. You have control of everything and you're just fine."

The man's black glance darted erratically around the alcove. He looked at Christy like he'd never seen her before. Then he looked again, surprised.

"Hey," he said. "Don't I know you? Come here."

"Stay put," Cain said softly. "Not one inch, Red."

She didn't move.

Johnny shook his head like a drunk trying to clear the cobwebs. Slowly he focused on Cain.

"Who's the bitch?" Johnny asked.

"Nobody you need to worry about." Cain's voice was gentle. "She's going to take a walk while we talk about old times."

Johnny thought it over, then spat again. "No. Bitch stays. Don't trust no one."

"You have to trust someone," Cain said. "You need help." He took a step forward, then another one, before Johnny reacted.

"Back off or I'll blow a hole through you!"

Cain stopped.

Christy saw that he was poised to move again, in any direction, at any moment.

"You still need help," Cain said.

"Bastards."

The comment seemed aimed at people in general rather than Cain in particular. The shotgun was much more focused. Its unblinking eye never shifted from Cain's chest.

Johnny coughed.

Cain inched forward.

The Indian spat blood into the darkness.

Cain moved again.

"I never shoulda got involved with those eastern assholes and their pretty-boy manners and their fancy dope," Johnny mumbled. "My head ain't been right since." He coughed.

Cain eased closer.

Christy held herself so tightly she ached in every muscle, screaming silently at him. *It's too far, Cain. Don't try it! He'll kill you!*

She wanted to scream it aloud, even though it wouldn't do any good. Cain knew the odds as well as she did. Better.

The gun was pointed at him.

"Did you do the dig for Hutton?" Cain asked.

"Hell, yes," Johnny said. He made a sweeping gesture with the muzzle of the shotgun. "I found the place. I dug the pots. I did it all. Pretty good for a no-good blanket-head Moki poacher, huh?" He grinned bloodily. "That'll teach you and all your fancy university friends. I found this ruin, me and Jo, and I dug it. Hell of a lot more than you can say."

Christy stiffened at the mention of her sister's name.

Johnny didn't notice her reaction any more than he noticed Cain's aching progress toward him, a quarter inch, stop and wait, a half inch, stop, a quarter inch . . .

Stop.

Wait.

"Would you have found it if I hadn't told Jo there had to be something around the Sisters?" Cain asked.

Christy's nails dug into her palms.

Johnny glared and swiped his hand across his mouth again. Then he grinned like a boy. "No, I wouldn't have found it. I didn't have to. I just let you do all the thinking and Jo do all the fucking. She picked you clean, got all your secrets."

"Did she?"

"She got the Sisters," Johnny said roughly. "After that, who cares what else you know?"

"What happened?" Cain asked. "How did you end up spitting blood?"

"All gone to hell. People dying, dead, more gonna die."

Abruptly he began chanting in a low voice. The atonal, alien words made the hair on Christy's nape stir.

"You need help," Cain said.

"Just some dirt, man. Just dirt and then get outta here before they catch me."

"Who's after you?"

"Sheriff. He'll never catch me if I get a head start. I know this country too good. As good as you." Johnny laughed, coughed, spat.

Cain inched closer.

"Was I you," the Indian said, "I'd go back in the mesa country and not come out for a time. They're planning on killing me and blaming you."

Christy threw a quick look at Cain. His expression hadn't changed. He looked calm, relaxed . . .

And a foot closer to Johnny.

"They?" Cain asked. "Who?"

"Find out the hard way. I ain't never seeing you again." Abruptly Johnny straightened and thrust the shotgun at Cain. "Back up!"

"I'm just trying to help you," Cain said.

Johnny drew a ragged breath and laughed like a demon in one of Hutton's paintings. "I don't need you. I got me a plan. I'll take care of that bastard Autry and all the rest. All I need is some dirt, and my BLM buddies will take care of me."

"You have friends in the BLM?" Cain asked. "That's a switch."

"Yeah, ain't it? I been a pothunter all my life, and now my only hope is the Bureau of Land Management."

With his injured hand, Johnny reached into his hip pocket and pulled out a small burlap bag like the ones natives used to sell Anasazi beans to tourists.

"Just dish me up a couple pounds of dirt from that hole over there," Johnny said, gesturing to the kiva. "Then I'll be on my way. Any questions you got, you ask Danner. He's about fifteen minutes behind me." Johnny tossed the burlap sack toward Cain. "Fill it."

Cain caught the sack with one hand. He seemed to hesitate.

No! Christy screamed silently. *He's still too far away. Don't do it!*

Chapter 31

Cain reached the same conclusion. Too far. Slowly he turned toward the kiva that had been used as a burial place for human bones. He dropped into the small chamber. Using his hands, he began filling the small bag.

"How many skeletons were in here?" Cain asked after a minute.

"Two."

Johnny heaved himself away from the rock's support and went to the grave to see what Cain was doing.

"Male, female, or both?" Cain asked.

"Both women. Prettiest grave goods you ever saw too. Turquoise, jet, abalone. I damn near rusted my zipper."

Motionless, Christy stood at the edge of the heap of broken timbers, trying not to attract any attention to herself. From the corner of her eye, she caught a flicker of movement, movement that was pacing every motion Johnny made.

Moki, belly flat on the dirt, creeping forward out of the shadows. He was gathered like a great, living spring, trembling and waiting for the moment of release.

Christy's heart beat so loudly she was sure Johnny would hear it.

"Did Hutton get everything?" Cain asked.

"Dunno. I took everything in sight, but I didn't have a chance to dig this baby out." Johnny wiped his eyes. He had trouble lifting his left hand. "The bitch got him too. She cut off his balls and fed them to him."

Cain stopped throwing dirt into the sack. "Who, Jo?"

Johnny didn't answer.

"Do you know where Jo is now?" Christy asked before she could stop herself.

He turned to look at her. "If she's smart, she's gone. Autry will kill her if he gets his hands on her."

"No," Christy said starkly.

The emotion in her voice caught Johnny's attention. He stared at her a long time. "Don't I know you?"

She looked away hastily.

Cain was watching her with dawning understanding.

And fury.

"Wait a minute," Johnny said. "You're the sister, the red-headed reporter from New York."

Ice slid down her spine.

"Autry thinks you were in on this with Jo," Johnny said. "She set it up to look that way. She's a cunning bitch. Was I you, I'd disappear."

"I'm not in on anything with anyone," Christy said.

Johnny laughed, coughed, spat blood. "No skin off my ass. Hutton's going to beat the truth out of you one way or the other. He likes bathing pretty women and putting baby powder on them and then hurting them where it doesn't show."

Christy felt the pressure of Cain's stare, but she couldn't make herself meet his eyes. His expression was a study in stark shadow and hard white light. He was utterly still.

"Do you know where Jo is?" she asked Johnny again.

"Why? She double-cross you too?"

"Something like that."

"She's a real snake queen, ain't she?"

Christy took a step toward Johnny, forcing him to cover her with the gun. The movement exposed his weak side to Cain.

It took a few moments, but Johnny realized that he couldn't cover both Christy and Cain with one shotgun.

"Back up," he snarled to her.

Instead of obeying, she took another step, opening the distance between herself and Cain, forcing Johnny to choose between them.

"Do you have any idea where Jo might have gone?" Christy asked urgently. She didn't let herself look at the gun barrel that veered between her and Cain.

And then the shotgun was pointing only at her.

"Get over with Cain," Johnny said. "Now, bitch, *now!*"

A savage, snarling shadow leaped from the darkness, going straight for Johnny's throat. The surprise was so complete that he couldn't bring the shotgun to bear on the dog. It was all he could do to throw up his injured left arm in self-defense.

Cain lunged up the rubble slope out of the burial chamber. As he shot out of the hole, Moki's jaws closed on Johnny's injured wrist. The big man screamed and twisted aside, flailing and stumbling under Moki's weight. But even as he staggered, he lifted the shotgun muzzle to the dog who was hanging from his wrist.

Barely three seconds after Moki attacked, the shadowy alcove exploded with the searing flash and savage thunder of a shotgun in a closed space. The blast beat against Christy. She couldn't even hear her own screams. Blind, deaf, she fought to reach Moki.

"Get down."

A second after he yelled, Cain knocked Christy out of the line of fire. Head ringing, she felt blindly in the dirt for a stone big enough to use against Johnny Ten Hats.

The Indian flung Moki's limp body aside and in the same

motion spun toward Cain. The shotgun came up, pointed right at Cain's chest. There was no way Cain could reach Johnny before he triggered a shot. There was no cover for Cain and no time to seek any.

Christy screamed in futile denial.

The shotgun's hammer fell on an empty chamber. Johnny hadn't had a chance to reload.

Cain didn't give him one. He attacked with the same snarling ferocity as Moki had. Instantly Johnny used the shotgun as a club. The blow caught Cain on his shoulder, knocking him to the ground. Furiously Johnny tried to work the shotgun's pump action, to reload.

His wounded hand slid off the pump, useless.

Christy's fingers closed around a rock the size of an apple. While Johnny cursed and tried to work the pump one-handed and Cain struggled to his feet, she hurled the rock at Johnny. The range was close and the target was big. The stone hit him in the side of the face with a solid thunk.

Johnny yelled and staggered backward, instinctively trying to get out of range. As he retreated around the ruined kiva, he clamped the shotgun under his left arm and tried to work the pump with his good right hand.

Cain raced along the tangled wreckage of the ruins. He caught Johnny in the window at one end of the alcove and lunged. Kicking and cursing, the men disappeared through the window in a tangle and landed on the rocky face outside the alcove.

From deep within the alcove came a spectral vibration that was more sensed than heard, as if masses of stone were slowly, slowly shifting. A timber groaned and exploded into splinters.

The sounds stopped.

Christy clawed to her feet, another rock in her hand. She reached the edge of the alcove in time to see Cain land a short, chopping blow on the point of Johnny's right shoulder. Abruptly the man's arm went limp.

The shotgun clattered on stone, bounced, then skidded down the steep slope to the sheer drop below. Seconds later, the gun vanished over the brink of stone. With an inarticulate cry of rage, Johnny threw himself at Cain and bore him down to the stony ground through sheer weight. Whatever damage had been done to the Indian's right arm was only temporary. Johnny grabbed Cain in a crushing bear hug.

The two men thrashed around on the stone lip of the precipice, rolling closer and closer to death.

Finally Cain butted Johnny's chin hard enough to daze him. Johnny had enough sense left to lower his chin and protect his Adam's apple, but doing that left his face wide open. A short, hammering blow from Cain's forehead broke Johnny's nose. Another blow in the same place made Johnny scream, yet he didn't let go of his crushing hold.

Instinctively Johnny turned his face aside, protecting his ruined nose. Cain wrenched an arm free and chopped across Johnny's throat. The Indian began choking and gagging.

And he didn't let go.

"Give it—up," Cain panted harshly. "You can't win—and you know it!"

Finally Johnny let go and rolled to his hands and knees, retching and fighting for breath. Cain got painfully to his own feet and stood with his head down, hands on his hips, breathing in great gasps.

"Cain," Christy yelled. *"Watch out!"*

He turned just as Johnny lunged for him. Cain tried to duck beneath the tackle. He almost succeeded. Johnny's weight landed on the backpack Cain still wore. Johnny's momentum threatened to sweep Cain over the edge of the canyon to a death on the rocks far below. With a raw cry of effort, Cain straightened his legs and back, using every bit of his strength to literally throw off the attack.

Johnny sailed out over the cliff like a massive black fledgling launched too soon from the nest. Seconds after he vanished below the stone lip, an eerie chant rose in his wake.

It stopped abruptly.

Christy ran to where Cain knelt, staring over the edge of the rock face. She took his arm and tried to pull him away.

"Get back from the edge," she said. "Damn it, Cain. Get back! It's not safe."

Slowly, he turned toward her. His eyes were coldly luminous. The wild exhilaration of survival was mixed with the bleak finality of having caused a man's death.

Then he focused on her. The look in his eyes changed to a contempt so deep that she backed up. He swept her with an icy glance.

"I shouldn't have worried about disinfecting Jo's clothes before I gave them to you, should I?"

Chapter 32

"**A**re you all right?" Christy asked tightly, ignoring his words.

In answer, Cain forced himself to his feet. Without a word he headed back for the alcove.

"I heard a timber break just after the shotgun went off," she said.

But as she spoke, she was grabbing the lantern and going into the alcove.

"Moki is back here somewhere," Christy said.

"I know."

"Moki," she called softly. "Where are you, boy?"

A faint whimper came from the darkness beyond the ring of lantern light. As she turned toward the sound, he grabbed the lantern from her and went swiftly to his dog.

"Easy, boy," he said gently as he knelt. "Let's see how bad it is."

Moki lay stretched out full length, motionless. Yet at the sound of Cain's voice nearby, the dog's tail stirred in a feeble wag.

"Hold this," Cain said curtly.

She took the lantern and held it up. The dog's front quarters were drenched with dark red blood.

Lantern light wavered, dipped, shivered.

"Hold still, damn it," he snarled.

"I'm trying."

He looked up. She was trembling all over. Her left arm braced her right in an attempt to hold the light steady. Tears ran silently, steadily, down her cheeks. She was as pale as salt.

"If you're going to faint," he said, turning back to Moki, "put down the lantern."

She hissed something between her teeth.

Very gently he probed in the bloody fur. Moki whined once and flinched. Other than that, the dog made no protest.

"Hold the lantern closer," Cain snapped.

When she leaned forward, the lantern light revealed a long furrow through the fur and muscle at the front of Moki's shoulder. White bone gleamed.

Steel clanged on stone as Christy set the lantern down.

"You faint and I'll leave you where you fall," he said.

"Kiss my ass." Her voice was strong and every bit as cold as his.

He looked up in surprise as she peeled off her jacket and handed it to him. "What's that for?"

"Moki."

Cain picked up the lantern and held it overhead, ignoring the jacket.

"Dogs go into shock just like people do," she said tightly. "He needs warmth. Put the jacket over him."

Instead, Cain stood up and peeled off the backpack and then his own shirt. The light transformed scrapes and bruises from his brief, brutal fight with Johnny Ten Hats into dark smears across bare skin. Cain folded his shirt into a broad, flat pad and very gently placed it over Moki's wound.

Without looking at her, Cain grabbed the jacket she held out. He was much more gentle as he eased the jacket beneath the dog and wrapped it around him.

When Cain finally did look at Christy, she wished he hadn't.

He hated her.

"I didn't dare tell you Jo-Jo is my sister," she said.

"Why the hell not? If you had, Johnny might still be alive."

"Bullshit," she snarled. "He was riding a one-way ticket to hell. You just happened to be the one who punched it."

Cain turned back to Moki. He worked quickly, for the alcove was cold and the dog looked very small against all the stone.

With an effort, Christy reined in her adrenaline-frayed temper. "I didn't know you. How could I trust you? Local gossip wasn't very comforting."

"Yeah, yeah, yeah," he said, disgusted.

"And . . . Jo-Jo had warned me that you were dangerous."

"*Shit.* Johnny was right. Whatever the scam is, you're in on it with your sister."

"No! Listen to me," she said urgently. "Jo-Jo called me, said she needed me, had to see me. I hadn't seen her for twelve years. How could I turn her down?"

"Ever tried the word *no*?"

As Cain spoke, he took a knife out of the backpack and slashed a slit in the back of Christy's jacket.

"If it had been your brother calling you," she asked, "what would you have done?"

Silently Cain tied the two new ends of the jacket into a tight little knot and looped the arms around Moki's neck. Then he made another knot to secure the dressing. Finally he looked up at her. His eyes were almost opaque.

"I've killed two men," he said. "Both times there was a lying little slut involved."

Christy drew a ragged breath and looked around the shadowy alcove. Jo-Jo and Johnny and Hutton had ransacked a thousand years of history. Now they were fighting over the spoils. They didn't care who got hurt in the battle.

"I wish," she said distinctly, "that none of this had happened. If I'd known what it would cost, I wouldn't have involved you."

"I kept you last night because I thought you needed help," he said as though she hadn't spoken. "What a laugh. Did Jo-Jo send you to finish the job Johnny botched?"

"You couldn't be more wrong about me."

He ignored her and talked softly to Moki, soothing him with voice and gentle touches. Then he eased his hands beneath the dog and lifted him carefully.

Moki whimpered and struggled a little when Cain shifted the dog's weight to his arms. A few words calmed him.

"I saw a canvas tarp in the first kiva, at the bottom of the ladder," he said. "Get it. I'll wait on top of the rim for you."

"What right do you have to judge me and—"

"Just get the tarp," Cain interrupted savagely.

She grabbed the lantern and headed for the kiva. She scrambled down the ladder, grabbed the tarp, and climbed up to the surface. When she reached the sandstone slab that had nearly sealed off the alcove, he was already climbing up the mound of rubble. He seemed to be moving effortlessly, finding his footing without a problem on the uneven slope.

She took a deep breath and wondered what Cain was using for nerves. Her legs no longer shook, but the whiplash of adrenaline still gave her hands a fine trembling.

Forcing herself to breathe deeply and evenly, she set down the lantern, stuffed the tarp in the backpack, shouldered it, and started after him. He was already walking on the ancient, deceptive steps that had been cut into the sandstone by Anasazi who understood their fellow man all too well.

Suddenly the rock in front of Cain exploded in a shower of shrapnel. There was a flat, keening sound, followed by the faint, unmistakable report of a high-powered rifle.

Christy froze in the act of stepping out from behind the cover of the sandstone slab.

There was no cover for Cain. He ran as fast as the steps allowed him to. The only safety for him was ahead, in the cleft that came down from the top of the mesa.

A second bullet screamed off the sandstone below Cain's feet.

Then a third.

In the shadows of the alcove, Christy held her breath and prayed Cain and Moki across the naked stretch of rock. It seemed like weeks before he reached the shelter of the tunnel.

It was forever before he set Moki down, went feet first into the narrow opening, and rolled over to drag the dog into the tunnel after him.

Shots keened and screamed around the rock as long as either man or dog was in sight.

Christy hugged the rocks of the alcove wall and peered down at the canyon floor, trying to see who was shooting. A thousand feet below, there was a vehicle on the road. A man was bent over the roof, using it to steady his rifle barrel. Sunlight flashed harshly on the telescopic sight. There were three block letters painted on the roof: RSO.

She'd seen a truck that size and color in Remington. Sheriff Danner had been driving it.

Another shot sang off the rocks where Cain had disappeared, then another and another, but the quarry was gone. The man stepped back, jerked open the door of the truck, flung the gun inside, and got into the driver's seat. Dust boiled up from the tires as the truck accelerated down the dirt road and disappeared around a bend.

Christy jumped out and ran across the sandstone steps with

reckless speed, intent on reaching the relative safety of the tunnel. She dove into the darkness, barely squeezing through with the extra bulk of the backpack. She was alone in the tunnel. Cain hadn't waited to see if she made it safely across the open rock.

She gathered herself and pushed through the tunnel on all fours at a frantic pace, ignoring the pain to her knees and hands. As soon as she could stand, she rushed forward, only to come up against the final, sheer length of stone that separated her from the rim.

Cain wasn't waiting there either. There were streaks of blood on the wall. He'd left her behind.

She made a low sound and shook her head, not wanting to know how he'd managed to carry the injured dog up a wall that was taller than he was. Then she took a breath and examined the bloody wall. She'd gotten down it with the help of gravity and Cain's strong arms.

There was no way for her to get up alone.

Chapter 33

Desperately Christy attacked the stone wall, scrambling and clawing for a handhold, a place to wedge a toe, anything to help her up. She fell and flung herself at the wall again. Thirty seconds later she landed on her back. Panting, she pushed herself to her feet and attacked the stone again.

Two bloody hands shot down and grabbed her flailing wrists just when she would have fallen again.

"Slow down before you hurt yourself," Cain said roughly. "Danner's an hour away from getting any help."

She looked up. There wasn't any comfort in his eyes, but he hadn't abandoned her. She drew in deep, tearing breaths, fighting for oxygen.

"Thank you," she said shakily.

"For what?"

"Not leaving—me here."

His eyes narrowed. He looked at her face where the dirt was streaked with tears and blood from a cut. Beneath it all, her skin was white and her pupils so dilated that barely any color showed around the rim.

He felt like a real son of a bitch, which only made him angry at her all over again.

"There's a crevice to your left," he said tightly, "and then a knob of rock on the right. See them?"

After a moment or two, she blinked away enough tears to see what he was talking about. "Yes."

"Put your boot in the crevice," he said.

She did.

"Now step up and find the knob with your right foot."

As soon as she stepped up, he lifted. She put her right foot out blindly, connected with the knob, and pushed upward. He pulled her out of the crevice like a cork out of a bottle.

And let go of her instantly.

She stood with braced feet, trembling, her arms wrapped around her body in a useless effort to get warm. The cold she felt was all the way to her soul.

Without a word he gathered up Moki and headed for the truck. His attitude said more clearly than words that he didn't care if she followed or not.

After a few deep breaths, she started walking. By the time she reached the truck, she felt like she'd never breathe normally again. Why should she? People in a nightmare breathed any way they could.

She peeled off the backpack and threw it on the ground. The tarp trailed out of the pack like a dirty flag. The look Cain gave her told her that he was surprised she'd bothered with any of it.

If she'd had the strength, she would have hit him.

He picked up the tarp, shook it out with a snap of his wrist, and laid it on the floor of the truck's cargo area. Gently he put Moki on half the tarp and folded the other half over, keeping the dog as warm as possible.

Moki neither whimpered nor moved.

"Is he dead?" she asked starkly.

"Not yet. But getting him through the tunnel and up that last pitch was rough. He passed out. Better that way."

She made a ragged sound. Then she pulled herself into the cargo area and braced herself next to Moki.

"Get in front," Cain said, his voice cold. "It's going to be a rough ride."

"Just shut up and drive. I'll keep Moki from banging around."

Cain gave her an odd look, started to say something, and then got in the truck. An instant later the big vehicle was moving. The ride was what he'd said it would be. Rough.

She wedged the backpack on the other side of Moki and held him as gently as possible.

"Did you say Danner was the one shooting at you?" she asked after a time.

"He's the only one I know who wears a white hat and drives a Remington Sheriff's Office truck."

"But why was he shooting at you?"

"He probably saw me kill Johnny."

"It was self-defense!"

"Maybe Danner hasn't figured that out. More likely, he doesn't give a damn. In the eyes of the local law, I'm what's known as 'bought and paid for.' Danner will kill me where he finds me and consider it a public service."

"Christ," she said in a raw voice. "What kind of hellhole is this?"

"It's just a place like every other place. The local cops know who's important and who isn't. Danner will do whatever he thinks he and Peter Hutton's money can get away with."

She absorbed that. "Now what? Make a run for Mexico?"

He smiled narrowly. "We've got maybe an hour before Danner gets back to a spot where he can call for help on the radio. If we're not back at the highway by then, we'll be cut off."

"Do what you have to. I'll take care of Moki."

She stopped talking and concentrated on making the ride

as easy as possible for the injured dog. The instant thcy reached the smooth blacktop of the highway, she checked the bandage. Both Cain's shirt and her jacket were soaked almost through. She didn't know how much blood the dog had lost, or how much more he could lose and still live. She only knew that Moki couldn't last much longer.

"I'll drop you on a little road that runs behind the hotel," Cain said. "Nobody will see you."

"Moki first," she said. "Go fast, Cain. Go really fast."

Closing her eyes, she fought for self-control. She didn't know what she should do after Moki was taken care of. All she was sure of was how badly she wanted to get her hands on Jo-Jo.

You got me into this mess, sister mine. You're going to get me out again. And Cain with me.

Somehow.

Christy bit back a laugh that would have been too close to hysteria. Jo-Jo had never helped anyone but herself. No reason to think that had changed. Not even a prayer.

Jo-Jo, for the first time in our lives I need you. Stop hiding from me.

No real prayer there either. If she wanted Jo-Jo, she'd have to run her to the ground like a fox.

"As soon as Moki is safe," she said, "I have to make some calls. My cell phone is back at your place."

He glanced at her in the rearview mirror. Whatever he was thinking, he kept to himself.

The veterinary hospital was in a little settlement outside of Remington. The community was no more than a weathered frame building, a gas station, a general store, and a handful of houses scattered along the highway. The windows of the store were blank and dirty. Obviously it had been closed for years. The gas station's two pumps squatted dismally in puddles of rainwater. The only sign of life was a muddy black dog.

Cain drove the truck around behind the frame building, where the vehicle couldn't be seen from the highway. He gathered up Moki in the bloodstained tarp. When Christy would have followed, he gave her a hard look.

"Stay here," he said. "The vet's office girl is the biggest gossip in Remington County."

Christy got back in the truck, but into the passenger seat rather than the cargo area.

Fifteen minutes later Cain emerged from the little clinic. He paused only long enough to pull on the shirt he'd borrowed. Afternoon light played across a livid pink scar in the middle of his back and an equally bright one on his chest.

Through and through, Christy thought, horrified at seeing evidence of his injury in bright daylight. *How did he survive? Who carried him away from the ambush?*

Cain looked exhausted and enraged at the same time. He tucked in the tails of the shirt with short, savage motions. Then he got in the truck and slammed the door behind him.

"Moki?" she asked instantly.

"About bled dry."

She bit her lip. Hard.

He looked at her, then looked away as if he couldn't stand the sight of her.

"It took Doc Tucker five minutes just to find a vein he could use," Cain said in a low voice.

She turned away. Being hated at such close range was painful. "But Moki's still alive?"

"Barely."

"Is Moki as tough as you are?" she asked huskily.

Surprised, he looked at her again. She was staring out the side window. "Tougher," he said.

"Then he'll make it. You did, didn't you?"

"So far. The divine Jo-Jo will be the death of me yet." He started up the truck and backed out.

"I have to make some calls," Christy said again.

"Why?"

"To find Jo-Jo."

"Why?"

"For God's sake," she said wearily. "She's my sister, she's in trouble, and—"

"So are you."

Christy shrugged impatiently. She didn't feel like explaining that she hoped Jo-Jo would get them out of trouble. She was pretty sure Cain would crack his face laughing.

"How long since you've seen Jo-Jo?" he asked after a moment.

"Years."

"How long?" he asked savagely.

"Ten years. No, wait, that was a phone call. A message, really. We didn't connect. So it's at least twelve years. Maybe thirteen." She gestured sharply with a hand that was smeared with Moki's blood. "I don't remember. What difference does it make? *She's my sister.*"

He flicked a glance at Christy and then concentrated on the dirt road he was taking.

"Younger sister," he said after a time.

It wasn't a question.

She answered anyway. "Yes."

He let out an explosive breath and shook his head. "Go back to New York, Red. Jo-Jo has finally bitten off more than her loyal older sister can chew."

Silently, blindly, Christy stared out the side window. She tried to swallow the fear that knotted her throat. She couldn't.

"You heard what Johnny said, didn't you?" Cain asked.

"Johnny said a lot of things."

"Jo-Jo did something to Hutton."

"Jo-Jo has done something to a lot of people," she said bleakly.

"Hutton may look like an angel, but he's not nice."

She remembered the demons hanging in his hallway. "I know."

"Go home. Let your little sister clean up after herself for once."

"She's not very good at that," Christy said. "She asked for me. She needs me."

And I need her to get us out of this mess.

"She doesn't need you. She wants to use you," Cain said. "There's a difference, honey. All the difference in the world."

The change in his voice made Christy feel like the steel bands around her lungs had finally fallen away. She turned toward him. "Then you don't really believe I'm in this—whatever it is—with her?"

He sighed and cursed at the same time. "I believe Jo-Jo wouldn't have sat in the back of the truck and cried without making a sound because she hurt for an injured dog. Jo-Jo wouldn't have given a thought for Moki's pain. She sure as hell wouldn't have dirtied her hands to keep him from bouncing around."

The savage contempt in Cain's voice when he spoke of Jo-Jo hadn't changed. Christy closed her eyes and clenched her fists until her nails dug into her hands.

She was afraid, terribly afraid, that he was right.

"You can't know that," she said.

"Can't I? You haven't seen her for ten or twelve or thirteen years. I have. Johnny has."

"You're men."

"Honey, you could be on fire and Jo-Jo wouldn't pee on you to put you out."

"I don't believe that," she whispered. *I can't.*

"Take off those rose-colored glasses and look at what your sister is rather than what you want her to be."

Guilt broke over Christy in a cold, nauseating wave. When

she spoke, her voice was raw. "I was able reach her some-times. I was able to reach her when no one else could get close. But I went east. And she went bad."

Cain's hands clenched on the wheel until white showed around his knuckles. "So you blame yourself for Jo-Jo."

"I—yes." Tears burned. She ignored them. She was too busy discovering why she'd let Jo-Jo avoid her for so many years. Sisters in name only.

And underneath, deep underneath, Christy had wanted it that way.

"You think you're responsible for what Jo-Jo became," Cain said.

Christy closed her eyes. Tears slid from beneath her dark eyelashes. "Yes."

"That is a crock of shit," he said, spacing each word. "Jo-Jo is old enough to take responsibility for what she is and what she isn't."

Christy didn't answer.

"Get out of here, Red. Get out while you can. Don't let her pull you down with her."

"I can't just turn my back on her, on what she's done, any more than you could leave Moki to die while you ran for cover."

"Jesus," he hissed. "What if I just dump you by the side of the road?"

"And do what? Look for Jo-Jo?"

The slight flinching of Cain's eyelids told Christy that he was planning to do just that. She didn't want him to find Jo-Jo. Not alone.

He hated her too much.

Chapter 34

"**W**hat are you going to do?" Christy asked after a time of silence.

And her tone of voice said she was going to keep asking until she had the truth.

Cain turned the truck onto another, smaller dirt lane before he answered. "I'm going to see a friend."

"Where?"

"Remington."

"That could be dangerous."

"So could being seen with me if Danner has given shoot-on-sight orders."

"I figured that out when the rock chips started flying."

Despite himself, Cain smiled slightly. "You're something else, honey."

She gave him a wary glance. "Don't tell me that. I've had all the excitement I can take for today."

He made a muffled sound and shook his head.

"After you've seen this friend, then what?" she asked.

"I start looking."

"For Jo-Jo?"

He nodded and turned the truck onto another country lane.

"Where are you going to start?" she asked.

"I'll think of something."

"I already have."

He didn't ask what.

"Don't you want to know what it is?" she said after a moment.

"What will it cost me?"

"We work together until we find her."

Cain gave Christy a sharp look.

She held her breath.

"You do realize that Danner is back in radio range by now?" Cain said.

"I'm not stupid."

"Yeah? Then think about this. I don't know how long I can stay ahead of the local law. It's either run like a rabbit or hunt like a wolf."

"Somehow I don't see you as the Easter Bunny."

"And I don't see how a woman like you is sister to a—" He stopped abruptly. "God must have some sense of humor."

Christy's mouth curved in something less than a smile. "Well?" she asked after a moment.

"Well, what?"

"Do we have a deal? I give you a lead and we look for Jo-Jo together?"

"You might not like where it takes us."

"I already don't like it. So what?"

A slow, cold smile spread across his face. "How do you know you can trust me not to take your information and then dump you on the side of the road?"

"I'll have to chance that."

"Yeah, Red, you sure will." Narrowing his eyes, he stared out the windshield.

When she couldn't take the silence any more, she said, "Is it a deal?"

He nodded curtly.

She let out a long breath. Then she dug around in her jeans pocket until she found the key. She held it up in the bright light coming through the windshield.

"Do you have any idea what this might open?" she asked.

He glanced at it, looked at her in disbelief, then back at the road again. "Yeah, I have an idea. Where did you find it?"

"Jo-Jo's room."

"Anything she had, Hutton knew about."

"Not this key. It was taped to the bottom of a drawer in her closet."

"How did you know where to look?" Cain asked.

"I spent my last six years in Wyoming searching Jo-Jo's room for forbidden fruit of one kind or another."

He took a hand off the wheel and reached for the key.

Christy didn't let go.

"If you don't trust me, you're better off alone," he said evenly.

She opened her fingers, giving him the key.

Without a word he reached down for the ring of keys that hung from the ignition. Deftly he fished one of the keys out of the cluster on the ring and let it dangle down his palm next to Jo-Jo's key.

They looked identical.

"I don't understand," she said.

"You've been in the city too long."

"Fine. I've been in the city too long. What does that have to do with these keys?"

"It means some country folks drive in to get their mail out of little boxes opened by keys just like these."

"You mean Xanadu doesn't get mail delivery?" she asked in disbelief.

"Sure it does. Makes you wonder what Jo-Jo was expecting in the mail that she wanted to hide from Hutton."

Cain flipped the key back to Christy.

A few minutes later he turned into a tiny, dusty ranch lane. A weather-beaten house was tucked away behind some big elms.

"Wait here," he said.

She watched while he walked to the door, knocked, and was greeted by a woman who was neither young nor old. She had dark brown hair with a dusting of gray and a smile that lit up the old run-down porch. She kissed Cain soundly, hugged him, and led him into the house.

A few minutes later he emerged with an armful of clothes and a paper bag full of food. He put the food behind the driver's seat, tossed the clothes into Christy's lap, and got in.

"Change into these while we drive," he said.

"What about you?"

"I'll do my best not to drive into a ditch watching you."

She tried not to laugh but couldn't help it. "I meant what about *your* clothes?"

"Out here, a man with dirty pants is no big deal."

"Where I came from in Wyoming, the women got just as dirty as the men."

"Were they wearing white designer jeans?"

"Point taken."

"Strip. I won't see anything I haven't already seen."

"In your dreams," she retorted.

He laughed and made a point of blocking his view with one hand so he couldn't see the passenger side.

Christy peeled off her filthy sweater and blouse and pulled on the soft, faded plaid shirt Cain had gotten for her. She kicked out of shoes and socks, pulled off the ruined white jeans, and put on a pair of Levi's that were as soft and faded as the shirt. Though loose, the clothes fit well enough. She transferred the contents of her pockets to her new jeans, put on her socks and shoes, and turned to look at Cain.

"I was wrong about not seeing anything new," he said blandly.

"What?"

"Nice underwear, Red."

"Stuff it."

He threw back his head and laughed. "You're more fun to tease than my little sister ever was."

Christy ignored him. She pulled her purse out of the console where she'd locked it away before hiking out to the Sisters. The purse was small, smart, and hopelessly Manhattan. She stripped out money, ID, and credit cards, and pushed them into her pockets. Then she sorted through the remaining clothes. A bandanna, a frayed quilted vest, and a faded red T-shirt rounded out the collection.

"Who should I thank for these?" she asked.

"Angie."

"Friend of yours?"

"Yes."

"She must be, to lend clothes to another—er, friend of yours."

Cain gave Christy a sideways look. "Angie is like every other human being. She gets lonely. So she'll cook dinner while I bore her with my latest Anasazi theories."

Christy made a neutral sound.

"Or I'll chop some firewood for her," he said, "and she'll swap ironing my shirts for some tutoring for her oldest kid. Angie never learned to read books, but she's a fine judge of people."

Christy's cheeks burned. "I didn't mean . . ."

"Sure you did. So I'm telling you. She's a friend. They're a lot harder to find than a piece of ass."

It was silent in the truck until Cain entered Remington on one of the dusty country lanes that crisscrossed the valley.

He kept off the main street and worked his way through town on the unpaved, unmarked back roads until he stopped in an alley a block and a half off the main square in downtown Remington.

Through a gap between two sagging old frame business buildings, Christy saw the second story of the Remington County Courthouse, as well as the rear side of the buildings that fronted on the square. In the middle of the block, an American flag snapped lightly in the afternoon breeze.

"That's the post office," he said, pointing to the flag. "All you have to do is figure out which box is Jo-Jo's."

"Wasn't the number on the—no, of course it wasn't. I would have seen it. How many boxes are there?"

"About a hundred."

She looked at both sides of the key again, hoping a number would appear.

It didn't.

"A hundred. God." She shook her head.

"Start at one hundred and work backward."

"Any particular reason?"

"The boxes with low numbers have been in the same families for the last century."

"Oh. Makes sense. Won't people get suspicious if I spend ten or fifteen minutes trying to open boxes?"

"They'd get a lot more suspicious if I tried it," he said. "I've had the same box for the last ten years. Most people in town know it. And me."

"I imagine most people in town know most everyone else. I'll stick out like a boil."

"Lots of summer folks rent boxes, and lots of summer ranch workers are transient. There's quite a bit of coming and going during the fall."

She looked uncertain.

He reached for the key.

"No," she said, jerking her hand back. "You'd be spotted for sure. Every woman in town looks up when you walk by."

He gave her an odd glance.

"Well, it's true," she muttered. "It's something about the way you carry yourself." She reached for the door handle. "Damned arrogant western—"

Her words ended in a startled sound as he casually dragged her back into the seat.

"You forgot something," he said.

"What?"

His long fingers slid into her hair. "This. Blazing red and damned beautiful."

"My hair?"

"Your hair. Looks like fire, feels like silk, and if you don't cover it up and get out of this truck I'm going to kiss you until neither one of us can stand up. That would be a really stupid thing to do."

"I—I don't have a hat," she said.

Without looking away from her eyes, he pulled the bandanna out of the clothes he had given to her. He folded the cloth diagonally, placed it over her hair, and tied it at the back of her neck. The stroking of his long fingers over her sensitive nape made her shiver.

"Better run, honey. Fast."

Chapter 35

For an electric moment Christy wanted to stay. Then she told herself it was the wrong time and the wrong man.

Well, wrong time for sure.

She opened the door and bolted out of the truck.

"I'll meet you in there when you're finished." Cain nodded toward the blank back door of a building. "Don't take long. I've got to ditch the truck real quick."

She read the rude sign over the building's door. "The Dew Drop Inn? I don't believe it."

"Believe it. Head for the booths in back."

She waved her understanding and walked quickly down the alley to the street.

Remington's sidewalks were busier than they'd been the day before. There was a crowd in the parking lot of the supermarket. The Greyhound bus had just unloaded across the street. A troop of trail bike enthusiasts sprawled in the shade of one of the square's huge trees.

The ranchers, townspeople, and tourists didn't give Christy a second look. Part of it was her clothing; a woman in old jeans, plaid shirt, and bandanna was unremarkable and natural in Remington. The rest of it was a surprise to her.

She felt natural too.

The town's rhythms and social nuances were as familiar to her as the lettering on the stop sign at the corner. She knew how to meet the passing glance of the cowboy and his wife so that they categorized her as a newcomer rather than as an outsider.

The lobby of the post office building had a musty pipe-tobacco smell. Someone was ignoring the rules and smoking in the sorting area. The customer at the counter was a sharp-faced Native American woman with two long beautiful black braids down her back.

No one gave Christy a second look. Most didn't even give her a first.

She went around the corner to a smaller lobby where the boxes were located. Cain was right. One hundred postal boxes stared at her like the prisms in the eye of a bee. Discarded junk mail littered the floor. No one was in sight.

Without looking around, she walked straight to Box 100. The key slid easily into the lock but refused to turn. Box 99 was the same. So was Box 98.

The key grated softly each time she tried a new lock. It sounded like a file on a live microphone to her, but nobody else seemed to notice. Certainly no one came to ask her if she needed help.

She tried three more boxes before she heard footsteps approach. Shielding the next box with her body so that no one could see the number, she tried it quickly.

No good.

Straightening up, she walked past a potbellied store merchant heading for his own box. There was a pay phone at the other end of the lobby. She headed for it, pulling change out of her pocket as she went. Her first call was to the hotel.

"This is Christa McKenna," she said. "Any messages?"

A sharp intake of breath followed by a pause told her that

THE SECRET SISTER   259

she was glad she hadn't gone back to the hotel for her own clothes.

"Er, where are you, Ms. McKenna?"

"Pocatello," she said blandly. "Any messages?"

"Mr. Hutton would most urgently like to see you."

"How sweet. Any other messages?"

"Um . . . er . . ."

She hung up. After a moment's hesitation, she used her *Horizon* calling card to pay for a long-distance connection. Someone picked up the phone immediately.

"*Horizon*, may I help you?" the voice asked.

"Hi, Amy," Christy said. "You're working late."

"So is Myra. Good thing you checked in. She's climbing the walls. Peter Hutton wants to see you, and he wants it right away."

"So I've heard. Any other messages?"

"Ask your boyfriend, Nick."

"Nick? Why?"

"Myra told me to give out his number to callers since you weren't checking in at the office."

Anger flashed through Christy. "I see."

"What should I tell Myra?" Amy asked.

"Go screw a chainsaw."

"*What?*"

"We must have a bad connection," Christy said. "I can't hear a word you're saying. I'll call back."

She hung up and punched in her calling code plus Nick's office number. He answered quickly.

"Hi, Nick. I hear you've been nominated as my personal message drop."

"Christa! Where are you?"

"West of Manhattan. Has anyone other than Peter Hutton and Myra been asking for me?"

"Ted Autry and someone who claimed to be a sheriff or

something called too. Got my number from Myra, for chris-
sake. What's going on?"

"Myra's rabies shot must have failed. Who else is after
me?"

"Me," Nick said. "Are you thinking about me?"

Cold washed over her. "What did you say?"

"Have you been thinking about me, darling? I've been
thinking about you."

"Oh, my God. It was you, not Jo-Jo."

"What?" he asked, confused.

"Did you leave a message for me at the hotel?"

"Of course I did."

Christy clung to the receiver and tried to fight the sick fear
washing through her as she remembered Johnny's words.

People dying, dead. People gonna die.

"Are you, Christy?"

"What?" she whispered.

"Thinking about me," Nick said impatiently.

"Right now I'm thinking about Jo-Jo."

"Jo-Jo? Your sister?"

"Yes. Has she called asking for me?"

"No. When do I get to meet her?"

"I'll be sure to introduce you if the three of us are in a room
together." But Christy didn't think that would happen. Ever.

Fear and nausea rolled coldly in her stomach.

"Dy-na-mite!" Nick said. "Can't believe I'm going to
meet her in the flesh."

"Don't hold your breath. I'm not likely to be in any rooms
with you in the future."

"Huh?"

"Nick," she said wearily, "it's over. Good-bye, *adiós, ciao,*
babe. I'm gone. You're free. We're history."

"What?"

"Don't make me repeat it."

"Does this have something to do with a man called Aaron Cain?" Nick asked abruptly.

"How did you—" She stopped.

"It *is* Cain, isn't it?"

"No. It's just that you and I aren't—"

Nick ignored her and kept talking. "Autry warned me about Cain. Says he's a real hand with the ladies. Especially the New York kind looking for a souvenir of the Wild West."

She didn't say a word.

"Christa?"

"Most of the time you're a nice man," she said. "Go find a nice woman to love you most of the time."

"Christa, I—"

She hung up before Nick could finish. For a long time she stared at the phone without seeing it.

Jo-Jo hadn't left any messages.

People dying, dead. People gonna die.

Grimly she straightened her shoulders and went back to the lobby where post office boxes waited in taunting array. No one was getting mail or watching other people get mail.

She tried a dozen more boxes, working the key as quietly as possible. She didn't want to make the pipe-smoking, mail-sorting employee on the other side of the boxes curious.

Two wind-burned women in rough work clothes like Christy's walked into the lobby chatting with each other. One opened a box while the other gave Christy the kind of casual yet thorough examination only one woman can give another.

Christy felt a momentary rush of uneasiness. She left the lobby, crossed the street to the hardware store, and pretended to window-shop while watching the door of the post office. A minute later the women came out, climbed into a pickup truck, and drove away. Christy started back across the street. She glanced in the direction of the courthouse in time to see a familiar truck pull into the space reserved for the sheriff.

Danner got out from behind the wheel and headed for his office. A man dressed in a business suit that would have been at home on Wilshire Boulevard or Madison Avenue met him on the sidewalk.

At first, Christy didn't recognize Autry. He'd shed his drugstore cowboy costume along with the barbecue sauce. Now he looked like what he really was, a highly paid corporate cop, a private policeman in the hire of a Fortune 500 company.

She fought a wild, primitive urge to break and run. Danner might not have seen her there on the face of the mesa, but Autry was hunting her for his boss. Watching Autry and Danner together, she didn't doubt that when it came to violence, the only difference between the two men was that Danner had been elected.

Turning her face away, she made certain the bandanna hid every lock of her red hair. Then she crossed the street, not as fast as she wanted, not as slowly as she should have. Just as she reached the sidewalk, a police cruiser with a light bar and state police insignia parked beside Danner's truck.

She ducked into the lobby and watched while a state highway patrolman climbed out and joined the other two men. Immediately Danner began talking, waving his arms around to dramatize his words. He pointed back to the mesa where the Sisters lay hidden from view. Then he made a falling, twisting, diving gesture with his hand.

Christy's hands clenched. Danner was describing the death of Johnny Ten Hats.

And Cain's part in that death.

The uniformed patrolman listened, then reached back into his cruiser and picked up the microphone on his two-way radio.

Her nails bit into her palms. The word was going out at the speed of light.

We have to get out of here.

But first she had to find the lock that fit Jo-Jo's key.

The lobby was empty again. Dropping all pretense, she tried box after box, working with grim efficiency. When a young mother pushing a stroller came in to collect her mail, Christy looked up and smiled.

"Forgot the dang number," Christy drawled.

The woman laughed sympathetically. "You can skip seventy-nine. It's mine."

"Thanks." She went back to shoving the key in slot after narrow slot, not looking up.

On Post Office Box 73, the key worked.

Chapter 36

The metal box was so full Christy had to fight to remove the thick wad of letters. Two fat rubber bands wound around the envelopes.

You don't come here much, do you, Jo-Jo?

Christy smiled to herself rather grimly. She didn't doubt that Jo-Jo would have been able to pass occasionally as a tourist or a transient ranch cook. She'd been raised like Christy in a small western town. There was also no doubt in Christy's mind that her sister had hated every instant of dressing down, of not being the sexual magnet that held everyone's eyes.

So what were you hiding here, sister mine?

The top letter was addressed to Christa Jody McKinley. Anger flared. Just what she needed. More grief.

Thanks a lot, Jo-Jo. Nice of you to point the finger at me.

The McKinley was like the rest of Jo-Jo. Half invented. Half real. All trouble.

Footsteps sounded in the main lobby. They were coming toward the post office boxes.

She stuffed the letters under one arm, closed the box, and

locked it. No one gave her more than a casual glance as she walked out of the post office, across the street, and through the front door of the Dew Drop Inn.

Inevitably the jukebox was playing Merle Haggard. Ignoring the irritating nasal music, she scanned the long bar for Cain. Several weathered outdoor types stared back with blunt masculine interest. Her clothes were loose, but nothing could disguise the female curves of her body.

She remembered that Cain had said he would be in a booth in the rear. She started toward the back.

"Hey, darlin', looking for somebody?"

The cowboy's dusty sweat-stained hat was pushed back on his head, revealing a shock of straw-colored hair. He was good-looking in a rawboned way and he knew it. He held a half-full beer glass in his hand. There were three pitchers on the bar in front of the men. The pitchers were empty. The cowboys were about half loaded.

She gave the blond man a quick glance. Something about him was familiar. She looked at his partner. The men reminded her of her past, of males who looked at a woman like one more farm animal to be appraised, discussed, and used when they got around to it.

Once, that look had enraged her, because she'd been terrified that the men were right. Now she knew just how wrong they were.

She met the cowboy's measuring gaze with an amused female smile. "Too late, cowboy. I've already found him."

The man's intent, predatory expression turned into a smile of simple masculine appreciation. "You change your mind, ma'am, you know where I am."

"Bet your wife does too," Christy said, still smiling.

The cowboy's buddies hooted, and so did he.

No one else tackled her while she walked to the booths in

the back of the saloon. As she approached, Cain looked up from a glass of beer that had gone flat while he waited. When his eyes met hers there was a cold, calculating light in them that burned like a laser.

Uneasily she examined the man who was sitting across the booth from Cain. The stranger was as tall as Cain but hadn't been fined down by injury and rehabilitation. When he glanced toward her, he smiled approvingly but without blunt sexual interest.

"This your lady friend?" he asked Cain.

Cain nodded.

The big man stood up, removed his hat, and waited to be introduced. Light glanced off the shiny five-pointed star that was pinned on his shirt.

Christy's mind went blank. For an icy instant she felt trapped, it was the alcove all over again, only now the stone was falling in slow motion.

"Christy McKenna, this is Larry Moore," Cain said. "He's the Remington town constable and brother of the man who owns a ranch up near the Sisters."

She gave Cain a glance that said he'd lost his mind. He smiled slightly, knowing what she must be thinking.

Moore swept his hat off his head and bowed with a flourish. His skin was weathered, and he sported a flowing, beautifully sculpted handlebar mustache with tightly waxed ends. He moved with remarkable grace despite a solid gut that struggled to escape over his ornate silver and turquoise belt buckle.

"Pleased to meet you, ma'am. Cain here is dead particular about who he keeps company with."

She looked away from Cain, swallowed, and said, "Good to meet you, Mr. Moore."

"Larry," he said easily.

"Uh, Larry."

She glanced around unhappily. Half the booths at the back

of the bar were empty, but there were still too many possible eavesdroppers for her comfort.

Cain slid out of his side of the booth. "Get in. Even in Angie's clothes, you put every man in here on red alert."

"Yeah, right," she muttered sarcastically.

"Would you believe yellow alert?" he whispered as she slid by him.

"I'd believe you've been doing tequila shooters."

Silently he pointed to his single, nearly full glass of beer.

As she settled into the booth, he tucked a lock of red hair back beneath the bandanna. The motion was frankly intimate, as was the smile he gave her.

Moore's revolver clunked against the side of the booth when he sat down again on the other side.

"Well?" Cain asked Christy.

She looked at him blankly.

"The box," he said.

"I took care of it."

"What was—"

"No," she cut in. "My turn. May I speak privately with you for a few moments."

It wasn't a question. It was a demand.

"Larry's a friend," Cain said.

"That's nice."

She stared at the constable's badge.

Moore smiled at her. "Don't worry about me, ma'am. I'm on Cain's side."

"Looks more like you and Danner are on the same side," she said flatly.

"I'd sooner side with a polecat," Moore said. "To our lord high sheriff, I'm just a fat old doorknob shaker who ought to be fired."

"Danner made a pitch to the town council to take over patrol duties in Remington," Cain explained to her.

"Luckily, I had the votes to put him off for the time being," Moore said, "or I'd be a jobless loafer like Cain."

"You're already that," Cain retorted. "If it wasn't for stray cats in trees and folks who lock their keys in their cars, you wouldn't have a single thing to do."

"That's why the council passed up Danner's kind offer," Moore drawled. "They couldn't see paying good money for what I do."

Christy glanced from one man to the other in disbelief. Despite Moore's shiny star and Cain's spotted past, the bond of friendship between them was real. They seemed as close as brothers. Closer.

Siblings didn't always turn out to be friends.

"Don't worry about Larry," Cain said. "For my money, he's the only honest lawman in southwestern Colorado."

Moore's face lit up at the compliment. "Yeah," he drawled, "and the lowest-paid, too. There seems to be a direct relationship."

Cain looked at her. "Spit it out, honey."

"I hope you know what we're doing."

"I do."

"I'm so relieved," she said acidly. "Because right now Danner is in front of the post office chatting up a Colorado state cop."

"Shit," Cain hissed.

"Was that jackleg cop Autry with them?" Moore asked. The drawl was gone. His lips were pursed as though he was going to spit on the floor.

"Yes," she said. "Danner and Autry drove up while I was in front of the post office. A state policeman arrived a few seconds later. I think he got a full briefing about—" She broke off and glanced quickly at Cain.

"I told him about Johnny," Cain said. The bleak look was back in his eyes, the look that said he'd killed a man.

She grabbed his forearm and said urgently, "It wasn't your fault."

"Dead is dead," Cain said. "What did the state cop do?"

"He got on the radio."

Cain and Moore exchanged looks.

"That'll make it a lot harder to move," Moore said. "The alert will be picked up in all four states. Inside of an hour, you're going to be hotter than a two-dollar pistol."

"Do you have a rental car?" Cain asked Christy.

"Yes, but Autry and Danner are chasing me too. They called my office in New York and my ex-boyfriend."

Cain gave her a sharp look. "Ex?"

"Ex," she said flatly.

"Do they know you're with me?"

"Autry suspects it. He warned Nick about you, what a stud you were with the ladies, especially the New York kind 'looking for a souvenir of the Wild West.' "

Moore snickered and shook his head. But an instant later he was serious again. "If they suspect you're together, they'll pull the tag number of the rental car off Christy's hotel registration."

"Yeah," Cain said. "The joys of a small town."

"You'll be nailed inside of a hundred miles," Moore added. "You sure as hell won't make Albuquerque."

"Why Albuquerque?" Christy asked Cain.

"Larry's given me a lead on a Bureau of Land Management investigator."

"So?"

"The BLM man might be able to explain why Johnny had me filling that bag with grave dirt."

"What good will that do?"

"I'll know when I hear the explanation." Cain tapped the bundle of paper underneath her arm. "Got something to share?"

She pulled the bundle of letters out and put it on the table. "I don't know what I have. I wasn't about to stand around in the lobby and read Jo-Jo's mail."

"Don't start here," Moore said to Cain. "You have a lot of friends in Remington, but Hutton has a lot more money."

"Yeah."

For the space of a long breath, Cain stared at the letters. Then he scooped them up and turned to Christy.

"It's too dangerous to stay with me, Red."

"No."

"Larry will see that you're safe."

"No."

"I could have Constable Moore here throw you in the city tank for a while," Cain said.

"For my own good, of course."

Cain's mouth thinned. "Yes."

"No," she shot back. "For *your* good. You just want to get your hands on Jo-Jo when there aren't any witnesses."

He became very still. "Do you really think I'd hurt her?" he asked in a low, savage voice.

"All I know is that when you talk about her, I'm afraid. You hate her."

Moore sighed loudly and took a sip of Cain's beer. "Flat," Moore said to no one in particular.

"Shit," Cain said.

"More like piss, actually."

Throwing Moore a disgusted look, Cain shot out of the booth, pulling Christy after him.

"Jo-Jo doesn't deserve you," Cain said savagely. "Let's go."

Chapter 37

"**H**old it," Moore said quietly.

Cain waited.

"No use going off half cocked," More said. "What are you going to do about a car?"

"There's a rental agency in Durango," Cain said. "That'll buy me a few hours."

Moore dug a silver key ring out of the watch pocket of his faded jeans. He flipped the ring to Cain. "Take my truck," Moore said.

"But—"

Moore ignored the interruption. "Camping gear and change of clothes are in the box in back. Sharon is shorter than Christy but wider in the beam. Maybe it will all even out. Where's your truck?"

"Out back," Christy said when Cain didn't speak.

"I'll take care of it," Moore said.

"But you can't—" Cain began.

"Bullshit I can't," he cut in. "I didn't carry you on my back off the Sisters mesa just to turn you over to the likes of Danner. Now get your stubborn butt out of here before you make me mad."

Cain hesitated, then accepted. "I owe you."

"Like hell you do." When Moore turned to Christy, his expression gentled. He tipped his hat and smiled. "Pleased to have met you. I do like a woman with sand."

The old western phrase made Christy smile.

"You all be careful, now," Moore added.

Cain grabbed Christy's arm and led her out of the saloon. He didn't speak to her again until they were in Moore's truck and safely out of town.

"Okay, Red. Let's have it. What was in Pandora's box?"

Christy pulled off the rubber bands and began sorting envelopes. "Letters, mostly."

Moore's police scanner connected with a transmission, held for three seconds, then moved on, seeking a new transmission. Cain turned down the volume until it was barely louder than the sound of the tires on the asphalt road.

"Sealed letters?" he asked.

"So far they've all been opened."

"Who are they from?"

"No return address. Same handwriting on the envelopes."

"Read one of the letters," he said.

"I'd rather not."

"Hell, honey, I'd rather be home in the hot spring with you on my lap, but nobody's offering me a choice."

She gave him a sideways glance. The smile on his face reminded her of the instant in the saloon when he had tucked her hair into the bandanna and caressed the nape of her neck at the same time.

She had liked that.

So had he.

Don't go there, she told herself. *Safer to read Jo-Jo's mail.*

She pulled the most recent letter out of its envelope, unfolded the notepaper, and began to read.

"Aloud," he said.

She started reading without really thinking about the meaning of the words. " 'Hi, babe, How's my creamy little fur pie?' "

Cain gave a crack of laughter.

Despite the red creeping up her cheeks, Christy laughed too.

"Good friends, huh?" he offered blandly.

"Sounds like."

"Keep reading," he said.

"I will."

"Aloud."

"I won't."

"Chicken."

"Cluck cluck."

"What happened to those wings you flew away on?" he asked, grinning.

"I molted." She took a deep breath. "Does 'fur pie' mean what I think it means?"

"What do you think it means?" he asked innocently.

She gave him a disgusted look.

"Yeah," he said, relenting. "It means pussy."

"Thanks—I think."

"Anytime, honey. Anytime at all."

She began reading the letter rapidly.

Silently.

Her eyes widened. "Good God," she muttered.

"Need a translator?" he asked hopefully.

"I may need one, but I don't want one. Apparently Jo-Jo was head over heels with this Jay character."

"Heels over head, more likely."

Christy grimaced and folded up the letter. Before she could set it aside, Cain plucked the page from her hands. He shook it open, held it near the steering wheel, and scanned the pages with the speed of a man used to reading dense, scholarly textbooks. His black eyebrows climbed.

"Find a new word?" she asked, deadpan.

" 'Poontang' is an old word."

"Same meaning, right?"

"Right."

"That boy—"

"Jay," Cain interrupted, looking at the signature.

"—has a one-track mind," she finished.

"Yeah. Tie 'em up, ride 'em hard, put 'em away wet."

She laughed. She couldn't help it.

Smiling slightly, he handed back the pages. "So she kept her lust letters under lock and key. Big deal. Anything useful in the rest of that pile?"

Christy sorted through the stack, dividing the correspondence into groups. The letters from Jay were the biggest stack.

"Mostly from her fur pie man?" Cain asked, glancing over.

"Looks that way. The postmarks span about eight months."

"Not a one-night stand, then."

"If the first letter was any sample," Christy said absently, "standing was the only way they didn't do it."

He gave her a startled look, laughed, and reached across the truck. A light tug on the bandanna and her red hair was free.

"It's a miracle I don't burn my fingers," he said, stroking a soft, flame-colored curl.

"It's a miracle you don't get them smacked," she said, but there was no heat in her voice.

Smiling, he released the lock of hair and concentrated on the road while she finished sorting through the contents of her sister's P.O. box.

Once she'd set Jay's letters aside, the rest of the papers were barely a handful. Jo-Jo had stuffed them into small manila envelopes with a word or two written on the outside. One of the envelopes was surprisingly heavy and had no label. It was sealed with wide, clear tape.

Reluctant to intrude on her sister's privacy any more than necessary, Christy put aside the sealed envelope and concentrated on the others. Pulling up the metal tabs on one of the manila envelopes, she shook out the contents. She flipped through them quickly, giving Cain a running commentary.

"AmEx credit card bills, correspondence with several upscale hotels around the Southwest, gas chits."

He grunted.

She opened another envelope. "Same stuff, different envelope." She got into the third envelope. "More of the same," she said, reaching for the fourth envelope. "She and Jay must have traveled to every— Hello, what's this?"

Cain looked over.

She fanned out a dozen smaller envelopes and held them at his eye level. "Recognize any names?" she asked.

"Scottsdale, Beverly Hills, Santa Fe, Dallas, Taos. Yeah, I recognize them. Galleries and art dealers."

"Fine art?" she asked, thinking of the demon paintings.

"Southwestern-style fine art. Except for the Sherberne Gallery in Santa Fe. He's almost exclusively Native art and artifacts."

"Anasazi?"

Cain shrugged. "Navajo. Zuñi. Apache. Moki. Any kind that sells is fine with him."

"Five letters from Sherberne."

"Read them aloud. Can't be any worse than Jay's, right?"

Christy organized the postmarks and went to work, opening the most recent first. As she unfolded the sheet, a slip of paper fell out. She picked it up, glanced casually at it, and then stared.

"What is it?" he asked.

"The voucher half of a cashier's check."

He looked at her oddly. "So?"

Wordlessly she held out the paper.

He took one look and whistled softly through his teeth. The check had been made out to Jay Norton and paid by the Sherberne Gallery. The amount was $537,840.

"What's the date?" Cain asked.

"Last week. The day before Jo-Jo started leaving messages for me in New York."

"You better read those letters, Red. We need to know what Hutton's jet jockey had to sell that was worth half a million bucks, wholesale."

"I could make a wild guess," she said unhappily, thinking of the alcove.

"So could I. We both could be wrong. Dead wrong. Read the letters."

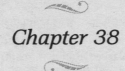

Chapter 38

For a few moments Christy fiddled with the letters, rearranging them without opening them. She really didn't like reading her sister's mail.

"Aloud, please," Cain said innocently.

"Bite me."

He gave her a slanting sideways look and a smile that was very white against the black of his beard. "I love it when someone talks dirty to me."

"Then turn up the scanner."

He laughed.

She flipped through the stack of mail again. This time she chose the oldest letter instead of the more recent ones. When she finished reading it, she put the letter back in its envelope, pulled out a new letter, and began reading again. She worked her way through five letters before he became impatient.

"Anything?" he asked.

"A postgraduate education in slang and ways to screw your employer's 'hot little whisker biscuit.'"

Cain smiled crookedly and said not one word.

She folded up the letter she'd been reading, put it in its envelope, and pulled out the next letter.

"You know," she said after a minute, "I think Jay really cares for Jo-Jo. His vocabulary is just a bit limited."

Cain gave her a look that said he thought she had lost her tiny little mind.

"He's about as subtle as a baseball bat," she agreed, "and has a one-track mind, but—" She shrugged.

"But what?" Cain asked after a moment.

"There's a sort of primitive energy in what he writes, as well as real affection. Coarse, but real. He worships the ground Jo-Jo walks on."

"More like the ground she sits on."

Christy ignored Cain. "Jay wants her obsessively, and Jo-Jo needs to be wanted that way. I think . . . I think she's always needed it, the way some people need heroin."

A disgusted sound was Cain's only answer.

"Reading between the lines," she continued, "Jo-Jo's long-time affair with Hutton was pretty well finished eight months ago. Jay caught her on the rebound."

"Or she caught him."

"It's a good match."

"As long as the equipment doesn't wear out."

"Oh, they've got more than sex going for them," she said.

"Yeah? What?"

"Some kind of hauling business."

"Ashes?" he suggested dryly.

"What?"

"Never mind," he said. "Just more slang. What's their business?"

"Packing, transportation, and delivery. Using Hutton's airplane, of course. Wonder what he thought about that."

"You're assuming that he knew. What were they shipping?"

"Something fragile and valuable. They don't mention what."

She went back to reading.

For a time there was silence except for the hum of tires on pavement and the occasional muttering of the scanner when it connected with a law enforcement radio transmission.

"It's the alcove," Christy said, looking up from a letter. "Jay mentions the Sisters."

"Yeah, I'll just bet he does."

She opened another letter. Pieces of paper fluttered out. "More check stubs."

"How much?"

Silence, then, "Almost half a million in this lot. A million, total."

Cain whistled.

"Was the alcove that good?" she asked.

"It was by far the most promising site I've ever seen."

"Why?"

"Protected. Hidden. And then there's Kokopelli." Yearning and anger combined in Cain's voice. An extraordinary site had been raped and ruined before it could be understood. "I've never heard of a kiva decorated with his symbol. That site was very special to the Anasazi. There would be very special artifacts in the kivas."

"But a million dollars in artifacts? Even at ten or twenty thousand a pot, that's a lot of pots."

"Not these days. The Japanese collect anything the Western world collects. And the Germans are absolutely nuts about Anasazi artifacts. They pay hundreds of dollars for a handful of sherds."

"Still, a million bucks—"

"Wholesale."

"—is a lot of money."

"Some foreign currencies have been strong against the dollar for a while," he said. "What we think is an outrageous price is a bargain to them, relatively speaking."

She shook her head doubtfully.

"Then there's the collector mentality," he added. "You get some rich, aggressive collectors bidding, and the outcome is big bucks for you and to hell with rational prices."

"That I can believe."

The scanner kicked in with a warning that a dead cow was a road hazard two miles inside the reservation's northern boundary, northbound side of the road.

When it was silent again, Christy let out a long breath. Each time the scanner came to life she was afraid she would hear about a man fleeing a murder charge in a white truck with a redhead by his side.

"The large kiva artifacts could easily have been worth a half million by themselves," Cain said after a moment. "If you throw in the grave goods from the second kiva, you've got quite a haul, even at wholesale prices."

"And they hauled every bit of it," she said unhappily.

"That must have been the richest find in the last thirty years." His voice was rough with anger for all that had been lost. "Was there any kind of inventory?"

Quickly she scanned the pieces of paper that had fallen from various letters. "They refer to 'your shipment' and 'the pieces' but never to anything specific. That's . . . odd."

"Damned odd. In legitimate deals, newly dug artifacts are photographed in situ and described millimeter by millimeter. The documentation becomes part of the value."

"Would this many dealers be involved in something illegal?"

"Most dealers don't give a damn about anything but a quick resale. The dealers paid in cashier's checks, right?" he asked.

"So far."

"That means they knew they could turn the artifacts around immediately and quietly. They didn't have to worry about getting caught with dubious goods."

"Jay went to just one dealer, at first," she said. "Sherberne. He offered to take everything off their hands, but Jay didn't like the price."

Cain grunted.

"So Jay went to some other dealers and solicited bids," she said.

The scanner crackled to life, muttering about a car upside down in a ditch two miles inside the reservation's northern boundary, southbound side of the road.

"They should try fencing their livestock," Christy said.

"The cow is worth more as roadkill than it was alive. Cash is hard to come by on the reservation."

"Was that why Johnny was looting his own history?"

"Johnny didn't think much about history, including his own."

Christy skimmed the page of angular printing that was becoming familiar. She flipped the page over and kept going to the bottom before she spoke again. "They ended up parceling out fifty-seven pots and twelve consignments of other goods."

"What goods?" he asked instantly.

She shook her head. "Jay doesn't say."

"Damn." Cain's hands flexed on the steering wheel. "I keep hoping for some kind of inventory, some way of knowing what was found. And lost."

"All I can say is that everybody paid by cashier's check and everybody would have bought five times as much if they could have."

His fist struck the wheel, a blow so sharp it made the tough plastic vibrate like a tuning fork.

"I wish I could have seen it, photographed it, catalogued it," he said savagely. "There must have been an entire village preserved behind that stone curtain. And so far north—it would have turned the Moki world upside down. So damned much lost. *Christ*."

"When we catch up with Jo-Jo, maybe we can recover—"

The look on his face made Christy swallow the rest of her words. His slicing sideways glance reminded her just how cold his amber eyes could be.

"I'll catch up with Jo-Jo, all right," he said, "but the artifacts are long gone. They're in Germany and Japan, New York and Los Angeles, locked up in private collections, hidden beyond anybody's reach."

Christy began reading again, grateful for the excuse not to confront his icy anger. After a few minutes she went back to a previous letter, pulled it out, and began glancing back and forth. She set both of them aside, opened a new letter, and read only partway through before she set it aside and opened another letter and yet another.

The quiet frenzy of reading and comparing letters drew Cain out of his angry thoughts. He reached for one of the pages.

"No," she said instantly. "Don't mix them up. I'm trying to check something."

"Give me some hints. Maybe I can help."

"When did you tell Jo-Jo about the Sisters?"

"The first time?" he asked.

"Yes."

"Maybe a year ago," he said.

"Don't you remember?"

"Contrary to what you believe, Jo-Jo wasn't a big blip on my scope. When Hutton got too rough for her, she'd call up and talk to me, that's all."

Something in Cain's voice made Christy uneasy. "What did she want you to do?"

"Kill him, probably."

"You can't be serious."

"Why not? She knew my past before she ever met me. Ex-con. Murderer."

"That's crazy. You're no more a murderer than I am."

He glanced quickly at her. "Red, you just saw me kill a man."

"Self-defense isn't murder."

There was a strained silence. Then Cain let out his breath.

"Besides," she added, "Hutton was Jo-Jo's meal ticket."

"Hutton was into bondage games. Real ones," Cain said, "not the satin whip kind of romp Jay probably talks about in those letters."

"I can't see Jo-Jo going in for that."

"You can't see Jo-Jo, period. You keep seeing the past. That little blond angel child is no more."

"She wasn't an angel," Christy said. "But she was . . . fragile, I guess. I always felt I had to protect her."

"Yeah, Jo-Jo's good at that game. She used it on all the local men. Get two men hot, complain to one that the other was hitting on her, and watch them fight."

"Don't give her all the blame. The men—"

"Have to be stupid enough to play her game," Cain interrupted curtly. "I know. I was, once."

"You were only eighteen."

"The other guy was only twenty. He never got any older."

Chapter 39

Christy took a long look at Cain's closed expression and gave up arguing. Silence filled the truck while she went back to reading her sister's mail.

"It looks as though Jo-Jo was planning to loot the alcove for at least eight months," Christy said finally. "Maybe more."

"Ever since I told her about the Sisters, I imagine."

"I don't know when she and Jay became an item—"

"Probably about the time she needed transportation out of Colorado for the artifacts."

"—but about seven months ago Jo-Jo talked Hutton into hiring Johnny Ten Hats to search the area around the Sisters for ruins."

"Using my information," Cain said.

"And the bowl Jo-Jo took from your cabin."

"How long did it take them to strike pay dirt?"

Christy sorted through various letters, reading quickly, her mouth a flat line of unhappiness.

"A few weeks, I guess," she said. "They took most of the good pieces before Hutton ever saw them. Lord, what they must have taken . . . The artifacts I saw in Hutton's house were incredible."

"Did Hutton even know about the alcove?"

"Oh, he knew. He didn't get those artifacts he showed me out of a Christmas stocking."

Cain waited, but she didn't say any more.

"What?" he asked.

"I read the *Horizon* file on Hutton pretty fast. I could be wrong."

"About what?" Cain asked impatiently.

"I think Hutton was in trouble financially as well as artistically. He'd started a new line of perfume and cosmetics. Those things require a huge amount of cash to get going."

"How are the new lines doing?"

"Too soon to tell," she said absently, looking at another letter. "The costs are all up front. The payoff is a few years down the line. If it comes at all."

She frowned and reread a section.

Cain waited.

"Listen to this," she said, and began reading aloud. " 'He'll go for it. Hutton is so desperate for cash, you're lucky he's not selling your platinum ass on street corners.' "

"Maybe Hutton was selling artifacts and forgetting to give Uncle Sam his cut," Cain said.

"It would fit. In any case, Jo-Jo planned to double-cross Hutton from the very beginning."

"Why? He was her meal ticket."

"She found out he'd been secretly interviewing models."

Cain's black eyebrows shot up.

"The spring line of clothes was going to be her last work for Hutton," Christy said.

"Any reason?"

"He told Jo-Jo she was too old."

Cain whistled through his teeth. "I'd like to have been there."

"So she came up with a scheme to steal artifacts from the alcove."

"Revenge?"

"Partly. Mostly she was broke."

"Broke! She was billed as the Million Dollar Body."

"Jo-Jo spends money as fast as she makes it. The future has never been real to her." Christy turned another page over. "Besides, Jay has expensive plans. This sounds like he's already bought one airplane. He wants several to start his own charter service."

"Any man who stays that long in the sack with Jo-Jo has earned it."

Christy ignored him and kept reading. "Somehow Hutton found out that Jo-Jo and Jay were skimming artifacts from the alcove. He threatened them both."

"When?"

She looked at the postmark on the envelope. Smudged. She tilted the paper several ways, trying different angles for the light. "Two weeks, max."

"What happened then?"

She read quickly and summarized. "He—Jay—thinks the threat is funny. Says Hutton is in it with them up to his ass and can't burn them without burning himself."

"How did they know which gallery owners to approach?"

"Johnny. He knew the private collectors too."

"Figures," Cain said, disgusted. "Jo-Jo had a real twist on Johnny."

"What was it?"

"His cock."

"What makes you think she was sleeping with him? There was Jay, remember?"

"Honey, Jay wasn't around all the time. Jo-Jo went bar-crawling in Montrose and took her trophies back to Xanadu for Hutton to enjoy. Ah, love. Ain't it grand?"

Christy winced.

"But then, maybe Jay was like Hutton," Cain said coolly. "Maybe he liked watching Jo-Jo do what she did best."

"Jay doesn't say anything about watching her model."

"I wasn't talking about modeling. Hutton liked to watch Jo-Jo in the sack with the local cowboys. It was the talk of the county."

Christy's head snapped up and she stared at Cain. "What did you say?"

"Don't look so shocked, honey. Jo-Jo liked strutting her stuff. Hutton liked watching." Cain shrugged. "It happens."

A shudder of distaste went through Christy. She set her jaw and went back to the letters. "I don't believe it."

"Long way from the High Plains of Wyoming, huh?"

She looked up. His expression was a mixture of sympathy and impatience. "A long way from anywhere I want to be," she said evenly. "Ever."

Without another word, she went back to the letters. A few minutes later she finished the last one, folded it, put it away, and leaned her head against the window.

"Anything new?" he asked.

"No."

The strain in her voice made him want to hold her, but all that would accomplish was to make him want her even more.

There was a long silence, broken only by the scanner's occasional mutterings.

Cain drove through a settlement that consisted of five wind-scoured houses, a one-pump gas station, and a store. The buildings were huddled at the base of the mesa. They looked old, beaten, gray without end.

Christy felt the same way.

Slowly, after many miles, the clean immensity of the land

seeped past the darkness of her thoughts. The air was so clear she felt like she could see all the way to tomorrow.

She let out a long sigh and leaned back, allowing the spare beauty of the landscape to ease the aching deep within her, the pain that grew whenever she thought of the past, the present, and the sister she'd always loved and would never understand.

Never *had* understood.

The last of the sunlight threw long shadows from a line of red-rock mesas. Cedar and juniper trees burned along rocky ridges like deep green torches. The steeply slanting light gilded ridges and set fire to slopes, giving a unique, almost ghostly glow to the land.

The truck came down a winding grade and into a narrow river valley where the leaves of huge black-trunked cottonwoods had already begun to turn a deep yellow. Sunlight and wind made the leaves dance like pieces of beaten gold.

Looking at the clean, vivid landscape, she could understand why the Anasazi worshipped the sun. It was more than a farmer's understanding that light was needed for corn and beans and squash. Sunlight was a blessing for the land, giving it a rich, warm beauty that never grew old, never corrupted, never was less perfect than it seemed.

The sister I loved never really existed. She never will. Accept it.

But a deep, stubborn part of Christy kept hoping, hurting, hoping, hurting . . .

With a long sigh she looked at the stack of letters on the seat. They made her feel old, used up, bleak. The sealed envelope that had no writing on the outside was buried beneath the others. She didn't want to pull it out, open it, and find out more things she didn't want to know.

Hoping.

Hurting.

She turned her head and looked out the side window, watching shadows lengthen and flow together, claiming the land.

The gentle caress of Cain's fingers on her cheek was so unexpected that she flinched. Instead of withdrawing, he simply repeated the slow caress.

"Sorry, honey," he said in a low voice. "I was out of line. There are some things about Jo-Jo you really don't have to know. I keep forgetting how much you love your sister, come hell or high water or human frailty."

Christy's breath came out in a long, ragged sigh. "If you'd known her as a child . . . Sometimes she just broke your heart, she seemed so sweet."

His answer was silent, another gentle stroking of his fingers over her cheek.

After a moment, Christy straightened, smiled wanly at Cain, and reached for the last envelope. It was so heavily taped that she ended up shredding it with her teeth.

Another, smaller envelope fell out. It had been rolled and taped until it looked like a fat pencil. With it came three folded envelopes. One had Jay's familiar, bold handwriting, but her eye was instantly drawn to the other two letters. Both were in plain white envelopes that had been addressed in big printed letters. They looked as if they had been written by a child.

"A new player?" Cain asked.

"I guess."

She checked the postmarks. One letter was three weeks old. The other had been mailed the same day that the big cashier's check had been drawn. Both envelopes were postmarked Las Alturas, New Mexico.

The letters inside were written in the same blocky, semiliterate hand as the envelopes. The paper itself had been ripped from the kind of cheap tablets schoolchildren use. The message was simple.

YOU GIVE ME SISTERS OR I GIVE YOU BIG TRUBLE

The note was signed by what looked like a brand consisting of a 10 with an arch over the number.

The second letter was even shorter.

YOU WANT TRUBLE YOU GOT TRUBLE

The same stylized brand was drawn at the bottom of the paper.

"I don't get it," she said.

"Let me see."

She held one of the notes out.

"Looks like Johnny was screwed out of some goods," Cain said after a quick glance.

"Johnny Ten Hats?"

"That's his sign. A number ten with a hat on it." Cain looked at the rolled, taped envelope. "Want my knife?"

As he asked, he dug around in his pocket for the small jackknife he always carried. When he handed the knife over to her, it felt warm against her palm, infused with the heat of his body.

"Thanks," she said, feeling oddly breathless.

As her fingers curled around the jackknife, she realized how cold she felt inside, a cold that Cain's masculine warmth somehow eased. She knew she should resist the elemental lure.

And she knew she wasn't going to.

Carefully she slit the tape and the envelope beneath. Another envelope was beneath. It wasn't sealed. When she opened it, gleaming chain spilled out into her hand, along with a pile of splinters. The chain was old, handmade, fragile. Delicate gold nuggets no bigger than peas alternated with the worn links.

"Gramma's necklace," Christy said huskily, fighting tears. "Jo-Jo kept it for me after all."

He looked at the splinters in Christy's palm, started to speak, and thought better of it. "Mind if I look at what came with the necklace?"

She gave him an odd look but tipped the small mound of fragments into his open hand. "What is it?"

"Bones. Old, very old."

Her hand jerked.

"Open the envelope again," he said. "I'll put them back in for you."

She pulled the edges of the envelope apart. A slim, pale green sheet of paper was hidden inside. She knew even before she pulled it out that she would find Jo-Jo's writing.

Hi, Sister.

If you got this far, I'm in more trouble than I thought. Help me get out and then I'll help you, because you're in a LOT of trouble. I left a trail pointing right at you, but I'll clear it all up from Rio.

Help me, Christmas.

Please.

Chapter 40

Christy's hands trembled, but her voice was even when she read the note aloud to Cain. It didn't take him two seconds to understand what Jo-Jo had done to her sister—she'd put Christy right on the firing line.

"Jesus." He flexed his hands on the wheel, wishing it was Jo-Jo's neck. "She really is a piece of work. What about the other letter?"

"What letter?"

"Lover boy's. The one she thought was special enough to hide away from the others."

Christy reached almost eagerly for the envelope with Jay's handwriting. His crude enthusiasm for Jo-Jo's body would be easier to deal with than Gramma's necklace wrapped in ancient bone fragments and a plea for help from a sister she'd never really known.

She pulled out the letter, expecting the familiar coarse endearments. What she found was a lament from Jay that he hadn't been able to finish Cain off before the Moore brothers showed up. Christy made a low sound and closed her eyes.

Hoping. Hurting.

And now just hurting.

"Honey?"

"You were right," Christy said raggedly. "Jo-Jo set you up to be killed."

There was nothing he could say without adding to Christy's pain, so he just nodded.

"But you were wrong about Johnny," she whispered. "It was Jay who tried to murder you."

Cain whistled softly between his teeth. "You sure?"

"I'm sure. Now what?"

"Find flyboy."

The flatness of Cain's voice made her feel even colder. It surprised her. She hadn't thought she could feel any worse than she did when she understood what Jo-Jo had done. Her secret sister.

Her deadly sister.

"How do we find Jay?" Christy asked.

"We'll start with Sherberne Gallery."

"Santa Fe." She sighed and rubbed eyes that felt like sandpaper. "How far is that now?"

"Too far."

She gave him a questioning glance.

"You're exhausted," he said.

"It doesn't take much energy to sit."

"We'll stop up ahead at Ghost Ranch," he said, ignoring her bid to keep going. "Ever heard of it?"

She smiled wanly. "Anyone interested in design, style, art, and women has heard of Ghost Ranch and Georgia O'Keeffe."

"Then you've heard of the Chama River Valley and Abiquiu."

"Sure."

"Look around you, honey. That's the Chama River shining off to the right."

The names triggered a flood of images in her mind, paintings from texts and museums: *The Road to the Black Place* and the *Church at Rancho de Taos,* the cottonwood series, and the black raven soaring like death and freedom over the landscape.

Cain pointed toward the hills ahead. "Ghost Ranch is right over there. It's a retreat for church groups now. A friend of mine runs it."

"Is Ghost Ranch as beautiful as I've heard?"

"Tell me tomorrow."

She made a questioning sound.

"We're going to sleep there tonight," he said.

A mile later Cain turned off the highway and headed up a gravel road toward the clay hills and stone mesas. Though not much of the establishment was visible from the paved road, the buildings weren't far off the highway. He drove into a small parking area and turned off the engine.

"It looks like a classy resort," she said.

"If you look harder, you can see the remains of an old working ranch." He got out. "I'll be back in a bit. Just rest, honey. You need it."

He was right, but she needed to stretch more. She got out of the truck and loosened up stiff muscles. Then she sat on the chrome running board of Constable Moore's pickup, watching daylight fade over Ghost Ranch.

She soon realized that Cain was right about the ranch, as he'd been right about so many things. Just beneath the new buildings of the retreat lay remnants of the old ranch. There were corrals and loading chutes, the stately, gnarled remains of an orchard, and overgrown irrigation ditches that fed water to fifteen acres of pasture and hay. The lines of the old ranch flowed together like a shadowy skeleton just beneath the surface of reality.

Then the last of the light drained away, taking the shadows

of the past, leaving only the present, where new buildings gleamed with artificial brilliance against the coming night.

Cain walked out of the long ranch house that served as offices for the resort and crossed the yard to the truck.

"We're in luck," he said. "Mack always keeps one of the old cabins in reserve for family visits and other emergencies."

"Which are we?"

The corner of his mouth turned up. "Both. There's even some food, if we don't mind cooking."

"I don't mind." She yawned once, then again. "Sorry. I don't know why I'm so tired."

"You're finally coming down off your adrenaline jag."

"Oh, God." She groaned. "Don't tell me I'm going to be run over by the adrenaline express again."

Laughing softly, he held out a hand. She took it, allowing him to pull her to her feet. Gently he stuffed her back into the truck and drove toward a cabin that was set apart from the other buildings in the mouth of a small canyon. Soon the headlights of the truck outlined a small adobe building with weathered vigas showing just beneath the flat roof. French windows looked out across the ranch toward the looming, mysterious mesas. The adobe had been sanded down by sun and wind and storm.

When Cain shut off the engine, the companionable chirping of crickets filled the night.

"Not much by Manhattan standards," he said.

"This adobe has its own standards and traditions." Christy smiled at the building. "It's part of time and the land, like the cliff houses of the Anasazi."

"You keep surprising me," he said after a moment.

"Probably because you keep misjudging me. You look at me and see East Coast, Jo-Jo, bitch-goddess, trouble . . ." Christy's voice faded. "Well, you're right about the trouble. I've been a lot of that."

"Not your fault. It started months before you came here."

"Years before," she said. "It started when I went east and left Jo-Jo rudderless in Wyoming."

"Bullshit, honey."

Wearily she shook her head. "I was the only one who could get through to her." *At least, I thought I could.* "I left anyway, and she . . ."

"Jo-Jo made her own choices," he said, getting out of the truck. "Every damned one of them. Her, not you. It was always her."

The door shut hard. He got around to the passenger side in time to help Christy down. She moved stiffly, drawn by a tension even fatigue couldn't loosen. Her knees gave slightly when her feet reached the ground.

"No more talking about Jo-Jo for now," he said. "You're nearly finished. If you don't let down, you'll fall down."

Christy didn't argue with his blunt assessment. For the first time in her life she felt fragile. She hated the feeling, but she couldn't ignore it any longer.

The cabin wasn't locked. He opened the door wide and flipped on a light. The adobe was a western version of an efficiency apartment. The single room still held the warmth of the day and smelled of dried flowers from a vase on the table. There was a kitchen in one corner, bathroom off in a closet, and a sofa that unfolded into a double bed.

She turned and looked at him, a silent question in her eyes.

"After dinner we'll flip to see who sleeps in the back of the truck," he said.

"On metal?"

"On a mattress. Larry's no fool." Cain opened the French windows to let in the cool twilight air. "We'll need a fire before long, I'll get the wood if you'll see what's in the kitchen cupboards."

"Any requests?"

"As long as it doesn't bite first, I'll take it. Hell, if it bites first, I'll still take it."

She knew just how he felt. It seemed like days since she'd eaten.

No wonder I feel fragile. I'm hungry, that's all. No big deal. A little food and I'll be fine.

It didn't take her long to go through the cupboards and the tiny refrigerator. Eggs, cheese, butter, and a small package of tortillas came from the refrigerator. A big can of *frijoles refritos*, a bottle of salsa, and a tin of coffee came from the pantry.

Since cupboard space was at a premium, the coffeepot and the cast-iron skillet were already on the stove. After a brief hunt, she found matches and was ready to go.

By the time Cain gathered wood and laid the fire in the small stone fireplace, she had *huevos rancheros* on the table. The corn tortillas were steaming from being warmed in a skillet with just enough butter to glaze the pan.

"Looks great," he said as he sat down. "Thanks for cooking."

Surprised, she glanced up from her own plate. "No thanks needed. It was nothing."

"Not to me. I love a home-cooked meal."

They ate quietly, watching the last purple light fade from the western horizon. Somewhere between the old adobe and the ranch house, an owl called several times. Another answered from a stand of trees across the narrow little valley.

Closing her eyes, she drew in a deep breath and let it out slowly, absorbing the peace of the valley. The sound of him pouring coffee into her cup was a variation on the sound of cottonwood leaves stirred by a freshening wind. A chair creaked as he sat down again.

"Why did you break up with your boyfriend?" Cain asked.

She shrugged.

"That exciting, huh?" he said dryly. "In that case, why was he your boyfriend in the first place?"

She opened her eyes.

Cain was watching her over the rim of his coffee mug. His eyes were the clear gleaming gold of scotch whiskey.

"Mistaken identity," she said. "I thought he wanted someone to take to concerts and exhibits and—"

"Bed?"

She shrugged again. "Sex isn't a big deal for either one of us. Then he turned forty and wanted home, hearth, and heathens."

Laughing softly, shaking his head, Cain asked, "What else?"

She gave him a puzzled look.

"Why did you break it off while I was talking to Larry in the saloon? That's what happened, isn't it? You told What's-his-name—"

"Nick."

"—to get lost."

"What should I have told him? That I'm raving around the Southwest with an ex-con who's wanted for killing an Indian called Johnny Ten Hats, who just happened to be trying to kill us at the time? That I saw a man die and heard a dog whine with pain and bleed and bleed and—" Her voice broke.

"Easy, honey. It's all right."

"No," she said bleakly. "It isn't."

She felt her throat tighten and knew she should stop talking, but she couldn't. The enormity of what had happened kept breaking over her in great dark waves, dragging her down in her sister's muddy wake.

"Maybe I should have told Nick that I'm looking for my sister, who happens to be the Million Dollar Body that Nick drools over whenever he sees a magazine layout."

Cain's eyes narrowed. "Nick liked Jo-Jo?"

"He'd never met her. He didn't even know we were sisters until this week."

"Why not?"

"I get damned tired of being the ugly sister, that's why."

"Ugly? Christ, honey, you're not—"

"Compared to Jo-Jo, I am," she cut in.

"Not to me."

She ignored him. "Or maybe I should have told Nick about Peter Hutton, who has demons on his walls and gets off watching my sister bang the local cowboys."

"Somehow I don't think Nick is up to hearing that."

Christy laughed a little wildly. "Neither am I."

With surprising gentleness, Cain took the coffee mug from her trembling fingers.

"The last thing you need is caffeine," he said.

"Then what do I need?"

He started to tell her, but thought better of it. Just because she watched him out of haunted, intrigued, and sometimes approving eyes didn't mean she wanted to be his lover.

Chapter 41

Cain stood, dumped the coffee in the sink, rinsed the cup, and went to the firebox in the living room. A moment later he pulled a bottle of brandy out of a nest of kindling. He poured half a mug and put it on the table in front of her.

"I can't drink all that," Christy said.

"I'll help."

She inhaled the aroma, sipped, and shivered. "It tastes . . . too good."

"Now who's the closet Puritan?"

She made a sound that could have been a laugh or a stifled sob. He stroked her hair once, then went about clearing the table without any fuss or wasted motions.

"I'll do that," she said.

"You cooked. I clean. Isn't that the rule?"

Slowly, she nodded. Then she just breathed in aromatic brandy and watched him move between table and sink with the unconscious grace of a wild animal.

When the kitchen was in order, he went to the fireplace, dropped a match into the tinder, and stepped back, watching the flames appear. Silently they spread across the hearth, taking delicate bites out of the wood. Soon the smell of burning cedar perfumed the air.

He returned to the table, picked up the mug of brandy, and looked at her. "Come sit on the sofa," he said. "Watching a fire is as relaxing as brandy."

If it had been more than ten feet away, she would have refused. But it wasn't, so she pushed herself to her feet. The couch was soft and worn. She sank into its embrace and leaned back. The gentle crackling sound of burning cedar and the chirp of crickets were the only sounds. Flames danced and flickered over the fragrant wood.

At first she just let the minutes go by as silently as the dance of flames. But finally she drew a deep breath and turned her head toward Cain.

As she'd sensed, he was watching her, not the fire. Silently he held out the mug of brandy. She accepted it, sipped, and returned the mug. When he took the mug from her, his fingers moved over hers in a light caress that reminded her of the previous night.

"You look like the adrenaline express just ran over you," he said.

"When you handed me the brandy, it reminded me of a lifetime ago, when you caught me on the way out of Hutton's house and took me to your cabin."

"A lifetime?" Cain smiled crookedly. "It was only last night, honey."

"It was a lifetime." Her voice was as tight as the lines of strain in her face.

"Take another sip," he said.

"Are you trying to get me drunk?"

"Could I?"

Something in his voice made her turn toward him. He was looking at her hair, her face, her mouth, her breasts, her hands. For an instant she was afraid to breathe, afraid to move from this moment into the next.

"It's a little late to be frightened of me," he said.

"You haven't looked at me like that before."

He smiled strangely. "I haven't looked at you any other way. You just haven't looked back at me. Until now."

Deliberately Cain set aside the mug of brandy. Just as slowly, he reached for Christy, giving her every chance to turn aside.

Instead, she came to him with a soft sigh and a shiver of anticipation she couldn't conceal. She was too tired to fight the pull toward him that she'd felt from the first time she saw him, an attraction that increased with every moment she spent with him. She knew him better than she'd ever known any other man.

She knew she could trust him.

Now she wanted to know all of him. She needed it with an urgency that was consuming her as softly and quickly as fire on dry cedar.

Another shiver rippled through her when his hard, warm hands framed her face. He looked at her for a long moment with hungry eyes. Then he bent and brushed her mouth with his, just once.

"Yes or no?" he whispered. "Tell me now, honey."

"Yes."

She felt sudden tension sweep through him. She smiled against his lips, enjoying the knowledge that she affected him as deeply as he did her. When his hands shifted from her face to her ribs, she sighed with pleasure.

"I like your hands," she said. "I liked them the first time I saw them."

"Did you? I sure as hell wanted to have them all over you."

He lifted her, turned her, and resettled her across his chest. She opened her eyes. He was watching her as though curious whether she would back away from the passion that bound them together as surely as the opposite shores of a river were bound by the water between.

"I meant what I said," she whispered. "I'm not a tease."

His head lowered even as she rose up to him, giving herself to the powerful currents that flowed between them. There was no hesitation, no subtle adjusting of bodies as they learned how to hold and be held. They blended together like longtime lovers.

The first taste of him went through her like fire. With a small sound, she moved even closer, winding her arms around his neck, needing him as she'd never needed another man. When she gave him her mouth, he took it with stabbing urgency.

As one they twisted down and around until they lay facing each other on the couch. The kiss turned deep and sensual, feeding the heat that seethed inside both of them. His hands slid down to test the resilience of her waist, then moved up her rib cage with tantalizing deliberation until her breath caught in her throat.

When he still didn't touch her, she tore her mouth from his and sank her fingers into the corded strength of his shoulders.

"Cain."

"This?"

Her breath caught as his thumbs traced the outline of her nipples. Sensation burst through her, surprising her, shaking her. She arched against his caressing hands and felt her body burn with unfamiliar fire.

Then his hands shifted and the buttons of her blouse slowly began to come undone. With a soft whimper, she sought his mouth again. She kissed him with a hunger so new she didn't know how to disguise or control it. Yet no matter how deeply she kissed him, his hands didn't hurry their careful unbuttoning of her blouse. She twisted against him, silently offering him the freedom of her body.

For long seconds he didn't take her gift. He simply deepened the kiss even more, until she was dizzy with his taste and with the slow penetration and retreat of his tongue.

Even after her blouse was finally undone, he didn't caress the breasts or the nipples that had turned into tight crowns at his first touch. His fingers stroked her neck, the hollow of her throat, her collarbones, her breastbone, until she moaned and twisted with anticipation and need. When his long finger finally slid beneath the sheer lace of her bra, she cried out with pleasure.

"God," he said hoarsely. "You're going to push me over the edge before I've really touched you."

She barely heard him. His fingertips were plucking delicately at the tips of her breasts, sending streamers of fire from her throat to her knees. Tiny sounds of pleasure and hunger rippled from her throat. When her bra loosened suddenly, she whispered his name even as she arched her back, giving herself to him.

His hands closed gently, taking the warm weight of her breasts while his thumbs teased her taut nipples. She felt the subtle textures of his palm and the calluses at the base of his long, elegant fingers as he pleasured her until her breathing was ragged and broken. Never had a man been so knowing, so careful with her.

She arched in sensual reflex against his hands, lifting her breasts to be kissed. The touch of his tongue was agonizing and delicious. When he took the sensitized nipple into his mouth, heat shot through her core. When he drew rhythmically on her, daggers of fire burst through her.

She moaned her pleasure and his name and felt the shudder that ripped through his strength. Even as he turned to her other breast, she felt the sudden release of pressure at the waist of her borrowed Levi's.

Cain's hand slid between cloth and skin. When his fingers

eased between Christy's naked legs, she shifted, allowing him to touch her. Demanding that he touch her.

The feel of his warm hand curling around her, cupping her, dragged a hoarse sound of need from both of them. She melted in his hand, moaning softly and lifting her hips in a sensual reflex that was new to her. She'd never offered herself so openly before. She was completely aroused, able to take him deep inside.

Cain knew it. He could feel it, see it, breathe it. He caressed her slowly, and the sound he made was that of a man in pain.

She understood, for the pleasure of his touch was so intense it was nearly agony. Blindly she lifted against him. Never had she felt so free and yet so enthralled. His name broke on her lips as flames coursed wildly through her, a fire started by the sweet friction of his hand between her legs.

Even as pleasure claimed Christy, she drew her nails down Cain's back in a silent demand that he finish the sweet torment he'd started. He answered with another slow caress, his hand sultry with her passion. The sleek, gliding touch made her cry out.

"I want you," she said raggedly. "All of you."

His answer was a throttled sound and a deliberate movement of his hand. Before she could draw another quick, shallow breath, she felt a gliding penetration as his fingers probed her with a violent kind of restraint. Her breath came out in a broken moan.

Blindly her hands sought the waistband of his jeans. She fumbled with the metal button for only an instant before his hand shifted, catching her fingers beneath his, preventing her from undressing him.

At first she was too wild with need to understand why she couldn't get the stubborn fastening open. Then she realized that he was preventing her from undressing him.

"Cain?"

There was no answer.

She tilted her head back so that she could see his face. His eyes were golden slits and his mouth was bracketed with effort. His expression was unreadable.

"What—what's wrong?" she asked. "Did I do something wrong?"

He closed his eyes and slowly dragged her hands up to his chest with a grip so harshly restrained it was numbing. Then he said something savage beneath his breath and opened his eyes.

"No, Red." His voice was rough with frustration and pent emotion. "You did everything right. Too damned right. I've never been so close to losing control with a woman in my life as I am right now."

The cold reflection of fire in his eyes made her uneasy. "Isn't that what making love is supposed to be about? Losing control?"

"Christy—" He swore bitterly and looked away from her flushed, bewildered face. "You've made it clear how much you love your sister. Most people care shallowly, if at all. You don't. You care all the way to your soul. It's a great strength."

Christy waited and felt an increasing chill that no hearth fire could warm.

"That kind of caring is also a great weakness," he said bleakly. "Jo-Jo figured that out and used it against you. I can't bring myself to do the same thing."

When Christy understood what he was saying, she felt like she'd been dropped into ice water. "You think I'm a whore."

The shock on his face would have been amusing if she hadn't been so coldly furious.

He grabbed her chin. "I never said anything like that."

"Really? What else do you call a woman who trades sex for something she wants?" She jerked free of his hand.

"Honey, all I meant was that you have a soft spot in your heart—and your head—for your sister. You'd do anything to—"

Christy wrenched herself free of his touch. Ignoring her open blouse and unbuttoned jeans, she reached in her pocket, dragged out a nickel, and flipped it.

"Heads," she snarled.

She caught the coin and she smacked it down onto the back side of her left hand. Without bothering to look which side was up, she jammed the coin back in her pocket.

"You lose," she told Cain. "Now get the hell off my bed."

Chapter 42

Abiquiu
The next morning

The crowing of a rooster in the corral came as a relief to Christy. She was beginning to wonder if she was the only thing alive on Ghost Ranch. The sun had pushed night from the sky what seemed like hours ago. The rooster was a late riser—and proud of it, if the continuous crowing from the corral was any indication. Or maybe she was just bitter because she'd spent too much of the night awake, her thoughts chasing around in smaller and smaller circles.

When she couldn't bear thinking about Jo-Jo any longer, she thought about Cain. Never had a man taken her up so high.

Never had she been dropped so hard.

Even now, in the clear light of dawn, her body seethed with anger and with memories of what it had been like to be fully aroused for the first time in her life.

Too bad he didn't feel the same way.

Tired of her own thoughts, she rolled out of bed. The air in the room was chilly enough to show her breath. Outside, in the open truck bed, Cain must have been cold.

I hope he froze his ass off.

She grabbed the coffeepot, filled it, and banged it down on the burner so hard that water sloshed over. With a hissed word, she moved the pot to another burner, scraped a match against the stove top, and turned on the gas.

By the time the coffee was perking cheerfully, she had a fire going on the hearth. She went back to the stove and began making scrambled eggs. While they cooked slowly, she wrapped the remaining tortillas in a damp cloth and warmed them in the oven.

Sun streamed in the back of the cabin, which had been built to take advantage of the southern exposure. An old wooden glider chair sat on the back porch. She opened the door, found the air delightfully warm, and went outside. Balancing breakfast in her lap, she ate and rocked slowly in the glider, letting the warmth of the southwestern sun chase the chill of the night from her body.

Just as she was eating the last bite, Cain appeared silently at the corner of the house. He was carrying a towel over his shoulder and his hair was wet. He was dressed in different clothes. The heavily faded chambray shirt might have belonged to Constable Moore, but the jeans had come from another source. They fit like a faithful denim shadow, reminding Christy of just how male Cain was. Her mouth turned down and she looked away. She didn't need any reminders.

She didn't want any either.

"Good morning," he said.

"It's morning."

He stopped at the corner of the little porch and looked out at the ranch. "The shower inside is broken, but—"

She interrupted. "I figured that out last night."

"—there's a small stream just up the canyon," he said, ignoring the interruption. "It's not as warm as the hot springs at my cabin, but it gets the job done."

"I took a basin bath last night."

"About last night. It—"

"Forget last night," she cut in ruthlessly.

He looked at her. "Impossible."

"Not at all," she shot back. "I'm quite easy. Scared the pants off you, didn't it? Well, not the pants. You hung on to them valiantly. Be sure to stick a gold star on both cheeks, if you can reach around that far."

With a muttered curse, he swiped a hand through his wet hair. "I shouldn't even have kissed you."

She lifted her coffee cup. "I'll drink to that."

"It's a bad idea for us to get involved. There's too damned many distractions in both our lives at the moment."

"Not to worry. Unlike some people I could mention, I'm not a tease."

His mouth flattened into a grim line.

"And I won't be a distraction in your life," she said. "So far as I'm concerned, last night is a *nolo*."

"What?"

"Lawyer talk. *Nolo contendere*. It didn't happen, and I promise it won't happen again."

"When this whole mess is cleared up, we—"

"Not in your lifetime," she said, cutting across his words. "Not even in your dreams. I'm not a closet masochist."

He muttered something brutal beneath his breath.

"Amen," she said clearly. Then she let out her breath. When she spoke again, her voice was nearly normal. "Your breakfast is in the oven."

"Honey, we can't act as though nothing happened."

"Why not, *honey*? Nothing did!"

She saw that he was on the edge of losing his considerable self-control. She smiled like a cat and waited for the explosion.

For a tense minute, Cain stared into the morning sky. Overhead a pair of hawks circled slowly in a rising column of warm air. Against the cobalt blue of the sky, the wild russet of their tailfeathers burned like fire.

The exact, beautiful color of her hair.

He turned on his heel and walked away. "We better get on the road," he said without looking back. "There's a lot of ground to cover between here and Santa Fe."

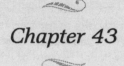

Chapter 43

Santa Fe
Midmorning

The plaza at Santa Fe and the streets around it were crowded with cars and motor homes. Flatlanders jostled one another for the best view of the Navajo jewelry vendors who had spread their velvet blankets on the shaded sidewalks in front of the Governors' Palace and the Museum of Fine Arts.

Canyon Road did business more sedately. The high-ticket galleries didn't hang out welcome signs or wait with open doors and cash registers. Canyon Road galleries invited only the most discriminating to enter and do business.

Or the most wealthy.

Cain cruised past the Sherberne Gallery twice before he circled the block and found a parking spot on a side street.

"Good," he said to himself, because he was the only one talking to him. "I was afraid it wouldn't be open for two hours."

"Do most of the galleries open after noon?" Christy's

voice was hoarse, like someone just waking up or a person who hadn't talked for hours. Both were true. She'd slept on the way and hadn't said one word otherwise.

"The snotty ones keep whatever hours they want," he said, looking at her almost warily. Apparently, when it came to business, she'd talk to him. It made a nice change.

"They're not going to be happy if you just walk in and start asking about stolen artifacts."

"As my cellmate used to say, if you can't do the time, don't do the crime."

She grimaced.

He opened his door. "I'll be back in—"

"I'm coming with you."

A single look told him he could have a screaming match at the curb or he could shut up and take her along. He wondered if it was too late to go back to the silent treatment.

"Do you have the letters that mention Sherberne?" he asked tightly.

She lifted a battered manila envelope.

"Are you familiar with the good-cop bad-cop routine?" he asked.

"Yes."

"Guess which you're going to be."

"Bad cop."

"Guess again."

He stalked to the gallery door with her hurrying along behind. The silver bell over the gallery door was delighted to announce their entry. A slim, tan, and sun-blond male in a white cowboy shirt emerged from the back room.

"Sherberne himself," Cain said very softly to her.

Sherberne's bolo tie was held by a chunk of turquoise the size of a hen's egg. His polite smile faded as he took in Cain's clothes. By the time the man catalogued Christy's well-used outfit, his welcoming expression had disappeared completely.

"May I help you with something," he said.

It wasn't a question. His expression said he didn't have anything they could afford to want.

Cain and Christy looked around the gallery. The decor was Santa Fe modern, white-on-white adobe walls, polished glass display cases, and intensely focused overhead lights. The cases were full of excellent artifacts, yet he catalogued and dismissed them with a single educated glance.

Good, but not unique.

"Mr. Art Sherberne, right?" Cain asked.

Sherberne hesitated, then nodded slightly.

Cain's easy smile turned hard. He went to the front door, snapped the deadbolt into place, and turned the OPEN sign around.

"What are you *doing*?" Sherberne asked in a rising voice as he took a step toward his desk.

"Forget your silent alarm," Cain said calmly. "The last guys you want in your lap right now are cops."

The gallery owner froze like a man who knew exactly what Cain was talking about.

"What do you have in mind?" Sherberne asked.

"I'm looking for some pots," Cain said. "Good San Juan Basin black-on-whites, ones that use Kokopelli motifs and maybe a tortoise clan symbol."

Sherberne's eyes widened fractionally. "I'm afraid I can't help you."

"Just like that? You don't even have to check an inventory sheet?"

"Items such as those you described are quite rare. I don't have any."

"You're certain?"

"I personally select every piece that passes through this gallery," Sherberne snapped.

Cain smiled like a wolf. "Then you'd be able to tell me whether you've handled any pieces like that in the past."

"That's none of your business."

"Don't bet on it."

Sherberne didn't like whatever he saw in Cain's eyes. The gallery owner looked away. "Who are you?"

Cain ignored the question and asked one of his own. "Have you handled goods using symbols of either Kokopelli or a tortoise?"

Sherberne's jaw worked. "No."

"Wrong answer." Cain turned to Christy. "Show him the letters."

She brought out the envelopes that had Sherberne Gallery in their return address.

Sherberne swallowed.

"Does the name Christa Jody McKinley mean anything to you?" Christy asked.

Sherberne's thin, tanned face turned as pale as his shirt. He looked at Cain with dawning horror.

"You're the—" Abruptly Sherberne regained control and stopped talking.

"I'm the what?" Cain asked.

Sherberne shook his head.

"Don't be a fool," Cain said. "These letters prove you're involved in the buying and selling of stolen property."

"Stolen?"

Sherberne looked genuinely surprised. He went to his desk, picked up a pack of cigarettes, and shook one out. After it was lit he stood and looked at Cain narrowly.

"So, you did handle the pieces," Christy said.

Blowing a stream of smoke, Sherberne nodded.

"Where are they?" Cain asked.

"Sold."

"Japan or Germany?"

The gallery owner gave Cain a hard look. "I don't discuss business with strangers. Unless, of course, you're the police and are carrying badges to prove it?"

Cain and Christy didn't say a word.

"Good-bye," Sherberne said. "It hasn't been a pleasure."

"We can get the police, if that's what you want," Cain offered.

"Listen," the other man snarled. "I vetted the documentation. It was adequate to the letter of the law."

Cain smiled thinly. "You know a lot about criminal law for a guy in the fine art business."

"I've bought and sold artifacts for years. I've been rousted by the Bureau of Land Management, the Navajo Tribal Police, and even the Federal Bureau of Investigation."

"Am I supposed to be impressed?" Cain asked.

"Nobody's ever caught me with a stolen pot or one whose provenance is suspect in the eyes of the law. And nobody ever will."

"That means you have documentation on the items the McKinley woman sold you," Christy said, forcing a pleasant tone and smile.

"Of course."

"Then they were legally dug," she said.

"That's what the paper said. It was notarized, by the way."

"Of course," Cain said under his breath.

"And you believed her," Christy said with a sad shake of her head for male frailty.

"Naturally."

"This Christa Jody McKinley," she said carefully. "Do you know where she is right now?"

"More or less." Sherberne shrugged.

"Where?" she asked instantly.

"Hell would be my best guess."

"What does that mean?" Cain asked.

Sherberne smiled maliciously. "It means the bitch is dead."

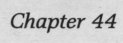

Chapter 44

Cain put a hand on Christy's arm, caution and reassurance at the same time.

"No," Christy said in a low voice. "Damn it, *no*."

Sherberne looked at her oddly.

"Are you sure?" Cain asked, drawing the man's attention.

The gallery owner took an impatient drag on his cigarette. "Yes."

"I don't believe it," Christy said. "She can't be dead."

"Why not?" Sherberne said with a shrug. "If ever a woman deserved it, she did."

Christy couldn't answer.

"Look, if you don't believe me, try the morgue," Sherberne said curtly to Cain. "Not that you'll be able to identify her. She and her half-smart boyfriend crashed his new plane over half the landing strip. Took a day just to pick up the pieces. At first it looked accidental, but now the cops are thinking sabotage."

Abruptly Christy believed that Jo-Jo was dead. A cold wave broke over her, loneliness and regret, guilt and despair.

Sweet child loved by everyone.

Beautiful woman loved by no one.

Color drained from the world first, then black ate from the edges to the center, shutting down her vision.

Cain caught her. "Breathe, Red. Deep and hard. Breathe!"

Blindly she reached for him, hanging on to his strength while the world spun sickeningly around her. She fought for breath, forcing air into her numb body, breathing deeply until the roaring in her ears stopped and color returned to her vision again.

With it came pain.

She bit back a cry and gathered the shreds of her self-control. The pain of biting her own lip helped. It told her that she was alive.

"At least Jo-Jo doesn't hurt anymore. Does she?" Christy didn't know she had spoken aloud until she heard Cain's low voice and felt the warmth of his breath against her ear.

"She doesn't hurt anymore," he whispered, stroking her hair. "Whatever demon was eating Jo-Jo alive died with her."

With a great effort, Christy lifted her head and looked at Cain. His eyes were watching her with an aching kind of sympathy, silently telling her that he would haven taken the pain for her if he could have.

"I'm sorry," he whispered.

"She was my sister."

"I understand."

"Do you?"

"She knew you as a child, when the future had no limits. And now she's dead and there are too many limits."

Christy fought against the tears she'd never cried for a loss she'd never before admitted. Jo-Jo wasn't within Christy's ability to heal now.

She never had been.

The funeral hadn't been held, but Jo-Jo had been dead to Christy for half her life. And Christy had been grieving for half her life. There wasn't much left now, of either hope or hate, love or grief. It was over.

It had been over for a long time.

"You can let go," Christy said quietly. "I'm all right now."

"You look pale."

"I always look pale. I'm a redhead."

Reluctantly he loosened his hold. But he stood very close, watching her intently.

"I'm fine," she said. "Just fine."

When he was certain she could stand alone, he shifted his attention to Sherberne.

The gallery owner took one look at Cain's face and backed up several steps before bumping into a glass case.

"What makes you think there was something fishy about the plane crash?" Cain asked.

"The plane was sabotaged. The police assume it was a drug-related killing."

"Why?"

"Because the two of them acted like cocaine dealers," Sherberne said. "Lots of cash, no class."

"When was the last time you saw them?"

Sherberne folded his lips and didn't say a word.

"Talk to me," Cain said, "or I'll do the kind of damage your insurance doesn't cover."

The gallery owner hadn't gotten where he was by being a bad judge of character. He started talking. Fast. "Day before yesterday. Just before they went to the airport."

"Were they selling stuff to you or just collecting money?"

"Selling. It surprised me. I didn't think they had anything left."

"Did you buy?" Cain asked.

"Yes."

"Do you still have it?"

Sherberne didn't want to answer, but he did anyway. "Yes. It's in the basement. They were in a hell of a rush."

"Let's see it."

"Mother," Sherberne muttered as he stubbed out his cigarette. "Sure. Why not?"

They followed him through his office into a basement work area that was as messy as the gallery was coldly ordered.

"It's not the sort of material I usually handle," Sherberne said with distaste. "Not on consignment. Not even on outright sale."

Cain looked around hungrily. Artifacts were scattered over tables and on chairs, heaped on the floor, and crowded shelves and cupboards on the walls.

"I didn't want it at all," Sherberne said, "but they were so desperate to sell, I took it for a flat fee on consignment."

"Where is it?" Cain asked.

Sherberne went to one of the worktables. As he started to lift the lid on a rectangular box that took up most of the table, he looked warily at Christy. "You're kind of squeamish. Maybe you'd do better upstairs."

"Open it," she said.

"Suit yourself."

He took off the lid.

The long box was lined with a plastic foam such as was used in packing photographic material. The foam had been hollowed to cushion long, darkly stained pieces of what looked like wood.

But it wasn't wood.

Empty eye sockets looked out from an equally empty skull. Arms, shoulders, and most of the rib cage were intact, as were the pelvic girdle and one leg.

Christy forced herself to look at the remains without emotion. Death wasn't fresh to these bones. They'd been a long,

long time in their grave before being dragged unwilling into the sunlight.

"I told the woman there wasn't a big market for human remains. She really wanted to sell. She said she'd take as little as five thousand."

"Five thousand?" Christy asked, horrified. "You can get five thousand dollars for a human skeleton?"

"Twice that, probably," Sherberne said. "Maybe three times that. Depends on the collector."

She looked at Cain.

"Collectors are a strange lot," he said. "They collect anything, including human bones."

"Lovely," she said.

"But I'm not wired into that end of the artifacts trade," Sherberne said. "She left this on consignment anyway."

Cain glanced around the workroom. "Judging by the goods I see here, I'm surprised anything is beneath you."

Sherberne shot him an angry look.

"I draw the line at bones," Sherberne said. "Ghoulish collectors and Moki sorcerers are not my thing."

"Moki sorcerers?" she asked quickly. "What are they?"

"Medicine men who practice the black arts," Cain explained. "They claim to be descendants of the Anasazi."

"What do they want bones for, stage dressing for their shows?" she asked Sherberne.

He didn't answer.

Cain did. "They use skulls for certain ceremonies. Some of them grind up bones to use for devil powder."

"Devil powder," she said neutrally.

"Soul poison. Some of the Navajo and Pueblo medicine men use powdered human bones to strengthen their curses."

A feeling of dread welled up. She'd felt the same thing the first time she saw the bone fragment in the alcove, and again when a gold necklace and bone splinters had tumbled out into her palm. She'd felt the clammy sensation in one other place too.

Peter Hutton's private gallery of demons.

The dread was primitive and soul deep, an acknowledgment that immense darkness existed just beyond the circle of firelight called civilization.

"Anything else I can do for you?" Sherberne asked with exaggerated courtesy.

"Yeah," Cain said. "When the police backtrack the blonde to your gallery—and they will—forget we were ever here."

Sherberne shrugged.

"In return," Cain continued, "we'll forget that we know where the blonde stole her stuff."

"My hands are clean."

"Good for you," Christy said. "I'm sure the reporters will point out how innocent you are."

"Reporters?" Sherberne looked unhappy.

"Right now, only the three of us know who sold off Peter Hutton's stolen artifacts," she said. "If you don't tell the police we were here, we won't tell the newspapers who sold the pots."

"And the bones," Cain offered. "Don't forget them."

"Ah, yes. The bones." She grimaced. "Headline stuff. Famous designer double-crossed by famous model. Sex and skeletons. The media will be slobbering. They won't care what kind of documents Mr. Sherberne says he has."

"You have made your point," Sherberne said. "I won't mention you to the police."

She looked at Cain and asked, "Does that cover it?"

"Almost."

Cain put the lid back on the box, picked it up, and tucked it under his arm.

"Wait a minute!" Sherberne said. "You can't—"

"It was on consignment," Cain said. "We're taking it back.

If you don't like it, think how much your customers would like having their names attached to the underground trade in human remains."

"Ridiculous. I've never—"

"Right," Cain cut in. "And now you never will."

Silently they walked out of the basement, through the gallery, and out the doors.

"Do you think it will work?" Christy asked when the doors shut behind them.

"Probably, until someone uses a better twist on him."

She didn't say anything while they walked to the truck. Nor did she say anything while Cain unfastened a corner of the vinyl cover that protected the open bed of the pickup, slid the box underneath, and fastened the cover again.

When they were both sitting inside the truck, Christy let out a long breath. "Now what?" she asked.

"Albuquerque and the Bureau of Land Management."

"Why?"

"Johnny thought they could save his ass. Maybe they can save ours instead."

Chapter 45

Albuquerque lay under a dirty blanket of smog. East-west traffic on Interstate 40 melded unevenly with the north-south flow on Interstate 25. When Cain walked out of a telephone booth in a service station for the second time that day, he looked at the sky unhappily. He was feeling edgy as a coyote on Main Street. Paranoid to the point of using public phones. The urban haze didn't make him feel better.

The fact that Christy was about as much company as the skeleton in the box didn't help. She wasn't so much grieving as emotionally spent, running on empty. Shut down.

"Larry got the investigator's name for us from some other cops," Cain said as he climbed into the truck.

She turned, looked at him, and nodded.

He realized it wasn't the silence that was getting to him as much as the shuttered pain and open exhaustion in her eyes.

"It's all set up," he said. "His name is Hoyt Jackson. He agreed to a deep background interview for *Horizon*."

"We're going to interview a *cop*?"

"Hoyt Jackson is more archaeologist than cop."

She didn't look convinced.

"You can go home anytime," he reminded her gently.

"You wanted to find out who tried to kill you," she said tonelessly. "You found out. Now I want to find out who killed Jo-Jo. Then I'll be able to walk away from it all." *Including the man I wanted who didn't want me.* "But until then, I'm your shadow."

He started the engine. "Just as well. I'd rather keep an eye on you until I'm sure you're safe."

"What a hero," she said under her breath. "First he saves me from myself, then he saves me from the world."

Cain's hands tightened on the steering wheel. He had a hard enough time explaining to himself why he'd pulled back last night; he sure as hell couldn't explain it to her.

So he stuck with what he could explain.

"No one knows about Jay and Jo-Jo," he said in a rough voice. "Johnny's death hasn't hit the news yet. Danner found my truck where Larry left it in the woods. If anyone has noticed you're gone, they aren't raising a fuss."

"No surprise. No one is left who cares."

"I care."

"Give me a break," she said wearily. "We both know just how much you care."

"Last night had nothing to do with caring!"

"Yeah, I figured that out all by myself."

"Honey—"

"Besides," she continued, talking right over him, "last night never happened, remember?"

"Shit."

"Amen." She put her head against the seat and closed her eyes.

He set his jaw and headed through the smog.

Neither one of them spoke again until they were inside

Hoyt Jackson's office. The BLM investigator's room looked like it belonged to a pack rat on speed. The tiny desk was stacked haphazardly with paperwork. The shelves of free-standing bookcases on three walls were crammed with boxes of potsherds and whole artifacts. Every box and artifact was marked with an official-looking tag that said EVIDENCE. The tags were the only sign of organization in the whole office.

Hoyt Jackson wore a khaki shirt with BLM shoulder patches, but the rest of his uniform was as haphazard as his office. His work boots were badly scarred and his Levi's hung low beneath a spreading belly. His face was tanned where it wasn't bearded. Metal-rimmed reading glasses sat crookedly on his big nose. He looked less like a cop than any cop Christy had ever seen.

Jackson cleared boxes of corrugated grayware sherds from two office chairs and motioned for Cain and Christy to sit down.

"What can I do for you?" he asked.

"I'm writing a piece on southwestern artifacts for *Horizon*," she said, letting professional reflexes take over. "Aaron Cain is acting as my guide."

"As I told Constable Moore after Joe got in touch with me," Jackson said, "I really ought to refer you to our public information office for any press interviews."

"This is strictly for background," she said. "I'm interested in the traffic in illegal artifacts from the Southwest to New York. Larry said you were the best man in the West on that subject."

The compliment pleased Jackson, but he still looked uneasy.

"I won't so much as mention your name in the article unless you specifically want me to," she assured him. "What I need from you is enough background to ask intelligent questions of the people who *will* be named and quoted."

He still looked a little skeptical, but finally he shrugged. "Joe said Larry was solid. Larry vouched for you two. I'll do what I can."

"Thank you," she said.

"Where do you want to start?"

"I'm particularly interested in the activities of a man named Johnny Ten Hats."

"Ten Hats, huh? Yeah, that ol' boy has a few tales to tell. Have you tried interviewing him?"

"He gave us your name," Cain said when she hesitated.

Jackson shifted like a man who wasn't comfortable.

"Johnny told me he was working with the Bureau of Land Management," she said, hoping her voice didn't show her strain.

"I hope the bastard—'scuse me, ma'am, but Ten Hats and I don't exactly get along."

She smiled reassuringly. "Was Johnny working with you?"

"He's not an employee, and he's certainly not an informant."

"How would you describe him, then?"

Jackson tugged at his chin whiskers and squinted over his glasses, first at Christy and then at Cain.

"You've already talked with him?" Jackson asked.

Cain nodded.

"Did he mention his aunt?" Jackson asked.

"He mentioned a lot of things," Christy said before Cain could open his mouth. "The point is, we don't know how much of what he said is true. What did he tell you about his aunt?"

Cain gave her a look of veiled admiration.

"Smart of you to check, young lady," Jackson said. "Ten Hats isn't the most trustworthy sort of man."

"That's why we came to someone with a reputation for integrity." Smiling encouragingly, Christy waited for the investigator to continue.

Jackson settled more comfortably in his chair. "Ten Hats has an aunt in Rio Arriba County, name of Molly. She got herself in some serious trouble a few months ago, digging where she wasn't supposed to be digging."

"I see," Christy murmured.

"She's really a fine old lady. She just doesn't understand that her people don't hold title to all this land anymore."

"Where was she digging?" Cain asked.

"Some ruin down near Chaco Canyon. One of our young patrol officers found her."

"Digging, huh?" Cain asked. "That means a felony charge?"

"Yeah," Jackson sighed. "What a stink. A more experienced patrolman would have handled it differently. . . ."

Cain made a sympathetic sound.

"Anyway," Jackson said, "Johnny Ten Hats came in to see me, trying to work out some kind of deal."

"For his aunt?" Christy asked.

Jackson nodded. "He wanted to provide information against someone else in return for his aunt's freedom."

"Is that sort of thing done?" Christy asked.

The BLM investigator looked uncomfortable again.

"All the time," Cain said. "It's called plea bargaining."

Reluctantly Jackson nodded.

"What did Johnny tell you?" Christy asked.

"A lot of bull, apparently. Said he would give me a big case involving lots of pots and famous folks from New York."

"Did he?"

"Not so far." Jackson grinned. "Matter of fact, that's the reason I'm talking to you right now, you being from New York and all. I figured you might be able to do me some good."

"I might," she said evenly, "if I knew what Johnny was after. What did he tell you?"

"Not one single hard fact."

"How many times did you talk to him?"

"Three times. Ten Hats would make vague statements about New York and then ask me how we connect a pot with one piece of land after the pot has been dug and sold and no one is talking."

She sensed Cain's sudden alertness, but he didn't say anything.

"I finally decided Ten Hats was just trying to learn how to be a better Moki poacher," Jackson said, "so I told him to get lost unless he had some hard evidence for me to process."

"When was that?" she asked.

Frowning, Jackson picked up a smooth, wedge-shaped black stone from his desk and hefted it a few times. "Not long ago. Frankly, I didn't like the way Ten Hats was acting. Thought he was crazy."

"Was what he told you that strange?" she asked.

Jackson sighed and put the wedge-shaped rock back down.

When the silence lengthened, Cain reached for the smooth black stone. "Nice gastrolith."

Jackson gave a little hoot of delight and approval. "Not many folks recognize a dinosaur gizzard stone."

"I've seen a lot of them in Moki digs."

"Why do you think the Anasazi carried these stones around?" Jackson asked eagerly. "I'm collecting theories."

"They probably used them to smooth out the marks on the inside of their pots," Cain said. As he spoke, his thumb described slow circles on the stone.

Christy watched and remembered just how sensual his touch could be. Color rose in her cheeks.

He saw it and smiled. "Or maybe," he added in a deep voice, "they just liked the satin feel of them."

Smiling, Jackson nodded. "Yeah, I kinda lean toward that theory."

"Are you still pursuing the case against Ten Hats' aunt?" Cain asked.

"Molly is an old lady." Jackson hesitated, then said, "Just between us, I'm going to lose the file."

"Where is Molly now?" Christy asked.

"Don't know for sure."

"Who might?"

Jackson thought a moment. He pulled open a drawer, found a file folder, and sorted through a dozen scraps of paper and bar napkins that were covered with notes. Finally he found a telephone number written on the back of an envelope that looked like it had once held a utility bill.

"Her full name is Molly Faces-the-Sun," Jackson said.

Again Christy sensed Cain's sudden intense interest.

And again he said nothing.

"Molly lives out beyond Cuba, between there and a spot called Counselors," Jackson said. "There's a little two-pump gas station just after you cross the county line into Rio Arriba County. Ask there. Somebody'll give you directions."

He tore a page off his calendar pad, wrote a telephone number down, and handed it to Christy.

"That's her daughter's phone number," Jackson said. "You might call her first, but I wouldn't do it until you're out there. Molly can make herself real scarce if she doesn't want to talk to you." He pushed back from the desk and came to his feet, signaling the end of the interview.

Reluctantly, Christy and Cain stood up.

"Thank you," she said, taking the paper. "We appreciate your time."

"You're welcome. If you really appreciate it, you'll tell me what Molly was digging for and why."

"She didn't tell you?" Cain asked.

"Not one word. She just clammed up."

"It must have been a religious matter."

"Think so?" Jackson asked.

"She Who Faces the Sun is the name the clan sorceress takes when she is initiated into her duties. If a woman with that name was digging in ancestral grounds, she was doing it for spiritual reasons." Cain smiled. "Losing her file is a good idea."

"Be damned. Thanks. I get so involved in old pots that I forget the modern tribes are people too."

Cain nodded and shook the hand Jackson was holding out.

"Was Johnny interested in any particular investigative method?" Cain asked as the handshake ended.

Jackson took the question, inspected it, rolled it over in his mind like it was a smooth stone. Then he looked right at Cain.

"He wanted to know how we proved that an artifact came from a particular dig," Jackson said, "even if the documentation said it came from somewhere else."

"Can you do that?" Christy asked, surprised.

Jackson grinned like a cop. "Yes, ma'am. We sure can."

"How?" Cain asked.

"Ask the lab boys up at Los Alamos—if you can get past the gate. As for me, I just send them the dirt and read the bottom line."

Cain doubted that Jackson was telling the whole truth, but didn't push. The BLM investigator had told them as much as he was going to.

As soon as they were out of Jackson's office and on the deserted street, Christy said, "Well, now we know why Johnny was ready to kill for a bag of grave dirt."

Chapter 46

Cain paused in the act of opening the truck passenger door. "You don't miss much, Red."

"I'm dynamite on the little things." She pulled the door the rest of the way open and climbed in. "It's the big things that nail me every time."

He circled the hood and came in on the driver's side. The truck door slammed behind him.

"What big things?" he asked.

"Like having a sister who is a murderer and not suspecting a damned thing. Like getting seduced by a man who couldn't hold his nose long enough to finish the job."

"Damn it, that's not—"

"*Nolo,*" she interrupted, rubbing her forehead. "My fault. I'm sorry. I'm not as tightly wrapped as usual. I really didn't mean to bring it up, and it won't happen again."

"Last night had nothing to do with how much I wanted you." His voice was as hard as his face.

"Last night had nothing to do with anything." She looked at her watch and remembered the map she'd read. "Is there time to get to Ruby or wherever before dark?"

"Yes."

"Good. The sooner this is over with, the sooner we can get on with our lives."

"Missing your boyfriend?" Cain asked acidly, starting the truck and pulling into traffic.

"I don't have a boyfriend."

"Then what are you in such a hurry to get back to? Your job?"

"My job?" With a broken laugh Christy leaned against the seat and looked out the passenger window. "I'll be shocked if my job lasts longer than the Hutton assignment."

"Then what's the rush?"

"What's the point of staying? Jo-Jo is dead. There's nothing here for me but the sordid history of a sister I always loved and sometimes hated and never really knew at all."

Cain would rather have heard anger than the bleak acceptance in Christy's voice. He glanced at her, wondering if her eyes held any less pain. Her head was leaning against the window. Though open, her eyes weren't focused on anything.

"You can't change the past," he said. "You can only change the future."

She wanted to tell him to go to hell, but it was too much effort. She rolled the window down a few inches, letting the cool afternoon air into the truck.

After many miles, the air and the austere beauty of the desert penetrated her fog of emotional exhaustion. She sat straighter and looked at the man she'd known only two days.

Two days. God. How can only two days have passed? Jo-Jo is dead. I've seen a man killed. Nick is history. My job soon will be.

And I'm on the run with an ex-con.

"Ready to talk?" Cain asked.

"About what?"

"Whatever you're thinking."

"I'm thinking that time is unreliable."

"Two days seem like two years?"

Startled, she looked at him. "How did you know?"

"I've had the same two days."

Her laugh had more sadness than humor in it, but it was still a laugh. "Yeah, I guess you have. But you don't look like you've been run over by a truck."

"It's a trick I learned in jail. When the big things get you down, think about the little ones."

"Does it work?"

"Most of the time," he said.

"And when it doesn't?"

"I get run over by a truck."

She took a deep breath and let it out. "All right. Little things it is. You first."

"Peter Hutton's treasure room was packed with so many extraordinary artifacts that he didn't notice when Jo-Jo and Jay skimmed off a million bucks, wholesale," Cain said. "Your turn."

"Johnny knew. He had to. He was doing the digging for Hutton."

"Right. I suspect he was also doing the skimming for Jo-Jo."

Christy frowned. "What went wrong? Why did Jo-Jo and Jay take off running?"

"Maybe Johnny asked for more money. Or maybe they didn't want to pay him at all." Cain hesitated, then added, "Maybe they figured a piece of Jo-Jo's action was all the pay Johnny needed."

"Whatever," Christy said, "they grabbed one last artifact and took off for Santa Fe. And then she died."

"If it was sabotage," he said in a matter-of-fact voice, "there are two possibilities."

She heard as though at a distance.

"Your turn," he said. "Little things, honey. Just the little ones."

She let out a ragged breath and gathered her thoughts.

"Who gained from the sabotage?" he prompted.

"Johnny, if he'd been double-crossed. And Hutton, who certainly had been double-crossed."

"But Johnny was blackmailing Jo-Jo and Jay," Cain said. "If he kills them, he loses a cash cow."

"That leaves Hutton." Christy frowned.

"He's my favorite candidate."

"Why?"

"I recently discovered that if Johnny wanted to kill someone, he would do it head-on."

"The way he was at the alcove?" she said.

"Yes. Sabotage isn't his style."

"But . . ."

"But what?"

"Hutton may have been selling artifacts and not reporting the income, but that's not worth killing someone to keep quiet."

"Jealousy," Cain said.

"From the man who liked watching Jo-Jo in bed with other men?" Christy asked, her voice rough with distaste. "Besides, he was through with her."

"Punishment for stealing from him?" Cain offered.

"Having Jo-Jo arrested for theft, stripping her of her position and her pride—that would have been punishment. Why didn't Hutton do that?"

For several miles there was silence.

"I'll bet Johnny knew the answer," Cain said.

"I wonder if Hutton has any half-literate notes in his file, signed by Johnny. Blackmail is a good reason for murder."

"You're forgetting something, honey."

"What?"

"I'm the one who killed Johnny. If there are any notes in Hutton's files, Jay or Jo-Jo signed them."

A long line of cars appeared on the highway ahead, coming out of the sun toward Christy and Cain. When they drew nearer, the reason for the tightly bunched cars became obvious. A New Mexico Highway Patrol cruiser was driving along at the exact speed limit—fifty-five miles per hour—which forced civilians to form a slow, sullen parade just behind him.

Both Christy and Cain held their breath and watched the truck's mirrors, half expecting to see the cruiser turn around and come after them.

The badlands convoy kept going and disappeared over a rise.

"I hope Molly Faces-the-Sun knows what Johnny knew," Cain said. "We can't keep running forever."

Chapter 47

Rio Arriba
Afternoon

The service station at the Rio Arriba County line was baked pale by the sun and haunted by wind. Cain parked beside one of the two old pumps and opened the door. As he got out, a pair of ravens flew off the branch of a cedar tree, cawing their displeasure at being disturbed.

Without waiting for the attendant, Cain started filling the tank. He was halfway through the job when a slight middle-aged man in a greasy coverall and a Stetson emerged from the tarpaper shack that served as office and service bay.

The attendant nodded a silent greeting and went to work on the windshield with a wet sponge and squeegee. There was a patch over his breast pocket that said he was HOMER. The man was clearly of southwestern ancestry—Spanish, Indian, Mexican, and Anglo, all intermixed in a weathered whole.

Homer barely noticed Christy when she got out to stretch her legs.

"We're looking for a woman called Molly Faces-the-Sun," Cain said casually. "I understand she lives around here."

For all the response Homer gave, he could have been deaf. He kept on working on the truck's window in dogged silence. When he finished one side, he looked at Cain for the first time.

"She lives out there," Homer said.

His chin jerked toward the general area of the desert beyond the tarpaper shack. With that, he circled around to the other side of the truck and began cleaning the second section of windshield.

" 'Out there' is a big place," Cain said.

"She likes big places because she don't like visitors."

Cain and Christy exchanged a glance over the back of the truck. He shook his head very slightly, silently telling her to leave it to him. He finished pumping gas and racked the nozzle.

An Indian woman appeared in the doorway of the shack. Dark and thick-bodied, her hair was absolutely black except for a few threads of silver at the temples. She wore a western shirt, jeans, and dark glasses that hid her eyes.

A distinct feeling of being watched came over Christy. She turned and nodded to the woman politely.

There was no reaction. The woman's stare wasn't friendly, curious, or even hostile. It was simply intense. Unreadable.

"It's important that we talk to Molly," Cain said, choosing his words carefully.

"Why?" the attendant asked baldly.

"It has to do with her nephew, Johnny Ten Hats."

The attendant glanced once at the woman in the doorway. She didn't move or make any sign. Homer laid down the sponge and went to work with his squeegee.

"Molly is too busy," the woman said in a clear voice. "And Johnny is dead."

"I know," Cain said. "I heard his death song."

The woman stepped forward and took off her dark glasses. She looked at Cain, then at Christy.

"How did he die?" she asked quietly.

"Police say he was pushed, Eunice," the attendant said. "Pushed by a white man."

Homer looked at Cain.

When Cain met his glance, Homer went back to cleaning windows. For a few moments there was no sound but that of the squeegee, the ghostly exhalation of the wind, and the two huge ravens settling back into their cedar tree.

"Johnny was acting crazy," Cain said. "He was going to kill both of us."

Eunice and Homer turned to look at Christy.

Cain was still talking. "We fought. When he tried to knock me over the edge of a cliff, I ducked. Johnny kept going."

The Indian woman's eyes hadn't left Christy, as if she was using the white woman's face as a lie detector.

"Cain didn't want to kill anyone," Christy said. "He risked his life trying *not* to kill. But Johnny—" She made a small, futile gesture with her hands, asking for understanding.

Eunice and Homer didn't say a word. They simply watched Christy's haunted eyes.

"Johnny wouldn't stop," Christy said in a low voice. "He just wouldn't *stop*."

The ravens rasped at the wind and each other, flaring their wings and walking on stiff, springy legs along a dead branch.

"Johnny was always a little crazy," Homer admitted.

He rubbed his hands on the legs of the coverall and went back to cleaning the window. But his expression was still sour, as if Johnny's craziness didn't excuse what Cain had done.

Eunice looked in Homer's direction. She seemed irritated with him, like a wife who thinks her husband is a fool.

"What can Molly do for the man who killed her nephew?" Eunice asked.

Again, her question was addressed to Cain, but it was Christy's face she watched.

"Johnny was involved in an important dig on a ranch in Colorado," Cain said. "Now Johnny is dead. There were others involved in the dig. Some of them are also dead. We want to know why."

"Why would Molly know anything about a dig so far away?"

"Johnny tried to get Molly out of trouble by selling information about the dig to Hoyt Jackson, who works for the BLM."

The raven-haired woman continued to study Christy's face for a few moments longer. Then she nodded and replaced her sunglasses.

And said nothing more.

"One of the others who died was my sister," Christy said.

Eunice became very still. She pulled off her sunglasses again and looked at Christy. *Into* her.

"Your sister?" Eunice asked.

"Yes."

"Did you know her well?"

Cain's eyes narrowed at the odd question. He stared at Eunice as intently as the woman was staring at Christy.

"I thought I did," Christy said. "But I didn't. She was a mystery to me. Now she always will be."

"The secret sister," Eunice whispered. Her breath came out in a hissing sigh. "She Who Faces the Sun must know. We have waited a long time."

The Indian woman turned and walked into the tarpaper shed.

Homer straightened, wiped the squeegee on his pants, and turned to Cain. "Wait here. She'll be back."

"What was that about the secret sister?" Cain asked.

Homer went deaf again.

Cain looked at Christy. She was rubbing her palms over her arms.

"Need a jacket?" he asked.

She shook her head. "Just goose bumps."

Without a word, he stepped closer and put his arm around her, pulling her against his side. She stiffened but didn't fight the intimacy. She was too frayed to turn away from the human closeness she needed right now as much as she needed air.

"Don't be afraid," he said softly. "Pueblo customs may seem strange to you, but they won't hurt you."

"It's unnerving to be part of something that belongs to a people and a religion I know nothing about."

His hand hesitated, then moved gently over her wild red hair.

"The Pueblo people look at the world differently," he said. "They don't separate things into categories. It's all of a piece. It could simply be that Eunice saw something in you that she liked. Therefore, you're her sister."

For an instant Christy closed her eyes. Then she let out breath she hadn't been aware of holding. "Sorry. I overreacted. I feel like I'm living inside out, every nerve exposed and screaming. No defenses."

His arm tightened. He wanted to protect her from what had happened, what might happen yet. And he knew he couldn't. The same ancient customs that worried her also prevented him from sending her away.

If she left, no one would talk to him.

"It will get better," Cain said softly.

She let out another breath. "I hope so."

For a time there was no sound but the wind.

"Honey?"

Her head came up sharply. He was watching with eyes that were both compassionate and unflinching.

"Are you sure you want to keep going?" he asked. "We can stop now."

"No."

He'd expected that. Now he tried to make her understand. "She Who Faces the Sun may not talk to a man. You may have to go to her."

"Alone?"

"Yes. Can you do it?"

She smiled uncertainly at him. "I'll get back to you on that."

There was nothing tentative about Cain's smile, or the approval in his eyes. For a few moments he tightened his arm, drawing her even closer.

Then the wind blew, summoning him. He let go of her and walked toward the cedar trees at the edge of the desert. Hands in his pockets, he stood and looked out over the wild land.

Restlessly, Christy jammed her own hands in her pockets. Her left hand found Jo-Jo's key. Her right hand found the smooth, large bead from the kiva alcove. She wondered if Cain was fingering the oddly shaped piece of turquoise and remembering the hidden alcove where they had nearly died.

And where Johnny Ten Hats had certainly died.

"Cash or credit?" Homer asked from behind her.

"Cash," she said.

She pulled a fifty out of her pocket. Homer made change from the grubby bills in his own jeans. Then he turned and went into the shack, leaving her alone.

When five minutes had gone by, she walked impatiently over to Cain. At her approach, the two ravens leaped into the air, scolding and croaking about being disturbed. But it didn't take long for the birds to settle on the cedar again, watching the humans with Kokopelli's shrewd black eyes.

When the birds stopped talking, she discovered that the wind had a different sound at the edge of the desert. Ancient. Solitary. Whispering of secrets better left unknown.

"Are we waiting for a sign?" she asked tensely.

"Patience, honey. These people don't waste words and they don't wear watches if they can avoid it. Relax and listen to the wind."

"I did."

"Listen some more. There's peace in it."

She listened.

She heard loneliness, not peace.

High overhead a jet drew a white line across the empty sky, telling of people hurtling toward life in a place far removed from the ancient dry land.

I should be on that plane. Away from here, going—where?

Home? I don't have one. There's no one in New York tied to me by blood or choice.

There's no one anywhere.

The shack's door banged as Eunice emerged from the station. She headed toward them, carrying her dark glasses in her hand. When she approached, she ignored Cain and looked Christy straight in the eye.

"She Who Faces the Sun will see you," Eunice said.

"When?" Cain asked.

Eunice didn't answer.

"When?" Christy asked quietly.

"Tomorrow at dawn."

"That long?" she said, dismayed. "Our business is urgent."

"Tomorrow at dawn," Eunice repeated.

"Where?" Christy asked.

"At the great kiva in Chaco, the one you call Pueblo Bonito."

Christy looked at Cain.

He nodded. "I know it. Now ask her why there and why to-morrow at dawn."

For the first time Eunice looked directly at Cain. Whatever she thought didn't show in her expression.

"Why—" Christy began.

"Dawn is sacred," Eunice said. "So is the great kiva. In it, all secrets are known to She Who Faces the Sun."

"We'll be there at dawn," Cain said.

Though the Indian's expression didn't change, Christy was certain Eunice was both amused and pleased by Cain.

"Good," Eunice said.

Then she looked past the white people to the desert. Her eyes moved across it easily, a woman enjoying an old friend's face, remembering old conversations and restful silences. . . .

A light touch on Christy's arm drew her attention back to Cain. Only then did she realize that she'd been staring out over the desert as Eunice had. Christy didn't know how long she'd been standing there. She knew only that Eunice was gone and Cain's hand was warm against her arm.

The wind lifted, combing cool fingers through her hair, whispering to her of time and distance, past and future, and life like a rainbow arched between, connecting everything.

"You're right," she said softly. "There's peace in a desert wind."

Chapter 48

Near Chaco Canyon
Late afternoon

The truck turned south off the narrow paved highway. The mindless rattle of tires on a washboard gravel road startled Christy out of her half sleep. She sat up straighter and looked around. Nothing she recognized looked back at her.

"Where are we?" she asked.

Cain pointed behind them, toward the north. "See those white peaks way off in the distance?"

The sky was like a huge inverted bowl of purest blue. It took Christy a minute to be sure she was seeing something more than faint clouds along the horizon.

"You mean those things that look like chips in the rim of the sky's upside-down bowl?"

"Those chips are the San Juan Mountains, where we started," he said. "The northern outliers."

"Outliers?"

"Outlying Anasazi communities."

"Outlying what?" she asked, looking at the empty land.

He smiled. "We're on the road to the center of the ancient Anasazi world."

She turned back to the distant peaks. They were outlined in brilliant light, as if freshly dusted with snow.

"How far away are they?" she asked.

"About a hundred and thirty miles."

"Wow." Then she thought about it. "The ancient ones lived in a universe that was only a few hundred miles across."

"It wasn't small to them. It was filled with spirits and signs and mysteries, a world more complex than any man or woman could know in a lifetime. If a world is beyond understanding, does it really matter how big it is?"

She thought about that while the land divided like a river and flowed around them. The farther south the truck went, the drier the country became. Juniper and cedar were limited to the ridges and a few arroyos. Bare dirt was everywhere. Rocks lay just beneath the thin layer of soil.

"Life must have been precarious," she said after a long silence.

"It was. Short growing season. Harsh winds. Numbing cold and killing heat. Summer monsoons that sometimes didn't come in time for the crops."

The road passed over a cattle guard and gave way to a dirt track that wandered off across the scrubland with no apparent destination.

"You're sure you know where you're going?" she asked.

"Are we talking philosophy or maps?"

She laughed, surprising both of them. "Yes, I guess the land does that to you. Cosmic and pragmatic at once."

Smiling, he guided the truck over a particularly wretched piece of road.

"Speaking in cosmic philosophical terms, I'm up for grabs," he said. "But I do know the way to Pueblo Bonito."

The track wound up a low rise that dropped away steeply toward another rock ridge a half mile ahead. A dusty, faded sign on a steel post beside the road announced that they were entering Chaco Canyon National Monument.

"This must be the back way in," she said.

"Yeah, but it's not much worse than the main route."

"Is the government trying to discourage tourism?"

"We've been driving across one of the richest archaeological areas on earth. Too big to fence. Too valuable to ignore. Too expensive to dig. Impossible to protect."

"So you limit access and hope for the best?"

"That's about it. If there's a bulletin out on this truck, they'd catch us at the monument gate or in one of the campgrounds, so I'm keeping off the most-used roads."

"What about right now?" she asked uneasily.

"This is the route an old Moki poacher showed me. Hard on man and vehicle but discreet."

"You, of course, have never poached here."

He smiled thinly. "That's right, Red. I've done a lot of exploring, though."

"Huh," she said, but she smiled. Having seen Cain's reaction to the destruction of the alcove, she didn't believe any longer that he stole artifacts from public lands or merely looted private digs

He pointed toward a distant ridge of rock, a splash of green perhaps half a mile away. "See that little stand of willows by the stock tank?"

"Hard to miss. It's the only real green for miles around."

"Look just to the left. See that notch?"

She leaned forward and shaded her eyes. "Yes."

"That's where the Great North Road came down from Pueblo Alto," he said. "It was the imperial highway from Chaco to the northern outliers. It runs all the way back to the San Juan River."

He slowed as the road dropped down into a ravine where a stock tank was serviced by a creaking old windmill. The metal blades turned mindlessly in the stiff breeze, drawing water up from an aquifer far below the surface. The overflow from the tank fed the willows and a small grove of cedars. Everything was lush with the luxury of year-round water.

The dirt track circled the grove and ended against a rock wall. He backed the truck into the cover of the cedars and shut down. The fitful wind died, bringing silence like invisible light over the land. Then the wind stirred and the windmill creaked its complaints to the sky.

When Cain got out, so did Christy, following him around to the back of the truck.

"What do you want me to do?" she asked.

"Count how many times the windmill turns."

For an instant she took him seriously. Then she smiled and shook her head. He smiled in return.

"Rest, honey. You've had a rough couple of days."

"What about you?"

"It's been interesting," he agreed dryly.

He wrestled Larry Moore's camp box within reach and began pulling out what they would need. A pair of sleeping bags, self-inflating mattresses, a tarp, jackets, a small ax, cooking gear, and a supply of canned and dried food were soon lined up on the ground.

"Nothing fancy," Cain said.

"Neither is hunger."

He looked over his shoulder at her and smiled. "Point taken."

While he began setting up camp, she went about gathering wood for the fire she knew they would need later.

The sun was sliding down the blue bowl of sky when Cain finished. He shrugged into a jacket that had seen better days and handed another, slightly smaller one to Christy. She put it on gratefully. Without the sun's heat, the dry land quickly cooled.

"Have enough energy for a walk?" he asked.

"How far?"

He pointed toward the notch on the ridge. "Be a shame to be this close and not enjoy the best view in the Chaco empire."

The climb to the ridge was easier than Christy expected. Cain stopped at the notch and stood looking out at the vast sweep of land and sky. She stood next to him, hardly able to believe the clarity of the air and the immense landscape empty of lights or wires or signs of man.

"What do you see that's different?" Cain asked after a time.

"No streets. No skyscrapers. No hustlers. No gourmet takeouts. No theaters. No hypes. No bars. No drunks. No five-star restaurants. No taxis. No world-class shopping. No street people. No fine museums. No—"

His laughter drowned out Christy's litany of the differences between the New Mexican desert and Manhattan.

"What do you see that's different for the *desert*?" he asked.

"Looks pretty normal to me. Empty. Immense. Dry. Rocky. Not very many plants." She hesitated. "Except over there."

She pointed to a ragged green swath of unusually lush sagebrush. The strip was about thirty feet wide. It marched up the hillside like a farm crop.

"That's the imperial road," Cain said.

"Looks more like an imperial roadblock."

A smile flashed against his dense, short beard. "Now, yes. The old roadbeds are acting as catchment channels for the rains. Plants love that extra water. Watching for green is the best way for us to follow the road across dry ground."

She began walking up the hill, following the path of the sage. He paced her, saying nothing, caught by the intensity of her eyes as they searched the land. Near the brow of the hill, wind had scoured away the topsoil, revealing the rocky bones of the land beneath.

"Look," he said, sitting on his heels and pointing to the bare rock. "Sandstone curbs like this run on the sides of the road for a hundred miles."

She knelt next to him and traced the cool surface of the rock, seeing the marks left by a stonemason long before Columbus set sail for India and found an unsuspected continent blocking the way. Awe shivered through her, a sense of touching lives long lost, of dreams unknown, of being part of a whole that was so much larger than she'd thought.

"A hundred miles of this?" she asked in a hushed voice.

"A hundred miles in this road, maybe three thousand miles in the entire system," he said. "We're just beginning to understand how little we know about the ancient ones."

When they reached the top of the hill, the sun was low in the sky. There on a broad bench lay an extensive set of ruins that commanded a view of the entire San Juan Basin. There were no fences, no restorations, no signs, nothing but hand-carved stones slowly melting back down into the land.

"Welcome to the center of the world," Cain said softly.

The La Plata and San Juan mountains lay straight north, pink in the fading afternoon light. Mesas and shadowed arroyos and red-rock spires lay east and south. Off to the west were more mountains.

The air was clear and pure. The last of the sunlight was warm, yet there was a bracing chill just beneath it, like a gentle bite hidden in a kiss.

"You can see four states from up there," he said, pointing to a low sandstone wall.

He mounted the ruined wall with an animal grace that she couldn't help admiring. Leaning down, he held out his hand to her. She took it and learned once again that, for all his restraint, Cain was a powerful man. She went up the stones like she had wings.

The wall was very thick. When she had her balance, he put his hands on her shoulders and faced her toward the distant San Juan Mountains. As he spoke, he turned her until she had made a full circle.

"Colorado," he said. "New Mexico. Arizona. And way off up there you can see the mountains of Utah."

Motionless, she absorbed the subtle voices of time and the wind blowing over the wild, empty land.

Only when the last bit of the sun slid beneath the dark horizon did Christy realize that she was standing so close to Cain that his breath stirred her hair and the warmth of his body radiated into her, replacing the vanished heat of the sun.

"We'd better get back to camp," he said reluctantly. "I didn't bring a flashlight."

He lifted his hands from her shoulders, both freeing her and setting her adrift in the fading colors of the day. She turned and watched while he descended the low wall, landing light and strong on the ground.

When she started down, he reached up and lifted her, pivoting, making her fly. The earth beneath her feet came as a faint shock.

He felt the hesitation before she regained her balance.

"Okay?" he asked, not releasing her.

"Yes. For a second there, I thought I could fly. Wrong life, I guess."

She turned away, leaving the memory of her bittersweet smile to haunt the twilight.

And Cain.

Chapter 49

Out of reach of the wind, the campsite was calm and scented with cedar. The first stars gleamed in the east, where the sky had shifted from blue to purple. Christy and Cain prepared a simple dinner, ate, and cleaned up in a silence that was companionable rather than stiff. When they were done with camp chores, she took off her walking shoes and sat on one of the sleeping bags he'd spread near the fire. The mug of coffee in her hands was spiced with brandy and smelled like heaven.

Cain poured himself a bit more coffee and moved to the fire's light and warmth. He sat on his heels in front of the flames and added several pieces of cedar.

From beneath lowered eyelashes, she watched every move he made. He had a muscular masculine grace that pleased her. There was something both new and familiar about him, as if she'd dreamed him long ago in an old house on the High Plains of Wyoming and now was remembering the dream in a New Mexican desert that was the center of an ancient world.

The flickering light of the fire bathed his hands in alternating tongues of gold and black velvet. His fingers were long, strong, deft. They fascinated her, as did the silky luster of his beard and the thick, straight black hair that he brushed carelessly back from his forehead. The reflected firelight made his eyes gleam.

He was watching her watching him.

"I want a second chance," Cain said.

Her breath hesitated, caught, stayed. She looked away.

"I was wrong about you," he said simply. "You weren't thinking about saving your sister last night. You really wanted me."

He waited.

She didn't speak or look at him.

"Know when I figured it out?" he asked.

Silence.

"When you threw me out of the cabin," he said.

Looking only at her coffee, she held the mug tightly to hide the trembling of her hands. It didn't work. Tiny rings rippled across the dark surface of the coffee. She closed her eyes.

"A woman who was looking for leverage over a man wouldn't have done that," he said. "And she sure as hell wouldn't have melted and run all over my hand like—"

"*Nolo,*" she interrupted harshly.

"Bullshit, Red." He came to his feet in a single flowing movement. "It happened. It happened hard and fast and deep."

"For one of us," she said in a flat voice.

"For *both* of us. Just like we were both wrong about each other."

She shook her head, making firelight gleam like liquid gold in her hair.

"I stopped because I wanted you too much, not because I didn't want you enough," he said, walking closer.

Then he was so close to her that he could touch her. He clenched his hands to keep from doing just that.

"I wanted you the way I haven't let myself want a woman

since I was eighteen," he said in a rough voice. "I'd have fought to have you. Christ, I'd have killed—"

"Don't," she said.

"—to have you," he continued relentlessly. "And it scared the hell out of me."

Shivering, she clung to the coffee mug and told herself that the raw hunger she heard in his voice wasn't real.

It couldn't be real.

Men didn't want ordinary women like that. That kind of male passion was reserved for women of extraordinary beauty.

Women like Jo-Jo.

Christy had never been that desirable. "No," she whispered, eyes tightly closed.

"*Yes.* And I still want you," Cain said savagely. "Too damn much!"

He snapped the dregs of his coffee into the fire. Steam hissed.

Her eyes opened, then widened in shock. The view she had of him profiled by firelight left no doubt that he was telling the truth.

For the space of several breaths, it was silent but for the sound of flames licking softly against the body of the night.

"You're staring, honey." His voice was half husky, half amused, and one hundred percent hungry.

"You're . . . worth staring at."

He gave a crack of laughter and sank slowly to his knees in front of her.

"You're the only woman I've ever known who could make me laugh and turn me on to the point of pain at the same time," he said.

She tried to speak, but he was so close she could taste his breath. His eyes were a smoky kind of gold that was as hot as the leap of flames.

"Give me that before you drop it," he said softly, taking her coffee mug and setting it aside. "Your hands are shaking."

"So are yours."

"Am I frightening you?" he asked.

"Not . . . quite," she whispered. "Am I frightening you?"

"Yes."

Her eyes widened. "Why?"

"We could just have sex and stay free. I don't think making love will be the same."

"Don't you know?" she asked.

"Never had the chance to find out. You?"

"Same here," she whispered.

"Want to find out?"

For an instant she closed her eyes.

Then she nodded.

His fingers slid deeply into her hair, caressing and holding her in the same instant. She felt the tremor of emotion that ripped through him, shaking his strong body.

"Cain?" she whispered.

"I don't have any defenses against you," he said. "And I don't care anymore."

His teeth closed carefully on her lower lip. When she gasped with surprise and racing pleasure, his tongue shot between her teeth, filling her mouth as he wanted to fill her body. His hands shifted and his arms closed around her, lifting her to him. Heavy, hungry, frankly sexual, his kiss told her more than words could have about his barely leashed need.

When she struggled in his arms, his mouth lifted just enough so that he could speak against her lips.

"Don't fight me," he said raggedly. "Please, honey. I don't deserve you, but I need you until I'm shaking with it."

The words went through her like lightning through a

storm. She wanted him the same way, no defenses, needing him as she'd never needed another man.

"I wasn't fighting," she said.

"You were trying to get away."

"No." She laughed a little wildly. "I was trying to get closer!"

His arms tightened suddenly, pulling her hard against him, arching her body so that she felt him from her knees to her mouth mated with his. Her arms went around his neck, holding him with all her strength while he kissed her like he expected to die in the next instant.

When the kiss finally ended they both were breathing in soft, rushing bursts. With two quick motions he unzipped her jacket and his own. The snaps on his shirt and hers came undone in twin ripples of sound. Firelight gleamed on naked skin and licked over black lace.

Cain's breath came hard and fast. Then he eased his index fingers beneath the straps of Christy's bra. Slowly his knuckles slid down.

Her breath broke when his fingers smoothed down the soft slope of her breasts, drawing the lacy cups aside until the cloth was beneath her breasts and they were naked but for the firelight gliding over them. Her nipples tightened in a rush, silently telling him of her own desire raging like a hidden, sultry storm.

With a low sound he bent and caught one nipple between his lips and then drew it deeply inside, shaping her, making her moan. When she was hard and moist from his tongue, he turned to her other breast.

Her nails dug into his arms while passion spiraled up like flames. The small pain of her nails was a sensual goad, urging him to strip away more of her control and his own until there was nothing between them but unleashed desire.

He turned his head from side to side, caressing her sensitized breasts. Their tips were dark, tightly drawn, and they glistened with firelight and the moist heat of his mouth.

"You're beautiful," he said hoarsely. "Just looking at you makes me want to—" He closed his eyes. "You're hell on my self-control," he said after a moment.

"Good."

The edge of her teeth on his ear made him bite back a curse of pleasure and restraint that was sliding away with each breath, each touch.

His hand slid down her body until his fingers curled between her legs. He flexed his hand deeply, savoring and caressing her at the same time, watching waves of pleasure claim her.

Eyes dilated until they were as dark as night, she looked at him. She felt dizzy, almost weak, yet her body pulsed with a relentless, restless heat.

"Cain?" she whispered.

"Don't be afraid, honey." He let out a rushing, hissing breath. "I won't hurt you. If you're not ready . . ."

He unfastened her jeans and slid his hand beneath black lace. Long fingers searched, probed, discovered, sank deeply into her sultry heat. The low, husky sound of his name breaking on her lips made him smile.

"Like fire and rain at once," he said in a low voice. "Hot, soft, wet . . ."

Her hands went from his shoulders to the dark swirls of hair on his chest, dropped to the cool sterling buckle with its turquoise eye.

And stopped.

"Keep going," he said huskily.

He dipped into her heat and then withdrew. A thumb slick with her passion circled the satin knot he'd drawn from her

softness. The broken, hungry sound that came from her made
him want to tear away clothes and sink into her.

Instead, he set his teeth and circled the sleek bud again.

Blindly, hands shaking, she traced the unfamiliar fastening
on his belt, a hook rather than a buckle. She tugged once, but
nothing came undone. She tugged harder. Same result.

Reluctantly Cain withdrew his hand from Christy's
clothes. His fingers closed over hers. For an instant she went
very still, remembering last night when he had refused to be
touched. She looked up at him with a question in her eyes.

"Don't you want . . . ?" she asked.

"I want your hands all over me. Everywhere, honey."

Her eyelids half lowered and she smiled as though the idea
intrigued her. "Your buckle is in the way."

"Move this hand over here," he said, guiding her, "and
then pull across and up with the other."

"Like this?"

The belt opened.

"Yeah, just like that." He grinned. "Now you know how to
get into my jeans anytime you want."

Her almost hidden smile was as sexy to Cain as the sound
of his zipper sliding down. Her hand eased into his jeans and
discovered that part of him had already escaped from his
briefs. Her fingers hesitated for a moment, then slid down the
aching length of his erection.

The frankly approving, purring sound Christy made as she
caressed him nearly undid Cain. A low curse came from between his clenched teeth.

"You're going to push me over the edge," he warned.

"Can I really do that?"

"You damn well know you can."

"No, I don't," she whispered. "But I'm going to find out."

His breath hissed between his teeth as the sweet pressure

of her fingers gave way to the harder pressure of her naked palm. She measured him once, twice, watching his eyes narrow and his whole body clench. Then she slid her fingers inside his briefs and knew the coarse silk of his hair and the twin spheres that were so tightly drawn with desire.

He stiffened and groaned as though she'd taken a whip to him. With a dismayed sound, she withdrew.

"I'm sorry," she said in a low voice. "You'll have to teach me more than how to undo your belt."

His eyes opened. There was little left of gold in them except a glittering circle around a dark, dilated center.

"I never really wanted to touch a man," she said hesitantly, "so I never learned how. But I want to touch you."

The soft confession was more arousing than any caress could have been.

"That did it," he said hoarsely.

His hands slid over her back and down inside her jeans. His fingers flexed, sinking hungrily into her hips, drawing a cry of surprise and sensual pleasure from her. Slanting his lips over hers, he sank into the sultry warmth of her mouth, penetrating her hungrily. One powerful arm closed around her back, lifting her.

In the next instant Christy felt her jeans and underwear stripped away. The sleeping bag felt cold against her back, but the heat of Cain's body covering her more than made up for it. As she lifted up to meet his kiss, her breasts rubbed tantalizingly against his chest. She twisted against him and shivered at the sensations streaming from her breasts to the pit of her stomach.

He pulled away and reached into his pocket.

"Cain?" she whispered. "What . . . ?"

Then she saw the gleam of the foil packet in the firelight and understood.

"Let me," she said, taking the packet and opening it with

fingers that were trembling. "That's one thing I do know. I've never done this any other way."

"Neither have I. But I came real close about two seconds ago. Wait. Let me take off my—"

His breath wedged and his thoughts scattered as slender fingers smoothed over him, caressing and sheathing him at the same time. Then she stroked down his length again, openly enjoying him, feeling just how much he wanted her.

"Honey, unless you want to be flat on your back with a half-dressed man between your legs, you better—"

A groan ripped from Cain when Christy's fingers eased between his thighs, caressing the violently sensitive parts of him that were still naked.

An instant later she was flat on her back with his half-dressed body between her legs. He parted her with his fingers, testing her readiness and increasing it at the same time. Her legs wound around his. The rough feel of denim between her naked thighs sent more wild sensations racing through her.

She tried to tell him how good he felt, but words became a moan as his hips flexed and he pressed into her until she thought she could take no more. Then he moved and a sensual rain swept through her, softening her even more. Her legs circled his hips, opening her body completely to him as she unraveled with a shuddering cry.

The heat and scent of her wild response burned away what little restraint Cain still had. His arm went beneath her hips, holding her so hard against him that he could feel the bones beneath her soft flesh. He took her mouth as he took her body, absorbing her wild cries, driving deeply, repeatedly into her, sparing her none of his heavy arousal.

Suddenly she arched like a drawn bow, shivering wildly, crying deep in her throat with every broken breath.

For an instant he was afraid that his unrestrained passion

had hurt her. Then he felt the rhythmic pulses of her body and knew he'd given her ecstasy rather than pain. He drove into her again, burying himself in her. His head came back and his body went rigid and he knew nothing but the deep, heavy pulses of his own release.

Spent, fighting for breath, they held each other for long minutes. She stroked his sweat-slicked back beneath his shirt, savoring the muscular heat of him while her breathing slowly returned to normal. He turned his head and bit her gently on the curve of her neck. Echoes of ecstasy shook her unexpectedly, making her moan and clench around him.

Laughing softly, he bit her again. Her breathing unraveled even as her body did.

"I didn't know . . . until now," she said.

He lifted his head and looked down at her with luminous eyes. "Know what?"

"Why women put up with men."

Laughing softly, he kissed her eyelids, the hollow of her cheeks, the corners of her mouth.

"It works both ways," he said against her lips as he slowly withdrew from her. "Pleasure like that is damned rare."

He rolled onto his side, taking her with him, holding her close, stroking her gently, being held and stroked in return. For a time there was no sound but the whisper of the fire.

Her fingers combed gently down his chest, enjoying the masculine textures of hair, muscle, resilient skin. When her hand drifted below the waistband of his briefs, she discovered that he was no longer sheathed.

And he was fully aroused.

"Don't tempt me, honey."

"Tempt you? It's a little late to be worrying about that, isn't it?"

The husky combination of laughter and sensual pleasure in Christy's voice made his heartbeat visibly quicken.

"I was afraid it was going to be like this," he said thickly.

"What?"

"You and me. The first time I saw you in the gallery I wanted you."

"And I couldn't stop looking at you."

"I know. It made me feel like I'd grabbed lightning. If it hadn't been for Danner . . ."

Cain closed his eyes and took a long, deep breath, trying to still the hammering urgency of his blood. He pulled off the rest of his clothes and turned to her, gathering her against his fully naked body for the first time. They fit each other perfectly.

"Damn, that feels good," he said.

Her answer was half laughter, half the low, purring sound that set his blood on fire. She pulled his mouth down to hers and kissed him slowly, deeply.

"You want me as much as I want you," he said, surprise and pleasure in his voice.

"Of course."

"There's no 'of course' about it. Even people who want each other aren't necessarily suited as lovers. Different needs. Different speeds. Different—"

His thoughts scattered as Christy's hand slid down his body, exploring him gently. He groaned and searched blindly in the pocket of his discarded jeans.

"I like the ways we're different," she said, cupping him.

"So do I. Put this on me, honey. I'll show you the way I like us best of all."

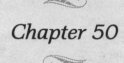

Chapter 50

Pueblo Bonito
The next day

Cain awoke an hour before dawn. The sky overhead was black and icy with stars. He and Christy were warm, lying like nested spoons inside the sleeping bags he'd zipped together. For a long time he didn't move, savoring her softness and warmth, trying to ignore the rational part of his mind.

The part that told him he was still a long way from cleaning up the mess Jo-Jo had dumped on her loving older sister.

He gathered Christy even closer and gently kissed her bare shoulder, wishing he didn't have to wake her at all. She looked so peaceful sleeping in his arms.

And he doubted that the coming day would have any peace.

People dying, dead. People gonna die.

Cain would do whatever he could to keep Christy alive.

"Good morning," he said gently as her eyes opened.

"Morning?" she said vaguely, rolling over to face him. "Looks more like night from here."

She burrowed against his warmth with a sigh and kissed

his chest sleepily. Within seconds her breathing changed as she sank back into sleep.

He slid his fingers into the silky tangle of her hair, tilting her head back. He nuzzled her lips and kissed her again.

"Morning is on the way," he said. "Listen."

Deep within the willow thicket around the water tank, birds were beginning to rustle, singing soft fragments of song, getting ready for the day.

She propped herself on one elbow and looked over him to the east. The sky had begun its slow transformation from black to the limitless blue-gray that precedes dawn. Shivering, she ducked back down into the sleeping bag and pulled him against her like a living blanket.

"She Who Faces the Sun will be waiting for you, honey." He kissed her hair. "Time to get up."

"What about you?"

"I'm already up," he said.

When Christy shifted against him, she realized that he was indeed up.

"When did you say dawn was?" she asked, her voice suddenly husky with more than sleep.

"Too soon," he said bluntly, shifting so that his erection wasn't rubbing against her.

"Oh." She sighed. "Do I get a rain check?"

"Anytime. Do I get one?"

"This is the desert. How about I give you a sun check instead?"

Laughing softly, he hugged her close, kissed her hard, and then shot out of the sleeping bag like his ass was on fire. Or something. He cursed steadily as he pulled on clothes chilled by a night on the ground.

"You make getting dressed sound irresistible," she said.

"At the moment, it's right up there with an icy shower."

Without getting out of the sleeping bag, she gathered up

her clothes, drew them beneath the warm cover, and began dressing.

Five minutes later, shivering, she followed the circle of Cain's flashlight to the ruins of Pueblo Alto. By the time they reached the tumbled stones and low walls of the ancient settlement, the sky in the east was light enough to reveal the outlines of mesas and the ragged rise of mountains behind Santa Fe.

A pair of meadowlarks burst from cover alongside the trail. For a few instants the world was full of the rushing sound of wings. Then one of the birds landed. An intricate, heartbreaking song rose into the dawn.

Motionless, Christy listened as the lark called again. It was a sound from her childhood, when life had been limitless. Joy and sorrow twisted through her like a double-edged knife. Tears filled her eyes, blurring the lines between night and dawn.

"I found the path," Cain called softly over his shoulder. "Light is coming on like thunder. We have to hurry."

She blinked, releasing the hot tears. Then she hurried to catch up with him.

The path led downhill from the ruins toward the rim of Chaco Canyon. The trail had been cleared and marked for tourists with small piles of stone in strategic places. Even in the half-light, Cain and Christy made good time.

Ten minutes below the remains of Pueblo Alto where they'd slept, the trail dropped over a small sandstone ledge. From there it skimmed along the broad stone lip of the canyon itself. Putting his arm around her, Cain stood with her on the brink. For a few hushed moments they watched the miracle of light emerging from darkness.

Gradually Pueblo Bonito condensed out of the night. Hand-hewn masonry walls made up a huge apartment block that rose two and three stories high. Countless rooms lay open to the sun and wind. The residential areas were laid out as a new-moon crescent with one curved and one straight side. The straight front was defined by a low wall. The body of the crescent was a plaza with open spaces the size of basketball courts. Within the crescent lay the circular ruins of kiva after kiva, an abundance of sacred places that announced the religious significance of Pueblo Bonito. In the shadows flowing out from the dawn, the circles seemed filled with the mystery of centuries.

One of the kivas was much larger than the others, first among equals.

As Christy's eyes adjusted to the fluid boundary between dawn and night, she saw that some of the old masonry walls of the room blocks had slumped with the weight of sunlight and time. Those walls were braced like the ones she'd had seen in the alcove.

"Twenty-four kivas," Cain said quietly. "Once, Pueblo Bonito was the most important building in the empire."

"But why so many kivas? Wasn't one church or temple or whatever enough?"

"Maybe each clan had its own kiva. That's the way some of the Pueblo people live now. Or maybe different kivas were used at different seasons." He spread his hands. "No one knows. Or if they do, they aren't talking to white folks."

She leaned forward, wanting to see into the past as well as into the dense shadows that remained like pieces of the vanished night. "What about the biggest kiva? Why is it different?"

"I don't know. It could be that's where everybody prayed ten hours a day during the long winter for the safe return of the sun in the spring."

Cain glanced at the sky. Polaris was just fading. He turned back to the ruins.

"When that straight wall was built," he said, pointing, "it was less than a degree off a true north-south line."

At first she didn't understand the implication of what he was saying. Then she remembered that the Anasazi had no metal, therefore no compasses. In ancient times, the polar star hadn't been the beacon of true north that it was today.

"How did they do it?" she whispered.

"Ask She Who Faces the Sun. It's one of the secrets she'll pass on to Eunice."

"Eunice?"

Cain gestured toward the ruins of the great kiva. Two human figures had stepped out of the shadows below the kiva's circular rim. One of the people lifted a hand in greeting.

Cain responded in kind.

"That *is* Eunice," Christy said after a moment. "How did you know?"

"Eunice is Molly's niece."

"Johnny's *sister*?"

"Yes."

Releasing Christy, Cain stepped away.

"We'd better go," he said. "She Who Faces the Sun wants to see you in the first light of day, when the sun first clears the rim of the canyon."

"After a night in the sack with you?" Christy said in a low voice, smiling but very serious.

His glance roved over her, remembering and memorizing at the same time. He smiled gently and held out his hand. "The ancients weren't strangers to the rhythms of life."

Lacing her fingers through his, she walked side by side with him until the path left the canyon rim. From there they had to walk single file. The trail dropped down into a narrow cleft between two rock faces that became a tunnel, recalling the trail to the Sisters alcove.

Cain and Christy stepped into the shadows of the cleft and began a steep descent down what amounted to a rude stairway. The stairs were faint, uneven, almost imaginary. Yet in places the walls were smooth with the passage of many, many hands. They were walking along pathways that had been old before the first Europeans came to the Anasazi lands.

She touched the smooth places on the stone walls and sensed time like a vast exhalation moving across the face of the land. Her skin shivered in primal response. When she looked up, Cain was watching her with eyes as ancient as fire.

Together they emerged from the cleft onto the flat floor of Chaco Canyon. The first faint colors of day were gathering low in the eastern sky. As the two of them walked toward the great kiva, he let her walk apart from him. With that, he became more guide than mate. She accepted the distance with the same instinctive understanding she'd accepted the stones smoothed by and infused with ancient lives.

The eastern sky was a radiant orange as they approached the long straight wall that ran along the north-south side of Pueblo Bonito.

"The entrance to the great kiva is on the other side of the wall," he said. "Eunice will show you."

With that Cain turned away, heading toward the ruined apartment block. He didn't look back.

Chapter 51

Christy waited until Cain was out of sight. Only then did she turn toward the kiva and She Who Faces the Sun, a woman directly descended from the ancients.

Eunice met Christy at a break in the north-south pueblo wall.

"Come," Eunice said.

Christy followed her through the wall to a spot where the kiva wall had collapsed, making the climb down a matter of only a few steps. Eunice gestured for Christy to precede her to the center of the sunken circular room whose roof was the onrushing dawn.

The woman who waited had the clothes and age of someone who could be Johnny's Aunt Molly, but she was as small as he'd been big. Less than five feet tall, she wore a faded denim riding jacket over a long gray velvet skirt and new white running shoes. Her gray hair was covered with a bandanna that was tied in a knot at the point of her chin. Her face was wrinkled with the passage of years and pain. Her clear black eyes were ageless.

She Who Faces the Sun.

Eunice said something to the old woman in a language that was utterly alien to Christy.

"This is She Who Faces the Sun," Eunice said to Christy a moment later. "She is the keeper of our clan's spirit."

"Good morning," Christy said, for she knew no other polite way to greet the keeper of a clan's spirit.

She Who Faces the Sun stepped forward, touched Christy's bright hair, and spoke in the language Christy couldn't understand.

"She likes your hair," Eunice translated. "She said she's seen sandstone that color in a small canyon near Mesa Verde."

Christy smiled.

She Who Faces the Sun took Christy's hand and tugged firmly. In response to the silent demand, Christy turned. Just as she faced east, the first direct rays of the sun lanced over the canyon rim, transforming everything in a single, sweeping instant.

A primitive awe shivered through Christy. She felt like an entire world rather than a day had just been born.

The old woman's hand tightened around Christy's. A low, shifting chant poured from She Who Faces the Sun. Christy couldn't understand the meaning of the words, but she sensed quite clearly that the prayer or incantation centered around her. When the chant finally came to an end, She Who Faces the Sun reached into a patch pocket on the front of her denim jacket. She brought out a pinch of pale yellow dust and scattered a trace of it over herself and Christy.

"Corn pollen," Eunice said quietly. "It's our way of blessing people. She likes what the dawn showed her in you."

Christy looked at the old woman's clear black eyes. "Thank you."

She Who Faces the Sun smiled. It transformed her face, making her Aunt Molly instead of an ancient holy woman.

She said something rapidly in the alien tongue.

Eunice smiled with sly humor as she looked at Christy.

"Aunt Molly likes your man too. She Who Faces the Sun called him Kokopelli."

Christy grinned and blushed at the same time.

Smacking her hands on her thighs with delight, Molly laughed with the vigor of a woman half her age. When she looked in the direction of the apartment block, she saw Cain sitting in the sunlight, watching the old kiva like a man watching a treasure room. She spoke rapidly again.

"She says Kokopelli settles when he finds the right woman," Eunice translated. "He looks pretty settled from here."

The old woman grinned, showing sturdy teeth. Then she turned and walked away from the center of the great kiva.

"She will talk with you now," Eunice said.

"Who will speak, Aunt Molly or She Who Faces the Sun?" Christy asked.

Eunice gave her a sharp look, then nodded as though Christy had just done something right.

"Molly," Eunice said. "Most of the time."

While they walked over to join the older woman, Christy spoke quietly to Eunice. "Please tell your aunt that we regret the death of Johnny Ten Hats."

"You tell her."

Christy stopped close to Molly and met her dark, clear eyes. "The sheriff blames Cain for Johnny's death, but I was there. It wasn't Cain's fault."

Eunice translated and Molly listened. Finally, the old woman nodded and began speaking. Simultaneously, Eunice translated, as though she did this often.

"Aunt Molly knows Johnny was a man torn by demons. He drank too much. He stole pots and grave offerings from the ancient ones and sold them to the white man. He spent much of himself trying to be a big man in a white world."

Listening intently while Eunice translated, Christy watched Molly's face. The old woman watched her in turn, nodding occasionally or gesturing fluidly with her hands to make a point.

"One of Johnny's demons was a yellow-haired witch," Eunice translated. "He stole for her. He spent his money on devil powders that he put up his nose. This made him more crazy, until he was a stranger to us."

"Cocaine?" Christy asked in a low voice.

With a curt nod of agreement, Eunice continued translating while Molly spoke.

"But enough of Johnny survived within the demon that he knew he was lost. He left the yellow-haired witch and came back to us for a time."

Both Indian women stopped talking and looked at Christy. Her mouth turned down unhappily, but there was no way to avoid the truth.

"The witch was my sister," Christy said simply. "Like Johnny, she lived with demons."

The old woman understood more English than Christy thought. It was She Who Faces the Sun looking at Christy, boring into her with eyes as black and bottomless as night.

"She witch all time?" the old woman asked, grappling with the foreign language. "Child. Woman. All witch?"

Christy shook her head. "No, not always. Once, Jo-Jo was a sweet little girl."

Then Christy shivered, remembering the past with savage clarity. Not so sweet after all.

Never.

She Who Faces the Sun narrowed her eyes as she saw the truth dawning in Christy.

"Jo-Jo saw herself much more clearly than she saw other people," Christy said in a low voice. "Always. All the time.

Yet she was my sister. Always. That will never change."

The old woman's eyes closed. She nodded once, slowly.

Christy waited.

She Who Faces the Sun was silent.

Christy turned to Eunice and asked, "When Johnny came back to you, did he break with the people in Colorado?"

Eunice and Molly talked back and forth for a moment, syllables and sounds without meaning to Christy.

"The witch who was your sister gave Johnny a powerful drug," Eunice said after a time. "It took him to a place where rocks had voices and the cedars walked like men."

"Peyote?" Christy asked.

"No. Much more powerful. Afterward, Johnny came to She Who Faces the Sun so that she could get his soul back from the demons. He brought her a gift from an ancient place."

"The alcove," Christy said.

Eunice hesitated. "He never told us. He simply stole it from the yellow-haired witch."

She Who Faces the Sun closed her eyes and began an eerie, sliding chant, ancient words rising and falling in the sunlight and shadow of the great kiva.

"The tortoise soul is very old, one of many such souls. Each made for and worn by a different She Who Faces the Sun," Eunice translated. "They were stolen from this kiva by a sister who wanted to be She Who Faces the Sun and hold the spirit of the clan in her hands. The other sister, the clan's She Who Faces the Sun, followed the thief."

"Where?" Christy asked urgently.

"North to the edge of the desert, where the land rises to a great mesa. Sister and She Who Faces the Sun fought. The sister was killed, but She Who Faces the Sun also was mortally struck. She knew she wouldn't have the strength to return her clan's spirit to the great kiva. Nor did she want to. She had seen in a dying vision that the clans were coming apart like kernels stripped from an ear of dried corn. The time of the sun was past. The time of the demons was coming."

The chant deepened, taking on a new urgency.

"The clan's spirit must be hidden," Eunice translated. "She Who Faces the Sun sealed her dead sister and herself and the clan's spirit in a kiva hollowed out of solid stone. And then She Who Faces the Sun called down the stone of the canyon itself to hide her clan's spirit in sacred silence."

As the eerie duet of Indian chant and modern English died, Christy once more felt the prickling chill of time blowing over her skin.

"The alcove," she said in a low voice. "I've been to the grave of the ancient She Who Faces the Sun. Johnny died there."

She Who Faces the Sun spoke again.

"Whoever disturbs the clan's spirit will die," Eunice translated.

"May I . . . is it permitted that an outsider see what Johnny brought to She Who Faces the Sun?"

Without waiting for Eunice's translation, the old woman opened her denim jacket.

Suspended from a thong around her neck was a tortoise pendant identical in shape to the effigy in Peter Hutton's display case. The turquoise inlays were similar in size and shape, but different stones made up different portions of the turtle body. The matrix that held the turquoise was white abalone shell rather than argillite. A single turquoise tile was missing. Instead of eyes made of turquoise spheres, one eye was a polished black sphere.

The other eye was missing.

Christy fought for the breath that time had squeezed from her lungs. She reached into her pocket. The black bead she'd found in the alcove was warm with her body heat and very smooth.

"Cain," she said urgently to Eunice. "Call him."

Eunice gave Christy an odd look, but She Who Faces the Sun was already turning to the place where Cain waited.

"Come," she called.

Moments later Cain was standing in the kiva next to Christy, his eyes luminous, curious, intent.

"The piece of turquoise we found in the alcove," she said. "Do you have it?"

Silently he reached into his pocket and brought out the oddly shaped tile. Simultaneously she pulled the bead out of her own pocket.

She Who Faces the Sun held out the tortoise on her palm. The tile fitted into place perfectly, completing the turquoise pattern. The bead slid onto a tiny stalk.

The tortoise was complete.

She Who Faces the Sun spoke softly over the pendant, caressed it with a gentle hand, and slipped it into a pocket for safekeeping. Tears of joy glittered in her ancient eyes.

Eunice let out a long sigh. "We have no way to thank you. The pendant is very important to our clan."

"There is another tortoise," Christy said.

"Where?" Eunice said sharply.

"It's owned by Peter Hutton."

"Who is he?"

"The man who owns the ruin where Johnny found both pendants."

"Not own," She Who Faces the Sun said harshly. *"Ours."*

"By your laws, yes," Cain agreed. "White law is different. But you might be able to bring enough political pressure to bear on Hutton so that he'll give up the bones, if not the grave goods, he found in the alcove."

Eunice translated rapidly, listened, and turned to Cain once more.

"Bones?" she asked curtly. "Were the pendants found in a burial place?"

"There were two skeletons. Female. The two pendants were found with them."

"They were buried in a kiva," Christy added.

"The Sisters," Eunice whispered.

Cain looked intently at the old woman, sensing the turmoil beneath her still surface. She spoke quickly, words tumbling out. Eunice translated just as urgently.

"She dreamed of the two sisters but saw only one when she looked in the dawn light."

She Who Faces the Sun turned away and walked across the hard-packed floor of the great kiva. Silently she went from niche to niche, staring into the empty places as though seeing a time in the past when each clan's spirit lay safely within.

Finally She Who Faces the Sun turned away from the niches where other people could see only emptiness and walked back toward the three who waited. Her seamed brown face was both serene and radiant with pleasure. As she approached, she did a small two-step dance of joy and laughed like a girl.

She spoke to Eunice.

"Aunt Molly wants you to bring the other tortoise to her," she said to Christy.

Cain and Christy exchanged glances.

"She Who Faces the Sun might not understand white property laws," Cain said, "but Molly does. By white law, the other pendant belongs to Peter Hutton. It was found on his property."

"No," the old woman said curtly. She spoke with equal bluntness to Eunice, demanding something.

For the first time, Eunice spoke exclusively to Cain.

"This place where you and Johnny fought," she said. "Was it close to two pillars of stone?"

"Yes."

"Why were you there?"

"Christy found Kokopelli's sign carved into the canyon rim. Below it was a trail leading to the ruins. We followed the trail."

"Was Johnny there?" Eunice asked.

"He came later."

"To steal more?" she asked bluntly.

"No. All he wanted was a bag of dirt."

"You fought over dirt?"

"I fought because he attacked me."

Eunice turned back to the old woman and spoke rapidly. The old woman listened.

And then she laughed.

At first Eunice looked shocked. A moment later she understood. Smiling, she turned back to Cain.

"The ruins you describe aren't owned by anyone," she said.

"What?"

"That's public land. Government land. Johnny was halfway through the dig when Peter Hutton figured it out."

A wolfish smile spread across Cain's face. "No wonder Johnny wanted to know how to identify the origin of artifacts."

"He was going to prove that Hutton's collection came from public land," Christy said, "and get the government off Molly's back in the bargain."

"Getting dirt from the site won't be a problem. Getting our hands on one of Hutton's pots, though—" Cain shrugged. "We need one that hasn't been cleaned."

"That must be why Johnny was trying to break into the room just off the main gallery," Christy said.

Cain nodded. His eyes narrowed as he thought about what had to be done.

Suddenly Christy wished she hadn't said anything. Johnny had been caught and badly beaten when he tried to steal the evidence he needed from Hutton's house. It would be different when she and Cain went back to finish Johnny's work.

This time Peter Hutton knew what he had to protect. This time he and his men would be even more dangerous.

This time Jo-Jo was dead.

Chapter 52

"**C**an't you get Larry Moore to help you?" Christy asked.

Cain didn't even look away from the road. He was driving fast and hard, holding the white truck to the road with ruthless skill. Ahead of them loomed the San Juan Wall.

"Larry's got to live in that town," Cain said. "He's already put himself way out on a limb for me."

"But—"

"No," he interrupted curtly. "Not until I'm sure I can protect Larry from the likes of Danner."

"How can you do that?"

"The same way Johnny was going to."

"You're going to steal a pot from Hutton's house." Her voice was tight, unhappy.

"You have a better idea?"

"Yes. Give it to the government."

Cain's laughter was as harsh as the look on his face. "You must believe in Santa Claus too. The first time Hutton gets a whiff of any official interest, those pots and grave goods are history, and you know it as well as I do. He'll put them down the garbage disposal and throw the switch."

"If there's a search warrant—"

"Not a chance," Cain cut in. "Without probable cause, you'll never get a warrant."

"But if we told what we knew, wouldn't that be probable cause?"

"Assuming the duly constituted authorities believe the word of an ex-con and an old Indian woman, it might be grounds for a search warrant. Then again, it might not. Either way, the news gets to Hutton. You want to take that chance?"

"What about *my* word?"

Cain's hands tightened on the wheel. "You heard what Johnny said. Jo-Jo left a trail of evidence pointing to you as her partner in theft. That's why Hutton and Danner were calling New York looking for you."

"But—"

"But nothing," he said savagely. "The second we go to the authorities, Danner will get wind of it. What Danner knows, Hutton knows."

"If—"

Cain kept talking. "The only way we have a hope in hell of clearing our names is by doing it ourselves. I wanted to drop you off in a safe place. You refused. End of argument."

He braked sharply and turned onto a dirt road.

"Isn't this the road we took three nights ago, when you grabbed me coming out of Hutton's house?" she asked. "Remember?"

"Yeah." Cain smiled, remembering how good she'd felt that night. And last night. "Oh, yeah. I remember."

She ignored him. Right now she didn't know whether to smile with him or yell at him for being a stubborn idiot. After a few minutes she sighed and looked at the man who had intrigued her from the first moment she saw him in the Two-Tier West Gallery.

"Did you ever imagine where it would lead when you saw me running down that hill?" she asked.

He gave her a sideways look. "I had hopes. The very first time I saw you, I knew there was a lot of woman underneath that hundred-dollar haircut."

She laughed. Then her smile turned upside down. "A lot of trouble too."

"Last night was worth every bit of it." He touched her red hair and soft cheek. "So was seeing She Who Faces the Sun hold that complete tortoise in her hand."

Christy kissed his fingertips and then braced herself for the rough part of the road.

He shifted into four-wheel drive as they entered the dry wash a mile from the ranch house at Xanadu. He drove the length of the wash and well into the streambed before he stopped. When they got out of the truck, the sun was high overhead. After the desert at Chaco, the mountain air tasted cool and hinted of winter. There had been a hard frost the night before. The leaves of a black-trunked cottonwood beside the dry stream had turned bright yellow. They rustled softly in the breeze.

"Stay here," he said.

She started to object.

"No," he cut in. "If I'm not back in an hour, run like hell to Larry."

"I know the layout of the house. You don't."

"You can describe it to me."

She didn't say a word.

"Or I can do it the way Johnny did," Cain said.

Silence.

He studied her face. His mouth flattened. "Once I'm out

of sight you're going to do what you damn well please, aren't you?"

"Isn't that what you're doing—what you damn well please?"

Without another word he started down the streambed. She followed, crouching when he crouched, standing still when he stood still, and moving when he moved. The sand of the streambed still showed their footprints from three nights before. They followed the tracks to the spot where they'd slid down the bank to escape Hutton's guards.

She touched Cain's hand, stopping him. She didn't want to set off to Hutton's house with anger between them.

"I should have known better than to hang around with you," she said softly, "after the way you lifted me down this bank."

For a moment, he didn't understand. Then he did. He circled her waist with both hands. Slowly his fingers traveled up her ribs and brushed against the sides of her breasts.

"You could have slapped me anytime you wanted, honey."

"I still can. I don't want to."

She stepped close and kissed him, holding him hard and being held even harder in return.

"Wait in the trees for me?" he asked against her lips. "If we're both caught in the house, we could be as dead as Jo-Jo and Jay."

For a long, taut moment Christy looked at Cain. "All right. But you have to come back to me," she added fiercely.

"It's a deal."

He kissed her hard and fast. And then he boosted her up the bank, following quickly. The spruce trees weren't far beyond. Inside the grove it was almost as dark as it had been at night. They stood side by side in the evergreens, watching and listening.

No one was working around the house or the barn. Only one airplane was tied down in the meadow. No one was using the target range. No cars were moving on the road from the gate. The barn and corrals were empty.

Standing alone, its doors and windows shut and draped, the big house stood like a modern sculpture on the brow of the hill.

"It looks deserted," she said in a low voice.

"That would be a piece of luck."

"We could use one."

He didn't argue. "Looks like Hutton has already closed up the place for the winter. I hope he didn't empty the display cases too."

"There was too much for him to move everything so fast."

Cain nodded. "Especially such fragile stuff. Even if he took the best with him, he had to leave something."

"Besides," she added unhappily, "it's not like the house is unprotected. The security inside is discreet, but it's there."

He didn't doubt it.

Together, they circled around to the back side of the hill, where the cedars grew thick and dense as fur on a dog.

No one called out to question their right to be on Hutton's land.

When they were within twenty yards of the deck Christy had jumped from to escape Hutton's guards, Cain stopped.

"This is far enough for you," he said. "Any closer and you wouldn't have much chance of escaping if something went wrong."

"Wait," she said when he would have turned away.

Using a stick, she quickly traced a floor plan in the dirt. "This is the deck," she said, pointing with the stick. "This is how you get to the grand gallery with the display cases."

He nodded.

"I don't know how much good those pots will do us," she said. "They were scrubbed and polished when I saw them."

"If the cases are empty or the pots look too clean, where's the room Johnny was trying to break into?"

She drew quickly, adding to the rough diagram. "Here. The skeleton of the other sister is probably there too."

"All right. I'll be back as quick as I can."

He gave her a hard kiss before he walked to the edge of the cedars, looked around, and then sprinted across the open lawn to the house. Once there, he plastered himself against the back wall next to a window in Jo's bedroom and listened. Nothing was making noise inside the house. He tried the window.

Locked.

Calmly he picked up a rock the size of his fist. He rapped firmly on the glass. It broke with a brittle, musical sound. He fished a few long splinters out of the window frame, reached carefully through the hole, and opened the lock.

The window slid back easily.

Pulling the curtain aside, he looked in and listened. Nothing came but the sound of his own breathing. He eased out a breath, held it, listened. Nothing. He reached up, caught the sill, and began to vault over it into the room.

"Gotcha, you son of a bitch."

The sheriff's face was triumphant. The mouth of his shiny chrome steel pistol was pointed right at Cain's head.

Chapter 53

Cain didn't try to talk his way out. He simply let his forward momentum send him into the sheriff in a kind of flying tackle. As the two of them fell back into the room, Cain's hand chopped at the sheriff's wrist. The semiautomatic pistol fired twice, wildly, and hit the floor.

Christy was running before the echoes of the shots faded.

And she was running toward the house, not away from it. The fear that Cain might be wounded or even dead wiped every other thought from her mind. She had just enough sense left not to burst through the window herself. Instead, she did what he'd done. She flattened out against the house and listened.

"You son of a bitch," Danner said in a strained voice. "I'll get you if it's the last thing I do."

"You'll sure complicate my life," Cain muttered. "Where's Hutton?"

"Fuck you."

"And here I thought you liked little girls."

There was a grunt followed by a thump and more grunts.

Christy risked a quick look through the window.

Sheriff Danner was flat on his stomach. Cain was sitting

on top of him. One of his hands was buried in Danner's hair, pulling the sheriff's head back at a sharp angle. Cain's other hand was wrapped around Danner's right wrist, dragging it sharply up between his shoulder blades. Just beyond Danner's right shoulder lay the pistol.

Stalemate.

Neither man could reach the pistol. But that could change at any instant. Danner had forty pounds on Cain, and only a few of it was fat.

"Cain?" she called softly. "I'm coming in."

"Red, you don't take orders worth a damn."

"I thought you'd never notice."

She scrambled in over the window ledge, grabbed the pistol, checked it with a few quick motions, and put the safety on.

Cain raised his black eyebrows. "Not your first pistol, huh?"

"I live alone in Manhattan. I can put ten rounds in the black at thirty feet."

"How are you on live targets?"

"With luck, I'll never know."

"So Hutton was right," Danner said angrily. "She's in this with that sister of hers."

"This?" Cain said sardonically. "Which 'this' are you talking about?"

"Theft, you son of a bitch. Your stock in trade."

"I'm a reporter, not a Moki poacher," Christy said.

"I'm talking breaking and entering, not pothunting," Danner said.

"Where?" Cain demanded. "When? What was taken?"

"As if you don't know, you—" Abruptly Danner began to make sounds like a man having trouble breathing.

"You can talk nice or you can choke," Cain said through his teeth. "Take your pick."

"Two nights ago somebody hit Hutton's house and cleaned

him out," Danner said in a strained voice. "Not a damn thing left."

Cain and Christy looked at each other in dismay.

"Is that why you're here?" Cain asked after a moment. "Looking for evidence?"

"Yeah."

"Find any?"

"No," Danner said grudgingly.

"What was taken?" Christy asked.

"You know better than I do, you little—"

Danner's words ended in a grunt as Cain yanked the sheriff's wrist up to the back of his head.

"Her name is Ms. McKenna," Cain said. "Now answer her."

"Pots," Danner said in a strained voice. "Beads. All that damn Moki stuff Hutton was so proud of."

"There's nothing left here?" she asked.

"You should know," Danner retorted. "You cleaned it out down to the dust in the glass cases."

"*Shit,*" Cain said, furious. "He's going to get away with it!"

"What are you talking about?" Danner demanded.

"Murder."

The sheriff made a rough sound.

"My sister and her lover," Christy said.

"Jo?" Danner asked. "Hutton's fancy piece of ass? She's your sister?"

"Yeah," Cain said. "Jo-Jo and Hutton's jet jockey died when their plane exploded on takeoff down in Santa Fe."

"I don't believe you."

"Jesus, Danner," Cain said in disgust. "Why would I lie about that?"

"Hutton said Jo, Jay, and the two of you were in on it. That you cleaned him out, Jay transported it, and—"

"Jay couldn't have transported a fly," Cain said brutally. "He was spread all over three acres of runway."

Christy drew a sharp breath.

"Besides, if we've already cleaned Hutton out, what are we doing breaking into a empty house?" Cain asked.

Danner said nothing.

"Well?" Cain demanded.

"I don't know."

"That's right, *Sheriff*. You don't know enough to pour piss out of a boot."

"I know I saw you trespassing on Hutton's property. I know I saw you murder Johnny Ten Hats. I know you're a Moki-poaching son of—"

"—a bitch," Cain interrupted sarcastically. "Well, one out of four ain't bad, I guess."

"None out of four." Christy's voice was as flat and hard as Cain's. "Self-defense isn't murder."

"What happened?" the sheriff asked. "Did Johnny jump you when he got tired of getting fleeced by the four of you?"

"Sheriff Danner," she said, "shut up and listen."

The sheriff would have objected, but he couldn't. Cain's grip was too tight.

"One," she said distinctly. "Until last week, I hadn't communicated with my sister for twelve years. Two. The alcove where Peter Hutton's 'Moki stuff' came from is on public land."

Beneath Cain's hands, the sheriff went very still.

"Three," she continued. "Jo-Jo, Jay, and Johnny Ten Hats were stealing from the alcove, from Hutton, and from each other."

Slowly the tension began to drain from Sheriff Danner's big body.

"Four," she said relentlessly, "Cain had nothing to do with any of it. Five. Jay shot Cain this spring. And no," she added sardonically, "it wasn't a hunting accident. Six. *Cain is not a murderer.*"

As the fight left Danner, Cain slowly eased his grip. He didn't let go entirely, because he didn't trust the sheriff not to make a lunge for Christy and the pistol.

"Seven," she said coldly. "Can you prove that you aren't an accessory to robbery, blackmail, and murder?"

"What?" Danner asked, shocked. "Lady, I'm the sheriff of Remington County!"

The outrage in Danner's face was so clear that she laughed and laughed and laughed.

And laughed.

"Easy, honey," Cain said, watching her closely. "It's almost over. Even a skull as thick as Danner's gets the point eventually."

She took a few deep, ragged breaths. "I'm okay. It's just that—you should have seen—his face—" She struggled not to laugh.

"Yeah," Cain said, smiling slightly. "I can imagine. You ready to negotiate yet, Sheriff?"

"You ready to surrender?" Danner retorted.

It took Cain a moment to realize that the sheriff was serious.

"Hell," Cain said. "Okay, but there's a condition."

"What?"

"Hutton's ass," Cain said. "Where is he?"

"Are Jo and that pilot really dead?" Danner asked.

"You don't believe me, call Santa Fe. They must have identified the scraps by now."

Christy winced.

"Let me up," Danner said.

Cain looked at her. She backed up until she and the pistol were well beyond Danner's reach. Cain let go of the sheriff and stood, watching him carefully.

"Damn," Danner groaned, rolling over and working his right arm. "No wonder Johnny was the one that took a header over the cliff. You're a lot stronger than you look." Slowly the sheriff got to his feet.

Christy backed up some more. She'd forgotten just how big Danner was.

The sheriff picked up his hat, reshaped it, and put it on. Then he looked at Cain for a long time.

"You really figure Hutton killed his model?" Danner asked.

"Or had Autry do it," Cain said. "He had the training."

"Why kill them?"

"Blackmail, likely."

"All because of a few ugly Moki pots?" Danner asked. "That's crazy."

"Hutton couldn't afford a scandal," Christy said.

Danner turned toward her.

"It's one thing to be inspired by ancient Anasazi designs found on your own land by experienced archaeologists," she said. "It's quite another to rape a unique, important archaeological site on public land just for some more fodder for the rag trade."

Danner shook his head slowly, but he wasn't disagreeing with her. He simply didn't understand. "Public land. Be damned."

"Jo-Jo and Jay knew Hutton had been digging on public land," Cain said. "At a guess, I'd say they were blackmailing him as well as skimming from the dig. Or else Hutton feared blackmail in the future."

"Well, you could be right," Danner said, "for all the good it will do you."

"What are you talking about?" she demanded. "Cain is innocent!"

"Sure," Danner said, shrugging. "I'll be glad to put it out on the wire. But as for the rest . . ."

She waited.

"Even if I believed you," the sheriff said, "and I'm not sure I do, Hutton has the money and Autry has the brains not to leave any evidence lying around."

"They left a whole alcove," Cain said. "I'll get the evidence I need."

"I don't think so. Hutton and Autry went upcountry about an hour ago. They took a couple of cases of dynamite with them."

Cain began swearing viciously.

With a resigned gesture, Danner tugged his hat into place. "Win some, lose some, some never had a chance. I don't like it, but there's sweet fuck all to do about it."

"I'm not going to lose this one," Cain said in a harsh voice.

"Sure you are," the sheriff said wearily. "Hutton and his like don't ever pay the piper. They just get in their fancy jets and fly off back to New York or Los Angeles. And we're the little people, the ones they fly over on the way."

A feral smile spread across Cain's face. "But they aren't aboard that private plane yet. They're still down here in the cedar and sandstone. And that's *my* country."

He turned and went out the same way he'd come in, through the window. As soon as his feet hit the lawn, he was running.

Christy went out the window after him, sheriff's gun still in her hand.

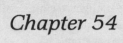

Chapter 54

By the time Cain parked Moore's truck within fifty yards of the Sisters, the rim of the mesa was already in deep shadow. Cautiously he went to the edge and looked over.

There must have been an easier trail to the ruins from the valley below. A Xanadu ranch truck was parked at the base of the rim far below, but no one was in sight.

He lifted his hand, signaling Christy to come closer. The sound of her approaching footsteps was almost lost in the long sigh of the wind through the cedars.

"They're still inside," he said quietly.

She let out a long breath. "All right."

"I still think I should take the pistol."

"When was the last time you shot a gun?" she asked.

"When was the last time you killed a man?"

"With a handgun at this range, killing won't be a problem. I'll be lucky to hit the alcove."

His smile flashed against his beard.

"But that stretch of open rock is dangerous," she said. "If someone is shooting at you, I can at least shoot back."

She was right and Cain knew it. He just didn't like it.

"You can come as far as the rock pile below the alcove. No farther, Red. I mean it."

Without waiting for her agreement, he lowered himself into the cleft. She shoved the pistol into her waistband and followed. Out of the sunlight, the air went from cool to chill. She gathered her jacket and zipped it up. The pistol felt cold and awkward against her stomach.

Slowly they made their way down the cleft until they reached the spot where rock steps had been hammered into the sloping front of the mesa. The way across was exposed and dangerous.

"I'll go first," he said softly. "You stay put until I find out what's going on. When I raise my hand, come in carefully."

She didn't answer.

He turned, took her chin in his hand, and said, "If someone comes sneaking up behind me, I won't be asking for ID. I'll just reach back and send whoever it is headfirst off the mesa. *Promise me it won't be you.*"

The bleak clarity of Cain's eyes left no doubt that he was serious.

"I promise," she whispered.

He looked at her, saw that she meant it, and nodded.

"But I don't like it," she muttered.

"That makes two of us."

He let go of her chin and turned back toward the alcove. But instead of starting across the rock, he froze.

Hutton and Autry were framed against the alcove's dark entry, facing one another. Autry was carrying a knapsack in one hand. Hutton carried nothing. He was standing nonchalantly, his hands shoved deep into the oversized pockets of one of his own designer jackets.

For a minute longer both men stood atop the rubble pile, talking urgently. Finally Autry reached into the knapsack and jerked out what looked like a two-way radio and began working over it.

A chill that had nothing to do with the cool air went over Cain as he thought of what Danner had said about dynamite.

"How good are you with that pistol?" he asked tightly. "Can you pick off Autry?"

Her eyelids flinched, but she said nothing as she measured the range. "From here?"

"Yes."

"I doubt that I'll hit him, but I can sure as hell give him a scare."

"Do it. *Fast.*"

An instant later a shot echoed.

Autry doubled over and staggered backward.

Christy froze in the act of pulling the pistol free of her waistband. "I didn't—" she began.

Another shot cut off her words. The sound of the report was tinny and flat, almost like the crack of a whip. It echoed into the alcove and out the other side.

Before the sound faded, Autry was on his knees. Peter Hutton stood over him, a gun in his hand.

While Cain and Christy watched in shocked silence, Hutton put the small pistol against the back of Autry's head and pulled the trigger a third time. Autry pitched forward and lay facedown on the rubble pile. He didn't move again.

Hutton climbed down to where Autry had fallen. Without hesitation, he put the muzzle of the small pistol against Autry and fired until there were no bullets left.

"Jesus Christ," Cain said under his breath. "I met some cold folks in prison, but nothing like that."

Christy closed her eyes and clenched her teeth against the nausea rising in her throat. "Don't ever call yourself a murderer again," she said through her teeth. "Hutton is everything you are *not*."

Hutton looked down at Autry, then shook himself like a man awakening from a dream. He put the pistol back in his pocket, bent down, and grabbed Autry's feet. Grunting with effort, he began dragging the slack body back to the alcove. When he got to the sill, he wrestled the body into a sitting position and hauled him up onto the rock.

Then Hutton rubbed his palms on his trousers with a gesture that said he didn't like getting dirty. He scrambled up onto the sill himself and tried to pitch Autry's body forward into the alcove.

It wasn't easy to do. Hutton pushed, pulled, jerked, kicked, and finally managed to shove the corpse out of sight. He followed it.

The instant Hutton vanished, Cain straightened up.

"What are you going to do?" she asked.

"Catch a murderer before he thinks to reload. Like Johnny. It's always the little things that get you."

Cain left the cover of the cleft and started over the sandstone in a controlled rush. Halfway across, he switched leads and swiftly covered the rest of the dangerous open space.

Christy was right on his heels.

When she reached the rubble pile, his hand shot out and pulled her down. His other hand went over her mouth, forcing her to be silent and very still.

Hutton was talking to someone inside the alcove. His breathing was ragged.

"I told you Jo—would get you. You thought you were so damn smart, fucking her and me at the same time. But I was smarter—than both of you."

There was a grunt and hoarse curses.

"Damn you, Ted. You weigh a ton. Pick up your feet."

Cain put his mouth right against Christy's ear. When he

spoke, his voice was a bare thread of sound. "Hutton's talking to himself."

She nodded.

"I want the son of a bitch alive," Cain said. "Just in case Danner has any doubts."

She nodded again.

"Stay here."

She didn't nod.

"Damn it, Red."

She kissed the hand covering her mouth and looked at him with steady eyes.

"Then at least stay here long enough to cover my climb," Cain said.

She nodded.

Slowly he slid his hand away from her mouth.

"Stay safe, love," he whispered.

Then he turned away and began climbing toward the alcove with smooth, powerful motions.

Chapter 55

Christy pulled the heavy pistol from her waistband, thumbed the hammer back into the fully cocked position, braced her elbows on a boulder, and took up a two-handed shooting stance. The muzzle of the pistol was aimed right at the point where Hutton would appear for his climb back down to the truck far below.

Phrases from Hutton's dialogue with the dead drifted across the rubble slope.

". . . kill her . . . vicious succubus . . . threaten *me* . . ."

Cain never paused. He moved steadily and carefully, a predator on the stalk, testing each rock to make sure it wouldn't move and make a noise.

Hutton's voice became fainter and fainter until finally it died away beneath the whisper of the wind. Apparently he was dragging Autry all the way to the back of the alcove.

The memory of stone shifting just a bit and a timber snapping echoed in Christy's mind. She wondered if the report of Hutton's little pistol had further undermined whatever was holding the massive wedge of sandstone in place.

Cain reached the sill and lay back against the wall, listening intently. He eased his head up, took a fast look, and ducked back down. After a long count of ten, he looked again, more thoroughly, his eyes probing the shadows.

He raised his hand.

Slowly Christy lowered the hammer on the pistol. She scrambled as quietly as she could up the rocks, following the route he'd taken. When she reached his side, she was breathing hard.

He pointed to his eyes, to her, and to the sill. Cautiously she raised her head until she could look into the alcove.

Hutton had managed to drag Autry halfway back to the frail supports bracing the sandstone flake. Now he was standing with his hands on his hips, catching his breath and staring down at the dead man.

"There really was no other choice," Hutton said. "I couldn't trust you not to tell. I couldn't trust anyone. If you talked . . ."

Hutton breathed heavily.

"Well, it just couldn't happen. I'm not like other people. I can't go to jail. It wouldn't be fair. It wouldn't make sense. I'm worth a hundred like you."

Hutton's voice was matter-of-fact, the voice of someone pointing out that the sun rises in the east and sets in the west. Nothing unusual. Everyone knew that was the way it worked. A simple fact of life.

Or death.

A chill seeped through Christy. For the first time she truly understood how terribly thin the line was between complete self-absorption and clinical madness. Hutton and Jo-Jo had been perfectly matched in more than their physical beauty. They believed they were the center of the universe. They believed they were too special for the rules that governed other lives. Rules were for the little people, the ugly people.

The flyover people in the flyover states.

Bending down, Hutton grabbed Autry's feet again. "Time to go. I've got a plane to catch."

With a grunt and a heave, Hutton resumed dragging Autry far back into the alcove.

Cain touched Christy's shoulder, drawing her away from the view of the alcove. He held his mouth so close to her ear she could feel his breath.

"He'll be out of sight in about thirty seconds. I'm going in after him."

Frantically she shook her head.

"It's all right," Cain said. "I've been watching him. He hasn't had time to reload. In any case, *no shooting*. Back in the alcove, even Hutton's little pocket pistol could bring the works down on my head."

Before she could say anything, Cain went over the sill and landed soundlessly inside the alcove. Heart hammering frantically, she watched him ghost forward.

"*Ciao*, babe." Hutton's voice echoed eerily inside the alcove. "Say hello to Jo and the Sisters for me."

In the silence that followed, a piece of debris rolled underneath Cain's foot. The sound was shockingly loud. Hutton spun around just as Cain ducked behind a ruined wall. Hutton saw nothing but a flicker of shadow flowing over darker shadow.

"Jo?" he called uneasily.

Nothing answered but the ageless silence of the alcove.

Hutton reached into his pocket. With the motions of a man performing a familiar task, he reloaded the small pistol.

"Jo? That you, babe? You want to play some more naughty games?"

A throttled scream ached in Christy's throat. Every step Hutton took brought him closer to the instant when he would discover Cain crouched and helpless behind the wall.

She pulled the heavy pistol from beneath her jacket. She sensed as much as saw the sharp, negative motion of Cain's head. She knew what he was afraid of, stone hanging by a thread, aching to fall.

But it might not.

If Hutton saw Cain, there wouldn't be any maybe or might. Cain would die. Before she let that happen, she would pull the trigger and take her chances on the ceiling coming down.

Tilting her head back, she spoke to the rock hanging overhead. "Peter," she called huskily.

The single word bounced off the red sandstone, echoing around the alcove until it was impossible to say which direction the call had come from.

"Peter . . ."

Christy used the second call to disguise the muted, distinctive snick and slide of steel as she cocked Danner's gun and circled to the left, trying to draw Hutton's attention away from the place where Cain crouched.

"Jo!" Hutton looked around wildly but didn't see anything. "Where are you? How did you find me?"

"I'll always be able to find you," she said in a low, throaty voice. "Just like lightning always finds the ground."

The voice came from a different place. Christy was still circling to the side, trying to lure Hutton away from Cain's hiding place.

"But you're dead," Hutton said in exasperation. "Ted followed you. He watched you walk to my plane. He punched the button, and ten minutes later you were toast."

"Yes, I'm dead."

The voice came from a different quarter. Hutton turned, tracking the sound.

"But you always liked demons, didn't you?" she asked huskily. "Well, here I am, babe. Your own private demon."

The voice was as elusive as a shadow in darkness. Hutton walked forward one step, then stopped.

"No," he said. "What fun is it if I can't see you?"

Slowly her finger tightened on the trigger. She hadn't been able to lure Hutton away from Cain's hiding place. At any moment he could be discovered.

The pistol was still in Hutton's hand.

"I can see *you*," she murmured, sliding off to the side.

But now Hutton's pistol was tracking the teasing voice with its familiar, exciting spice of malice. He turned and took a hesitant step toward the voice.

Relief swept through Christy. If he kept turning, his back would be to Cain. All she had to do was keep moving and pray Hutton didn't start shooting at ghosts.

"Don't be afraid," she said in a low, sultry voice, moving farther to the side. "I brought the baby powder."

"But there's no bathtub," Hutton complained. "And you haven't just banged some guy. If I can't wash you afterward and powder you and play with you, it's just no good, babe."

His voice was thin, peevish, the voice of a child whose ritual had been disturbed.

Christy opened her mouth, but no words came out. She didn't have any more ideas about how to use the fractures in Hutton's soul against him.

Cain did.

He unwound from his crouch in a long, low tackle that knocked Hutton far back into the alcove. Flailing for balance, Hutton tripped over Autry's corpse and fell backward. His head slammed up against one of the supporting timbers. The crack of skull meeting wood echoed in the alcove.

Hutton fell forward in an oddly graceful, boneless sprawl.

As Christy ran to Cain, he ripped the little pistol from Hutton's hand.

"Is he—" she began.

"Just unconscious," Cain said, cutting across her question.

"Thank God."

He gave her an odd look. "I didn't know you cared for good old Peter."

She shuddered. "I don't. He deserves to die. But you don't deserve to be his executioner."

The back of Cain's fingers brushed over her cheek with surprising tenderness.

"What now?" she asked.

"Now we wake up Golden Boy and tell him all about the new designs in his future."

"Gray bars and prison orange?" she asked, trying not to laugh. Because if she laughed, she didn't know if she'd be able to stop short of screaming.

"More like white jackets and rubber rooms," Cain said. "The guy is certifiably crackers."

She shuddered. "I noticed."

"You see a lantern anywhere? I can tell Hutton is breathing, but not much more."

She looked around, spotted a gleam of metal in the middle of the supporting timbers, and started for it. As she bent down to pick up the lantern, a very faint glow from the deep crack in the stone over her head caught her eye. She looked up. Froze.

"Cain."

The stark fear in her voice brought him to his feet. "What is it?"

"Oh, God. Autry—the plane—"

He punched the button, and ten minutes later you were toast.

Cain pulled Christy back and looked up into the crack.

It was crammed with dynamite, wires, and an electronic package with faintly glowing digital numbers counting off an unknown amount of time to explosion.

Autry had triggered the bomb before he died.

"Out!" Cain said.

She didn't have any choice. His fingers were clamped around her upper arm like iron bands, forcing her through the darkness without a care for the rough ground beneath their feet. He yanked her up and over the low wall, dragged her over the pile of rubble, and rushed her across the exposed sandstone steps at a reckless pace.

On hands and knees, she scrambled through the tunnel, straightened, and dashed through the cleft, only to be brought up short by the wall at the head of the mesa. Smears of dried blood showed plainly.

He bent and held out his linked hands. "Put your foot—"

She was already doing it. He straightened and lifted his hands at the same time, boosting her up onto the plateau with enough force to send her rolling up and over the lip at the top.

As she staggered to her feet, he shot up out of the cleft, grabbed her arm, and set off at a dead run away from the mesa edge. The ground flew beneath their feet.

A sharp, dry thunder rolled through the canyon.

Moments later, the mesa answered. With a prolonged grinding roar, sandstone pulled away from the mesa edge. For a timeless moment the ceiling of the alcove hung unsupported. And then it came down, dragging a piece of the mesa with it, destroying the alcove in one crushing instant.

Hutton and Autry were dead and buried under a mountain of fractured stone.

"She Who Faces the Sun was right," Christy said as the last rumble of shifting stone faded. "Whoever disturbs the Sisters dies."

Chapter 56

The hot spring steamed and seethed gently around Christy and Cain. Overhead the Milky Way burned like a ghostly silver bridge between the undiscovered past and the unknown future.

Moki slept next to the spring in a nest of blankets that were carefully arranged to accommodate his healing wound. She reached out and eased a corner of cloth over the dog's neck so that the chill night air was shut out. His tail wagged beneath the blankets and a long pink tongue slid over her hand.

"You're spoiling him," Cain said.

"Yeah. Fun, isn't it?"

He laughed softly and pulled her through the water until she was sitting on his lap, facing him, her legs straddling his.

"Want to spoil me too?" he asked.

"What do you think I've been doing for the last two weeks?"

"Spoiling me thoroughly."

"Thoroughly?"

"Addictively."

Whatever she'd been about to say was lost in the husky sound she made as his hands slid up to her breasts.

"Have I spoiled you a little bit too?" he asked against her mouth.

"Why do you think I've been hanging around?"

"Moki."

Laughing softly, she ran the tip of her tongue around Cain's lips.

"Danner?" Cain asked, smiling.

"Wash your mouth out with soap."

"Oh, Danner didn't turn out so bad."

"Was that before or after he started whitewashing Peter Hutton?"

Cain's shrug sent currents of water stirring between Christy's breasts. He didn't care.

She did. "Now in the eyes of the world Hutton is a modern *artiste* who gave his all for his designs when God blinked and an alcove vanished," she said bitterly.

Cain made a neutral sound.

"And Autry becomes a scorned lover who killed Jo-Jo rather than lose her to another man," she continued.

"Don't forget that She Who Faces the Sun also got something out of the deal."

Christy took a deep breath and let it out slowly. "Yes. I'll never forget her eyes when we handed her the second tortoise."

"Like watching the sun come up twice in one day," he agreed softly. "A little whitewash isn't such a big price to pay for that, is it?"

A quiver of heat that owed nothing to the pool expanded through Christy as Cain's hands moved beneath the water, slowly stroking her.

"Not a big price at all," she admitted.

"Beats explaining to the sound-bite set that your beautiful

famous sister was a thief and a would-be murderer," he murmured against her neck, "and that Peter Hutton was a whacked-out killer with the face of a Greek god."

"And that Danner was a fool?"

"So was Jo-Jo. Flyboy spent every last cent of their money." Cain shrugged again, sending currents stirring. "We're all fools, one way or another."

"You aren't," Christy said.

His breath came in with a soft, ripping sound as he felt her hands sliding down his torso, curling around him, savoring his naked strength. Blindly his right hand searched along the edge of the pool until he found the foil packet he'd left on a rock.

"Oh, I'm a plenty big fool," he said, "such a fool that I'm thinking of asking a woman who hates the West to marry me and live here."

"Funny," she said, her breath catching. "I was thinking of asking a man who hates the city to marry me and live there."

He went still. Then he fitted his mouth to hers in a hungry kiss that was both elemental and complex. When the kiss finally ended, both of them were breathing hard. Silently he held out the tiny packet, a question in his eyes. She eased it from his fingers . . .

And threw it away.

Foil gleamed in the instant before it vanished beneath the black water of the hot springs.

Then she was sliding over him in a slow, sleek union that was like nothing either had ever felt before. The intimacy was stunning, perfect, hotter than the seething water.

He groaned and fought for self-control.

"Which will it be?" he asked through his teeth. "West or East?"

"Yes."

"What?"

"Both," she said against his lips. "Summer here. Winter

there. I don't have a job at the moment, but I still want to tell
New York a thing or two."

"And when it's not summer or winter?"

She moved over him with a long, shivering sigh. "We'll
negotiate."

"One of us will lose."

"No. We'll both win."

And they did.

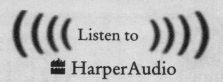
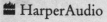

Carnival Pride℠
April 2 - 9, 2006.

7 Day Exotic Mexican Riviera Itinerary

DAY	PORT	ARRIVE	DEPART
Sun	Los Angeles/Long Beach, CA		4:00 P.M.
Mon	"Book Lover's" Day at Sea		
Tue	"Book Lover's" Day at Sea		
Wed	Puerto Vallarta, Mexico	8:00 A.M.	10:00 P.M.
Thu	Mazatlan, Mexico	9:00 A.M.	6:00 P.M.
Fri	Cabo San Lucas, Mexico	7:00 A.M.	4:00 P.M.
Sat	"Book Lover's" Day at Sea		
Sun	Los Angeles/Long Beach, CA	9:00 A.M.	

ports of call subject to weather conditions

TERMS AND CONDITIONS

PAYMENT SCHEDULE:
50% due upon booking
Full and final payment due by February 10, 2006

Acceptable forms of payment are Visa, MasterCard, American Express, Discover and checks. The cardholder must be one of the passengers traveling. A fee of $25 will apply for all returned checks. Check payments must be made payable to **Advantage International, LLC** and sent to: **Advantage International, LLC, 195 North Harbor Drive, Suite 4206, Chicago, IL 60601**

CHANGE/CANCELLATION:
Notice of change/cancellation must be made in writing to Advantage International, LLC.

Change:
Changes in cabin category may be requested and can result in increased rate and penalties. A name change is permitted 60 days or more prior to departure and will incur a penalty of $50 per name change. Deviation from the group schedule and package is a cancellation.

Cancellation:

181 days or more prior to departure	$250 per person
121 - 180 days or more prior to departure	50% of the package price
120 - 61 days prior to departure	75% of the package price
60 days or less prior to departure	100% of the package price (nonrefundable)

US and Canadian citizens are required to present a valid passport or the original birth certificate and state issued photo ID (drivers license). All other nationalities must contact the consulate of the various ports that are visited for verification of documentation.

<u>**We strongly recommend trip cancellation insurance!**</u>

For complete details call 1-877-ADV-NTGE or visit www.AuthorsAtSea.com

---

For booking form and complete information

go to <u>www.AuthorsAtSea.com</u> or call 1-877-ADV-NTGE

Complete coupon and booking form and mail both to:

Advantage International, LLC,

195 North Harbor Drive, Suite 4206, Chicago, IL 60601